10 DAYS

A Dee Rommel Mystery

by
Jule Selbo

© 2021 by Jule Selbo

This book is a work of creative fiction that uses actual publicly known events, situations, and locations as background for the storyline with fictional embellishments as creative license allows. Although the publisher has made every effort to ensure the grammatical integrity of this book was correct at press time, the publisher does not assume and hereby disclaims any liability to any party for any loss, damage, or disruption caused by errors or omissions, whether such errors or omissions result from negligence, accident, or any other cause. At Pandamoon, we take great pride in producing quality works that accurately reflect the voice of the author. All the words are the author's alone.

All rights reserved. Published in the United States by Pandamoon Publishing. No part of this publication may be reproduced, stored in a retrieval system, or transmitted in any form or by any means—for example, electronic, photocopy, recording—without the prior written permission of the publisher. The only exception is brief quotations in printed reviews.

www.pandamoonpublishing.com

Jacket design and illustrations © Pandamoon Publishing
Art Direction by Don Kramer: Pandamoon Publishing
Editing by Zara Kramer, Rachel Schoenbauer, and Forrest Driskel, Pandamoon Publishing

Pandamoon Publishing and the portrayal of a panda and a moon are registered trademarks of Pandamoon Publishing.

Library of Congress Cataloging-in-Publication Data is on file at the Library of Congress, Washington, DC

Edition: 1, Version 1.00
ISBN 13: 978-1-950627-36-3

Reviews

"In her debut crime/mystery series, Jule Selbo delivers a tense, nail-biter of a detective story. 10 DAYS, A Dee Rommel Mystery has everything - including Dee as the unlikely investigator, reminiscent of Jack Nicholson in Chinatown. She's in rehab for a life-altering injury, she's got a penchant for drinking – and through her seasoned eyes, we see the underbelly of Portland, a cast of quirky and dangerous characters, along with a riveting crime story that is so compelling and cinematic it cries out to be made into a Netflix series. It's that good." — **Jamie Cat Callan, Creator of The Writers Toolbox, author of** *Bonjour Happiness* **and** *French Women Don't Sleep Alone*

Jule Selbo's *10 DAYS* boasts a high-octane plot introducing Dee Rommel, a streetwise protagonist whose personal creed drives a compelling narrative. Despite a permanent injury that impacts her mobility, Dee stands up to power brokers and thugs. She and the rest of Selbo's deeply human characters are so real and compelling you'll wish The Sparrow was your local. But it's Dee's personal courage and loyalty to her tight circle of friends that gives this debut novel its power and will have fans signaling for another round. — **Brenda Buchanan, author of the Joe Gale Mysteries**

10 DAYS is an action-packed story that bristles with raw energy. I tore right through it. Using the mean streets of Portland as her canvas, Jule Selbo has created a fascinating and complex protagonist in Dee Rommel. A great read for lovers of crime fiction! — **Joseph Souza, best-selling and award-winning author of** *The Neighbor, Pray for the Girl* **and** *The Perfect Daughter.* josephsouza.net

10 DAYS is riveting and fun and inventive, and best of all, it features Dee Rommel, a tough, fearless, beautiful sleuth with an intriguing past. Warning: this book will induce a powerful craving for a fried haddock sandwich. And you won't be able to put it down until the suspenseful and totally satisfying conclusion. — **Kate Christensen, PEN/Faulkner Award-winning author of** *The Great Man* **and** *The Last Cruise*

In this engaging and fast-moving story set on the coast of Maine, Selbo gives us a damaged heroine dedicated to protecting others and struggling to protect herself as she finds her way forward after a devastating injury. — **Kate Flora, Maine Literary Award-winning author of the *Joe Burgess Series***

Packed with richly detailed characters, we root for policewoman Dee Rommel to bring the bad guys out of their holes and into justice. *10 DAYS* author Jule Selbo deftly contrasts the criminal elements of working-class vs high class, hi-tech vs low-tech. She knows the world and clearly illuminates Dee's own demons as she struggles to right humanity's wrongs—and decide the path of her own future. — **Susan Merson, author of *Oh Good, Now This***

Dedication

For Mark, for 5,204 reasons (see list in my head)

10 DAYS

CHAPTER ONE
Wednesday

My goddamn leg thinks it's whole again; the knee thinks it's connected to a calf and ankle and foot—thinks it has muscles, tissue, fat, tendons, veins, arteries, and bones all in place to keep blood flowing from my left extremity to my heart and beyond.

Of course, I know it's my brain dipping into the past; imagining the tickle of fresh sheets and the heat of a calloused hand stroking the length of my leg.

Wake the hell up, I tell myself. My hair has fallen over my face, I sweep it off with my hand, its thickness especially heavy this morning.

Then I feel the warm body beside me, rolling onto my arm, breath hot on my cheek, fuzzy face close. I push him away, moaning, the hangover thick. A sleepy dog-yip escapes from his throat. Bert is a fifty-pound labradoodle. He belongs to my boss who's out of town right now. He must have climbed into my bed when I was in my drunken sleep, making himself at home.

I force my eyes open, even though the excessive amount of Rittenhouse I drank last night at Sparrows wants to keep me submerged in a semi-conscious purgatory. Sparrows is a beloved neighborhood place in Portland, not far from my apartment. Pat Trangle is the owner of the bar and he lives above it, his whole world in this community's watering hole. His biggest talents are his taste in vintage rock 'n' roll and sensing when to cut people off. What happened to his reading me last night?

The night started with a meeting to button up a case. The client had gone away happy with the information that there was physical evidence—explicit photos and intimate recordings of infidelity—and he could now proceed to a quick and nasty divorce filing. I stayed for another drink to drown out the disappointment of seeing another example of humanity's vindictiveness and greed. And more evidence that love can go very, very wrong. Pat's song choice, *I Want to Know What Love Is,* the Foreigner version from the eighties, seemed apt. A middle-aged liquor salesman, hoping to sway Pat's allegiance from his regular distributor, settled in close to me at the bar. His bulbous mid-section challenged the buttons on his green polyester shirt.

Ten Days

He invited me, in a suspect lilting accent, to sample the Belvenie Doublewood Single Malt Whiskey, said it was the real good stuff. He introduced himself with a silly name, like MacAngus or MacBugger. But when he opened his fat wallet, crammed with hundreds, I saw his driver's license. Name was Thomas Charles Beene. New Jersey. Registered organ donor. God help the person who might hold out hope for his liver.

MacBugger Beene used the excuse of reaching for the napkin holder to get his fleshy arm against my breast. "Sweetheart, you're my target audience. Women hitting thirty—no offense—are you thirty yet?"

"None of your business." I pointedly rearranged my fleece vest to make it clear his high school behavior hadn't gone unnoticed.

Beene laughed. "Ladies with sass and attitude. You're our new bull's-eye. Independent and ready to kick ass. Likes to keep up with the boys."

He went off, leaving a scent of greasy highway food, to pour a sample round for a couple by the fireplace table—out-of-towners. I could tell they weren't Mainers because of their self-conscious accessories and expectations of prompt service. I'd bet money they were from New York City.

Pat had been distracted. His usual dancing shoulder, a holdover from his days in a fiddle band, was gone. When he leaned across the bar for a private conversation, I understood why. He muttered, "Billy Payer just got released."

Pat's eyes were worried—I remembered Billy Payer slamming Pat's face onto the corner of the bar last New Year's Eve, breaking his nose in three places. Pat pressed charges and the volatile prick got prison time. I was reassuring. "Billy won't be thick-headed enough to come anywhere near you. Plus, I heard he got religion."

Pat wiped his nose with his now-ever-present bandana handkerchief. "Hired him for insurance."

"Who?"

He nodded towards the corner. A guy I'd never seen before, in a leather jacket, dark jeans, and black Timberland boots sat behind a pitcher of beer. He had a thick hardcover open, a flexible gooseneck book light illuminated its pages. His hair was pulled back in a ponytail, a massive neck was visible, about the size of my right thigh. He hadn't raised his eyes, but he knew I was checking him out. The Reader exuded presence.

And now it's the morning. I groan as Bert pushes his cold wet nose into my back. "Yeah. Yeah. Need a sec. Just a sec."

I put the heel of my hand on the bedside table and muscle myself upwards. I balance on my good leg, slip my half-leg into my iWalk and tighten the straps. Count a slow five, the time needed to focus on balance.

Bert bounds off the bed and lands on his four good legs, sniffs around the bedroom. My open-cuff crutches rest against the folded-up wheelchair, my vacuum-system, shock-absorbing LiteGood prosthesis is on the top of my dresser, my peg leg tossed on a chair. I'm aware my bedroom looks like that of a woman who can't make up her mind—but it's not the 'what-to-wear' dilemma, it's the 'how-will-I-travel-today' question.

My prosthetist tells me it'll all feel second nature soon. I tell him that it's been over a year and ask how long does 'soon' take?

Bert gives a sharp bark, doesn't want me to forget him. "Okay. Come on, boy."

We move through my darkened living room to the kitchen door that opens to stone steps that lead to my backyard. Bert slips out into the cool June morning and races up the steps to the lone tree he favors for bladder relief.

I prop the door open and call after him, "Be ready in thirty. I gotta get to the office."

Bert's food sits in a plastic storage box on my kitchen counter. My boss packaged its contents for me, not trusting me to properly feed his best buddy. I thumb through the pre-measured, all-organic portions, find the right day and date on the plastic baggie. Dump it into the bowl.

I clomp-step into the living room and pull back the curtains on my eye-level windows. A basement apartment is not usually on the list of must-live places, but it's good for me. Out the long low windows are grassy tips of lawn, a quiet street, and a view straight out to Casco Bay. Dayboats head out to bring in the catch of the day.

Bert pads in for his breakfast, I head back to the kitchen, lock the back door, and appreciate the sound of the latch bolt sliding into place.

"Taking a shower," I tell Bert, as if he cares about anything but lapping up his food.

I keep my showers short to defy the natural swelling of tissue in wet heat then step out of the white-tiled stall, unstrap the iWalk, lean my weight back on the sink, and use a towel to give a rough massage to the half-leg. My hair dryer, on top speed, attacks any remaining moisture. I grab the cuff crutches, catch a foggy glimpse of myself in the full-length mirror on the back of the door: too thin, maybe ten pounds underweight for my nearly six-foot frame. My ass is flat, typical white girl; no matter how many curls or lunges—high and rounded glutes escape me. I contemplate my lone long leg and wonder if I'll ever look familiar to myself.

I dress from shoulder to crotch. Then pull on my liner and my 2-ply stump sock and don my LiteGood, use the vacuum pump to tighten the fit, slip into my jeans, add a high-topped Nike boot over my plastic foot with its anatomically correct toes and a right boot to the foot that can feel.

Ten Days

* * *

Bert and I move down the hill into the bustle of town. There's a crisp morning chill in the air. We pass Victorian houses whose rear windows look out over the bay, past the 19th century brick buildings that were once machine shops geared towards boat builders. The high-end refurbishing of Portland's historic district has pushed them out. A Silversea cruise ship is in place at the docking terminal. Its gangway is weighed down with passengers as they move off the ship; some will get on a bus to the massive L.L. Bean store located in the middle of discount venues in Freeport, some will wander Portland for the day, and then get back on their ship and be gone by sunset.

I grab a take-out coffee at Nivas Cafe on Thames Street.

"Your dog." The voice comes from behind me, the accent is German.

"'Scuse me?"

He wears a baseball cap, sunglasses, and a nylon runner's jacket. Zero body fat. Binoculars peek out from a pocket.

"Your dog rope. Stretched here. It is blocking my entry to get coffee."

Bert sniffs a fire hydrant, as far away from me as he can go on his leash.

"Sorry." There's a birdwatching book in the German's hand. I slip past him and give a gentle tug to Bert, signaling him that we're on our way again.

At Gretchen's Doggie DayCare, my friend's staring at her phone. She forces a smile, but she's frazzled.

"Whazzup?"

"Trying to reach Karla." She moves around the counter to greet Bert. "Hey there, big silly guy, you come to play?" She opens the gate and Bert, the streaking fur ball, speeds through to the play area already populated by canine slobberers.

"So rude. He sleeps with me, I make him breakfast, let him use my outdoor toilet and not even a 'later, lady.'"

"You're good with a dog."

"Stop trying to convert me." Gretchen pulls her watch cap lower on her head. Something's different. "What're you hiding?

She takes off her cap to reveal lavender-streaked hair in a new pixie cut. "I thought shorter would make me look more fun. Someone should have told me it makes my face look fatter."

"You don't have a fat face."

"I'll never have cheekbones like you. And you have a real chin. Mine looks like a marshmallow attached to a jaw."

"Is this low self-esteem day?" Gretchen and I have known each other since first grade. She's getting more and more fretful about what she calls 'Her Future with a capital 'F.''

Gretchen grabs a cart packed with thick rubber toys. "All I want is a life-long partner who will binge on tv shows with me, want to heave-ho at least four times a week, sleep next to me the whole night, and get my name right in the morning."

"There's probably someone out there fitting that description."

"For you, too."

"You're worse than my mother." I study her new haircut. "You know what? That short hair does make you look like a bedroom-super-athlete."

She tosses a dozen brightly colored balls to the happy barkers. "That's the idea. But I'm thinking of freezing some eggs just in case." She moves back to the counter. "Karla told me Billy Payer wants to see her so he can apologize."

"She didn't fall for that, did she?"

"For her—he's got some magic action."

I shake my head. We'd met Karla at University of Southern Maine; she never declared her major but we kidded her that she was the head of the Department of Party. She opened her own hair salon on India Street a few years ago. She's always after me to donate my straight locks so she can make a strawberry blonde wig from human hair.

"I'll guilt her into meeting us for a drink at Sparrows. Six?" Gretchen writes the time on her wall calendar as a reminder.

"She's not going to listen."

"Dee, we have to try. He's dangerous."

CHAPTER TWO
Wednesday

I'm a block from the office. Produce trucks are parked in the center lanes of the street, drivers quickly unload foodstuffs for the restaurants on the wharfs. Seagulls sit on top of the nearby buildings, cawing, hoping for spilled boxes and ready food.

"Dee. Got something to tell you. *True Romance* is one of my favorite films—it brought Tarantino to everyone's attention. My girlfriend doesn't like violence though…"

Malio, the self-appointed morning greeter on this section of Commercial Street, always shares the details of the movie he and his girlfriend watched the day before. "Morning, Malio."

"What'm I g-gonna do?"

"Watch something else."

Malio nods as if he hadn't thought of that. Then he jerks his head towards the corner of the street. "Beefcake waiting." A broad-shouldered driver with a cubic head leans against a sleek black Escalade. "He's been upstairs for t-twelve m-minutes."

"Who went upstairs?"

"Mr. Upstairs sat in the b-backseat behind Beefcake."

I take the elevator to the third-floor hallway. A man with a rigid gait and a precisely trimmed beard paces in front of the embossed logo: G&Z Investigation. He's in his early forties, wears a gray jacket, gray khakis, and gray suede Chukka sneakers; he holds a gray oversized umbrella in his hand.

"Help you?" I ask.

"Dee Rommel?" He's about my height and has thick ginger hair. His brown eyes, protected by steel-rimmed glasses, are slightly magnified and cautious. He radiates impatience, as if whatever brings him to this office is keeping him from taking care of everything else and time wasted pisses him off.

"Maybe," I tell him.

"I have something I need G&Z to take care of."

Ten Days

"Office is closed for regular business for a month."

"Not closed to me," he says.

"Got a good reason for thinking that?"

"Gordy said to come."

The code words for immediate entry.

Maybe he's lost sleep lately. Maybe what I thought was impatience is anxiety.

"Can we go inside?" He taps the door with his umbrella.

"If you'll step back, I'll arrange that." He retreats a few feet and checks the orange Swatch on his freckled wrist. I unlock the security box; under its cover I punch in numbers, press my thumb on the touch pad, hear the familiar click and then use the QwikZeus key to unlock the door.

"Triple protection." He's assessing the efficacy of the shields.

"Gordy insists on it."

"Kept the bad guys out so far?" He's serious; it's a real question.

I move inside and reach for the switch that raises the blackout shades. Seconds later, morning light shines through the large windows. He puts his umbrella in the stand. I tell him the sky's clear. No rain in sight.

"In the next hour, we'll get a squall." He's very sure of himself.

I rarely check daily forecasts. Unless I'm going out on a boat. Weather can change every five minutes in Maine.

"When did you talk to Gordy?" I ask.

"When I told him I had to find out who my daughter is marrying."

I turn on my desktop monitor, enter my password, activate the coffee maker, and continue with morning set up. "How does it happen a father isn't informed on something like that?"

"I have the pissant's name, where he works. It's not enough. This wedding can't happen." He dips his hand into his jacket's pocket, reacting to the vibration of his cell phone. He reads the text. Punches in a response. Then back to me. "It's scheduled for June 22. The marriage ceremony."

I glance at the calendar in the corner of my computer screen. "That's ten days from today."

"That's right."

"Sorry, it's a bad time. Gordy's not available. He should have told you. And Zandrick—he's been dead for ten years. There's no one available to 'get busy.'"

"I talked to Gordy last night. He told me you can do it."

I'm surprised. And not pleased. "I'm his bookkeeper."

"He says you were a cop."

"Notice the past tense."

"And that you're smart."

"My job at G&Z is to keep things organized and do the bookkeeping. Doesn't take a huge intellect."

The landline rings. The phone's readout: Gordy. I pick up the receiver. "Gordy, someone here says he knows you."

The man in gray raises his voice loud enough to be picked up by the receiver. "Gordy, she doesn't know who I am, does she?"

I instantly resent anyone who cries entitlement.

"Damn it, Dee," Gordy growls. "Google Claren. Philip P."

I blame last night's Rittenhouse again because I feel I'm about to look like a fool. I type in the command; the Wikipedia page pops up. First line reads "…*on the list of the top one hundred technology entrepreneurs in the world.*"

Shit. That's why he's familiar. The reclusive golden boy of Portland who invests heavily in the city and its small businesses, sits on the boards of the civic institutions but is shy of being the 'face' of his endeavors. He's a local legend—Claren grew up in Portland, his middle school teachers felt they couldn't give him the attention he needed and contacted Fremont Academy in Andover, Massachusetts. The academy gave him free tuition, room and board, and kept the tech lab open-on-demand for him. Two years later, he accepted a full scholarship to MIT and breezed through undergrad, graduate, and doctoral programs in five years. He holds over 900 patents, mostly in the areas of semi-conductor memories and circuit transistors. Not quite the profile of a Jobs or Gates or Musk; he's a muted presence. I slide my eyes over to Claren to compare the reality to the Wiki mugshot—the prominent freckles, the unruly reddish hair falling forward, the eyes analytical and wary. Yeah, all there.

"Tell Phil to give us a minute," Gordy tells me, his words coursing across the lines from Florida.

I look at Claren. "Gordy wants to keep it between boss and bookkeeper. I'll put him on speaker in a second."

Irritated, Claren moves to the window to gaze out over J's Oyster Bar and Restaurant and the Portland harbor. He holds his head high and straight, moves like his body is an unwelcome appendage to the head—and like it sometimes gets in the way.

Gordy's talking. "Now listen to me, Dee. I want you to do this."

"Stop a wedding? Not in my job description, boss."

"I'm giving my brother a goddamn kidney. What are you doing with your life?"

"I'm babysitting your poodle."

"Labradoodle."

Ten Days

"He's more poodle than Labrador. He's very sensitive and a little girlie."

"Bert's not girlie. He misses me." Gordy sighs. "Dogs get attached to people. Something you should think about."

"Let's not get personal today, Gordy."

Gordy gripes. "I'm hungry. Haven't eaten since midnight. And I don't like hospitals."

"When's the operation?"

"They're coming to get me soon. I'm all primed to be hooked into the IV crap. And I got a ball-buster nurse. Thought I might rate a pretty one."

"Pretty ones are always trouble for you."

"Back to the request at hand. There must be a reason. Give Phil some peace on this. I owe him."

"For what?"

Gordy's evasive. "I can't get into that right now."

Claren clears his throat, he's had enough of being on the outside of the conversation. I tell Gordy, "I'll send your friend over to Screw-up and Dingbat."

"I'm not putting ten thou in their pocket for a day's work."

Did he say ten thousand? My curiosity accelerates.

Gordy tells me to put him on speaker. I activate the landline's option. "Hey, Phil," Gordy says.

"This isn't the reception I was expecting. You told me she was very sharp."

"Well, she's not perfect."

I resent them talking about me. "I'm right here."

Gordy is exasperated. "Dee, damnit. You can keep twenty percent."

"If I did take this on, it would have to be forty percent."

Gordy sounds pained. "I have overhead."

I'm his bookkeeper, I know the details. "Three rooms. Bathroom down the hall. The rent hasn't been raised for twenty years."

There's a rumble in the sky outside. Dark clouds have gathered. A few large raindrops collide with the window.

Gordy rasps, persistent. "You gotta say 'yes' to life, Dee."

Gordy's addicted to daytime talk shows. "Stop watching *The View*."

A bossy woman's voice comes through the phone connection. It's deep and I imagine a nurse built like a linebacker. She's telling Gordy to give her his phone. He speaks fast. "Dee, gotta go. I'll be in surgery for the next few hours and don't count on talking to me for the rest of the day—I plan to take advantage of happy drugs. Take me off speaker."

I click the speaker function off. Claren, irked, turns back to the window. The rain splats against the glass.

"What, Gordy?" I say.

Gordy puts on his persuasive voice. "Dee. What if I die today and I haven't seen you get back in stride?"

"You're not going to die. And my stride is fine."

"This could be the last favor I ever ask you."

"Don't play that card, Gordy."

The ball-buster nurse announces she's now taking Gordy's phone. The connection is broken. A sudden wave of anxiety fills me. Gordy stepped in after my father died, he's the one who forced me to show up at my rehab appointments; he'd sit and read the newspaper while I struggled to re-find strength in my body, deal with my inner screams and my not-so-inner vocal curses at the physical therapists who were too fiercely encouraging and too relentlessly cheery and optimistic. Gordy would tell me to stop being a baby. I know he hates hospitals, but he's giving up a kidney to help his brother regain quality of life. He'll be fine. I won't even consider the possibility that Gordy will not be back in Portland soon.

The wind's whipping now, lightning flares in the distance. I stretch across the desk and turn on the desk lamp. Claren turns to me. "Are you going to take this on?"

I decide to barter with the universe: I'll do this in exchange for the speedy return of Gordy, less one kidney, but still bossy and opinionated.

And a rich payday would come in handy. I've got medical bills. And I need a new car.

I meet Claren's eyes. "Okay. Let's get started."

CHAPTER THREE
Wednesday

"How old is your daughter?"

"Bunny Luce is twenty-two." Claren sits in the chair across from my desk, his back to the window.

"Bunny Luce?" I immediately feel sorry for her. Shitty name. No matter how much money her father has, that name invites bullying.

"Her name is Lucy, named after my mother. I called her Bunny when she was born so there was no mix-up at the rare family gatherings and then—it stuck." He brings up a picture on his cell phone. "Took this about a year ago." Bunny's half-turning to avoid the camera; she's round-faced, with a soft double-chin. Midnight black hair cut in a bowl-cut bob, pale lips and pensive dark eyes behind heavy-framed glasses.

"She dyes her hair?"

"Bunny thinks her natural red makes her too visible." He's apologetic, like his genes disappointed.

I notice green flecks in his brown eyes. I don't know why but they make him seem less genius, more human. "Your daughter's an adult. Even if she makes a mistake and marries a jerk—she's got the right to do that."

"The job is to figure out why this guy. Why this guy now."

"But what if the situation is legit and the love is real? Will you accept it?"

Cynicism—or is it anger—pulls his lips back. "Don't tell me you're a romantic."

"No." My response comes quickly, and truthfully. I notice he's not wearing a wedding ring. "Is there a reason you think your daughter's upcoming marriage is not about true love?"

"Chebeague."

"What?"

"The place means something to us."

Ten Days

A group of seventeen islands in Casco Bay makes up Chebeague. Great Chebeague is the largest; it's about ten miles by water from the Portland docks. Four hundred people live there year-round—in the summer the numbers triple. My dad used to load picnics into our 23-foot Grady-White, we'd head to the island. He told me Chebeague's a Native American word for 'cold springs' and referred to the fresh water deep under the surface of the islands. We kept our lobster pots off Little Chebeague, the uninhabited island that, at low tide, we'd access by walking across a connecting sandbar from Great Chebeague. When I was a kid, I thought it was a magical pathway that showed itself just for me.

I lean in. "Explain why the word 'Chebeague' is a trigger."

"It's part of our cryptograph." Claren takes a plain white business-sized envelope from his jacket's inside pocket. "We spent a month there—every summer—when Bunny was little. Swimming in the coves, picking blueberries, looking for red foxes, biking around. I'd set up a workshop so I could keep up with work and communications were delivered by boat twice a day. One year we found some arrowheads and buried them on our spit of land. She asked why we couldn't live on the island full time. I knew her mother—we were divorced by then—wouldn't go for that so I told Bunny we had to cherish the time we had. We decided—if she ever faced trouble, or needed me, to send me the code—cryptograph: 'Chebeague.' And that I'd move hell to get to her." He hands me the envelope.

"You haven't talked to her? Asked her what's going on?" The envelope was posted from New York City, marked as leaving the city three days ago. Snail mail, pretty old-fashioned. I open the envelope and take out a piece of typical printer-grade paper that's tucked inside.

"She was in New York for a conference. Never went back to her condo in Boston. Or LC Lab at Claren Tech. She's not responding to email, phone, or texts. Her mother's not returning my calls. I tried every number again this morning. They go to voicemail—or nothing."

I unfold the sheet of paper and read:

"Dad. Getting married. June 22. Bunny's Point. Chebeague."

"Maybe it's simple; she thinks Chebeague's a pretty place for a happy nuptial."

"Bunny Luce got access to over twenty patent profits two weeks ago. When she turned twenty-two."

"What're profits on these patents worth?"

"In a good year—three to four million—give or take."

Sometimes, like right now for a split second, I'm positive I belong to the Unlucky Club. But that passes because I remember the look in Bunny Luce's eyes as she tried to duck before her photograph was taken.

"I've talked to our lawyers," Claren says, gliding his glasses up higher on the bridge of his nose. "There's no pre-nuptial agreement that we can ascertain. She's never had a serious relationship. Why would she suddenly get married?" He pulls a glossy tear sheet from a magazine from his pocket, puts it on my desk, taps it with his finger. "This is the guy. The fiancé." I glance at the photo; Bunny Luce, again nearly turned from the camera's eye. "The issue of *Social* hit the public today." She's thinner; dressed in a long burgundy dress that hangs on a bony frame, her face is drawn, and her glasses are huge. Next to her is a twenty-something reed in a matte black suit, a scarf around his neck, an architectural haircut that droops in various angles over a pale face. The lights of the cameras hit two reflective points on him: one on the excessive Rolex on his left wrist and the other on his shiny, pointy, steel-toed boots. He looks like an arrogant dickwad. The photo, apparently, is documenting their presence at the VIP Event in New York, three weeks ago. The caption reads "Tyler Peppard of Yarborough Inx and his Claren heiress fiancé."

"When did she lose the weight?"

"Excuse me?"

"Her face is much thinner." I tap on the cell phone picture, then the tear sheet.

"Don't know. My ex-wife is always suggesting diets. Maybe Bunny…"

I bring up the obvious. "You have a prominent business, Dr. Claren. Don't you have people on payroll to find out things for you?"

"Yes, I do."

"Why pay extra to an outsider?"

"This is not business. Has to stay private. And I trust Gordy."

"And he owes you. Why?"

Claren ignores my question. "Are you going to find my daughter?"

Lightning cracks. The clouds open and rain pounds against the wide window behind Claren.

"Let's make it official." I move to a cabinet to extract a standard deal memo. Claren's eyes are on my back and a prickle stings my neck, signaling that my digenetic animal sense is at work, that invisible canniness that warns of someone or something observing too closely.

"No paperwork. You never know what the media will glom onto."

He takes another envelope from his jacket pocket. This one is thick manila held shut with a Velcro tab. I wonder how many bills are stacked within it.

"This is a deposit. Cash."

He's being careful. Okay. "You and Gordy agreed?"

"We go back."

"Gordy's a lot older than you. What's the connection?"

"Met him when I was seven. He was the Portland Boxing Club champion then; big deal in our neighborhood."

"And?"

"Isn't relevant to this."

"Okay." That's all I'm getting. "I'll want to use a few accessory sources. Ones Gordy and I trust."

He hesitates.

"I suggest you don't handicap me. We don't have a lot of time."

He nods.

I walk to a boat-scape Gordy found in a dusty antique shop on Route 1; it hangs on the wall behind the desk. I lift it up to reveal the wall safe. I plug in the code, press my thumb against the scanner. The safe clicks open. I take out two burner phones. "The red one is mine. The black one is yours. G&Z's number is already programmed in, we'll add yours. Keep phone communication to these devices."

"Hackable but not necessarily traceable." I'm not surprised he sees the advantage.

"Always new ways to harvest data but I like to think I can heighten the level of difficulty."

A tight smile tugs at his mouth. "Level of difficulty. Yes. Very important to raise that whenever possible, in many areas of life. We agree on that."

We activate the phones and I retrieve his umbrella for him. "Well, you were right about the weather."

He looks at my left leg. "How's that working for you?"

That prickle in my neck returns. "How's what working for me?"

"What're you wearing? The Jeiner or the LiteGood?"

He's asking me like he's asking who designed my jeans. "LiteGood."

"Gordy told me about your accident."

"Right. My accident." My jaw is tight.

"The specific carbon fiber making up the pylons in your prosthetic—we did substantial preliminary work on it in our lab."

"So, I'm wearing one of your patents?"

"Project was focused on maximizing strength while concentrating on lightness."

"Well sometimes it feels real heavy." Screw you, I want to say.

"Yes, I suppose it's successful only to a point. Work continues in the area."

I go to the door, open it. "I'll be in touch."

CHAPTER FOUR
Wednesday

I immediately get Jade booked on research. She's a stay-at-home mom who lives in Kennebunkport—a few miles from the waterfront compound of the Presidents Bush. A walking Fort Knox of secrets, she learned how to file-away-and-toss-the-password when she worked for Homeland Security. Now she uses a system of multiple electronic brains set up in her basement office to dig through real and fake and alternate news, social media posts, and photo galleries, gain entry to phone records, use pre-texting to gain credit card histories, real estate transactions, tax records, online buying habits, voting practices, and other fingerprints left in day-to-day lives. Not all of the information could ever be used in court—because all are not legally available. From these Jade sets up predictability charts. Things like location predictables, buying and service predictables. Jade's my constant reminder that, in the age of access, privacy of any kind is nearly impossible. She's aware that I hate the idea of strangers knowing my preference for organic toothpaste, Buzo amputee socks, and aisle seats on airplanes. 'Concentrate on the important stuff,' she tells me. 'The grid is there, you can't shake it. Live the life you want.' She's done that, totally happy being super hack-mistress—with the perk of being within shouting distance of her pre-school kids.

And making good money doing it. Jade's expensive. But Claren's footing the bill and he wants things fast.

"I need anything on Lucy Claren, a.k.a. Bunny Luce Claren, daughter of Philip P.; concentrate on the last two months. And anything on a mid-twenty-something Tyler Peppard." I spell the name. "He works at Yarborough Inx in Manhattan. Seems like there's a quickie marriage plan and maybe it's not a fairytale romance. Or then again, maybe it is. Whatever you find might give me a direction. Lots of unknowns right now. Bunny Luce was in New York City last week at a Bio-Engineering conference. But she's MIA now."

Ten Days

Jade is up for the task. "Hey, my kid is on the wait list at the Claren School. I registered him two years ago, when he read 'The Bells' by Poe to me as a bedtime story."

"Not exactly a poem to encourage sweet dreams."

"It's exhausting; I'm doing double duty. I have to sing 'Wheels on the Bus' ten times a day and also talk to him about the concept of internal rhyme. Not that I'm complaining."

"How does a kid pick up Poe's greatest hits?"

"Chubby little fingers randomly plucking at the family bookcase."

I laugh. Back to business. "Jade, this job's sensitive. High on the hush factor. And there's a clock ticking."

"I'm hanging up now so I can get started." Jade clicks off and I imagine her alerting her nanny that she's about to pad down the carpeted stairs to her basement control center.

I open a fresh TrueCrypt file on the computer and log in the time of Claren's request for hire, my acceptance of his cash deposit, my conversation with Jade, and a few questions I want to follow up on. I leave off identifying components and simply call it 'Chebeague.'

The cryptogram could be a cry-for-help. Or a way for Bunny Luce to tell her father she doesn't want his interference in a quickie marriage that might be naïve—or true—romance. And a picturesque island merely a nice place to make a love-for-life promise.

***

Jade will dig deep, so I start on the surface. I type Yarborough Inx into my search engine. It's an international public relations and marketing firm; clients include mid-level hotel chains, private jet companies, super-yacht builders, tech companies, media start-ups, and more. Not exactly a targeted clientele. I look up the names of the top executives of the firm. No Tyler Peppard listed, but that doesn't surprise. He's young, probably mired somewhere in the support pool. I browse the client list; my eyes stop a quarter of the way down the list of Yarborough's clients. Destiny Leader.

I check out the page torn from the magazine again, the photo of the heiress and stringbean Peppard. The banner behind them reads, 'Destiny Leader, part of the Wolff Conglomerate, proud sponsor.' I click on the link. Destiny Leader is one of the top companies in Artificial Intelligence Expansion. Yarborough states its task is to provide Destiny with actionable guidance in tech sectors. 'Actionable.' What the hell does that mean?

I call the main number of Yarborough Inx on my burner cell and ask to be transferred to Peppard. I'm told he's on vacation.

"When will he be back?"

The woman on the other end of the phone ignores my direct question and asks if I want to leave a message. I decline and hang up. I snap a phone photo of the tear sheet, put the original in the Chebeague file.

One of the obvious phone calls is to the Chebeague Inn. Winston Barry won all the spelling bees when we were in elementary school and he's now the assistant manager at the inn and has committed to living year-round on the island. That makes for a busy summer and a near-hermit-like winter. He tells me his connection to the inn is deep, he figures he must have had a seminal experience there in one of his past lives. Winston believes in the inn's ghosts, the famous one being a young woman, who, the day before her wedding in the 1920s, stared from a high window, expecting to witness her fiancé's arrival from the mainland. But his boat capsized and he drowned. The bride never left the inn after that; she eventually died there. Winston insists she haunts the place, hoping for her love to rise from the waters.

"Good morning. Chebeague Inn."

"Winston, it's Dee. How's your Gram?"

"Nicotine's still mother's milk to her. Ninety-eight years old in a few days and puffs a pack a day. You coming out?"

"Might. Kind of busy right now."

"You called just to say 'hey'?" He knows better.

"I met someone whose daughter plans on getting married on the island. June 22."

"We're booked for the Chen/Kennedy nuptials. That her?"

"No."

"Zemberski and Holden on the 20th, Fibli and Gonzalez on the 24th. Those names grab you?"

"No. Maybe she's using a private residence. You hear of anything?"

"No one's asked our kitchen for catering help."

Great Chebeague is only three miles long and one mile wide. Most of the homes are privately owned. And most are not grand.

Maybe Bunny Luce Claren does not do grand.

Winston makes a suggestion. "The wedding could be booked on a yacht. Maybe the plan is to anchor off the island and hope for good weather."

"I'll check around." A yacht could be chartered from anywhere up and down the coast. Or it could be privately owned. Tracking this option is problematic.

Ten Days

"Any news, Dee?" Winston wants to get a bit deeper, personal. He wants to know if I'm still on medication. If I am getting out. If I'm dealing with my anger issues.

"Crazy happy. It's tough to stop dancing on the pier."

"Sarcasm doesn't suit you," he chides. "Come out. We have a new chef. Very creative with all things haddock."

"I'll try. Thanks, Winston." I hang up.

I do a surface search on Lucy Claren. Not much available for the nosy, incidental viewer. Daughter of Philip P. Claren and Renae Claren. Five years at Massachusetts Institute of Technology, where she scored her first patent for a device that aided in the advancement of 3-D printing technology in Myoelectrics. Whatever that is. Doctorate in Biological Engineering. Head of the LC Labs on the Claren Tech campus.

I'm reminded how the influential and rich can keep details off public access. I once researched the founder of *Graze*—one of the biggest search engines—and saw he was listed as having two children. The ages and sex of the progeny were not included. No family pictures available for the casually curious. I wonder how much oversight—or money—it takes to maintain this kind of privacy.

I search for images of Lucy Claren. Two photos. The first shows a chubby girl, age five or so; she's on her father's shoulders in front of a banner declaring the opening of Claren Gifted in Portland. Her bright shock of red hair shines in a blue sky. The other was taken when she was pre-teen; she wears large red-framed glasses, her hair falls over her round, full-cheek face, her plumpness decked out in a yellow sack dress and red Keds. She stands like the winner of the odd child contest, next to her mother. Renae Claren is toned, bleached, and botoxed, and clearly not afraid of the camera. Her smile reveals arctic-white teeth, her hip is thrust out at a modeling angle and her eyes challenge the viewer to find any faults.

I push back my chair and roll a nearby footstool into place so I can extend my leg. The lift of the four-pound prosthetic goes well, my thigh and hip muscles appreciate the elevation just fine.

So. Bunny Luce Claren, stuck with a silly name, a genius father, and a ready-for-the-camera mother. Keeping clear of the spotlight and maybe wanting her superstar intelligence to be the only thing anyone notices. Or not to be noticed at all. But I need to shine a spotlight on her—that's the job. Find a poor little rich girl so her protective, worried father can step in and save her—if necessary—from a greedy wolf salivating over a tasty bank account.

Is it simply a case of a parent unable to relinquish control? Wanting a chance to force his will? Or is it something else? I go back to the magazine tear sheet again; Bunny Luce's sunken shoulders, bony arms, and thin face. All youthful baby fat is gone.

"Dee? I am here, at the moment you expect." It's Abshir's voice coming through the intercom.

I buzz him in and he enters in a rush, all lanky six feet, five inches of him. He drops his immense student backpack on the floor, unzips his hooded sweatshirt, and lands a plastic container on my desk. Smells of garlic, cumin, and ginger. "Leftovers. My *hooyo* says you told her you like cabbage. It has in it Kashmiri chilies and sesame seeds."

"Did you forget Gordy said you could take the week off?"

Abshir pulls his laptop from his backpack. It has University of Southern Maine stickers on it as well as stickers from all the latest Marvel movies. "I have a final this afternoon, American Political Systems, where the professor will try to trick us into wrong answers. I do not want to worry about it, *walwal me leh*, so I prefer to work here on anything you need. How is the boss?" Gordy had met Abshir when he spoke at the University's Career Day. Abshir insisted on volunteering in the office, stating he wanted to see American justice served. Gordy told him private investigation was a lot of paper-pushing, snooping, and sometimes sidestepping strict legalities, not everyone's idea of justice. Abshir grinned, "As long as it is truth-seeking, it is for me." Gordy quickly recognized Abshir's willingness to do everything from getting lunch to adding coins to parking meters to doing late night surveillance. He added him to the payroll.

"Gordy's in the operating room."

We're interrupted by the sound of sirens. Without warning, quiet Portland is pulsing with distress. Abshir and I look out the window to Commercial Street; the rain is now a drizzle. Fast moving clouds allow shards of sun to shine on the black and white Portland Police cruisers as they turn onto Widgery Wharf. Motorcycle blues glide into strategic spots to re-route traffic.

A familiar feeling pulses inside me—sternum to brain—it's like a magnetic pull. "I'll be back in ten." I put the burner cell and my personal cell into my pocket. "Oh—and we have a new client. Start a list of charter companies that specialize in yachts, Rhode Island up to Maine. Phone numbers and ports of call. Can you do that while you consider the trick test questions on political theory?"

"I can do that. *Dabcan*."

I lope quickly to the elevator, curiosity leading.

* * *

The post-squall air is heavy, promises a growing humidity. The Crime Unit, in their yellow jackets, stretch police tape across the wharf's entrance. My old partner, Marvin, next to his motorcycle, is stiff and defensive. He's got sunglasses and a helmet on, resembles a robotic insect. He sees me approach. "What're you doin' here?"

"Just breathin', Marvin. And wonderin'."

"You can't help yourself, can ya?" His voice has an edge to it. He's never gotten past the fact that I outclassed him in the academy's PAT and PPQ trials—a girl besting him in four out of five physical tests rubbed him the wrong way. He never expected to excel at the written, but he hated it when it was announced—as a joke—the lowest scores were being partnered with the highest scores to amortize the talent in the squad car. Our mean-spirited captain got a laugh from the graduates—but not from Marvin. Our partnership never coalesced, even after a year of having each other's back during a couple of tight situations.

"What's goin' on here?" I ask.

"Police business."

"Heard your brother Billy got out."

"You got an opinion on that?"

"Me? No. Like to be friendly." I nod towards his ride. "You're on a bike now."

He lifts his chest. "And I can't talk. Got work to do." He strides over to corral a group of tourists who have gathered, cell phones held high, hoping to phone-video a freaky event.

I move to the southern side of the wharf where I'll get a better view. The seagulls are hovering, swooping down, squawking. Two members of the Portland PD's dive team surface, shepherding a body being brought up in a net. Three other cops in Crime Tech windbreakers disconnect the net from the winch and lay the large dead weight on the wet dock. A beam of startling sunshine breaks through a thin cloud and lands on the deep gash in the man's head; it starts at the hairline and cracks through the nose and chin. His face would split in two with a strong pull. What the hell did he fall on? Or get pummeled with? The guy's basketball-sized abdomen has popped the buttons of a familiar green shirt, the thick torso hair is matted like seaweed on his blue-ish white belly. The water temperature today is probably in the mid-forties. An obese man descending into that would quickly go into cold shock and lose coordination as the blood collected in his core. Cardiac arrest would follow. But, then there's that face chop, maybe he didn't have time to panic.

Robbie Donato, my training sergeant in my first months at Maine's Criminal Justice Academy, is there. He's a Portlander, four years older than me; our high school tenures never crossed but his reputation as captain of four sports—football, basketball, sailing, and cross-country had lingered in the school's hallways for years. He's got broad shoulders and a lean, runner's body. In the Academy, I was aware of his steady blue-gray eyes taking patient inventory of all information. He walks over. "Hey."

I state the obvious. "You have a floater."

"That's the word."

"Accident?"

He's candid, probing. "You got that look. Like you know something."

I nod towards the human blubber. "Well, I met that guy—not officially. He got in body-odor distance of me last night. At Sparrows. Really loud and obnoxious."

"What was he doing there?"

"Trying to sell Pat on switching suppliers."

"There's no ID on him. Catch a name?"

"He claimed MacScottish something. But I saw his driver's license when he gave Pat a really suck-o tip. Thomas Beene. Double 'e' in the middle. New Jersey somewhere. Morristown, if my memory stored it right."

"That 'noticing' of yours was always impressive." Donato writes it down in a small black notebook.

"The wallet was fat."

"Fat?"

"Lots of hundreds."

Donato nods. "Okay. Might've been tempting." He settles back on his heels. "So—your life?"

What kind of question is that? I deflect, "Last time I checked I had one."

He laughs. "Rommel, you know what I'm asking. When you comin' back to work?"

"I work."

"You can still be a cop, Rommel." His blue-gray eyes squint, one of the corners of his mouth has turned upwards into a challenging half-smile. "You're missed."

"By who?"

"Well, I'm one of the people noticing you're not livening up the place."

A forensic tech calls from dockside. "Donato? You wanna take a shot of this."

Donato puts his notebook in his pocket. "Gotta go." He calls over his shoulder as he walks off. "We'll talk more about Beene."

"That's all I got," I tell him.

"Never know."

CHAPTER FIVE
Wednesday

I'm back at the office. Abshir puts aside his research on yacht-rental companies. "The list is long. I will resume after my test at the University."

"How do I say 'good luck'?"

"*Nasib wacan.*"

"Back at you."

Abshir slips out. There's a ding from my phone. It's a text from Jade. She's sent me information via the secure Dropbox: Bunny Luce has had no credit card activity in the last week. No bank card withdrawals. High percentage of her bills are on automatic payment. No cell phone activity. She has no recent use of personal accounts, has not logged into GPS or any travel sites. Bunny Luce does not own a car, there's no license plate to track. Her whereabouts remain unknown.

Jade reports that the New York City conference was focused on Bio-Engineering and Artificial Intelligence. Lucy Claren was a keynote speaker. The blurb from the private gathering of forward-thinkers:

Lucy Claren initially caught the attention of the Bionics community with her work in Myoelectrics. Lucy Claren is now the head of LC Labs at Claren Tech, leads a research team focused on the pros and cons of AI in regard to privacy issues and its place in Bionic Technology.

The next item stops me. Bunny Luce's lab was shut down a week ago, and the main switchboard at Claren Technology was not forthcoming with any information as to when it might be re-opened.

Jade notes that she'll work on predictables and send more information as she finds it.

Why would Bunny Luce drop out of contact with her father? Expectations of disapproval? She'd sent him the note, but it was an 'after-all-decisions-have-been-made' alert and no way to contact her. Basically, she's giving him a chance to show up and observe her fait accompli. No discussion. What kind of father-daughter relationship is this?

My dad had been gentle. After my mother left us and settled in Boston—I remind myself she would never use the term *left us*—she preferred to refer to the event as *her relocation*. When she *relocated* to Boston for a job that demanded enormous time and effort and did her best to fit in short visits to Maine to convince herself that we were thriving without her, I felt my role was to make sure my dad didn't sit alone in his recliner, his eyes glazing over during never-ending reading on naval battles off the coast of Maine. I'd accompany him at least once a month to the Maine Maritime Museum in Bath—an hour away—or the Great Harbor Maritime Museum in Northeast Harbor. Or we'd head up to the Maine Lighthouse Museum in Rockland and to all scheduled naval lectures within a 150-mile radius of Portland. My dad's parenting style was buddy-ish. We hung out. I can't imagine I would've ever wanted to cut him out of my life.

And why did Bunny Luce shut down her lab? What does it have to do with her dropping off the grid?

* * *

I pick up Bert at Doggie DayCare and we walk up the hill towards my apartment. The air is muggy, feels gloppy. A thin film of sweat—on my neck and back—forms quickly. We head to my favorite bench at the highest point on the Eastern Promenade. I'm wishing for a breeze. No luck.

"Come on, Bert. It's your dinner time."

He yips and trots across the street beside me.

Bert's nose twitches as I prepare his dinner in the special bowl with Gordy's picture on it. Gretchen has told me dogs categorize the world according to smells. The smell of food, the smell of an animal that could be friend or foe, the smell of danger, smell of a warm resting place in a sun-filled room. They're supposed to have an advanced kind of olfactory bulb in their noses—about forty times more efficient than a human's. Bert's snout is a good one—and he's enjoying smelling the poached egg on top of his soft turkey kibble. It's gotta be a fabulous life.

My neon-pink PhysTherapy notebook is on the counter. It's so bright and ugly I can't miss it. I lean cuff-crutches against the counter where I can reach them and clear my water bottle off the dining table. The table's solid heaviness has come in handy; my dad made it of two, seven-foot slabs of thick, old barn wood. I roll out my yoga mat on its surface, discard my jeans and hop up onto it. I take off my LiteGood, keep the liner and sock on because I'm going out again later.

I go through my exercises. Hamstring stretches for the whole leg. Turn onto my stomach, place the rolled towel under the stump. Stretch the hip flexor muscle, thirty reps. Rest in this position for five minutes. My PT complimented me on my dedication to strength. I told her the only way to get pity out of people's eyes is to get stronger than I was before.

There's a ding, it's coming from my phone. It's a text from Jade. I grab the crutches and head to my computer.

More dead-ends await. Contact attempts with the five employees in the LC Lab have not been successful. They had all put in for their vacation time. I shoot an email back to Jade, asking her to track down personal contact numbers and addresses.

I make a note to check with Claren. He should be able to get me into Lucy's lab, if that's what I need to do. After all, he owns the company.

Jade has forwarded a pdf file of the Claren Labs Employee Newsletter. I read the list of recent award-winners, an article on the new menu in the cafeteria and the latest carpool and parking options. There's also a short letter from the boss, Philip Claren, noting that all government contracts, in light of the newly-elected administration in Washington, DC, will now be subject to review. He closes, extending an eagerness to welcome everyone at the company picnic in July.

'Government contracts will now be subject to review...' That doesn't sound friendly.

Finally, I reach the starred information at the bottom of the page and my spirits spike—the first good news: Renae Claren, Bunny Luce's mother, has made a reservation at the Westin Hotel in Portland. She arrives tomorrow, early check-in scheduled for late morning. Seems plausible the mother of the bride is coming to town to take care of bride and groom details.

Maybe a quick conversation with Renae Claren will clear up the mystery.

I smile. This time tomorrow the case could be closed. And I might be able to start checking out the used car lots.

* * *

I claim my favorite stool at Sparrows so I'll be able to see Gretchen and Karla as they walk in. *My Sharona* plays at the perfect volume—not so loud you can't hear yourself think but loud enough that you don't feel like an ass not talking. Pat pours me my first beer and I lean into him. "Did you hear that the MacLiquor salesman from last night was found floating off Widgery Wharf this morning?"

"That tall detective was in here asking about it."

"Corduroy jacket, khakis, kind of a long face?"

Pat nods. "A guy who listens. Takes his time."

"That's Donato."

"I gave him the business card the drunk jerk left with me." Pat catches himself. "I guess I shouldn't speak ill of the dead."

The beer is cool and bitter in my mouth. "Being dead shouldn't put angel wings on everyone."

"How stupid do you have to be to get soused and weave around on a wharf at night?"

"Stupid."

"How's Gordy?"

"Got an email from his sister-in-law. Operation went well, the kidney transfer's successful, and he's healthy enough to complain. That's good, right?"

"Sounds like he's back to normal," Pat mutters, wiping the bar with a cloth. "I know you were worried, Dee."

I snort. "Not."

"Course not." Pat's agreeing, but he's got a challenge in his eye.

Reader is here again at the corner table, ponytail and biceps stretching his leather jacket. "Pat," I say, "you think maybe it's a waste of money to pay a guy to sit in your place and read a book?"

"Peace of mind." Pat heads off down the bar to refill wine glasses for a couple who look like they hate each other. I sip my beer, wonder why people bother trying to make coupledom work.

Someone perches on the stool next to me. I turn, come face-to-face with the Reader. He must walk on cat's feet. I try to mask my startled twitch. "Gonna hit the john," he says.

"Information not needed." I notice the corners of his olive-green eyes are scored with squint lines—they are lighter than his tanned and wind-marked face.

"Keep an eye on Pat—for five. Can you do that?"

"Who's asking?"

"Me." He raises a thick eyebrow.

"Name?"

"Asking you to keep your eyes open. Not asking for a date."

"Which is not even in the arena of possibilities."

"Understood. You're way too hot for a guy like me."

He speaks in a monotone. He's funny. I ask, "Do you want me to give a little girl squeal if a big bad guy stomps in?"

"Sounds like a plan."

Jule Selbo

He leaves his book on the bar. *Great Expectations.* A Dickens guy? I read it in high school—my teacher was an avid Dickens-as-a-social-justice-chronicler, always pointing out how the rich and powerful make unilateral decisions that affect the working poor who are often too uneducated, tired and hungry to stick up for themselves. This book doesn't jibe with my assumptions about the Reader—but then, what was I expecting? *Men Can Rock Ponytails* or *Bodyguarding for Dummies*?

I take out my pocket notebook, it's full of details of Jade's initial grab into Tyler Peppard's life. Brief rundown: born in Omaha, Nebraska, parents (now deceased) owned a steakhouse. He washed dishes as a kid, bussed tables as a teen, waited on customers during summer breaks. Married in the middle of his senior year in high school, four months later became a father to a daughter named May. A year later, a divorce was granted and Peppard, who may have always been hankering to get to the big city, moved to New York. He started night classes at Manhattan College, focusing on business and marketing and started to work days in Yarborough Inx's mailroom. A year later he was assistant to a vice president named Vincent Kern; he worked for him for five years. I did a search on Vincent Kern; he was a regular in the clubs that cater to the trust fund and celebrity crowds for over a decade. He resigned from Yarborough Inx two years ago; became a co-founder of a fancy drug rehab facility, Barriers Broken, located in Hyde Park, New York. Its website documents Kern's problems with substance abuse and how he thanks the Lord for giving him the strength to kick his habit. Barriers Broken is Kern's way to give back and help others.

A tap on the bar next to me. It's the Reader, sunk into his monotone. "All good?"

"Negative on incoming," I tell him.

"Good job. Wasn't sure you'd be up for it."

I laugh. "Screw you."

"But we're not even dating." He picks up his book, leaves my side, and regains ownership of his corner table. Opens his Dickens.

The door swings open. Gretchen, wearing her cap, comes in; Karla's behind her. They wear slickers and sparkling drops of light rain bead on their shoulders.

Pat nods, he knows a pitcher of Shipyard IPA is in the plan. "Got it."

Karla, her hyperactivity in full force, leads the way to the back booth, dancing to the bass line of *You're So Vain*. I'm about to slide in next to Gretchen when Karla gets defensive. "No fair. Two against one." She hangs her damp slicker on the booth's hook and skootches over to make room for me. "I don't want you two ganging up on me." Her sparkling eyes are framed in dark eyeliner; spangling earrings drop from her lobes.

Ten Days

Pat puts the pitcher and two more glasses on our table. Karla blows air kisses at Pat—and then at us. "Hi, honeys."

Gretchen parks her slicker and keeps her cap on. Her grin is a bit forced. "We have to do this more often. Girl bonding."

Karla pours the beer. "Dee, talk to any of your old cop buddies? Was the guy they found at the wharf a jumper or a drunk who took a wrong step?"

"No details yet," I tell her.

"I sure don't want to die drownin'—it's a disgusting, scary way to go. That's what people say." Karla shudders, her high spirits have an edge to them. She turns to Gretchen. "Why are you wearing that ugly cap? You don't love the new cut?"

Gretchen hedges. "I like it—getting used to it."

"You two are way too cautious," Karla complains. "What's 'getting used to it' worth? It's your life. Your hair. Your body. Your feelings. We're wired, right? Not like we can control who we are, what we want."

"Come on, K," I laugh. "You think it's all fate? Are we—the supposedly intelligent life on the planet—incapable of making any of our own decisions?"

Karla has a tendency to preach pseudo-psychology from *Cosmo*. "Sure, you can decide not to be happy. But what good is that?" She slurps her beer.

Gretchen speaks slowly, wanting to get Karla settled down a bit. "I don't know, maybe the universe presents possibilities and then it's our job to weigh stuff. The good. The bad. Get a pool of opinions. Maybe check on how friends see stuff."

Karla ignores Gretchen's attempt to lead the conversation and grabs her shoulder bag. "I brought presents." She pulls out plastic sandwich bags, the kind that have a zip-it seal. They're filled with samples of hair products—mini-bottles she gets free at the salon.

"Gee, thanks, Karla." She always tries to buy love—figures gifts can secure affection.

Karla reaches into her bag again. "Those are jokes, setting you up for the real thing. Look what I found at Flea-For-All." She takes out a small box, opens it to reveal three vintage brass pins, the kind my grandmother used to wear on her coats. Each is a cupid ascending, wings akimbo, pointing a bow and arrow upwards.

"For luck in love," Karla says.

Not my style. But I don't want to burst her camaraderie bubble.

Gretchen pins one on her purple satin baseball jacket. "Thanks, buddy."

"Silly, sure, but there were three of them. And three of us." Karla blows us each a kiss and approves when I pin it on the strap of my bag. She places hers in the center of the felt flower that's tacked onto her cardigan. "Give me your phone, Dee. Mine's out of battery and I want to take a picture." She grabs my phone and opens the camera app. "Lean over, Gretch." Karla stretches her arm out to get the group pic and we all point at the cupid presents. "Say 'love you, Karla!'" We obey and Karla punches the photo button with her thumb. "Got it."

Gretchen settles back on her side of the booth. "Maybe we should plan a trip. Head up the coast this weekend. Find some white sandy beach. Eat lobster. Talk about things."

"About Billy?" Karla challenges.

"About deciding whether you want to hang with him again or not."

"Don't worry about me, honeys." Karla's hackles show.

Gretchen leaves us to bring the empty pitcher over to Pat for a refill. Karla lets her head fall onto my shoulder. "Dee, sorry, I haven't found the time to check in lately, got so busy with the salon and expanding—growing the business. But I'm a phone-call away. You'll have fun again." Karla's mood shifts. She laughs and sits up. "I'll make it happen. That's me. Miss Fun." She elbows me. "I gotta pee."

I let her out of the booth and she heads to the bathroom. I notice Reader's not reading, his attention is on something outside. I follow his gaze. Billy Payer, driving a white Chevy pickup, has pulled up behind Karla's lime-green Camry. The driver's side window is open; he lights a cigarette and blows out a mouthful of smoke. He reaches an arm out of the truck to feel the rain. His cut-off sweatshirt leaves his muscled arm exposed; seems he's taken advantage of the prison's gym. And then I see Karla, her cardigan pulled up over her head to keep the rain off her hair, slip across the street.

Gretchen arrives back with the pitcher of beer.

"Karla went out the back door," I say.

Gretchen looks out the window. Karla gets into the passenger seat of the Chevy truck.

I sigh. "Told you she wouldn't listen to us."

Billy tosses his cigarette onto the street and the white truck pulls away.

NINE DAYS

CHAPTER SIX
Thursday

It's morning. I gaze out of the eye-high windows of my subterranean home. The rain has let up but gray clouds hover low in the sky. Sometimes knowing I'm in a room dug out of the earth gives me a sense of stability. Sturdy, packed ground surrounding my four rooms and hallway; front and back entrance, double-locked. Secure. Solid.

The plan is for an early meet-up with Claren at the office. I don't have anything concrete to give him—he wants location, access, and reasons and all I have are biographical tidbits and 'probables' that are not panning out.

But I do have questions.

"Come on, Bert. Playmates await." Bert's just finished his morning bites; his long tongue laps all the extras trapped around his hairy mouth. I land my favorite Portland Sea Dogs baseball hat on my head, anticipating rain. We head up the short ramp to lawn level; a twelve-year-old dark blue Volvo, plagued with rust, mud, and water spots, pulls up to the curb. It's Hilary, the newly-graduated and now official Mercy Hospital Emergency Room nurse who rents an apartment in the Victorian next door. I joked with her once that her spiffy crisp scrubs, spotless clogs, and fresh, twenty-year-old face didn't jibe with her car's exterior. She'd grinned and shown me the interior with pride. It was a study in what a dust-buster, sham, Windex, and fabric cleaner could accomplish. Every inch shone like a new quarter. She'd told me it made her too crazy to try to control the exterior, waste of time and money, due to Maine's rain, snow, slush, wind, and falling leaves—elements that sometimes crowd into the same day. Now, whenever I have the urge to wash the rust-spotted, metal skin of my Subaru Outback, I think of Hilary's common-sense attitude and think twice before heading to the car wash.

"Long day at work?" I know Hilary's helping her sick mom pay off debts so she's been taking on extra shifts.

"Jerk shot off his toe."

"Geez, that's not attractive."

"People don't care how they destroy their bodies," she vents. "I mean, you put an overload of any chemical into it and your body's gonna get mad, swat at you, kick you around, or…" She sighs, "Sometimes, just give up."

"Sorry."

"I try to sympathize—but there's too many self-destroyed nasal passages and knife-cuts and shot-off toes." She throws her hands in the air. "Don't they care there are a lot of people who are trying to take care of themselves who need medical attention fast too—that those people have to wait while we deal with the bozos?"

"Maybe there should be a line for the 'reckless bozos' and a line for the plain 'bodies falling apart.'"

"If I had my way." She laughs, but it's a tired sound.

"You get to snooze now?"

"Long snooze." She heads to the Victorian. "See ya, Dee."

Bert and I walk down the hill for coffee at Nivas and I pick up a newspaper. Lurid headlines focus on the body pulled up at Widgery Wharf. I sip at my extra-large caffeine boost as we head to Doggie DayCare. A frazzled Gretchen waits at the glass doors—she rushes out. "Karla didn't show for work. Two of her stylists came over 'cause she'd told them I have the extra key. I had to open up. Customers were waiting outside—Karla's special customers, too. She does the early bird appointments on Thursday."

"Maybe she overslept."

"Not answering her phone. She never screws up her business. You know that."

Karla can be a flake as a friend, but Gretchen's right, she never misses a beat with her salon. She's finally saved up enough to rent another location in nearby Westbrook, her first step in building her franchise.

A child calls out, "Gretchie! Here's Jaws!" A boy, probably the nerd of a kindergarten class, opens the back door of a just-parked red SUV. He's literally pulled out by a cocker spaniel. The boy's father stays behind the wheel of the car, his eyes buried in his cell phone.

"Hey, Danny! Hey there, Jaws!" Gretchen tries to replace her worried face with a happy one. She reaches for Jaws' leash. "I'll take Jaws and bring him inside. You have fun at school today."

"Only a week left and then it's summer vacation, Gretchie." Danny bends down and hugs the dog. "See you after, Jaws." Danny races back into the red SUV. "Come on, Dad, get off the phone. I gotta get to school."

Two businessmen approach from opposite directions with their dogs. One is straining a pinstriped suit and the other is well into his fifties, a Rotary pin gleaming on his lapel. They're like poster-men for the study that asserts owners resemble their dogs. Mr. Pumping Iron strides with a lean, muscular boxer and Mr. Community Involvement moves alongside a kind-eyed golden retriever. They hand over their leashes to Gretchen and head off to their jobs.

Gretchen, dealing with three dogs, lets her worry pour out. "I have a feeling, Dee." She pats her purple satin baseball jacket; the angel pin is in its place.

"Okay, I'll go by Karla's apartment." Bert's pawing at me to let him inside doggie heaven. I unclip his leash and he follows Gretchen inside, cantering behind the trio of canines.

I head back up the hill and unlock my Outback. I fold in, pull my left leg in after I settle in the seat. This is when I'm particularly aware I've got no feeling below the knee on the left side. Just dead weight decked out in a slip-on boot resting on the rubber mat.

I drive past Sparrows and check the street for Karla's lime-green Camry. Not there.

She lives a few miles away, near Deering Park, in a second-floor walk-up with a view of the pond. In the winter, she appreciates the ice skaters gliding over frozen water, in the summer she's close to the ducks and geese and the weekly Farmers' Market. I find a parking spot on Grant Street and walk towards a tired brick building with flaking brown shutters. I check the street for a glimpse of Karla's Camry. No sign of it. Someone is exiting the front door of her building, spooning cereal from a bowl into his mouth. This guy's stubby skeleton is supporting an enormous amount of flesh; the torso is enveloped in a food-stained Techno Shack hoodie and his sweatpants are stretched over a jiggly-jelly butt. He squints his red-rimmed eyes against the morning light and slurps liquid from the bowl. I wonder if he's using beer to wet his morning cornflakes.

"Excuse me." I inch up the brim of my Sea Dogs hat to get a better glance at him. "You live here?"

"Why?" His lips are fleshy and his jowls hang past his jawline.

"I'm looking for Karla—she lives on the second floor."

"Haven't seen her. But when you find her, tell her I can return her blender anytime. Don't like making those shitty veggie shakes." He licks his spoon. "They're a pissy way to start the day."

I head up three steps to push the buzzer with Karla's name on it. No response. Press again. Nothing.

The guy's eyeballing me. "She's probably frizzing up someone's hair. She's got a hair place on India Street."

"She's not at the salon. She's got customers waiting."

Ten Days

"What do I care?" He moves to a rusted Tahoe. I call after him, "Could you let me in? I'm a friend and I'm worried about her."

"Maybe she doesn't want to deal with people's dead hair today."

"Excuse me?"

"Hair is dead. It's got no blood or nerves or nuthin'. Grows, sure, but it's dead. It's weird stuff."

"You know a lot about hair."

He turns his cereal bowl over, shakes a few soggy flakes onto the street. Obviously, he thinks someone will clean up after him. He reads my appalled face. "I pay taxes."

I push down my judgmental nature and try to appeal to his humanity. "You said she lent you a blender. Return the favor. Let's make sure she's okay."

He sneers. "She gave me that blender as a big hint. Recipe book with some shitty title like 'Stop Looking Gross. Veggie Yourself to a New Look.' Yeah, the word was 'gross.'"

He opens his car door, tosses the bowl into the passenger seat. He sits his butt in first, then wedges his doughboy legs in under the steering wheel. The seat's back as far as it can go but that makes his legs too short to reach the pedals. He forces the seat forward as much as his gut will allow, slams the door and drives away.

Asshole.

I call Gretchen. "Karla's not answering the buzzer."

"I think she left a key with the guy who lives below her. His name is Henry or Hector…"

I notice the name next to #1A. Hector Manfred. "Well, this Hector's not inclined to help out. Maybe Karla went health-nut on him."

"There's a tree in the back—outside her bedroom window."

"So?" I get what she's suggesting. I just don't want to consider it.

I head to the back of the building. The compact yard features wet, wheat-hued grass with early summer spurts of green and a single, sturdy oak tree. An empty, hard-plastic recycling container is against the fence. I hope it won't collapse under my weight. I place it strategically under the lowest, thickest limb of the tree. Standing atop it, I reach up to the branch, use my three reps of ten-chin-ups-a-day strength to pull myself up. I swing my good leg up and use my abs to lift the rest of my weight. Hurts like hell. I reach for the next limb. Heave upwards. Then two more branches, dragging my LiteGood up and working to balance. I'm finally opposite Karla's second story window. I lean against the damp trunk and swing my high-fiber appendage across the branch so I'm straddling it. I look inside the second story window. Karla's room is painted yellow, her bed is made, the bedspread is rose-colored and lavender lace pillows are arranged artfully at the headboard. I lean forward, get a glimpse through the open bedroom door into a hallway that leads to the living room. No one moving around. I scooch ahead on the limb and bang on the window—as hard as I can without toppling over.

No response. Damn.

I look down and my stomach tightens with resentment. It's going to take more effort to reach earth again than pulling myself up off it. I hold onto the trunk and descend towards the lowest limb. I don't want to risk a jump, worried my prosthetic might jam into my residual leg and create more problems. A one-legged dismount brings up insecurities on balance issues. I consider my ability to land light as a cat and execute a tuck and roll but the ground is hard and rocky and I have no circus training. I mutter encouragement to myself, "This is why you kill at the gym. Use it." I wrap my arms around the tree limb and hug it to my midsection and slowly slide down until the lower half of my body, from abdomen to toes, swings free. My biceps and triceps burn, my back feels it and I think—damn—all I need is to tear a rotator cuff. I stretch my good leg—toes downwards; my boot scrapes the top of the recycle box. I try to lower another inch. My hands are too small to get a good hold on the branch, I'm slipping and my swinging prosthetic hits the plastic container and knocks it out of reach. Damn it. I allow my hands to slip off, land as light as I can on my good leg and bend, deep as possible so my rump hits the ground, then roll onto my back and shoulders and finally hear the boot on my prosthetic hit the dirt. My Sea Dogs hat falls off and my hair spills out. I grouse under my breath; the wet dirt and sodden leaves press against the back of my head.

I lay there for a moment to assess various parts of my body. I used to take everything for granted. Physically, I'm fine. Mentally, I'm disgusted with myself.

Back in the Subaru, I check the time. I've got less than an hour before I meet with Claren at the office.

Time for one more stop.

CHAPTER SEVEN
Thursday

I make it in ten minutes to my ex-partner Marvin's garage apartment in East Deering—he's living within spitting distance of his mother. She's been married four times; I'm not sure if Mister Four is still sticking around. I climb a flight of outdoor stairs and pound on the apartment's door. "Marvin?"

No answer. Give it one more hard series of raps. "Marvin?"

The kitchen door of the main house opens and Billy stands there, in boxers and a t-shirt. He's eating peanut butter out of a jar. His eyes squinch into the daylight. "So, it's Raging Rommel."

A nickname from my high school athletic career. I didn't like to lose, and when faced with the possibility, rage was my go-to emotion.

"Haven't seen you since my trial."

"That was a special day."

"For you? Bet it was." He scratches his belly. "Marv's off protecting Portland. Not here."

"But you are. Felons don't usually live with their cop brothers."

"I'm living with my mom. And he keeps his gun locked up over there…" He waves towards the garage apartment. "Don't worry. He told his captain."

I come down the stairs, reach the driveway.

His eyes graze over my legs. "Shame about your accident. Feelin' different?"

I ignore the mean, satisfied tone. "I saw Karla meet you last night—outside Sparrows. Get into your truck."

"So."

"You know where she is now?"

"Karla and me went to the Tavern for a beer. I abstain from Pat's place out of respect."

"And 'cause you're banned from there," I remind him.

"What happened—that was the old me. I have repented."

Ten Days

"Karla didn't show at work today. Went by her apartment, doesn't look like she slept there last night." I try to peek around him into the house, but he stretches to fill the door.

"I dropped her back off at Sparrows so she could pick up her car. She's hot for me, talking love, love, love. Told her no time to get serious, got some self-work to do before I can give to anyone else."

"That sounds like prison-shrink talk."

"Taxpayers paid for my therapy. Shouldn't they get their money's worth?" His eyes are widely innocent and his lips form all the right words. But it seems like he practiced that line for the parole board.

"Billy. You got any idea where Karla is?"

"No."

I press. "If you see her—tell her I need to talk to her?"

"Not planning on seeing her." He closes the door—hard—like he wishes it would hit me.

* * *

I slide into a parking place near the Ferry Terminal and resent the Pay to Park. I'll move the car back up the hill after my meeting with Claren. The Silverseas ship is gone, replaced by a Princess Cruise ship, a regular in the Portland harbor. Its passengers board in New York or Boston, head north to Portland, onto Bar Harbor, and then to the windswept shores of Nova Scotia to take in the more unpopulated landscape, a relief from America's fast pace. Maybe the passengers fantasize it's a place to disappear, to get off the grid.

The sky's gray and teasing rain. Malio is there, holding court with the regulars who've left the shelter for the morning. He's talking about his DVD viewing from yesterday, pontificating about the merits of the special effects in the *Titanic* film. "I had to w-watch it 'cause of my g-girlfriend. She cried, not me. Didn't get my t-tears. No way." They seem impressed with his macho stance.

I cross the street and head towards the office. A black Escalade pulls up next to me; the back window is powered down. It's Claren. "I have a meeting I have to get to, so I'd appreciate it if you could fill me in as we drive? Roger will bring you back after he drops me off."

My reflection in the window reveals remnants of crumpled oak leaves on my hat. I brush them off as Roger, the cube-headed 'Beefcake,' gets out of the car. His hair is cropped military style and he wears a black polo shirt and black jacket and a wristwatch that tells time on multiple continents. He opens the back door.

"Fancy," I say, sliding in and brushing against the soft leather. I can smell Claren's citrus-inspired aftershave.

Roger puts up the soundproof glass between the driver and the back seat and moves into traffic. Claren's got a folded newspaper on his lap; he's looking at the picture of the victim, Thomas Beene. "Fished him out yesterday morning," I say.

"Accident?"

"Haven't heard."

He pushes his glasses back towards the high bridge of his nose. "Do you miss being on the force?"

"I like working for Gordy. Fine for now."

He gets to the point. "What do you have to tell me?"

I take my notebook from my pocket and go over Tyler Peppard's background, his growing up in the Midwest, his quick, early marriage, his child, his move to New York City. Yarborough Inx and its clients. His former boss' reputation as one with a drug problem. "Peppard could have been part of the New York club scene with his boss. Do you think…"

"Bunny Luce doesn't do drugs."

"More common than you think…"

"She wouldn't waste her time. Too many other things that take focus."

"Have you noticed she's lost weight? She's not looking as healthy as…"

"I'm telling you, drugs is the wrong thing to consider." Claren's jaw tightens. "Bunny couldn't accomplish what she's been doing at the lab without full use of clear faculties."

"She looks thinner than her Claren Tech photo on the company website." Is he really seeing his child? It's clear he loves her, but is he really seeing her? "So, you're sure she's been focused on work. What's her latest project?"

"Confidential at this point."

"Does she have any vice? Over-shopping? Gambling? Alcohol?"

Claren snorts. "She runs a high-profile lab. Like I said, she doesn't have time."

Clearly, Claren's holding onto his version of his daughter. He might be right. Or he might not be considering her youth, her access to anything money can buy, maybe a desire for love. Love can become a powerful addiction, if one gets bit hard by it. I know Claren doesn't want to consider this, so I carry on with my list of questions. "The tear-sheet from *Social*—you gave it to me…"

"Yes?"

"The photo was taken at an event for a Yarborough client—a business called Destiny Leader."

Ten Days

Claren's voice gets hard. "This is what I want to know: where is Peppard? Is Bunny with him? How did he get a hold on her? And why is Bunny not paying attention to what's important?"

"Some background could help me locate her."

"Some social event she attended a month ago can't be important at this point."

He's wrong. Every action is important, each is based on previous events. We are what we do. "Her entire lab was closed down last week."

"I was alerted."

"You didn't tell me that yesterday. All you said is that she hadn't shown up for work, not that she had shut down her entire operation."

"She's got complete autonomy. It was part of our agreement when I suggested she put her labs on the Claren campus. That means she can put her work on hiatus whenever she wants."

"Do you think it's weird that she did?"

His shoulders slump. "Damn it. Nothing feels right at the moment."

We're traveling south on I-295. "Any reason your daughter would be dodging you because of a work issue?"

He rubs his temples. "No reason that I can think of."

"Does Bunny Luce like to play games? Pull your chain? Get your attention by disappearing? Has she done this before?"

"No. No. No." And. "No."

His energy dissipates with every negative, as if his bewilderment and sadness are multiplying. I notice we're moving off the highway, following the exit sign to Portland International Jetport. "Your meeting is at the airport?"

Roger turns the Escalade into a private aviation area. Claren powers down his window, shows his ID to the guard. We're waved through. Claren puts his ID back in place, slips his wallet into the inside pocket of his suit jacket. He keeps his hand there, over where his heart beats. "My meeting's in DC"

"Can you postpone?" I put my notebook back in my pocket and play my one good card. "I should have led with this. Your ex-wife is supposed to check into the Westin hotel in a few hours. It makes sense that the mother of the bride would be arriving to finalize wedding details. Bunny Luce might be with her. If so, problem solved. You could be there."

Claren takes his glasses off, polishes the lenses with the soft cloth he takes from his pocket. "But you're not sure Bunny will be with her?"

"No."

"They're two very different people." He's weighing the possibility. "Don't spend a lot time together. Lately."

"Wedding plans can bring mothers and daughters together."

"But you don't know for sure that Bunny will show."

"No," I repeat. "Not for sure."

The Escalade has stopped next to a private plane. The pilot and flight attendant are at the bottom of the staircase leading up to the jet. Claren's torn. "I can't cancel my meeting."

"Postpone it?"

He hesitates, then shakes his head. "Can't. But I'll be back as soon as I can…" He stops. At the top of the mobile stairway, in the doorway to the plane, is a rail-thin man in a perfectly tailored suit. He's got silver-gray hair cut close to his head. Why is he familiar? My brain lands on it. *'Your dog rope…blocking my entry to coffee.'* It's the German. Here now, sans birdwatching book and binoculars.

"When you find Bunny Luce," Claren says quickly, "Tell her we need to talk. As soon as possible."

Claren gets out of the SUV and climbs the stairs.

The German slips back into the plane's interior.

* * *

Portland's Westin Hotel sits at the peak of High Street, its upper-level rooms have a view of the harbor, the lighthouse, and the Whitehead Passage that leads out to the ocean. Its lobby is modern, it caters to those who value service, amenities, and cool, square spaces. I'm dressed to fit in—after a quick sponge and towel off, I went to the back of my closet for a blue linen shirt, pleated black pants, and blazer. The kind of things my mother buys me for birthdays. She's got an aversion to Maine's flannels and plaids.

I cross the hotel's gray stone floors to the shining white reception counter.

"May I help you?" The hotel clerk is perky. Her name tag reads 'Colleen.'

"I'm here to meet with Mrs. Renae Claren. She hasn't checked in yet, has she?"

Colleen scans her computer. "No. Not yet."

"If it's all right with you, I'll wait." I give a pat to my bag. "I've brought work—so I'll sit here in the lobby."

"That's fine."

Ten Days

I move to the back corner of a carpeted space, sink into a leather chair situated behind a pillar. There's a clear view of the sliding glass entry doors and I'm partially blocked from the clerk's eyes. Maybe Colleen will forget about me.

I keep one eye on the entrance and open my bag, move the compact umbrella to get to my iPad. I go over Jade's research again: Renae Bennard Claren grew up on a tough side of Boston. Never made it through the community college, apparently too focused on frat parties at the more elite institutions. Claren was twenty-one when he promised a lifetime to her. They had a daughter when he was twenty-two and they divorced when he was twenty-three. I remember Claren's guttural growls when romance came up in our first meeting. Can't help but think that Renae's sting must've been deadly.

There's a whoosh of the glass entry doors opening. Out-of-towners enter—the two I saw at Pat's that were happy to accept MacScottish's whiskey pours. The couple have Starbucks coffee cups in hand; they look like they're recovering from another hard night of drinking. They head towards the bank of elevators and the guy presses the button for service. I move to the lobby's gift shop, situated across from the elevators. The woman scowls at the digital readout on the side of elevator, impatient with its slowness. "You've got no spine, Chanel," says the guy, adjusting the scarf that's below his perfectly trimmed beard.

Her temper is sharp. "You're afraid he goes both ways. And that payday is winning."

"You don't know anything about anything," he sounds sure of himself. "I'm not worried."

The elevator doors open and they get in. The carriage stops on the eighth floor.

The Press Herald and its "Death on the Wharf" story rests on the newspaper rack in front of me. Maybe these two were among the last to talk to Thomas Beene. I shake my head, tell myself it's not my business anymore. My uniform is packed away, deep in the corner of a closet. But it's ingrained. I take out my cell and punch in the familiar number and ask for Detective Robbie Donato. I'm transferred to his line, hear his recorded message. "Robbie Donato. Tell me whatcha need." I supply my name and cell phone number.

And then settle back into the leather chair and wait.

It's a half hour later. Hotel guests have walked by with city maps, preparing to take in Old Portland's highlights. Mail has been delivered. Personnel has changed at the reception desk. I've read the Press Herald cover to cover and, after finishing *What to do in Portland in June*, I make a mental note to get my ticket to the Maine Brewers Festival, the pinnacle event for those into craft beer.

Renae Claren strides into the lobby, her chin leading. Her cinnamon-colored, long cashmere coat catches the air and flows out behind her. She wears a white silk shirt, black jeans, and four-inch patent-leather heels. I can see out to the street. A Lincoln Town Car is at the curb. The driver opens the trunk and takes out a set of hard-shell luggage, golden in color.

Renae Claren stops at the reception desk. I can head her thin, breathy voice. "Mrs. Philip P. Claren."

A reedy clerk is at the check-in desk, his fingers peck at the computer keyboard. "Welcome, Mrs. Claren. We're very pleased you've chosen our hotel. I have a note that you're here for a week."

"I've reserved three suites," Renae says, clearly not interested in chit-chat.

"Right, I have a request for an early check-in. But, ah…I'm afraid that…" He sneaks a glimpse at the clock on the wall behind her. "I'm sorry, the guests occupying the suites have not checked out. We did guarantee them for you by noon, and it's ten thirty now and…"

"You're kidding." Renae's tone becomes sharp enough to slice someone's throat.

The clerk is skittering, wants a way to make things better. "We're happy to comp you a breakfast in our restaurant. We serve an extensive menu…"

Steam seems to rise from under the collar of Renae's cashmere coat. "I have a meeting scheduled in half an hour. If the suites are not ready, as I requested and *expected,* I will require a *private* space."

The clerk's relieved he has a solution. "I can make our business conference room available at eleven, Mrs. Claren, and make sure there's coffee, tea, and water. Would you like us to arrange for anything else?"

"Veuve Clicquot, Grand Dame. I notified the hotel to have some chilling in my suite."

"Yes, Mrs. Claren, I have that noted. I'll arrange for the same champagne to be brought to the conference room."

Renae commands, "Put in an order for a soft-boiled egg, unbuttered toast and espresso. I'll wait in the restaurant."

"I'll do that." The clerk's already on the phone.

Renae strides down the hallway towards the restaurant, her long, highlighted hair swinging on her back and her heels clicking loudly on the stone floor.

I wait five minutes to let Renae Claren get settled with her fancy coffee. Then I mosey to the restaurant. She's at a corner table, her back is to the entrance. I've read that celebrities have a habit of not facing out, keeping their backs to other diners, with hopes of not being recognized. Maybe she's employing the same strategy, putting herself at the same level as a pop star or movie actress. I move to her table and go for super friendly—a wide smile. "Mrs. Claren? My name is Dee. I'm sorry to bother you, but I saw you come in."

"How do you know who I am?"

"From pictures. In the newspapers, I guess."

I expect she'll be flattered, but she's wary. "I'm trying to have a bite to eat. Not to be taken advantage of."

"Of course, of course. If you could help me get in touch with Lucy…"

Renae's eyes narrow. "Why are you interested in my daughter?"

I keep it general as I compound my lies. "A lot of us in bio-engineering, at the University of Southern Maine, would love to invite her to talk about her work. It'd be an academic coup if you might put me in touch with her."

"She has an office."

"I haven't been able to get a response from her office."

Renae's golden-brown eyes harden. "He sent you, didn't he?"

"Excuse me?"

"My ex-husband sent you."

"I only want to talk to Lucy about coming to the university…"

She stands and hisses into my face. "He pushes her. Has no idea how fragile she really is. It's all about control with him. He expects everyone—me, his company—and especially our daughter—to do what he wants when he wants it. Tell him she's made a decision and she doesn't need or want his approval. Tell him to stop pushing her, that a mother knows when her daughter is close to breaking." She grabs her Vuitton bag. "Tell him he doesn't own her." She heads out of the restaurant, announcing loudly to the manager that she's being harassed. She takes him to task as she exits, "What kind of place allows this?"

The flummoxed manager, frowning, steps towards me. I defend myself, "Total exaggeration, but sorry." I veer towards the street exit of the restaurant. "Sorry."

Outside, I'm pissed at myself. I screwed that up. What was I thinking—that I'd be greeted warmly and that Renae Claren would be happy to be my go-between with Bunny Luce? Apparently, not so. A blown opportunity.

CHAPTER EIGHT
Thursday

The low, resonant burring horn of a ship's arrival in the port drifts up the hill. A couple approaches, I recognize Sean Prinn, local celebrity chef. He's in jeans, a checked shirt, and fleece vest, not dressing to show off his success. He's with a woman whose platinum-colored hair is arranged in a perfect tight topknot; her pencil skirt and the spike-heeled ankle boots scream out-of-town. Portland's filled with brick sidewalks tortured by years of weather and trees whose roots have proven stronger than man's plan and make walking in four-inch heels not practical. She's perturbed. They pass me without notice and enter the main doors of the hotel. I trail behind and slip through the glass doors, make a show of checking my cell phone near the valet office. Pencil-skirt puts her business card on the reception desk. "We're here for Mrs. Renae Claren."

The reedy clerk is ready. "Excellent. Mrs. Claren is waiting in the conference room." He points the way. "Up the short stairs and to the left."

They head off. The clerk looks at me expectantly. "May I help you?"

I move to the reception desk. The elegant business card is still there.

Shannon at Shannon Styles Ltd.
Event Planning
Boston, Massachusetts

"Beautiful hotel," I say. "Some of the rooms must have stunning views of the harbor."

"They do."

"My friend, Tyler Peppard, said he might leave a message for me?"

The clerk checks his computer. "Hmm. I don't have him registered as a guest."

"I must have the wrong hotel. I'll check with the Hyatt down the street."

"Have a nice day." The clerk's eyes are back on his computer.

Ten Days

The elevator dings. I look over my shoulder. Chanel's bearded, snarky companion, now in a tailored suit, light pink shirt, and carrying a leather folder under his arm, exits through the elevator's sliding doors. He quickly moves to the hallway that leads to the conference room. I turn back to the clerk. "How many conference rooms do you have here?"

"One. It's very nice. We have two small offices also, that guests can use."

"That's a real plus," I smile.

"We're full service."

I head back into the crisp, cool day. My car's parked on a residential side street, facing the hotel. I roll down its window to take in the salty air. My personal cell buzzes. I recognize the Middle Street Station prefix. "Dee Rommel."

"You called?" Donato's calm, steady.

"Random information," I say. "You interested in talking to two of the people MacDead was chatting up at Sparrows?"

Donato takes a moment. I imagine him reaching for his notebook and pen. "I would be."

"They're staying at the Westin."

"And you know this how?"

I stretch the truth. "I was meeting someone for breakfast. Happenstance. I noticed them. The woman's name is 'Chanel.'"

"You notice a lot, Rommel."

"Being a good citizen. That's all."

"Aren't you due here in the afternoon?"

How does he know this?

Donato continues, "I'd appreciate it if you check in with me after your appointment with Fogel. I need ten minutes."

I'd been thinking of taking a no-show at my weekly appointment at the department's mental health office. I'd pretty much decided I wasn't planning on going back to active duty, but Gordy has a habit of haranguing me to keep each session; stating that my compliance leaves the door open for a re-think of my decision. Besides, he asserts, everyone should talk about themselves and their feelings at least once a week. I was sure he'd heard that on *The View*.

"See you after shrink, Rommel. Okay?" He clicks off.

Donato has a way of getting people to do things they don't want to do, even while they think they have a choice in the matter. The night of my graduation from the Police Academy, he'd arranged for cider and a giant sheet cake from Two Fat Cats Bakery to be delivered to 109 for a celebration with his trainees. It was a chocolate cake, topped with low-bush blueberries, the best of the summer season.

Donato had caught me as I tried to slip out. "You don't like blueberries, Rommel?" Sure I do, I told him, but Gordy was waiting for me at Sparrows. I'd hurried out before he could guilt me into raising a glass of cider with my peers. A half hour later he'd shown up at the bar with a hefty wedge of the cake, three forks and called for Pat to set us up with a pitcher of beer. Gordy took Donato's worming into our own mini-celebration in stride, ate the berries and cake with gusto and we all ended up talking about the Donato family farm, its acres of blueberries. Donato surprised me with his knowledge of soil acidity, irrigation, and propagation; I remember thinking his passion for farming was striking—and that I wanted to get the story of why he chose law enforcement. But Christine Poole had come in, the news anchor for WMFT. A buzz rushed through the customers in Sparrows: a celebrity was among us. Her eyes landed on Donato and she joined us, taking hold of his arm. She graciously congratulated me, "Well, my guy thinks highly of you." The way she said it did not sound like a compliment, and Gordy snorted into his beer.

Donato and Christine left Sparrows ten minutes later and I never had the chance to ask Donato more about his farming techniques.

And then, life took an unexpected turn.

I punch in a call to Abshir. I ask him to bring the Chebeague file, the office's camera, plenty of snacks and join me in my car across the street from the Westin.

* * *

Abshir parks his rusted minivan behind me on the side street a block away and jogs to my car. He slips in, takes a file out of his jammed backpack and hands me his research on private yacht chartering companies. He tells me that some of the companies have fleets of over twenty boats, some have less, some even more. He'd called a few, got the expected answer: it's not permissable to give out information on their clients.

I get him up to date, show him pictures of Bunny Luce, Renae Claren, and Tyler Peppard.

"Text 'yes,' Abshir, if you notice any of these people. Just 'yes.' I'll get back here as soon as I can."

"*Fahmaan*. Got it," Abshir nods and heads back to his vehicle.

I pull out, and he moves his minivan into my space.

* * *

Ten Days

If I'd been blindfolded, driven around in circles for a day, and dropped off at this location, I could've identified it instantaneously. The smell of 109 Middle Street. Pungent whiffs of aggressive floor cleaner, abused coffee machines, and microwaved burritos, grunts, farts, sweat, and adrenalin. I take the elevator to the top floor, walk the linoleum-tiled corridor, pass the door to where the detectives in Criminal Investigations live. Random phone conversations and shout-outs eliciting, for the most part, good-natured curses fill the bullpen.

I take a hard left; Doc Fogel's weaselly assistant waves me into his office. The only window provides a view of four lanes of Franklin Arterial traffic. In the distance is Micucci's Italian Grocery on India Street. One of Micucci's roasted turkey and salami sandwiches would taste good right now. I toss my blazer over the end of the lumpy leather couch and sit in its corner. It feels like the safest place in the room.

Doc Fogel is situated behind an indestructible pressed-wood desk that has as much personality as the brown wall-to-wall carpet. His graying hair is in tight curls, his frayed polyester brown sport coat hangs on his narrow shoulders, his face is lined and spotted from exposure to wind and sun. He unlocks a drawer of a file cabinet, takes out my paperwork, slides the drawer back into place. Locks it. "How's your mental health, Officer Rommel?"

"You can write down 'fine.'"

"My paycheck depends on me doing more than that."

Therapy offices, I had assumed, were supposed to be places to cushion feelings, but this place is all lumpy bumps and smashed edges and a carpet that smells as if it had been woven with old gym socks. Fogel's doctoral certificate in Counseling Psychology is on the wall, along with pictures of him smiling, his hair blowing curlicue in the wind, on his sailboat. It's a Benetau 361; he's told me about it—bought used, it's his prize possession. Because of its needs, he's dedicated to a Wal-Mart and Goodwill wardrobe. His thrift has led to a healthy collection of sailing trophies lining his windowsill.

"Remember, we're moving our weekly up to Wednesday next week. I'm in the All Class Race at Penobscot and won't be able to make our regular time."

"Sure."

He scratches his sharp Adam's apple and checks his notes from our last session. "How's the stress level?"

"From one to ten? I'd pick three. Which is lower than the daily national average according to the American Psychological Association, which states that thirty-six percent of all Americans experience feelings of high stress on a daily basis."

"Don't repeat the statistics I gave you in our last session."

"Then let me say I'm kicking back—hanging loose."

He shoots a warning look at me. "Let's make this time together worthwhile, shall we?"

Since Fogel's job is to evaluate police officers' abilities to do their jobs, recommend promotions, demotions, and discharges, I choose to adjust my behavior. Ultimately, I want him to give me a clean bill of psychological health so the decision to go back on duty—or not—is my choice—not anyone else's.

But I don't like anyone moving into my mental space. He's been telling me for months we have to go beyond the night when my leg was crushed. He tells me that how a person reacts to a crisis situation has everything to do with former factors, and how a person heals is reliant on support systems—ones that we've built over time for ourselves and new ones we gain from outside sources. I usually nod, act compliant and impressed with the wisdom coming at me. I don't say I think it's bullshit and that my belief is that it's best to move on to the next day and take it as it comes. The trick is to learn to be okay with…whatever's handed to you.

"Dreams? Of falling?" he asks.

"No," I lie. "Actually, in the last week, I've been sleeping through the nights. Wake up excited for the day, ready to feed the dog."

"Dog?"

"Gordy's. I'm taking care of his dog."

He's interested. "You think the dog's presence is contributing to the unusual good nights of sleep?"

I cross my arms, and even in doing so I recognize my body language is shouting that I reject his idea.

He goes on, "Consider what the dog adds to your home life. You're not alone. You have protection."

"He's part poodle."

He ignores my snarkiness. "Maybe getting your own dog—after Gordy gets back—is a good idea."

"I'm not a dog person." My statement sounds sharper than I expected.

Fogel shuffles his papers. He's only doing his job and I'm not letting him in. Shutting people out has become a familiar, knee-jerk reaction.

"How long has it been since you've felt safe?"

Here it starts. The broken record.

He lets the question hang.

I let the hang elongate.

He changes the topic. "Your job? How's that?"

"There's a puzzle I've been asked to solve."

"You like puzzles." Fogel forgets nothing.

"Yeah. I do."

My cell phone vibrates in my pocket. It could be Abshir. Had someone arrived at the Westin? I look at the clock. Shit. Thirty-five minutes left in the session.

"And Gordy?"

"Recovering. Should be home in a week."

"How do you feel about that?"

Does everything I share have to be examined? "I'll be glad when he's back."

"Because Gordy's your 'family'?"

The phone vibrates again.

I grab at my stomach. "Damn it. Must've eaten something bad. Can I hit the jill-john?"

"What?"

"You might not like it if I stay."

Fogel waves me towards the door. I race down the hall to the ladies, slip into a stall, and check my phone. The text is from Abshir. "My class starts at four." Miffed, I text him that I'll relieve him in time for him to get to the University and don't text if there's not a warranted 'yes.'

The cold metal of the stall feels good against my forehead. Think. What's my plan? Sit outside the Westin for a week, waiting for Bunny Luce to show? Hardly seems the best use of my time. I want to put this task in Gordy's 'win' column, in my 'win' column.

I splash water on my face and grab a couple of paper towels.

Back in Fogel's office, with wet paper towels bunched in my hand, I continue the charade. "Amazing how the body warns you to expel demons." I wipe my forehead, just for effect.

Fogel's bored with me. And I can't make myself care. He checks his notes, goes on to the next question. "We're close to our one-year anniversary, Officer Rommel."

"Should I bring a cake next time?"

He ignores my desire to shift away from serious conversation. "Decisions are going to have to be made. Just a reminder. How's your personal life?"

"I have my neighborhood spot."

He's sarcastic. "Nothing more intimate than drinking at a 'neighborhood spot'?"

"It's okay."

"Anyone special?"

"No."

"Heard from your boyfriend?"

"Ex. He's long gone. Reno, Nevada agrees with him. And his newly acquired wife keeps him busy."

"Did you tell me your ex-boyfriend now has a wife?"

"My friend recently saw it on Friendline."

"How do you feel about that?"

"I don't feel any way about it. Haven't seen him for over a year." A month after my fall, he loaded his yellow kayak on the roof of his car, ready to head west. Gordy drove up as the car and kayak disappeared from sight. Gordy had snarled, "Never thought he was good enough for you." For me, it was sad relief—now no one was going to be expected to love an incomplete me.

I assure Fogel again—because I want it to be an absolute truth. "It's okay."

He sighs. "Fine. You know what's next."

I lean forward and put my head in my hands and close my eyes. It's time for visualization. Fogel thinks my inability to recall the moment-to-moment events that led up to my fall is keeping me from coming to terms with my anger. He reads from my former statement, setting the scene again. "December, year and a half ago. There were four of you—you and your partner, Marvin Payer, and two others, Heckley and Shappen. Marvin stayed on the ground, the three of you ran up the six flights of stairs at the new construction next to Prosper Building on Marginal Way. Each flight contained twelve steps to a landing, then there was a change of direction and another twelve steps to reach the next floor." My mind goes to that cold night, the clomp of our solid winter boots on the concrete stairs. The heaviness of my police-issue parka. "You're heading to the roof." Fogel instructs me to slowly inhale and exhale. I tend to flick off this exercise, but there have been rare times I do concentrate and pick up a fragment of memory. Then my heart races. He prompts, "You reach the door to the roof and you reach out your hand for the handle…"

"Heckley's breathing on my neck," I mumble. "Reminds me, for the tenth time, that we have no idea what we're going to face on the roof." I told him we had a job to do—the assholes had run a kid over, a kid crossing the street after a Kung Fu class—an added piece of crap-action after hog-tying Fred Doyle, the manager at Doyle's Brew and Food and crashing his skull with a cast iron skillet and making off with the cashbox.

"Who opens the door?"

"I do."

We take out our guns.

The sleety snow felt like claws ripping into my cheeks. I'm trying to see in the darkness. The roof was icy and slick under my feet. Large metal containers holding the heating and cooling systems for the new building dotted the rooftop along with unused building materials. Tarps, tied over bundles of supplies flap, the tie-down ropes arch and snap in the wind. Headlights of the few cars on the highway, a half a mile away, look like giant colliding fireflies. A late-night Pine Tree garbage truck, its safety beeps loud over its diesel engine, was backing up somewhere in the vicinity. I couldn't hear any movement on the rooftop. Was there an escape route on the other side of the building? We didn't know. I nodded at Heckley and Shappen that it was time to separate, I signaled that I'd go to the left. I do. Ten steps, maybe twelve. Out of the darkness, I saw—too late—a four-by-four inches from my face. I dodged, it whooshed through the air above me but another came down on my back and another on the top of my head and my boots don't find traction on the ice. My feet scrambled, scratched at the slickness. I'm trying to steady my hand, steady the gun. It was strangely silent, except for the whoomph of wood hitting my parka, the crack of a home-run swing on my jaw. I stumbled back, realized a moment too late I was at the roof's edge as another board plunged into my stomach—my feet left the roof. I was propelled over the side of the building. My gun flipped out of my hand, descended out of my sight. Then it was slow motion, the feeling of being in a dream where I never hit the ground, being stuck in an elongated, constant fall. And then the wonderment—the panic—the short steel beam that was tossed after me and its heavy, dead weight descending towards me. I remember anticipating hitting the ground and breaking bones and spasms of pain and then the amazing realization that this was the way I was going to leave this world.

There was a dumpster, full of unused shards of sleet-drenched dry wall and insulation and garbage. I hit its hard, metal lip, heard my shoulder crack, a bone fractured instantly, as I flipped into the debris. My lungs were jolted, my breath nearly knocked out. I heard the sound of the steel beam crash—an explosive whack—onto the wide lip of the dumpster, resoundingly smack the metal structure. I squeezed my eyes just as the solid, gray, massively dense beam spun and catapulted into my lower leg.

And then I was in the ambulance.

"Marvin saw no one?" Fogel had asked this question before.

"He was in the front, waiting for more backup." I'd learned later that Heckley had been downed by a crack on his head, didn't get a bead on the bad guys. Shappen, in the instant we had all separated, had decided law enforcement was not for him, had skittered back down the stairs. The next day he'd moved to Mexico and no one has heard from him since.

Fogel's always hoping I'll remember more sounds, or a face, or a voice—something.

My memory blips forward, to Marvin sitting next to me in the ambulance, the sound of sirens whirring. My partner's face was pale; he was sweating in the icy cold.

"Marv…M…" I said. "Catch any…anyone?" I sometimes think he was about to say something but I couldn't listen because I was slipping into a blackness.

* * *

The clock strikes the hour. I grab my coat. "Well, this was…as always."

Fogel's eyes soften. "Next week, Officer Rommel. Until next week."

CHAPTER NINE
Thursday

Donato leans his rangy frame against the wall outside Fogel's office. He straightens when he sees me. "How was it?"

"Fogel-time." Always unsettling.

"Productive?"

"He wants new stuff. And so do I. But there's nothing more." It's disappointing to everyone. Parents lost a child, Fred Doyle was eating through a tube, and the bad guys got away. "How come you're waiting? I know the way."

"Didn't want you to forget."

"No faith in me?"

"Oh, I have lots of that. Maybe I needed to get off my chair and you were the excuse."

"Glad to be of use. What pictures do you want me to look at?"

Donato puts his hand on my back for a moment and points me towards the bullpen. He walks at my pace. One of the things I miss is the sound of my solid footfalls, a rhythm I'd taken for granted. It's not there now, no familiar cadence of weight hitting the ground. He doesn't seem to notice. "Talked to the New Yorkers staying at the Westin," he says. "Chanel Forchet and Murphy Duncan. Duncan's the one with the trimmed beard, he did the talking. Works for Yarborough Inx, his client is a company called Destiny Leader."

My attention sparks. "Really."

"They confirmed the liquor salesman offered them a tasting of the scotch he was pushing. They thought he was a jerk."

"They were happy to take his booze."

"Most people don't say 'no' to free booze."

"Did they mention why they're in town?" I'm hoping they might have brought up a wedding.

Ten Days

"Here for a break—lobster rolls, ferry rides, clean air. The usual. They thought it was pretty cool to be asked about a dead body. They wondered how I happened to find them."

"You said?"

"I told them Portland's a small town."

"And no one can keep secrets here."

"Not for long," he says.

"Chanel's leaving to go back to New York tomorrow morning. Duncan's here for a few more days—checking out a work opportunity and Portland's 'food scene.'"

"Destiny Leader. Pretentious name for a company."

"They said the company is full of computer geeks hired to bring the web to countries who want it or not. These two—they're in sales."

"Thus the fashionista vibes. Gotta make an impression in sales."

"If you say so."

Chances are Murphy Duncan had nothing to do with Renae's meeting in the conference room and simply availed himself of one of the Westin's small offices. I was hoping for an easy connection, that these members of Destiny Leader's salesforce were here to support Peppard's entry into marriage. Still, it's something check out. Later.

We enter the bullpen. Cubicles dot the large room; they're mostly empty right now. Interview rooms are also empty. But the case boards, stacks of files and photos, the gold stars slapped on the wall for closed cases are visible. I had planned to take the detectives' test the beginning of this year—I'd been pretty sure I'd be slapped down—too green, too young, too female. But the plan had been to take it every year until the brass got used to the idea.

"You okay?" It's like Donato senses that I ache to be part of all this.

"Sure."

He pulls out his desk chair for me. "We've got photos of the crowd around the wharf where Beene was pulled out. Just in case any of the lookee-loos might have been at Sparrows that night. You recognize anyone?" He's got the photos up on the computer; he clicks on one, brings it to full screen.

I settle in, move from photo to photo. My eyes scan over the groups. Some observers have raincoats over their arms because the squall had blown over. Some sip coffee from take-out cups. There are a few joggers and bicyclists who have stopped to gawk. Nobody stands out. Wait. "Behind the pink lady." I point to a spot next to a very large woman dressed from head-to-toe in pink athletic gear.

Donato leans in; his face is inches from mine. "Skinny guy? Nylon zip-up jacket?"

"Saw him in town, near Nivas, that morning. German accent—or something like it. He carried a birdwatching book and those binoculars."

"He was at Sparrows when you saw Beene?"

"No." I didn't comment that the reason he stood out to me at this moment was that I saw him this morning in an expensive suit, about to take off in a private plane with Philip P. Claren.

"So?"

"Sorry—he made an impression—crossed paths at Nivas Coffee and he didn't seem to care for my dog."

"You got a dog? I have a beagle." He points to a photo of an eager-eyed pup tacked on the foam board in his cubicle. "That's when he was younger. Thor."

"That's the name of a movie."

"And a Nordic god. And my dog."

I get up from the chair. "Are you leaning towards accident?"

"Waiting for the autopsy report."

"If it wasn't an accident—any motive rearing its head? Robbery?"

"Why do you say that?"

"Beene's wad of hundreds. Anyone could've caught him waving his wallet. And I'm assuming a car full of high-end whiskey. Find his car?"

"Near Spotty's on Commercial. Stripped down. Empty."

I grimace. "Doesn't give Portland a good name. Anything else?"

"Not now. I'll walk you out."

"No need."

"But I like the idea. You head to Boston to catch any Celtics games live this year?"

"One. They were embarrassed by the Bucks."

He laughs. "They always are."

We get on the elevator. It's not quite comfortable being next to him. I search for conversation. "Playing basketball?"

"Every Monday night. Eight o'clock. At the Rec Center."

"Competitive?"

"We try. Usually head over to Salvage for beer and barbecue after."

"Best coleslaw in town."

"Come by if you feel like it. I'll let you share my slaw."

"Wouldn't want to deprive you." I didn't add that Christine Poole, Donato's long-term girlfriend and news anchor at WMFT was not my favorite person and I didn't want to think of chewing on BBQ with her.

The elevator opens to the lobby just as a swift breeze pushes through from the main entrance. Marvin enters, tucking his motorcycle helmet under his arm. He sees us and hesitates—then abruptly heads down the hallway towards the squad rooms.

Donato stops, surprised. "What was that?"

Ten Days

"Probably pissed at me. Something to do with his brother. Billy and Karla spent time together last night. She didn't show up for work today and I was asking around this morning."

"Asking who?"

"Billy."

"In what capacity?"

"As Karla's friend—who wants to know where she might be."

"Careful, Rommel."

"Billy thinks I'm a pain and I think he's a shit. But she's my friend. I had to ask."

"You don't have any authority."

"I didn't pretend I did. Billy told me he respects Karla and regrets he had to let her down gently last night. He doesn't want romance to take time from his focus on being a fine, repenting citizen. Does that sound plausible to you?"

Donato grunts. Like he doesn't believe Billy Payer either.

* * *

There's a parking spot across the street from Karla's Hair and Beauty. The salon is on the first floor of a red brick row house and the lights are on. I prepare a litany of annoying lectures on thoughtlessness, including harangues like 'you're an ass to run out on us like that' and 'you don't deserve the friends you've got' and 'you've got Gretchen worried half to death' and I hope Karla's there so I can use them. I push through the door. A chipmunk-cheeked hairdresser I've never seen before sits at a manicure station, painting his fingernails with a dark purple polish. A thick lock of his jet-black hair drops over his forehead, Elvis-style. His eyes are framed with blue eyeliner and they're locked on me. "Cut? Blow-dry?"

"Have a question."

"Mani-pedi? Lime green's the color of the month."

"Not a favorite color."

"I have time for a walk-in."

"Not today, thanks."

He waves his white, hairless hands in the hair to dry the polish. "Then what do you want?"

"I'm a friend of Karla's. Hoped to meet up with her here."

He rolls his eyes. "She called in, said her mom's sick. Her cell phone died, but she wanted us to know she's in boring Augusta with a sickee." He blows on his nails. "Maybe you want to make time for a manicure?"

"Another time." I head out. "I'll call Karla at her parents'."

"Whatever." He grabs a *People* magazine, flips it open as if it's a lifeboat in his sea of boredom. I expect it will do what it's intended to do. Fan his discontent.

* * *

I park a short distance from Abshir's minivan. The entrance to the Westin is clearly visible in my rear-view mirror. Abshir strides over and I roll down my window. He hands me the camera. "Pictures of all activity coming in and out. There's time code on them."

"Okay. Go to class."

"You will need me after?"

"I'll text if I do. Thanks."

"*Mahadsanid.*" Abshir jogs back to his vehicle and then he's off—heading towards Deering Park and the University of Southern Maine.

I swipe through the photos. Shannon of Shannon Styles and Chef Prinn left the hotel an hour ago. No sign of Renae Claren leaving. No sign of Bunny Luce or Tyler Peppard arriving.

The possibility of failure always makes me anxious; I never liked it in sports—never liked it in any area of my life. Doc Fogel suggests it's because, deep down, I haven't come to terms with my mother moving away from the family. I told him that was bullshit. He told me to think about my need to prove worth to myself. He'd rubbed his Adam's apple, said it was his job to point to things that might be important to discuss. I told him I didn't like placing blame. He jumped on that. Had he said 'blame'? Who was I blaming? My mother? Father? Myself? The world? I tuned him out.

I take out my notebook. Read through my notes again. How does someone, without living in a sleeping bag in the desert or under pine cones in a forest, step off the grid? What's entailed? A person has to stay off personal computers and phones; send no emails or texts, conduct no searches. Avoid signing into a personal Smart TV. Avoid accessing apps connected to GPS tracking systems. Avoid use of credit cards, use cash. I star this and check Jade's notes. Bunny Luce's latest bank withdrawal was one week ago. Is that important? Was it one week ago, when deciding to send the snail mail to her father, that she knew she was going to be living a cash existence? What else had she planned? One how-to possibility: piggyback on someone else's trail. Hide behind their digital footprint. Who could Bunny Luce piggyback? Jade's done a complete search on Tyler Peppard and he, too, has left no traces in the past week. Could Bunny Luce and Peppard be piggybacking on the same third party?

I call Jade. "Anything new?"

"Only that my list of 'probable-nots' is growing. Probably no commercial air travel. Homeland Security has landed on sexy ways to get us to turn over tracking information like offering priority boarding if we agree to fingerprinting, facial recognition, and background checks. They've convinced us to trade privacy for convenience."

"Private planes?"

"Different kettle of fish. Sometimes there are no tickets. A person's name is supposed to be on the manifest but—rarely policed. Some airports require PPRs—that's Prior Permission Requirements. But those are high security areas, not the usual protocol."

"Jade," I grumble. "I need something."

"I'll check out the newer surveillance products—they can activate laptop webcams and cell phone microphones…"

"Wait. Just anyone's?"

"Know you detest the idea. But not sci-fi anymore. You understand what Ed Snowden is in exile for—his argument about personal rights…"

"What's this about cell phone microphones? Is it true they can be recorded and there's voice ID?"

"If Lucy Claren's lectures were recorded and posted on some site like YouTube—I could try to access the viable technology. But there's nothing."

"Bunny Luce's in tech; she'll know everything to steer clear of."

"Luck can decide not to be a stranger." Jade shuffles papers. "On a related topic: Were you aware that Philip Claren is meeting with the Justice Department in Washington DC today?"

This is fresh news and it stops me for a moment. "I knew he went there."

"Did he imply why?" Jade asks.

"No."

"No information available on this end," Jade tells me. "Yet."

"Okay, Jade. Later."

The 'probable-nots' are strangling me. I need something to report to Claren. I use my personal cell to call the office of 'Prinn's Bounty.'

"How may I help you?" The question is friendly.

"I'm planning a wedding and wanted to know if…"

"We don't cater weddings, I'm sorry."

I create a fiction. "It's more like a private celebration. I can't tell you who's on my guest list but it does contain a few European royals and an ex-President."

There's a pause. "If you give me more details, I can talk to Chef Prinn."

"We're considering one of the close islands as a location."

"That can be problematic—depends on access to an acceptable kitchen. Call us when you decide."

I want to keep her on the phone. "I was thinking about Chebeague. Is that a possibility?"

"Only with a floating kitchen."

"Floating?"

"A vessel with proper facilities. And we don't arrange those things. That would be up to you. We should talk further after you've made your final decisions. Thank you for considering us." She hangs up.

Floating kitchen. Okay. Prinn's Bounty is likely readying food for the event on a boat. Where's the connection? How could that info-bite get me closer to finding Lucy Claren?

The red cell phone buzzes. I answer. "Yes?"

Claren's gruff. "I'm on my way to Boston. Bunny Luce's lab has been broken into."

A shiver nestles at the base of my neck. "Anyone there when it happened?"

"No one."

"What was taken?"

"I'll know more when I get there. How long will it take you?"

CHAPTER TEN
Thursday

It takes a quick phone call to alert Gretchen that Bert will need a place for the night. I tell her Karla might be with her sick mom in Augusta.

"Might?"

"That's what one of the stylists at her shop said. But I called—no one's answering at her mom's house. Can you try later tonight?"

"Where are you going?"

"Boston. Have to do something for Gordy. You'll call Karla's mom?"

"Yeah. Dee, I'm worried."

"I'm sure Karla will show up."

I pack quickly—jeans, t-shirt, sneakers, silicone-based lotion, and second skin bandages in case the prosthesis starts an ache, Advil, pair of Agile-Tech collapsible forearm crutches.

I've got my phone on speaker and I'm finally connected to Donato. I can hear the buzz of activity in the precinct room. I ask if he'll do me a favor.

"What?"

"Can you add Karla's car to the vehicle locate list?"

"How long has she been out of touch?"

"Day and…well…"

He sounds distracted. "You really thinking there's a problem?"

I don't want to sluff it off and be wrong. "Could you add it to the bulletin? In case she was in an accident, maybe ended up off the road."

"I'll get someone to scare up the plates. Text me a description of the car." He gives me his cell phone number. "So does this mean you owe me one?"

"Name it." I zip up my long duffel.

"Wouldn't leave that offer so open-ended, Rommel." He calls to someone in the bullpen to wait up for him. Then he's back to me. "You're not active on this, are you?"

"You told me I had no authority."

"You don't. Keep that in mind."

"I have to go to Boston for Gordy. Okay if I check in later?"

"You have my cell. Call any time." He clicks off.

I make the turn onto South I-295 and head towards Boston. I've been clinging to the idea that Bunny Luce's disappearance was straight-forward, the direct result of a dysfunctional family; a daughter aching for independence, a father worried about his brilliant daughter's emotional and financial welfare, and a mother who'd do anything to stick it to her ex-husband.

But the news of the break-in at Lucy Claren's lab doesn't set well. The timing does not feel right.

My EZ Pass allows me to take the no-stop lane onto the 95. I tap my phone, connect to a stored number. The ring comes through my speaker and there's the click of connection.

"Dee? Honey. Everything good?" My mother's voice is concerned.

We don't talk a lot on the phone. Neither of us is good at chit-chat so a personal call always raises the adrenalin. "I'm fine," I assure her.

"Good. Good." She waits, expecting to hear the reason for the call.

"I'm headed to Boston. Work."

"Can you stay overnight?"

"Not sure."

"Have dinner with us?"

"Doubtful." I'll reach Claren Tech before sundown. But I have no idea what might be waiting there.

"You know the front door code. Stay the night. The three of us can have breakfast."

The 'us' referred to her new husband. Despite the fact that Chester Forbright wears pink oxford shirts and double-breasted blue blazers and his Harvard class ring forty years after graduation, he's a good guy. He sits on the boards of museums, raises money for causes I agree with and he accepts that my mother will do her own thing.

"Mom, I have a quick question."

"Okay."

"In your very posh life…"

"Dee, don't start, it's not…"

"Question coming." I want to keep this on track.

"What is it, honey?"

"I was wondering if you might know of an event planning company in Boston called Shannon Styles? Maybe you've used them to cater an event?"

"Do you need someone to cater something? I can search out excellent people for you in Portland. It's usually advisable to use local talent."

"Mom, are you seriously asking if I'm throwing an event?"

"Life is full of surprises, Dee. And life evolves."

She retains hope, I give her that. I have no idea what she envisioned for me, but being a Police Academy graduate was not at the top of her list. I tell her I need the info for Gordy. "Have you heard of this 'Shannon Styles'?"

"Mmm," she says. "There are so many party planners in Boston. Chester's assistant, Nella, might know. She arranges our events. Do you want me to ask her?"

"Sure. But don't make a big deal out of it."

"All right. I'll call Nella. Hope to see you tonight, honey."

I'm moving into Massachusetts and traffic slows. My mother will come through, she prides herself in that. High school basketball games, every Friday night. We'd be warming up, running drills and I'd have one eye on the gym's doors. Fifteen minutes before the start of the game, she'd walk in—just as promised. She'd be in her Boston fashion—heels and tailored suit. Her eyes would search the stands, find my dad who always sat three rows behind the team. He'd wave. That was the moment I'd be able to let everything else go and concentrate on winning the game. Same thing when I played on the University of Southern Maine's team. Never outgrew it, always resented it. My mother *administrates,* specifically the Cancer Research Center of Boston. She can juggle timetables, finances, personalities, and charm donors to open their wallets. She can *persuade* people. I begrudged the fact that my father couldn't fall out of love with her, I saw it was a weakness on his part. There were plenty of single moms of my high school friends who continually asked us over to dinner. They saw a steady and kind man who deserved better. He wasn't interested. One day, while driving to Bath's Maritime Museum, I got up the courage to ask him about it. "Don't you want her to belong only to us? Be with us all the time?" He'd said, "Dee. Let's take it as it comes. We're doing fine, aren't we?"

Nearly three years after my dad died, my mom married Chester. Over time, I've come to admire Chester's patience. They'd been friends—not lovers—who attended the symphony, ballet and society events together during the week and he'd never asked her to make room for him on the weekends—the time she spent with us. When she became widowed, he gave her space to feel sad. To put in some time with me. Then, he made his move. It took another year for her to agree to marriage, but he was sanguine. My mother generates loyalty—from the men who love her, from her office staff, from her donors.

After my fall from the roof of the Prosper building, she had wanted me to move into the elegant townhome off Chestnut Street and connect with the medical community in Boston. She'd said, "Your father would want you to be with me." But I couldn't leave Portland, it was my home.

So, while I was in the hospital, she got permission from my landlord to retrofit my apartment—add railings to the back steps, widen doorways to accommodate a wheelchair, change up the shower for easy access, and add grab rails, a bench and non-slip mat. I came to a realization that being motherly, to her, meant *administrating,* organizing and arranging for her child. The fact that day-to-day presence didn't seem as important to her was a topic that was never broached between us.

Dusk is stretching over the Boston skyline. I leave the highway and turn onto a road designated as Claren Drive. A half mile later, I face a large gate. A guard station is behind it; one of the duo expects compliance, "Please turn to the camera on the pole to your left and state your name."

"Dee Rommel. Philip Claren expects me."

A moment later, the gate swings open. The Visitors' kiosk is another quarter mile. Two big-and-tall uniformed guards greet me. I'm instructed to park. "We'll have an Electro Buddy take you to the lab."

"Electro Buddy?" I half expect a robot. But a fully-roofed, four-door electric cart, manned by another hulky guard, pulls up to my parking space.

There's no sound as the Electro Buddy moves onto the smooth and narrow campus pathways. We pass several angular, dark buildings. We take a hard right; ahead is one made of concrete and glass. The Electro Buddy pulls up to its wide entrance. Here, all the lights are on.

The two-story lobby of LC Labs is spacious, colorful. The floor is white with orange and blue flecks—and smooth—the kind of surface that makes moving equipment easy. There's a massive stairway on one side of the building, it's painted a shocking golden yellow, the treads are a royal blue. Claren's in a small group, still in his gray suit, but the tie is gone. He holds onto his briefcase. His forehead is creased with worry, as if a new fear is settling into his brain.

A stern presence steps out from behind Claren and he makes introductions. "Dee Rommel. Meet Prudence Lopez; she's head of our security."

Lopez is in her early forties and has the Pilates and health-food look. Her dark hair is pulled back into a severe low knob, a well-tailored suit hugs her fit figure. Her large brown eyes are full of questions—clearly, she's wondering why Claren has brought me into this situation. Her phone buzzes and she lifts it to her ear. She turns to Claren. "They're ready for us."

Lopez leads, we head to a bright orange door off the reception desk area. It's got no doorknob. She runs a fob down the side of the frame. There's a *tick* and the door swings open. We're in a large room, filled with computer screens. A wiry guy with sunken cheeks, wearing a Red Sox baseball cap and t-shirt, sits in the center focused on a bank of display screens. He steps aside so Lopez can man the main console. The feed comes up on two of the top screens. Today's date and time of the break-in is embedded in the corners of the screens. The twenty-four-hour clock marks it at 3:16. Just after three o'clock in the morning.

"Why wasn't this reported right away?" Claren asks.

"The system was compromised and the footage masked. We were able to retrieve it an hour ago." She points to two figures, dressed in loose, dark clothing, silhouetted against the skyline. "They entered in through the roof access. The alarm did not activate because there's an indication that a fob was used for access."

"How is that possible?"

"We're working on that." Lopez adds, "I've left messages for Dr. Lucy. But, as usual of late, she has not communicated. It is very difficult to do my job if she will not…"

"Let me see her office." Claren sidesteps Lopez's complaint and does not offer information about his own experience with Bunny Luce's lack of connection.

Two oversized, overstuffed chairs flanking a coffee table are overturned; the bottoms slashed, coils and fabric tossed aside. A couch is upended and leaning against a wall like a blob of wood and stuffing and fabric that has forgotten its purpose. A long desk-table with graceful legs is shoved out of its place, its slim drawer pulled out and its contents dumped on the floor. Papers, files, and books are strewn on the floor next to the empty bookcase—framed photos, with glass broken, have been tossed and added to the sea of debris. A French armoire has been broken open to reveal an open safe inside; it's empty.

"Nothing else in the lab seems to be disturbed," Lopez reports. "Only this office."

"Looking for something small?" I ask.

"Why do you ascertain that?" Lopez queries, her eyes are not friendly.

I point to the mess. "Something that could be hidden? Behind a book, in a drawer, behind a photo frame?"

A meticulous man, in a customized power wheelchair, rolls in. He's thirty-ish, his mahogany hair hangs to the collar of his crisp white shirt. His dark trousers are creased and folded under the remains of legs amputated above the knee. His eyes are stormy, but his voice is calm. "What do we know?"

Claren eyes the self-possessed man. "Dr. Hogan? What're you doing here?"

He's got a white-ish scar breaking through his left eyebrow, it crosses his temple towards his ear. It's healed now—and leaves a dull mark of experience on his face.

Lopez is quick. "Dr. Hogan's on the LC Lab emergency call list."

"Since when?" Claren's clearly perplexed.

"When the funds were re-arranged, Dr. Claren." Hogan holds onto his respectful but cool tone.

Lopez reminds Claren, "Your daughter made that change two months ago after Dr. Hogan installed the Virtual Privacy Network. You received the update."

Claren looks momentarily frazzled, as if he's upset there's something he's forgotten.

"Good news," Lopez continues. "Dr. Hogan's VPN was not breached."

He nods to Lopez. "A word?" They step outside Lucy's office.

Hogan and I are alone. Silently, he surveys the mess in Bunny Luce's office. I venture, "I've read about you in the Claren Technologies newsletter. About your work in biometrics with Lucy—you two received an award. And your service in the Military Intelligence Corps in Afghanistan."

Hogan shifts his gaze to me; his eyes are green, there's a warm gold in them too. His eyelashes are thick. "Have we met?"

"I'm Dee Rommel." I want him to assume I'm in the loop. "Bunny Luce must be upset about this."

"At work, she's 'Lucy.'"

"Is she on her way?" There's no answer. "The head of security said Lucy's been alerted. She must be on her way."

"Have no idea."

"Do you think it's odd she's letting wedding plans take precedence over the work of the lab? Over a break-in?"

Hogan's about to say something; he catches himself.

I press. "I haven't met her fiancé yet. Have you?"

The corners of his eyes twitch. No comment.

"Nice picture."

"What?"

I point to a broken photo frame on the floor. A photo that had been slipped behind an LC Lab group shot was now freed. It's of Lucy and Hogan, at a beach bar holding martinis, a foot-tall glass obelisk next to a cupcake with a birthday candle in it. "Who's birthday?"

"Lucy's. She turned twenty-two."

"Where was the photo taken?"

"Miami. We were at a Festival of Ideas."

"What's the crystal award thing between you?"

"Called the Near Future Prize."

"Sounds like a big deal. You must be a good team."

He doesn't respond. It's as if he's not listening.

"Any idea what someone was looking for here? Or if 'it' was found?"

"'It'?"

"Something's worth breaking in and trashing things…"

He puts his right hand—it's thickly veined, with well-groomed, long fingers—on the control panel of his mobile chair. "I need to check my office." He activates his vehicle, heads out of the office and to his right.

I move out to the hallway and observe Hogan wheeling himself into the office next door to Bunny Luce's.

CHAPTER ELEVEN
Thursday

A half hour later, members of Lopez's security team pack up their gear. I walk with Claren through the lobby. "Obviously, circumstances have changed," I say.

"Let's talk over dinner."

"I could communicate what needs to be said right here. And pretty quickly."

"I prefer to talk over dinner."

Technically, if I'm going to bill for a full day, he's got me for a few more hours. "You're the boss."

The security guard opens the back door to the loading dock. Roger's holding the door of the Escalade open; he must have driven down from Portland too.

A short while later, we've traveled a delivery road that led to a back exit off Claren Tech campus. We wove through back streets and entered a warehouse district. Roger turned into a dimly-lit alleyway. Finally, he stops the Escalade in front of a high brick wall divided by a filigreed iron gate.

A slim, middle-aged man in a tuxedo appears and we're ushered inside to a muted, sconce-filled cavern-like dining room. The music is classical, the lighting soft on red brick walls. Each table is private—high, thick leather screens are used as partitions. The maître d' shows us to a corner table.

"You have any food allergies?" Claren asks me.

"No allergies."

"Wine?"

"I drink it."

"I usually let the Chef pair the wine with the food."

"That's fine."

The maître d' nods and moves off.

I ask, "Does this place have a name?"

"Only if you're a member." Claren takes a long sip of water from the crystal goblet in front of him. "There's an understanding here—no table-hopping, no journalists, no photos. Simply excellent food. And peace and quiet." He settles back in his chair. "Lucy and I come here for holidays."

There's the soft tread of waiters on the polished wood floors, the mellow clinking of silverware and glasses. I forge ahead to what's foremost in my mind. "What I wanted to say back at Claren Tech is this: the break-in brings up more possibilities and questions about why Bunny Luce might be MIA. Technology and the work in LC Labs are foreign to me—no expertise in this area."

"I've already instructed Lopez to bring in the right team."

"Oh." I'm surprised. "Okay. Good." It's senseless—he's only agreeing with me—but a feeling of inadequacy rears its head. "You really didn't need to buy me dinner to tell me I'm fired."

Claren lifts a thick silver fork, absentmindedly presses its tines into the thick white tablecloth. "You're not off the hook, Dee Rommel. I expect you to stay on the personal side. I need to get in the same room with my daughter. Sooner rather than later."

If eyes are tunnels to truth, I witness a flash of desperation in Claren's before they shift away to nod to the arriving wine steward. He holds a bottle of French wine, the label's calligraphy too florid to read. Our glasses are filled with golden liquid.

"But there's a problem," I say as the steward moves off. "There could be overlap. While I'm trying to find Lucy, I could get in the way of the investigation at the lab."

"I want you and Gordy to stay on it."

Two servers approach, each carrying a plate topped with a shiny dome. They place them in front of us and, in unison, lift the cloches. The fragrance of small poached fish filets wafts into the air. "Dover sole, in lemon, wine, and bone broth," utters the taller server. "Bon appetit."

The tip of my fork touches the sole; it flakes into a perfect portion. I spear the piece and let it rest on my tongue, the citrusy broth is a delicate tingle of flavor. I notice that Claren eats automatically—wonder if he's appreciating it all.

"Maybe Bunny Luce got too used to keeping secrets," he says. "She had two lives when she was kid—she was my daughter—and Renae's daughter—never *our* daughter. Bunny and I talked science and its usefulness. The desire for work to be beneficial. All I knew about her life with Renae was that she traveled in fashionable, rich company. I should have asked more questions—known more." The guilt is consuming him. "I don't know what friends she might have from childhood—where she might land—to be out of touch."

"Your ex-wife insinuated that you push Lucy, want too much from her. That she might be cutting off contact with you because of that."

"Renae has no idea what she's talking about."

"I got off on the wrong foot with your ex. My fault."

He frowns. "I'm sure it wasn't. She only steps out with those who have power or money, or if she wants something."

"At least she's consistent."

He sips the wine, doesn't find any humor in my observation. "She is."

"Renae sees Lucy as fragile; she's worried her daughter could be at a breaking point."

"It's drama. Renae likes to paint me as the villain. A year ago, Bunny decided to take a break; Columbia University invited her to do a residency for a year. Teach, work in their labs on her projects, mentor students. Lucy wanted the opportunity. It was her decision to accept the offer and take a place in New York City. Would I have preferred her to stay at Claren Tech full-time and focus on projects there? Of course. But she's got autonomy."

"What projects?"

"Her interest is in extending the realms of bio-memory."

Whatever that is. "You two don't work together on projects?"

"She has her own work."

"And it never conflicts or feels redundant?"

His countenance makes it clear that I don't understand his world. "No."

"So, at age 21, she's teaching classes, not taking them. Mentoring students probably her own age."

He nods. "Sure, that was part of the draw. She graduated MIT young…never fit into college life, I suppose."

"Like you."

"It all works out. Eventually." There's no sureness in his observation.

"She met Peppard during that time? Maybe their paths crossed in the city."

Claren half-smiles. "Have no idea. Didn't think to have her followed every minute or anything."

I snort. "I suppose every parent would like to be able to do that."

"Of course. She's very—special. And important to me."

That truth hangs for moment. Then I forge ahead, "You must have some idea of what Lucy's working on? Something that would trigger a burglary?"

He holds the stem of his wine glass and moves it in a circle, observes the liquid spinning. "She doesn't inform me on every element of her projects. When I was young, I didn't want interference either—I wanted all my decisions to be my own. Or at least feel as if they were. 'Course, there is the big picture."

"What's the big picture?"

Ten Days

He drinks, empties his glass. The servers appear to take away our plates and pour light red wine into thin crystal. Another duo arrives, holding plates topped with shiny cloches. When they're lifted, slices of rare duck, drizzled with a purplish-rich berry sauce and nestled on a circle of pureed turnips, are revealed. Sparrows' duck hash comes to mind. It's topped with a poached egg—a tasty, muddled, comfort food that sticks in your stomach for the whole day. If Sparrows' food is like a best friend, this is a gift from angels.

I'm trying to find connections. "You were in Washington DC today—dealing with the powers there?"

Is there a flash of anger in his eyes? He snaps, "The place where clout trumps all."

"I read in the Claren Tech newsletter that your company has a few contracts with the Pentagon and other government agencies."

"The government has deep pockets. Construction, science, communication, transport. Shall we infer they're into everything? Why not? When we were a young company and we got our first government contract—we thought we'd struck gold. At that time, it made sense to chase them. But Claren Tech has gone through a re-think."

"What's that?"

"Last year eighty percent of my company signed a petition asking to be allowed input on company decisions—concerning licensing or sharing of work—that might cross ethical lines."

"Whose ethics?"

He gives a short laugh. "You hit the heart of it. Whose ethics—that's always the question." He slips his knife through a slice of duck, it cuts like butter. "Obviously, Claren Tech is not a democracy, I'm the final decision maker. But eighty percent of researchers, scientists, support staff can't be ignored. The thought of losing my talent pool is not pleasant."

"They'd quit if you didn't agree to consider their input?"

"My people are at the top of their fields. They have their choice of where to do their work." He notices I'm not eating. "Please. We cannot disappoint the Chef, she'll come out here if our plates are not properly consumed."

The duck, paired with the creamy pureed turnip is a complex taste, and holds rare-for-me flavors. "My mouth is doing a happy dance."

Claren stays on his train of thought. "It's not just Claren Tech. Other tech companies are getting the same push from their employees. Innovators face the possibility that—even tangentially—they might be responsible for a violation of personal safety—physical or mental—against humanity. Could be, even tangentially, responsible for a disaster or atrocity. Think of those involved in nuclear fission in the '40s and the atom bomb—many had intense, disquieting remorse. From the Los Alamos group to those who contributed from university or personal laboratories. And that's despite recognizing the later positive uses—like using nuclear power to launch satellites and provide a capability to put a man on the moon. Like bringing power to remote areas. For its medical uses. Now that we're in our second nuclear age and access to using its energy is expanding beyond the United States and Russia—add India, Pakistan, Korea and others—decision-making gets more complicated. Therefore, at each juncture, we, who are always searching for the new, have to continue to ask ourselves: does the good outweigh the bad?"

"But would any company turn their backs on enormous profits?"

"Obviously a question worth debate."

"Why would a company make the decision to stop progress?"

"What is the definition of progress? Is it about finding new ways to control our environment and its inhabitants? To lessen the sometimes tedious work of mankind?"

"That sounds like progress…"

"Perhaps we need to use our muscles, our time, and not shirk labor. Not to jump on technology that invades privacy simply to streamline existence?"

"I'm not comfortable with the invasion of my life. In fact, I hate it."

"Listen to your gut, Dee Rommel." He takes another bite of the tender duck meat. "Many questions circle the work in Artificial Intelligence and how it's changing our landscape. And the 'if'—would these changes be for the better?"

"And if they're not?"

"Knowledge does not have to be shared."

"You'd withhold something that could make you rich?"

"Richer?"

I'm reminded that Claren has multiple well-financed subsidiaries, foundations, and resources that, negating a catastrophic financial doomsday, would provide sustenance for generations.

"That's what you—and Lucy—are working on? AI?"

He holds up a finger. "I told you, Bunny Luce and I don't work together."

"Right." Why is he being so insistent?

He chews his last taste of duck, swallows. "Decades ago, ethical responsibility was not a top priority in the labs. It was science for science's sake—with one eye on profits down the line, of course. But ultimate use was often left to policymakers and the capitalists. Now the decision of what to work on and who to share it with—is becoming a scientist's concern. Novel neural engine chips are advancing capabilities. Everyday models allow for facial recognition, animation, language translation. Influencers and 'best friends' like 'Alexa,' 'Assist,' and 'Siri'—are tech innovations that know more about you than you know." He sips his wine. "In the past, scientists explored and they discovered. Policy makers, such as the military, corporate giants, and lobbyists, decided which applications to implement. Bunny—and others—including me I admit, are actively asking 'should it be so'? We humans are at the top of the food chain not because we have muscular strength or the sharpest incisors—but because we have intelligence. Is it intelligent for us—the innovators—to ensure our work be used in productive, helpful, safe ways? In ways that align with our own personal, political ideology. Or should innovators solely celebrate their abilities to open the next envelope—and not be concerned with consequences?"

"I'm out of my depth…"

"You work on a computer in Gordy's office."

"It's unavoidable."

"And you've noticed—if you do a search for a shoe or a dish detergent or a drone or an AK-47 that, within moments, you've been identified—via cookies—as a potential customer for relatable items. These cookies—named after innocuous treats, of course—are part of a pervasive data harvesting system. It's a progressive information collection system. For example, Friendline created those extraordinary connective tissues to bring together customers. They made the world 'smaller.' People can now make 'friends' in China and New Guinea and the Antarctic. The public, initially, saw the technology as warm and fuzzy. Even the developers of Friendline, we can hope, did not foresee its use as a site to plan hate crimes and manipulate minds. It's impossible to predict what those with questionable intents might make of new ventures."

"Was the break-in at LC Labs—in some way—involved in this question?"

"I don't know."

"Is that why you were in Washington?"

He finishes his wine. The steward appears with two large-bowled, stemmed glasses. "A burgundy you have enjoyed with us before, Dr. Claren." He pours the wine and moves off.

Claren eyes me. "You get to the base problem quickly. This week we've decided to stall on a lucrative offer because it's not clear if our latest project could be fashioned in ways to enhance lethality."

"Enhance lethality?" The term was like a gut-punch. "Is that business-speak for 'killing a lot of people'?"

Claren presses the bridge of his glasses against his nose. "The 'problem' we face, as innovators, is the addiction to the challenge. AI is exploding. But what's the endgame? Consider history, for example, World War II. Nazis recognized an early computer tech group's ability to develop a system to peg, organize, catalogue, and disseminate Jews. Basically, the Nazis got a Holocaust road map. Today things like facial recognition ware—it's logged in enough false positives to create problems. Innocent people have been detained and have faced unjust aggression. Anti-encryption glitches. Consider the consequences of the Five Eyes Nations' decision to share private data and information without the public's knowledge. Now, in all endeavors—we have to ask—what's the endgame? That is why, at Claren Tech, I've recommended all applications be examined and investigated to ensure approval for specified usage—and only those usages—before patents are licensed."

"Can that ever be enforced?"

Claren doesn't answer, he focuses on tasting the deep red wine.

"The man in the blue suit, who was waiting for you on the plane. I saw him in town the day before. He had birdwatching paraphernalia."

"Birdwatching?" He sounds surprised—and confused.

"Was he at your meeting in Washington?"

Our plates are whisked away and replaced with those offering a small, plump filet of beef. He glances at his plate, as if surprised it's already time for the next course. "This is Kobe beef from farms in Wisconsin, the cows descend from the Japanese Black cattle strain. The chef's proud of it."

We eat. There's a perfection in the juicy lightness of the meat. "Wow."

He scans the elegant, refined space. "This is a refuge for me, place to think things out. But it is nice, sometimes, to have someone with me at the table."

I imagine Claren sitting in this private space with a younger Bunny Luce, discussing his hopes—their hopes?—for being positive contributors to a changing world. Was she his acolyte for years? And then, eventually, formed her own opinions? Perhaps Claren has not come to terms with her pulling away from him, a desire to control her own LC Labs. Maybe that's the only reason Lucy doesn't want to discuss her wedding decisions with her father.

"Tell me about Hogan," I say. "A photo of Bunny Luce and Hogan fell off the bookshelf, I saw it on the floor of her office. Getting some award."

"They met at Columbia, when Bunny Luce led her lab there. Bunny gave him space at LC Labs a few months later, he'd just finished his doctorate; they had co-authored an AI project and paper together."

"What kind of AI?"

"I didn't get all the details." The deflection is clear.

"In the photo—they look like they get along well. Was there a more personal relationship there—deeper than co-workers?"

He raises his eyebrows, as if my assumption is too quick and definitive. "They shared a common interest and goal."

"He's on that emergency call list."

"Ms. Lopez appreciated his revamping of some of the systems in the LC Lab. That must be why he's on Bunny Luce's call list."

It's clear Claren wants to think of Lucy as a colleague, a woman—albeit a daughter—interested only in work. I let it go. "Will you arrange access for me—would like to see her condo."

"I've been over it. Nothing pointing to where she might be."

"Better to be thorough."

"I'll get someone to meet you there in the morning. Let you in."

"Appreciate it."

Claren reacts to the vibration of his cell phone. "Sorry." He takes the call. Listens. And then one word. "Tomorrow." He clicks off. I wait for him to let me know if this call has anything to do with Bunny but, apparently, it doesn't. He checks the time on his orange Swatch, now anxious to leave. "It's late. Let me get Roger to book you a hotel in Boston for the evening."

"I'm all set—giving my mother a treat. Staying at her place."

The maître d' appears and pulls back my chair. There's no asking for a check, no credit card changes hands. We're simply ushered out, with wishes that Dr. Claren visit again soon.

*　*　*

The gate at the perimeter of the Claren Tech property is opened and I drive through. A hundred yards later, I pull to the side and punch an address into the phone: the location of Bunny Luce's Boston condo.

In less than thirty minutes, I'm there. In front of me is a caged community; high iron fence work and a gate to protect a row of pristine brownstones. A surveillance car is parked across the street. A security guard is making his rounds, walking the path in front of the homes' entrances. Claren has told me there's twenty-four-hour coverage. And that Bunny Luce's home security system has not shown any activity in the last week.

It looks as if nothing has changed.

CHAPTER TWELVE
Thursday

I let myself into my mother's Beacon Hill townhome. There's a soft ripple of sound, the subtle alert of an approved entry. I step onto the black and white checkerboard marble floor. I hear the muted sounds of vinyl spinning on the turntable in the library—the sounds of Big Band, Jim McNeely on the piano.

"Dee?" My mother steps out of the wood-paneled library. She's in fuzzy slippers and a slim robe with a fleece collar. Her blonde hair, even now, is smooth and perfectly tucked as it brushes her shoulders. She moves her glasses off her nose, slips her paperback into her robe's pocket. She hugs me. I feel my height—my father's genes—as I tower over her by six inches.

"Are you hungry, honey?"

"No, Mom, I've eaten. It's midnight, you didn't have to wait up."

"A good book makes it easy. Can you come sit by the fire for a bit? I'm sure you're tired but maybe you'll give me a few moments…"

I put my duffel down. We sit on chairs facing the fire. I smell the polish that's used to keep the centuries-old paneling burnished, the scent of potpourri resting in bowls on the antique tables.

"Chester's in bed. Poor thing has a head cold. He apologizes he couldn't sit up and wait with me."

I'm always taken by how comfortable she is in this elegant place. The bookshelves are filled with first editions, bookended with vases and small bronze statues. The tie on her robe is in a perfect bow. Her nails are perfectly painted one shade darker than her flesh. She wears no make-up; her skin is flawless.

"Here, put your legs up." She gets up and moves a footstool over to my chair. "I checked in with Gordy's sister-in-law. I'm glad the kidney transfer was successful."

"All good so far."

"You look nice, honey. I like that jacket."

"Didn't you pick it out for me last Christmas?"

Ten Days

She smiles. "It fits well." She reaches into the pocket of her robe. "Nella, Chester's assistant, says she'll call you after she talks to her friend at Shannon Styles about their upcoming events. Here's her name and number in case you need it." She hands me a folded piece of elegant note paper. No Post-Its for my mom. "I haven't seen you for two months. Too much travel, too many conferences."

She's often scheduled as an expert speaker at these conferences. The work that bifurcated her time with us when I was growing up.

"I've got a conference in Tokyo end of next week…"

"What's in Tokyo?" I ask.

"New research on bone cancer. Trying to get the global community on the same page."

"You like Japan."

"But after that," she promises, "I'll get some dates on the calendar for a break. Later this summer? Maybe we can get up to the cottage." The small, three-room, un-winterized 'camp' on Goose Lake was the only place I ever saw my mother completely unwind. The only heat came from a wood-burning iron stove and the old quilts thrown over our shoulders at night. The lake trout and perch my father and I caught in the morning was cooked on a campfire on the narrow beach. Sunset swims were chilly and magical but, even in August and September, after the water had had a chance to warm all summer, the initial dip took your breath away. It's time to go up there, clean out the cobwebs, and see what damage the squirrels did over the winter.

She cocks her head, leans forward a bit. "How's Gretchen?"

"Doggie DayCare's doing well."

"Is she dating?"

"No. I don't think so."

She wants to ask if I'm dating anyone. There's a pause, a hope for a personal morsel. But she won't pry.

We sit for a moment. Wistfulness takes over her face. "Waiting for you tonight…it brought back memories of my own mother telling me that she sometimes had an insane desire to crawl into my mind and under my skin. Because I rarely told her what I was thinking. Or feeling." She taps her manicured nails on the arm of her chair. "But, of course, she knew—and I know—that independence is good. It's excellent, in fact."

"I'm okay, Mom." I can feel her longing to get closer. But I can't help her out.

"Any thoughts about going back to the force?"

"Not sure."

"I always thought you might like law school. You have a strong desire for justice. To right wrongs. Put the world in order."

"Whatever, Mom. Not thinking about it right now." I rub my eyes, I'm tired. "Mom, have you run into Philip Claren—here—in Boston?"

"The tech multi-millionaire?" Her lips purse as she digs into her memory bank. "Chester introduced us at a museum opening—a few years ago. Our paths crossed at the Symphony, once. Or twice. Oh, and the Davenports socialize with him—so once at their home for a fundraiser." She's satisfied she's retrieved the information and adds a commentary. "He's been divorced a long time. And there's a long line of women who've tried to batter down the wall into his private life. I don't think anyone's been successful." She sips her tea. "He's done a lot of good things for Boston—and Portland—but, from what I've seen and heard, he doesn't engage well. And that can make a person isolated and—detached? He strikes me as lonely." She cocks her head. "Why do you ask?"

"He and Gordy are friends. Or—well, there's a mysterious history there."

"Something to do with Gordy's gambling."

"What?"

"Your father didn't go into details. But Gordy had a problem. When he was so upside down he couldn't figure how to get back up—Phillip Claren was there for him."

Gordy's gambling was history, as far as I knew. "Dad didn't tell you more?"

"You know your father. He didn't like talking about anyone else's business. And Gordy was his best friend."

My father was fishing with Gordy when the heart attack came. Gordy got the boat back to shore, had called ahead for the waiting ambulance and sat next to him at the hospital when he'd taken his last breath. Somehow, I feel my mom's thinking of the same moments we had both missed.

"Another log on the fire?" she asks.

"Pretty tired."

"I have an early morning too. Do you need anything?" She doesn't ask if I need help. She's smarter than that.

"I'm good."

I plod down the long hall to the back of the townhome to the guest suite she's renovated for me. The bed is covered in a fluffy blue and white coverlet. It takes too long for me to get under the covers, but I go through the routine methodically. The strip down to nakedness—with no foreign object attached.

My final task is to lean the crutches against the bedside table. And then, the moment my head hits the pillow, exhaustion pulls me into sleep.

EIGHT DAYS

CHAPTER THIRTEEN
Friday

Coffee and sausage. An excellent motivator for getting up in the morning.

The sunlight streams into the room. Chester, dressed to go out into the world for his various obligations, sits at the long pine kitchen table, happily digging into a Boston breakfast. Emma, the housekeeper, sees me. "Good morning, Miss Rommel."

Chester gets up and pulls out a chair for me. "Dee, I'm sorry I wasn't able to wait up last night."

"How's your cold?"

"I think the god-awful concoctions your mother comes up with have conquered it."

My mother enters, she's dressed in a coral-colored St. John suit and beige, suede heels. Ready to manage her team at the Cancer Research Center.

Chester pulls out her chair. "Gayle, I've asked Emma to prepare eggs, Boston beans, and sausage this morning."

She kisses his cheek. "You're using Dee as an excuse again."

"As a lovely opportunity for a hearty morning meal." Chester winks at me.

My mother accepts her veggie drink from Emma and holds it up as a toast to us. "Here we are, together. I do love it."

The doorbell sounds and Emma heads out to answer it. Chester spoons the last of his beans onto his toast. He smiles at me. "Will you be able to stay for a while?"

"I have to get back to Portland this morning."

Emma returns. "A gentleman is here, asking for you, Miss Rommel. A Dr. Philip Claren."

Chester and my mother startle; curiosity is killing them. My mother turns to Emma. "Please bring coffee to the library for Dee's guest."

I head to the front entry. He's there, in jeans, a gray tweed jacket, and light gray shirt. "Gordy told me you were Gayle Forbright's daughter, and you did mention you'd be staying here. I'm sorry for stopping by unannounced but I wanted to speak to you directly."

He follows me into the library. Emma arrives with a tray, two coffees mugs, cream, and sugar. Claren waits for her to leave. "Your points last night were good ones. As you said, no need for investigations to cross each other. I've decided it's best to keep everything in-house now."

"Meaning?"

"I won't need G&Z Investigations any longer."

What's going on? "Any reason for this quick change? Did Bunny Luce show up?"

He avoids a direct answer. "I believe I'll see her soon."

"But you're not sure? I have a few things to pursue today." I'm hoping he'll give me a clue for the change of heart. Gordy will want to know.

"No need, no need for your time anymore," he says. "I'll settle with Gordy."

"If you haven't talked to Bunny Luce yet…"

"It's under control." He hasn't touched the coffee. "I need to get to my office."

"Excuse me." I'm frustrated, it doesn't feel good to be taken down a notch, to be viewed as superfluous. Plus, Gordy will want an explanation. "Can you give me more—why change your mind now?"

"I'm late for a meeting." He heads out the door, gets into the Escalade.

The SUV moves down the street. Something's off. But, clearly, I've been fired.

"Honey?" My mother's coming down the hallway. "Can I ask why Philip Claren's come to call on you?"

"Mom, you sound like some old-fashioned Victorian whatever…'call on me'?"

She stops at the hall closet, gets out her light coat. Waits for an answer.

"It wasn't a social call," I say. "Sorry, can't tell you more."

She searches my face for a moment; the struggle to not ask more questions is evident. She slips into her coat, and pulls me into a hug. There's the fresh herbal scent of her cologne. She mumbles in my ear. "Drive carefully, honey. Call me if you need anything."

My mother's off to work. Chester's retired to his workspace on the second floor. In the guest room, I throw my overnight needs into my duffel.

* * *

The early morning drive north is easy. Traffic's light as I pass the edges of the big city, its low, rundown mini-malls, its tattered auto-body shops and tired motels. I go over Claren's visit again in my mind. How stiff his shoulders were, how clipped his decision sounded. What had happened between midnight and dawn?

I cross into New Hampshire. The pines, black oaks, ash, sycamores, and birches thicken, proudly taking up more space. Wind rustles the branches and the sky's brightness is threatened by a large, dark cloud bank in the west—moving east.

My phone pings. A number I don't recognize. I answer. "Who's calling?"

"This is Nella, Chester Forbright's assistant. Is this Dee Rommel?"

"It is."

"Your mother asked me to give you call?"

"Oh. Right."

"About a wedding scheduled on June 22? On an island?"

I was off the case. But I couldn't help my interest. "Right. Chebeague. Close to Portland."

"I would do any favor for your mother. She's so elegant—and smart, don't you think?"

I've heard this all my life.

"My friend at Shannon Styles told me a bit about the event on Chebeague Island. We love to talk weddings." She shuffles papers, seems to be reading off a list. "Several good-sized homes next to each other have been rented. There's going to be a lobster bake on the beach, steaks on the grill, seafood salads, a five-tiered lemon and vanilla cake, Cliquot La Grande Dame champagne, a company called Sawyer is bringing flowers across on the ferry that morning. My friend is excited because she'll be on site, her boss has put her in charge of making sure the tent is filled with sparkling lights and candles. The cool thing is that one of the guests has funded helicopter rides for anyone interested for the afternoon." She confides. "I've been living with my boyfriend for five years and my friends get that I want the perfect ceremony. But a perfect wedding like this, I could never afford."

"Perfection doesn't have to include helicopters."

"Of course." She giggles. "Also, there's a private security company hired for the event—means the guest list must be interesting. Of course, she couldn't share details on that."

"Understandable. I appreciate your call."

"Well, your stepfather, Mr. Forbright, is my boss. This is the best job in the world. And like I said, I would do any favor for your mother. Personally, I think something's very weird—the bride didn't even do an online wedding page. For her guests to check out. Details. Wedding present suggestions. Who doesn't want to share news of love and marriage and make a list of perfect presents?"

"Maybe she doesn't want anything."

"That's crazy. There are so many wonderful things to want."

Ten Days

We click off. I didn't think Claren would care if the nuptials were going to feature sparkling lights and candles, steak and lobster, and lemon cake. He wants to see his daughter. Talk to her, plain and simple.

And I wasn't able to make that happen. No tick in the 'win' column.

Large and gunky raindrops land on my windshield just as I pass the sign:

Welcome to Maine

The signs along the highway bring back memories. Sailing with my father out to the Goat Island lighthouse in Kennebunkport. The magical beaches created at low tide in Ogonquit. Biddeford's Palace Diner, one of the best breakfasts in Maine, served to fifteen lucky customers who sit at a narrow counter in a renovated old railway car. I stay to the right and head north on I-295 and soon I'm in Portland, passing the Sea Dogs stadium. My season pass is on my refrigerator. When Gordy gets back, we'll go to the Double A baseball games. If he's not too pissed that I've lost a client.

An advantageous free space at the curb in front of my apartment; I thank the parking spot god. I grab my duffel and head through the rain. I'm about to reach the key into the lock when I notice a piece of torn paper, folded into a tight, damp bundle, stuck in the door's frame. I pluck it out, stick it in my pocket.

Inside, I drop my duffel in the living room. I hang my wet blazer in the bathroom, grab a towel to dry my hair. My stomach growls, I head to the kitchen and open the jar of almond butter. I spoon a mouthful and rummage in my pocket for the folded piece of paper. There's something inside it, it's lumpy. I unfold it on the counter.

It's a brass angel pin—one of the wings broken off.

My throat goes tight. I read the first-grader-ish block handwriting: *PemaPond, Route 32. #5. By the hour.*

I punch in Gretchen's phone number. She answers and I ask, "Hear from Karla?"

"No."

"Still got your angel pin?"

"On my jacket. Why?"

I get a sick feeling in my stomach. "I'll call you—call you—later." I click off.

Moments later, I park in front of the G&Z office building, pull the hood of my slicker over my head and rush to the door of the building. Malio is there. "You f-forgot to put money in the meter."

"I'll be right down."

Malio calls after me, "I will p-protect from p-parking cop!"

Abshir's in the office, eating from a Tupperware container. A spicy and meaty aroma fills the space. "My mother sends you sambusa."

"Are you free right now?" I grab a folder full of maps.

"*Haa.* Yes. I have no school."

"We'll need access to Google maps too. Pack a charger. Don't forget your raincoat. We're heading up the coast."

He recognizes my agitation. "I am with you. *Adiga.*"

* * *

Pemaquid is the former name of the town of Bristol in Lincoln County. There's the Pemaquid Harbor, Pemaquid River, Pemaquid Park, a lighthouse, a beach—dozens of sites named after the area. The name translates to 'situated far out'; it's famous for the ancient shipwrecks found off its point.

"Abshir, anything called PemaPond?"

Abshir's got the iPad open. "Looking. Looking."

Route 32 winds for sixty some miles from Waterville south into the area near Bristol. We're hoping to find Karla anywhere on this far-out route, all the way to the southern finger of land. What is Karla doing out here?

Abshir calculates the size of our search. "The Pemaquid Pond—the body of water—is almost twenty-five miles long. It is between Route 1 and Route 32."

"Let's get to Waldeboro, that's pretty much the top of the Pond. We'll go south, stick to the east side."

"*Haa.* Okay."

"See if you can get hold of the Chamber of Commerce near Waldeboro."

Abshir's fingers fly over his iPad. He calls the number and we get lucky. Someone answers. "Beautiful Maine. How can I help you?"

Abshir puts the call on speaker. "Hello, very kind of you to answer. We want to find a place, on Route 32. It is called PemaPond? Maybe a motel."

"Let me check. Hold please." The volunteer's probably a senior citizen who lives in the area and wants to put in a few hours of social time, proud to share insights to the best camping sites, beaches, and lobster shacks. "PemaPond Motel," she says. "Mm. Oh dear me, nothing under Pemaquid Pond Motel and…nothing—oh no—nothing, nothing, nothing under Pond Motel or Pema Motel. Some places of course are not on our register, we encourage every business to register with us but some do not take advantage. There are other places for you to stay on Route 32, if that's where you're headed."

Ten Days

"Thanks for your help," I say. "Could you recommend something not too expensive?" The note in my door said 'by the hour'—probably not a high-priced place.

Abshir writes down a few of her recommendations, and we disconnect. He looks at me, "Didn't you testify against Billy Payer? Help put him in prison."

"Yeah." I was one of the witnesses in the case against Billy, along with Hilary and Pat, his nose now permanently crooked and causing his nasal passages to be on constant drip. Karla was also called to testify, the prosecution wanted to know what had gone on that night, before Billy had arrived at Sparrows. No one felt safe; Billy, at the defense table, glowered at us as we testified. Marvin, Billy's brother and my stodgy partner, sat in the courtroom, head down. I wondered if Billy insisted on loyalty from Marvin.

"All of Billy Payer's group follow him, he is the leader, he is a bully. They come to the park near where I live and shove all the young kids off the basketball courts. There are other places for them to play but they choose this place. Why is it possible for your friend to even talk to this Billy Payer? He is not a good person."

"I don't see the charm either."

* * *

Route 32 may be labeled a state highway but it's more like a two-lane, winding country road. Miles of trees and an occasional farmhouse. Pemaquid Pond is to the west of us, there are multiple turn offs that would get us closer to the water's edge—some of them dirt roads that probably lead to summer cottages. Perhaps they could lead to a motel, but there's no signage.

The sky is darkening.

Abshir straightens. "There is a campground. Down that road. Called Hawk Puddle."

"We'll come back to it if we don't find anything on the main road."

The winds are picking up, bending the trees unmercifully. Rain bursts from the gray clouds as if the clouds are impatient to rid themselves of heaviness. The deluge clings to the Outback's windshield and the glass fogs and, for a moment, I'm driving blind.

Abshir presses the defrost button, it sputters and whines. "What is going on?"

"Car's old, gets cranky," I say.

He leans forward, scans both sides of the road. "We could ask someone, maybe. Someone who lives here. *Haa!* Over there! There—to the left side—an old market. It's open. There are lights on in the window."

I swerve into the cracked blacktop parking lot. Abshir points. "Could be a motel behind."

There is. It's a long, low building, stretches the length of a football field. Painted yellow, the doors of each unit are painted blue. The roof is blue shaker tiles, quite a few have fallen off. The neon sign in the office window glows dimly *'PemaPond Motel. Easy Rates.'*

I drive past the office/grocery store towards the motel. Karla's lime-green Camry is there. Parked in front of a door with the number 5 hanging off one nail. We get out of the car and I open the trunk to grab my baseball bat.

The blacktop is slick. I force myself to stride purposefully, lift my left leg high, pound it down. My gait is jerky. I pound on the door.

"Karla? Karla, are in you there? It's me, Dee."

Someone's fumbling at the doorknob. My hands tighten on the bat, my elbow is cocked.

The door opens, the safety chain is on. Karla's puffed and discolored eyes allow for only a slit of sight. Her forehead is tinged a nasty bluish-purple, her hairline is jagged; someone has pulled out chunks of what were once dark, soft locks.

She fumbles at the safety chain. Disconnects it. She's got a sheet wrapped around her naked body and she's bent at the waist, as if it's too painful for her to be erect. There are dark marks on her shoulders, left by a hammer fist, her neck and chest are brown with bruises. Her jaw is twice its normal size.

"Oh geez, Karla. Oh geez."

She rasps. "Dee."

I want to take her into my arms, console her but I'm afraid touching her might cause more excruciation. She's unable to form full words. I can make out some of it. "Want...home. Dee. Dee. Home."

I drape my raincoat over her shoulders. There are tiny punctures in the skin; are those bites? "I'm here. I'm here. Who did this to you?"

Abshir is behind me. We get her to the car. I open the trunk again, push aside my toolbox, my rain gear, down vest, and binoculars and grab the blanket I keep in a plastic pouch. I toss the blanket to Abshir, tell him to stay with Karla, make sure she's warm. I head to the side door of the market where the office sign sits in the window and slam through to shock the most hunched and ugly man I've ever seen. It's like cauliflower-ear has spread over his entire face. "Room 5," I bellow.

"What about it?" He doesn't lift his neck, only his eyes. He's got a wrinkled Penthouse magazine in his hands.

"Who checked in there?"

"Who are you?" he fumes.

"A friend of the beat-up woman in Room 5 who is ready to call the cops."

"Cops?"

"Who booked Room 5?"

"Paid for. Cash. Two nights. Hundred-dollar bills. Cash. I got a right to take money."

My cell phone is focused on his face. He tries to turn away but he's not quick enough, I get the bastard's mug.

"Describe the person who gave you the money."

"Don't remember faces."

"If you touch that room, there'll be trouble. Room 5 is a crime scene." I step closer, the counter my only barrier. "It's a crime scene. Do you hear me? I'm taking pictures of it and if one thing is moved, you're in jail. Don't you give a fuck what happens on your property, asshole?"

He wears the familiar expression of a man who resents a female telling him he's not worth the shit that drips out of his ass.

I let the door slam and head back to Room 5. The boot on my prosthesis slips on the slick blacktop of the parking lot and a pinching crick shoots through my thigh. I step inside, snap pictures of the trashed bed, overturned chair, blood on the sink, Karla's torn shirt, ripped skirt, slashed and ragged tights, and discarded panties.

A long gray rat scurries out from under the bed, heads to a hole in the floor molding—and disappears. I swallow the bile that rises in my throat.

CHAPTER FOURTEEN
Friday

The closest police force is probably in Brunswick, more than a half hour away. There might be a sheriff assigned to the area, but I don't want to take the time to locate and rouse the person. Cell reception is iffy; I decide that when I'm back on the highway, I'll put out an alert. First thing is to get Karla medical attention.

She's stretched out in the back seat of my car. Abshir's covered her with the blanket. A low moan rumbles in her throat.

It's only a half hour past Brunswick to Portland's Mercy Hospital, to doctors Karla knows. The horseshoe drive in front of the Emergency Room is clear and Abshir leaps from the car to hurry inside. Moments later, aides push a gurney to the car and once Karla is transferred to it, she's rushed through the sliding glass doors towards an examination room.

I've called Donato and he's brought a photographer to document Karla's black eyes, the discolorations on her arms and back, the swelling on her knee and the contusions on her face and hands. There are rodent bites on her legs and shoulders, one bite is torn open, as if the rat wanted to dig deeper into her flesh. I pace, on high boil; I want to slam out of there, avenge Karla—confront the prick who did this to my friend—whose dream was having a few salons and a solid, friend-filled life.

Hilary's on duty, goes through her protocol of making Karla as comfortable as possible. Karla's moans soon quiet. Hilary comes out to the hallway. "What happened, Dee?"

"Last time I saw her she was getting into Billy Payer's pickup truck."

Hilary's face turns ashen. "Was it him?"

"Nothing's for sure."

She grabs my arm. "Why did they let him out?"

"Wheels of justice, Hilary, sometimes don't roll the way they should."

She's paged. "Another drug overdose," she mutters. "I'll check on Karla again when I can." She hurries down the hallway, her body tight, her shoulders slumped as if shielding herself from incoming.

Donato joins me. "It'll be in the Brunswick police jurisdiction. Under Detective Stinner. He got to the motel."

"You won't be overseeing it?"

"Can't be me," Donato says. "Crime scene is in Brunswick."

* * *

Two hours later, Detective Mike Stinner of the BPD, comes out of Karla's room and beelines to Donato. "Robbie. Not getting anything from her. Just mumbles and groans."

Donato introduces us. "Stinner, this is Dee Rommel. She was the one who found Karla Ackerman at the motel."

Stinner's hair is parted on the side like a first grader at church. He flips his notebook open. "Robbie says you're the one who took the photos."

"On my cell," I say. "I did them quick—wanted to get Karla to the hospital."

"I've got forensics in the PemaPond motel room. Did you touch anything? Move anything before you took the pictures?"

"Left everything as it was. I touched the door to the room—and I told the creep in the office not to go in there. Keep the crime scene intact."

The doctor joins us, tells us a rape kit has been administered, that there are no broken bones, there could be a slight concussion. He leaves us to check on the patient.

Stinner finishes taking my statement—how I happened to find Karla, the note in the door, the angel pin, Abshir and my search, the call to Chamber of Commerce. I suggest he rustle Billy Payer out of whatever bar or hole-in-the-wall he's in and arrest his ass. Stinner's countenance gets colder. "Don't tend to jump to conclusions. Best to gather evidence first."

I immediately dislike Detective Mike Stinner.

"Where is this note that was stuck in your door?" He asks.

It's been crumpled in my pocket and the thin notepaper is damp. I hand it to him. "My prints will be all over it."

"And this angel pin?"

"The broken part that was wrapped up in the note is on my kitchen table." My pin is attached to my shoulder bag. "When it's not broken, it looks like this."

Stinner takes out his cell, takes a picture of the pin.

The doctor rejoins us. He tells us that he suggested to Karla that she spend the night. The idea upset her. He asks, "Does she live alone?"

"Yes, she does." In a second-floor apartment, above Hector, her hefty, uncaring neighbor. "If you think she can leave the hospital, I'll bring her to my place and keep an eye on her."

The doctor nods. He tells us the report will be ready in the morning and then he leaves us.

Stinner tells me he's got a Victim's Advocate in with Karla. "Name's Rita Smith. She'll be assigned to Karla, from tonight onwards. She's supposed to keep checking in with her through the emotional rollercoaster sure to come." He tells me he'll be by in the morning to talk to Karla. He turns to Donato: "You and TV Christine at the stage where you can be civil?"

"She's a professional. Why?"

"Wanted to know if you had her ear—even though you parted company."

This is news to me.

Maybe it's old news to him because Donato doesn't seem bothered. Or maybe he's masking heartbreak.

"You know, Christine covered the announcement on me getting named for the Governor's Award," says Stinner.

"Your drug bust thing."

"Biggest one in Maine."

"New drug—what was it?"

Stinner's chest puffed out. "Good to be recognized."

"Sure. Congrats," says Donato.

"But we don't need television coverage on this," says Stinner. "Can you get Christine to back off on this one?"

"Doubt there's enough for her to sink her teeth into—yet," Donato tells him.

"Hope so. 'Til I figure it out." Stinner walks off.

I let out a breath. "He likes to be top dog."

"He's not a bad guy, Rommel," Donato says, reading my quick dislike. "Don't think he sees this bringing awards his way, it's simply an addition to his 'to-do' list."

"That's how it works."

"Can you keep the media away?" I ask.

"He thinks I have some pull. But I don't—and never did."

Ten Days

The smell of the place gets to me—the hardy and potent cleanser mixed with sickness, grief, fear, harsh laundered scrubs and sheets and decades of disease. "I need to get Karla out of here."

* * *

Hours later, Gretchen was waiting at my place, Bert at her side. He had whined when he saw me; I figured he was complaining because he hadn't had Gordy's special meals for a day and a half, and it was well past dinner time. But Bert went silent when Abshir helped Karla into the living room, it was like he knew he had to give over being the center of attention. I moved my crutches and the coffee table; we got the sleep-couch pulled out. Abshir and I put the sheets on, and Karla sank into the mattress, turned her head to the wall.

Donato had stopped by to bag the broken angel pin. He'd moved around the perimeter of the property—and found nothing.

Now we're all in my living room. Gretchen sinks into a chair, her eyes on Karla, who has not talked since we've gotten to the apartment. "Dee," Gretchen declares. "I'm staying here tonight."

I punch a number into my phone. "I'll order take-out."

* * *

The chicken noodle soup is in my take-out bag and the pizza is being taken from the red-hot stone oven. Pat is behind the bar, serving customers who have eyes glued to the television, cheering for the Red Sox as they make a comeback against the Yankees. It's warm and convivial, as if this community is united and bad things never happen. A wave of depression washes over me.

"Who's that?"

It's Reader. He's behind me, looking out at Donato waiting by his department-issue Ford Taurus. He'd insisted on escorting me on the food run.

"A friend."

"He's a cop, isn't he?"

The pizza box is placed in its cardboard box. I reach for it. "Detective."

"How come you're striking me as—I don't know—what it is—mad? Sick? Like you're holding in something."

"Just rage."

"Good meal choice then. Pizza goes well with rage."

"You seen Billy Payer?" I ask.

"Hasn't been around." Reader waits. Like he expects another question.

"Keep an eye on Pat. Billy might be getting back in stride."

Reader raises an eyebrow. "You wanna tell me something?"

"Not now. People are waiting for me."

"Good people?"

"Hurt people."

I step around Reader and make my way out. Donato's holding the car door open for me. Reader's in the window, peering at us.

* * *

Karla's sitting up, her back against the cushions of the pullout couch. Donato's left and Gretchen is changing cable channels on the television. She can't land on a show, they all seem inane and inappropriate for the gravity of the moment. Karla closes her eyes, sinks down, turns her face to the wall.

Gretchen joins me in the kitchen. "What can we do?"

"That's it for right now. The Brunswick team is finishing with the motel room. They'll be going through her car. Maybe we'll have something by morning."

I take a bowl of soup out to Karla. "You gotta eat, keep your strength up."

Karla moans, her fingers twitch, but she doesn't hear me. She's slipped off into a ragged sleep.

Out my window, I see a white Chevy pickup parked across the street. The driver's side window is down, there's the tip of a lit cigarette, smoke being blown in the air. Billy Payer, in a denim jacket, steps out of the truck, leans against it.

"Shit."

Gretchen comes out of the kitchen, alarmed. "What? What?"

I'm already storming out the door. I move over the short ramp, over the grass, hell-bent on reaching Billy Payer. The grass is slick, my good foot loses traction, I lose my balance and I'm down, hitting my hip hard onto the ground.

"Got a problem there, cripple?"

I roll over, shove the heels of my hands into the earth, get on my good knee and extend my prosthesis the side.

His voice is cold. "Takes a bit of time? To get up?"

I extend my good leg so I'm on the toe of my shoe and walk my hands back until I'm in pyramid position. Keep walking my hands back until I can stand on my good leg and use my abs to straighten up.

I can hear a constant click of cell phone—the asshole is taking pictures.

Ten Days

There's a debilitating tremor that shoots to my pelvis. I breathe deep, grit my teeth. Billy, cigarette between two fingers, walks across the street towards me.

"What're you doing here?" I ask.

"Heard Karla got hurt. You know I care about her." He's full of sing-song arrogance, so confident he's alpha and basking in the aphrodisiac of power.

We face each other.

"Tell my little pet I was here. You do that. She'll wanna hear I was asking about her."

Billy jogs back to his pickup truck. I can see the skull patch on the back of his denim jacket. He flicks the cigarette onto the street. And drives away.

SEVEN DAYS

CHAPTER FIFTEEN
Saturday

What sleep there was must have come in spurts. I spent the night listening for Karla's breathing. Gretchen had fallen into deep snooze-land in my one overstuffed chair with mismatched footstool. She stretched, huddled back into a fetal position and then stretched, huddled and stretched. She slept like a lavender-haired cat.

I had left three phone messages for Donato. No callbacks. A reminder that I had no place in the information-share. When I was active on the force, I saw how criminals screw up. They'd leave something behind, they'd brag, they take a trophy of their deed. I ached to be among those in the motel room as the space was photographed, as evidence was collected, vacuumed for fibers, and surfaces searched for any bits of body scree on doorjambs, sheets, and bedside tables.

Something had to point directly to Billy. But he hadn't looked the worse-for-battle, no visible marks on his face or arms when he showed up last night. I held out hope for the rape kit—that DNA would seal his fate.

Where's the justice? Why is it so unfair—that charm and a movie-star-worthy face are bestowed on a predator? Shouldn't people come with warning labels? Why couldn't Billy Payer's handsome facade be turned inside out to reveal the putrid monster inside?

It was in the early morning hours when Bert curled next to Karla on the pull-out couch. Initially he'd been confused about the sleepover but then, feeling the gravitas in the air, had settled in as protector. He'd lowered his chin onto his front paws and, with half-opened eyes, fallen into a half sleep. I could hear the periodic hum of the city bus passing by—twice an hour—connecting the East Bay and the West End of the city. I imagined it rolling through the empty streets, turning on Congress, the main thoroughfare, and moving past the lights of the late-night clubs and barely disturbing the seagulls that spent the dark hours pecking through garbage or snoozing in doorways.

Finally, dawn arrives. I muscle my way up and out of the low-slung chair that had been my father's favorite place to read. The hamstring of my left leg ached, I must have pulled it last night, trying to get up off the grass and duck Billy Payer's cell phone photos.

Bert raises his head and follows me to the kitchen; he's quickly out the back door to shake himself fully awake and pee and sniff around the edges of the fence. Moments later he's back inside and I lock the door.

"Did you sleep?" It's Gretchen, yawning in the kitchen doorway.

"Not much," I say. "You okay if I take a shower?"

"Go ahead. Bert's on high alert and...." her voice trails off. "I am too."

The smell of the moldy walls and stained wall-to-wall carpet of PemaPond Motel lingers in my nose. I head to my bedroom and sink to the edge of my bed. I massage my thigh, get a hot pad ready to put warmth on my hamstring. I take off my LiteGood.

I let the hot shower water beat against my body. Wash away the memory of Billy Payer's face—his malevolent triumph after I'd fallen in front of him. His underestimation will be his downfall.

There's a knock on the bathroom door. It's Gretchen; she calls through the closed door. "Dee? Someone's here for you. He says it's urgent."

I'm in a long terrycloth robe, supported by my cuff crutches, looking through the peephole of my front door. It's Reader, a newspaper tucked under his arm. Karla's awake, she's pulled the blanket up to her nose, keeping her swollen jaw out of sight. Gretchen's curious and tense. Bert's parked nearby, growling.

"It's okay, Bert. It's okay, buddy." Bert whines and sits on his haunches. I tell Karla I met our visitor at Sparrows—that Pat vouches for him. I unlock and unchain, and Reader steps in.

"Morning." He's sunny and irritating.

"How'd you find me?" I ask him.

Reader smirks as if it's a silly question. He examines the door. "Interesting. Three locks and a chain. Fort Knox vibe here." He breathes in through his nose. "Ah, coffee." His eyes glide to mine. "Let me pour you a cup?"

This is my turf, I want to stay in charge. "You show up for coffee and don't bring donuts?"

"My mother didn't raise me right." He turns to Gretchen and Karla. "I make social mistakes all the time. Apologize." Then he's back at me, pressing his request. "Coffee smells good. Where's the kitchen?"

I lead the way. Once we're inside, Reader slides the pocket door closed, so it's just the two of us.

"You played the urgent card," I say.

"Felt compelled to check in." He opens a few cabinets, finds the coffee mugs. His jumbo-sized hands make the over-sized mugs seem small. The veins in his wrists and forearms are prominent. A sign, along with his strong neck, that he's a weight lifter. "Milk? Sugar?"

"I like it bitter and plain."

"That sounds like you."

He's got a wryness that keeps me off-center. This morning it also pisses me off.

"Heard about your friend. Coupla nurses from Mercy ER had a nightcap at Sparrows."

"News travels fast."

He pours coffee into two mugs. "Heard she was one of Payer's main squeezes before his lock-up." He puts a mug near me on the counter.

"Heart's a weird thing."

"It is," he agrees. "Sometimes it's wrapped up in whatever bunk we're thinking about ourselves. Self-worth and all that."

"Is that a bullshit way of saying Karla brought this on herself?"

"No. Just that maybe she's got iffy taste in guys."

My jaw juts out, I resent any implication that Karla is at fault. "To be clear, my friend doesn't think she deserves this." Karla's mistake is thinking she can bring goodness and light to a bad man's nature.

"*Can Love live against all reason, against all discouragement?* That's a Charles Dickens' question—trimmed down and paraphrased by me."

"You not only read, you memorize. Should I be impressed?"

His sharp blue eyes glint. "I'm working hard to make that happen." He sips his coffee. "You've got a pretty high wall built around yourself. Ever let anyone in?"

I lean against the table, take my arm out of one of the cuffs so I can raise the coffee mug to my lips. "Like my privacy."

"Pat told me about…" he nods towards my leg. "That no one got arrested that night. That the bad guys got away."

"They did."

"Sucks."

"Yep," I confirm. "Not the focus of my concern right now."

"Right. If Billy's the guy on this thing with your friend," he says, "he's gotta be put away."

"We agree on something."

"Pat's my responsibility. Billy's not getting to him."

"Has he shown himself around Pat—or near Sparrows?"

"Not yet. That shit's got a Flitter account. He announces every day he's not drinking or eating at Sparrows. That the place sucks. His watering hole of choice is now the Gull's Roost—off Veranda. Has your friend pointed a finger at Billy?"

"She's not really talking. She'll come to her senses."

"Gonna stay here with you?"

"Her parents are coming to get her today. She'll go back to Augusta with them."

He takes another sip. "Also, heard a note was left for you. Someone wanted you to find her. Coulda been a trap."

"Thought about that." In fact, that realization was one of the reasons I was up all night. That, and Billy's unexpected visit.

Reader takes in the kitchen—at the unused stove, the bare countertops, the pristine, rarely touched knife rack. "Cook much?"

"No."

"Probably a good thing," he says. "They say the best food is cooked with love."

"I've never seen 'love' sold in the grocery store."

"No. Might be too expensive anyway."

I'm impatient. "I guess I should thank you for checking in…"

He interrupts. "You rescued your friend, right? And that's why you had a cop escort last night?"

"You got all this news how?"

"Sparrows attracts news and gossip."

"That's true. Well, I'm okay, if that's why you came by."

My robe is thick, and its belt is wrapped tightly around my waist. I'm aware he's taken in the crutches and made assumptions about what's missing under the terrycloth.

He puts his mug down. "For a bad-ass, you look good right out of the shower." He moves to slide open the pocket door.

"Call first next time," I say. "I'll put on a ball gown."

"No need."

"Where did Pat find you?" I ask.

"He didn't tell you?"

"I didn't ask."

"I'm his nephew."

"You're getting a bodyguard and a family discount at Sparrows?"

He crosses his arms, as if in exaggerated petulance. "You didn't even ask, and I thought I was a contender."

"For what?"

"For a smidgen of your interest."

"Stop playing around," I snap.

He takes a step closer to me. "Let me paraphrase again from Dickens. *The pain of parting ain't nothing compared to the joy of meeting again.* You know where I am. In Sparrows, or upstairs with my Uncle Pat. Thanks for the coffee." Reader moves, slides open the door, and walks into the living room. Bert is at his heels, shepherding him to the front door. Reader nods to Gretchen and Karla. "Sorry to disturb you, ladies."

By the time I get my crutch in place on my wrist, pick up the newspaper Reader's left on the counter, and traipse after him, he's gone.

Gretchen's eyes are big. "Who the hell is that?"

CHAPTER SIXTEEN
Saturday

The Saturday newspaper headlines are about Governor Mills' news conference on Maine's summer economy. In the lower half of the front page, in much smaller bold type, there's a headline followed by a report on the body found near Widgery Wharf. The article states that the coroner has determined the death was not due to drowning, but as a result of foul play, and a murder investigation is in progress. The article does not mention Thomas Beene's skull being nearly split in two, but I fill in the blanks—the brain must have been halved before Beene was dumped off the wharf.

What the paper does not report is the assault of one Karla Ackerman, discovered bloody and spent at the PemaPond Motel. The news came in too late? Or had Donato been successful in keeping the Emergency Room news squashed?

I slip a light sweater over my t-shirt, do a quick pull on my bedcovers to lend a semblance of tidiness to the room. I wonder who might be coming to pick up Beene's body. No one was mentioned in the newspaper report. How quickly a murder becomes a separate thing from the people who are affected. Did Beene have a grieving wife? Children? Energies pour into finding the perpetrator, the chance to place a feather in a detective's hat, move a case to the closed column. Stunning how quickly a battery or a rape becomes separate from the victim; how crime swiftly becomes a timetable, a list of clues and, in Karla's case, a judgement of a woman who found herself in the wrong place, at the wrong time, with the wrong person. Or persons. Who took her into Room #5? If she was driven there, who followed with her Camry? Who parked her car in front of Room #5, hung around for—or participated in—the assault and then left her to fester—possibly to die? Who put the note and angel pin in my door? Who wanted me to find my beaten and defeated friend?

Gretchen sticks her head into my bedroom. "Dee? I have to get to Doggie DayCare. Karla's asleep."

"Can you take Bert?"

"We're all set." Her eyes well up with tears. "It's not fair."

I wrap my arms around her to settle her shaking shoulders.

She lifts her head from the curve where my neck and shoulders meet, wipes away one of the tears that has slipped down her cheek to her lip. She mumbles, "Be careful, Dee."

* * *

I'm in the kitchen, sipping on cold coffee and listening to Gordy vent. "Why didn't you tell me what happened with Claren?"

"Got a crisis here. Karla…"

"Called the office. Abshir told me about Claren—and about your friend."

"Karla," I snap. I want him to think about her in the specific.

"'Course I know who she is. She even cut my hair once, good job too. Sorry about what happened. But the cops are swarming, I bet. Let 'em have it."

"Billy Payer did this."

"You can't go off half-cocked, making accusations. It's too dangerous. Step back."

"Don't want to."

"Need to let the cops take care of it. We'll stay on Claren."

"We're fired. Claren said he was going to call you."

"Why would he want us to back off?" Gordy's sister-in-law, Janette, is in the background, asking if he wants a yogurt and banana milkshake. He yells at her that he's on the phone and besides, he likes to chew food. Then he's back, grousing at me. "So, tell me. What do you think? What's this quick turnaround with Claren?"

"Doesn't make sense." I fill him in on the break-in at LC Lab and that Claren, initially, said he wanted me to stay on, to focus on finding Bunny Luce before the wedding date. Then, the next morning, he'd shown up at my mother's place, said he'd changed his mind and told me he'd settle the bill. "He said that Claren Tech's in-house team would now handle all aspects. There's this woman, Prudence Lopez, head of his security…"

"Doesn't feel right. We need to stick with it."

"The client doesn't want us, Gordy. And I've got Karla here."

He hardens his tone, just enough to remind me he's not just family friend and my self-appointed Cerberus; he's the boss. "We're gonna stay on Bunny Luce."

"Is this because you mysteriously 'owe' Claren? What's this big debt?"

"I'll be there Sunday night."

"You're supposed to stay in Florida for the entire week."

"Calling my doc now." Gordy starts to yell at his sister-in-law again and hangs up. I slam my near-empty coffee mug on the counter and start to punch in Gordy's cell phone number to tell him the surgeons must have also taken cerebral matter when they harvested his kidney. There's a knocking on the front door. I quickly move to it; don't want anything to wake Karla. I glance through the peephole. It's two men. One looks apologetic and one looks scared.

Moments later, we're in the kitchen and Abshir puts his backpack and laptop on the long dining table, avoiding my glare. "Gordy told me to come," he whispers. "Said I should stay with your friend because you have other work. This I have to do because Gordy signs my paychecks." He takes three ten-pound textbooks from his backpack. "Gordy says you must press ahead. That it is a point of honor."

"His honor."

"He is counting on you," Abshir says. "He said to say that."

"Okay, okay." I can hear Gordy saying exactly that.

Winston leans against the counter, holds up a bag from Standard Bakery. "Karla's favorites. I thought about these all the way over on the ferry from Chebeague. Cinnamon biscuits. And croissants. And sticky buns. And cookies." There's fear in Winston's voice. He feels useless, incapable of correcting the horror that our friend endured. He hates that he's part of a world where cruelty co-exists with friendship and ferry rides. He's plaintive: "Where's the magic wand, Dee? I just want to turn back time for her."

Abshir taps one of his textbooks. "My criminal psychology book—says in the book that sympathy and empathy are senses like smelling or hearing or seeing. And most people have those senses. But there are psychopaths—they inflict pain in others and it brings them a pleasurable feeling. My professor says many can't fully understand this aberration."

Winston shudders. "I can't."

Abshir opens the textbook. "But it is real. I can let you read."

"No one needs to read it, Abshir," I say. "We get it."

"Remember the story about the dog when we were kids?" Winston says. "Billy was supposed to have hung Marvin's dog in the family garage and then made Marvin witness his dog die?"

"That was an urban legend," I mutter. "When we were kids."

Abshir frowns. "Maybe it is a true legend? Billy Payer and his friends torment the kids on our neighborhood basketball court. He doesn't need to play there, except he likes to scare and be powerful." He unwinds his cord and plugs in his computer, glances up at me. "They have proof it was him? Has he been arrested?"

Ten Days

"Think I would've heard. So—the answer to that, I assume, is 'no.'"

Karla's flailing, coming out of a deep sleep. "Who's here? Who's here?"

We move out of the kitchen. "Karla, it's Dee. You're at my place. In Portland. You're safe."

Winston sits on the side of the couch. "Hey, honey. Came in from Chebeague to visit you." Karla ducks her head, as if she could hide the bruises. "Brought bakery treats. I'll get you anything you need."

Karla's eyes fill with tears. "Don't want…anything…anymore. What's the point?"

"Your friends care about you. We're here for you." My heart's sinking, because I recognize her disillusionment. Our experiences are different, but there's a common denominator—we both thought we were going to die at the hands of someone who did not value us. Stuff that gives you nightmares. "Karla, I'll be back as soon as I can. Someone's going to be here with you all the time. You're not alone."

I grab my shoulder bag; I can feel the cold metal of the angel pin against my hand. I head out to my car.

* * *

Stylists are at work at Karla's salon, trimming hair, layering on foils and color. The one who is not busy has dark, copious sideburns, he's focusing on straightening a stack of gossip magazines. His eyeliner-ed eyes glance at me; there's a recognition. "You want that manicure?"

I take a business card from the plastic holder on the counter. "This you?"

He points out the unique spelling. "Name's L-vis." His purple eyeshadow sparkles.

"That's your real name?"

"My professional name."

"Short for what?"

"Who wants to know?"

"Cops will. They'll want to find out why you told me Karla had called and said she was in Augusta with her sick mom. She wasn't in Augusta. She was beat up and raped and stuck in a trash motel."

His pale hands flutter to his neck. "She okay?"

"Ludicrous question. No, she's not." I take a step closer to him. "Who told you to lie?"

L-vis' eyes dart to the window. Donato's Taurus pulls up to the curb, a Portland Police cruiser is behind him. Two uniforms follow Donato into the salon.

"Got your text," Donato says to me.

I introduce him to nervous L-vis and add, "Not a loyal employee of Karla's Hair."

"Really."

L-Vis' face is beet red and his hands cover his crotch, maybe afraid if he says the wrong thing he'll get kneed. I could've told him Donato doesn't resort to violence, but why make his life easier? Donato invites L-Vis to have a private chat in the back room. L-vis stutters and leads the way down a hallway. Donato apologizes to the other stylists and customers. "Get back to beauty. We all appreciate it." He nods to me. "Wanna hang outside?"

Fifteen minutes later, Donato joins me on the sidewalk. "What did he say?"

"That he lied. Because you showed up asking questions and didn't want a cut or a manicure and he just wanted to get you out of the shop and stop wasting his time."

"He was reading trashy gossip magazines—half of the articles and pictures are lies." What a jerk. Didn't sit right. "Do you believe him?"

"He has a big chip on his shoulder. Seems to think his time is pretty special."

I'm processing. "He really made up a lie to get rid of me?"

"Technically he can lie to you. But not the police. He said he was sorry—didn't fathom Karla was in trouble."

"Jerk."

"Can't charge him with anything. You know that."

"Yeah."

"Rommel, Stinner plans to check in with Karla again today. He wants this solved. You're impatient but you need to let him do his job."

"Guess it's good I can't stick around."

"Where you going?"

"Gotta do something for Gordy."

His gray-blue eyes study me for a moment. "Be safe."

* * *

Ten minutes later, I'm back on the road to Massachusetts.

Jade has found an address for me in small community of Lincoln, about forty-five minutes northwest of Boston. Fine homes are built on two to three acres of land and enjoy elegant isolation.

It's mid-morning when I pull to a stop next to a low, stone fence built hundreds of years ago. The well-kept, century-old farmhouse is painted a deep red, has sage green shutters and a black asphalt shingled roof. There's a barn to one side, also painted red. The New England summer, late in coming this year, is showing off; Mother Nature has graced a plum tree with pale pink blossoms, the maples lining one side of the driveway have unfurled burgundy leaves, their silver undersides shimmer as the breeze catches them. Warm temperatures have encouraged the sweet peas and begonias to bloom in the pots near the front door.

A shiny green Volvo SUV is in the paved driveway. A long, wide wheelchair ramp leads from pavement level up to the slightly elevated side door.

No sidewalks here, no steady traffic. There's no way to hide my approach. Edges of curtains in a living room, a lamp on a table near a window. These farmhouses often have kitchens in the back, overlooking fields or gardens. I head up the driveway and glance inside the SUV, notice the customized hand controls, the added mechanics to manage the loading of wheelchair and driver. Needed elements to hold onto an independent life.

The side door of the home opens and Brad Hogan, in his powerchair, motors down the ramp. He's in jeans and a deep blue, long-sleeve polo shirt. "I wondered how long you were going to sit outside my house," he calls to me.

"We met at the LC Lab. The day of the break-in. Two days ago. Dee Rommel."

He waits.

"You don't like living in the city? Closer to the lab?"

"Too much noise," he says. "If something happens out here, I hear it."

"What do you expect to happen?"

He doesn't answer—just repeats, "Can I help you?"

Since I'm technically no longer employed by Claren, I stretch the truth. "Wanted to ask you a few questions about what happened at the lab. No one seems to be able to find a trail that leads to Lucy."

"She doesn't need to check in with me."

"Her father's trying to get in touch. He needs some peace of mind. Parents are like that."

"Can't help him." He turns his chair. "Got work to do in the garden. I'm busy."

"The lab at Claren Tech—being shut down—must be affecting your real work."

"The mind doesn't stop."

"Your mind's in constant work mode on the project you and Lucy are working on?"

His eyes narrow and I'm aware, again, of the scar creasing his eyebrow and stretching to his temple. "You're making assumptions. Who told you we had a project together?"

"Assumed. Festival of Ideas award in Miami. You two looked pretty happy in that picture in Lucy's office. Why stop working together?"

He frowns. "Come to the back garden. We can talk there."

I follow him on the pathway past the barn to the back of the house. The wide door of the barn is open; he wheels inside and grabs a sturdy flat filled with containers of seedlings. He puts the flat onto his lap and uses his levers and controls to return to the garden.

"You must like to cook," I say. "Or at least eat a lot of vegetables."

Hogan doesn't reply, definitely not interested in small talk.

A gardener, about seventy years old and hunched from constant bending, is aerating the soil in a raised bed. A hat with a large brim is plopped on top of his head; only gray whiskers and a pointed chin are visible. Another tray of seedlings is nearby; I recognize the leaves of tomato plants, eggplant, onion, and squash.

Hogan speaks to the gardener. There are rows and rows of apple trees on the back of the property, their branches starting to bud. By October, Hogan should have a large crop. In the other direction, there's a large deck off the back of the house. A bank of windows to catch the light. Containers of basil, sage, and oregano are set in planters on the deck, close to the sliding glass doors that lead to the kitchen.

Hogan finishes conferring with the gardener and heads back to the barn. I follow, trying to engage him. "Lucy's father tells me he was surprised by Lucy's sudden plans to get married. He's concerned; he doesn't want her taken advantage of."

"By anyone but him?" He puts the flat tray on his lap.

"Can I carry one of those?"

"No need."

He motors off.

"Dr. Hogan, what do you think the break-in at Claren Lab was about?"

He doesn't stop, doesn't answer.

"Did they find what they wanted?" I'm interrupted by a sound. Something has fallen inside the house—there was a loud clank and thud of a chunky object hitting a tiled floor. Through the back windows of the house, I glimpse a small woman moving in the kitchen. Large glasses. Jet-black hair.

I hurry towards the deck, climb the three steps, and reach the back door.

Hogan yells after me, "You can't go in my house."

My hand reaches the doorknob but it's in lock position. Bunny Luce is shoving a laptop and a notebook into a carryall. I rap on the glass. "Lucy. I'm Dee Rommel, I came here hoping to talk to you. Can you open the door?"

Her hair shields her face, she's intent on sifting through a pile of papers spread out on the table. She finds a sheaf of papers, folds them in half, and puts them in her bag. I call through the glass. "Lucy. Your father wants more information about the event on Chebeague—wants to know if you need anything."

Ten Days

Anxious eyes dart up to me. Her skin's dry, her lips are chapped and colorless.

"Lucy. Open the door. Let's talk."

She scribbles on a piece of paper in a small spiral notebook, tears it free, hurries to the door, and opens it a crack. Her skin is dry, stretched tightly from her cheekbones to jawline. Her eyes are huge, her speech low, raspy. "He's coming to Chebeague, Bunny's Point, tell me that," she says.

"He wants to talk to you before."

"I...have it." Her hands are trembling, her pupils, magnified slightly behind her glasses, are large—they seem to tremble in the center of her green eyes.

"Have what?"

Lucy pushes the paper out the narrow opening, I take it; she quickly closes the door. "Chebeague. Tell him he has to be there."

Just then, Tyler Peppard enters the kitchen. His legs are like sticks in tight black jeans, his torso is contained in a maroon t-shirt and black jacket. His hair is swept upwards—a good two inches up off his scalp, a Rolex glints on his wrist.

Peppard moves to the table, takes the carryall. His eyes slide to the window for a moment; he coolly takes note of my presence. So this is the midwestern guy who now struts the slick, New York City vibe. He whispers something in Bunny Luce's ear. She ducks her chin. Peppard puts his hand on her elbow and she allows him to lead her out of the kitchen, towards the front of the house.

I hurry around the side—the ground's soft from the recent rain, I have to move carefully. Rounding the corner, I see Peppard's holding onto Bunny Luce as they jog towards the country road. Her clothes, sizes too big and too loose on her thin body, billow around her frame.

A white Chevy pulls up to the end of the driveway. Peppard opens the back door. His hand is on Lucy's back, guiding her inside. The door slams shut and the car speeds off. The sound quickly becomes a memory. Everything is refined and country-quiet again.

The piece of paper in my hand. I look down at it. One word: *Einstein*.

What the hell am I supposed to do with that?

The breeze has come up and there's the sound of a door banging. Lucy and Peppard have left the front door of the farmhouse open.

* * *

I enter Hogan's farmhouse, hesitate in the entryway. Take a moment to listen. No movement. I step lightly into the living room. There's a well-worn leather couch and two chairs. The wood, destined for the large stone fireplace, is piled in a raised cubby. The hearth has been re-built—raised to just below waist-high—easier for Hogan to tend. The living room has a wide, arched opening that leads into the state-of-the-art country kitchen.

There's a wide hallway leading to a bathroom and bedroom on the first floor. A twin-sized bed, with assist rails, is against the wall, a desk with three computer screens dominates the rest of the space. A Connect Tru-Lift—an open elevator large enough to move a wheelchair from the first to second floor has been built into the corner.

On the far east side of the living space is a stairway, its pine steps are well-worn. At the top of the stairs is a landing and a long hallway that extends the length of the house. I pass a bathroom, then an area that must have once been a closet; it's now the space relegated to the Connect Tru-Lift.

I move on down the hallway, pass by a bedroom. Its walls are blue, the curtains made of white linen. A suitcase is opened on the window-seat. A few shapeless dresses hang in an open closet. The bedcovers are pulled back and it's clear that only one side of the bed has been slept on. I move inside the room to the desk. There's a notepad, nothing has been written on it. I pull open each of the three drawers. Nothing but used pencils and pens. The trash can under the desk is empty.

I move through a door to a connecting room; it's painted a deep gold. Boots with steel toes, black jeans, and a leather vest hang in the closet. Another unmade bed, this one reveals twisted, olive-colored sheets. So, Lucy and Peppard are not sleeping together. My idea of their upcoming vows being a tribute to true love has taken another nosedive.

I pull open the bedside table's drawer. A sleep mask, loose change, and a photo strip—black and white images from a cheap photo booth—one you might find in a drugstore. The pictures are of Peppard and Murphy Duncan, one of the guests at the Westin that I had first seen at Sparrows. Peppard and Duncan have wrapped arms around each other; they're grinning and the last photo on the strip shows them in a lip-lock.

I take a cell phone photo of the strip, leave it where it is. The tip of a small shiny object, jutting out from under the top photo, catches my eye. I lift the edge of the photo booth strip, there's a super compact, silver flashdrive. I mark its location with a cell photo. Hesitate. Instinct tells me to put it into my pocket, logic and law insist I leave it where it is.

I slip the flashdrive into my pocket.

At the farthest end of the hallway, is a bedroom. Here, everything is buttoned up, military style. A large, wide Adaptive Freedom bed, with hydraulics and assist rails, sits in the center of the room. The corners of the blankets are sharply tucked under the mattress, the pillows stacked precisely in the center of the bed. There's a desk and a computer set up, and a wall of bookshelves filled with academic journals.

The backyard is visible through the window in Hogan's room. The gardener is bent over the vegetable bed, but I don't see Hogan. Where is he? I decide to hurry back down the stairs and out the front door. But then I notice the poster-sized, framed photo of Albert Einstein, circa 1950, on the hallway wall. Einstein is in shorts and a t-shirt and sits on a sea wall, his head lifted to the summer sun. Under the photo is a quote: *"Let us not forget that human knowledge and skills alone cannot lead humanity to a happy and dignified life."* I take a cell phone picture of the poster and its apt warning, then run my hand over the poster, feel the underside of the frame. Nothing. I lift it off its hook. Attached to the hanging wire on the back is a clear plastic baggie containing at least two dozen small, aqua-colored pills. I lean the frame atop the hall table and take another photo; zoom in for a close-up of the pills. There's an imprint on them—a plump, smoochable lip. The baggie is partially opened, I reach in and pluck one out.

There's the whirr of a powerchair behind me. "You're trespassing."

My hand goes into my jacket pocket and deposits the single pill in a secure spot. I choose offense, point to the baggie. "Yours?"

His brow creases, he powers forward for a closer look. "No."

"Pretty good hiding place, I suppose."

I show him the note. "Lucy gave this to me before she ran out. Obviously thinking—maybe hoping—that these would be found. Why?"

"No idea."

"I'm here to help Lucy."

"She didn't ask you to come here and 'help.' You barged in." His tone is sharp. "Do I have to call the sheriff?"

"At the kitchen door, she asked if Claren was going to meet her. June 22. At her wedding. She made it sound imperative. Seems like there's more than family dysfunction going on here."

His lips are set in a straight line. No comment.

"What kind of pills are these?"

"Don't know."

Is he telling the truth? "Saw a lot of MDMAs when I was on the Portland PD. Different colors, go under the names of Ecstasy, X, Love Drug, E-tarts. Popular at the clubs, at parties. These fall into that category?"

"They're not mine."

"Are they Lucy's?"

A muscle in at the side of his mouth twitches. He averts his eyes.

"She doesn't have a healthy glow right now. She having a problem with drugs?"

No response.

"You think Peppard stashed these drugs? Or did Lucy?"

"You can weave all the scenarios you want, but I don't know how those pills got behind my poster."

"Why is Lucy hiding from her father?"

"Ask him."

"Maybe you think of Claren as a bad guy or a controlling father—think that however Lucy is treating him is his own damn fault."

"It's their thing."

"Eight months or so ago, at the conference in Miami, when you two won some prize, she was at least fifteen pounds heavier, a lot happier. Now she looks like she's a member of the Addam's Family and could blow over if you waved a hand in the air. Is she taking these pills?"

"Told you to leave." He takes out his cell phone. Maybe he will call the sheriff.

"I'm trying to get a bead on Lucy. Does she like to play games with people's heads?"

"You've ten seconds to get down the stairs and out my front door."

I put a G&Z business card on the hallway table next to the Einstein poster. "My personal cell's on the back. Have to tell you, I'm pretty tired of not getting to any truth here and not being able to flush out whatever crap is going on. You care about her, don't you?"

He doesn't answer.

"You looked like you did in those pictures taken in Miami."

He stabs at his phone with his finger, punches in a few digits.

"You believe this quote?"

He looks at the poster, confused.

"*...human knowledge and skills alone cannot lead to a happy and dignified life.*"

"What if I do?"

"Lucy does not look dignified—or happy." I'm pissed that he's not forthcoming, so I trek to the staircase and, holding onto the handrail, descend noisily. I let the door slam shut behind me.

CHAPTER SEVENTEEN
Saturday

I've started my Outback and frown at the flashing 'need oil' light. I call the burner phone I gave to Claren when he first came to the office. It buzzes, a series of staccato attention-getters. But no answer. Maybe he's no longer carrying the phone. I try the main number for Claren Tech. A live person answers and tells me Philip Claren is not in his office. After requesting a callback, I ask to be transferred to Prudence Lopez, head of security. A moment later, there's a connection.

"Lopez."

I remind her of how we met.

"How can I help you?" she asks.

"It's important I speak to Philip Claren. Could you help facilitate that?"

"I'm not his social secretary."

Okay, so Lopez has no idea why I arrived at the lab the night of the break-in. Obviously, Claren hasn't shared any information with her.

"It's about Lucy. Will you tell him?"

"What did you say your name was again?"

It was a dig, a reminder she doesn't consider me worthy of her full attention. "Dee Rommel. Please tell him it's important." I click off.

Jade's left a message on my phone, wants to see me in person. Since I'm heading north from Massachusetts, towards the Maine border, I send a message that I'll be at her place in an hour. And that I have a favor to ask.

* * *

Exit 25 off Highway I-95 takes me towards Kennebunk. The small village and its sister, Kennebunkport, share a population of about 15,000. In the early 18th century, it was a township for shipbuilders, fisherman, and farmers. Now it's tranquil and sophisticated, working people mix with residents of multimillion dollar estates.

Ten Days

I turn onto Main Street, pass graceful two-story colonials, some painted yellow, some white, some soft green. Many of them have dark shutters and look proud of their centuries-old heritage—housing families with joys, heartaches, and stubborn Maine principles.

Main Street takes me to Summer Street, and then to Route 9. I deny myself a stop at Gooch's Beach to grab a moment of peace walking on its soft sand. I drive onto Farburke Lane. There's Jade's rambling house. It had been connected to its barn fifty years ago and when Jade moved in, she and her sculptor husband reconfigured the footprint; the barn door is now a double-door front entry. At this moment, Jade, dressed in her normal all-black, her eyes framed with large, clear-rimmed glasses, is in the open door, waiting. Why is she so anxious to meet with me?

"Welcome to Bedlam," she quips in the chaos of her mudroom as I hang up my jacket. Worn sneakers and boots in kiddie and adult sizes, raincoats and windbreakers, hats and earmuffs, umbrellas and walking sticks clutter the room. The walls are covered with innocent art done in crayon and finger-paint and gluey-glitter.

"You look frazzled," she says.

"Lots going on."

"There's more."

She pads, in her fuzzy slippers, into her massive living room—over-full with colorful rugs and ample couches covered with quilts and toys and socks. A pup tent is set up in the center, a flag perched at its peak that reads: 'Kids Only.' Her husband's sculpting studio is in the far back, behind a series of primary-colored stained-glass doors. One long wall is full of bookshelves; this is probably where her son discovered Poe and the onomatopoeia of *The Bells*. "You have a favor to ask?"

"A three-parter. First, do you have a small plastic bag I could use?"

Her two boys make macaroni and cheese with the housekeeper in the kitchen. They both have pickles stuck up their noses. Jade opens a drawer and takes out a plastic sandwich bag. "This do?"

I thank her and take the aqua pill out of my jacket pocket and drop it inside the bag.

"Part two?" she asks.

"Can we go to your office?"

Jade leads me down the stairs to the basement; we stop at a steel and concrete blast-resistant door. She punches in a code and we go inside. Free-wheeling interiors vanish, it's all sleek consoles, touch screens, locked file cabinets, and computer-controlled paraphernalia. I drop into a chair, prop my LiteGood up on a footstool. Feels good to re-allocate the weight.

"I'll go first, if that's okay," I say.

"All right." Jade's curiosity is gentle, her patience remarkable. I fill her in on my visit to Hogan's home, my interaction with Lucy Claren, Peppard's controlling presence, sussing out the sleeping arrangements, the photo booth strip of Duncan and Peppard and finally finding the pills behind the Einstein poster. I get to Part Two of my ask: "Can you arrange for this pill to be analyzed? Not sure if I'm correct but I believed Hogan when he said the pills were not his. Bunny Luce clearly hoped I'd find them. Has to be something connected to why she's eluding her father."

"Perhaps." Jade always tries to keep an open mind.

"These little pills can be a combo of a number of things. And the strength of the dosage is critical."

"I know. Kids don't realize that. I'll arrange for a test," she says. "My chemist's set up for spectroscopy and chronograph. Should give a thorough analysis. He works at a lab in York—but he also sets up in a trailer at concerts and festivals, people can have the drugs they plan to take checked out."

"People bring in contraband and have it checked out?"

"Part of the Harm Reduction Movement, putting safety first. Shared that info to let you know he's used to going fast; I'll check how jammed up he is."

"Part three."

"Ready."

I hand her the flash drive. "I lifted it from the bedside table in the room where Peppard has his stuff. Have no idea what's on it."

"No guesses?"

"Could be nothing that can help us. But Lucy, in the ten seconds I talked with her, said something about 'it.' She said tell my dad I have 'it.'"

"What's 'it'?"

"Could be work-related something?"

Jade looks at the flash drive. "You think 'it' could be on here?"

"Wish I had the answer."

"I'll see what I can find."

"Lucy looks anxious. Not in control. Maybe the 'why' she looks so weak needs to be discovered before the meet-up with her father can be arranged."

"The news today probably won't make things better. My turn." Jade moves to a large console; three screens are mounted on the wall above it. "Claren's being targeted."

"What? Who's targeting him?"

"The zero point is not clear. But it's going viral. Already a group of investors are calling for him to step down as CEO of Claren Tech."

"Why?"

"Rumors about misconduct."

"In business?"

"In social and sexual arenas."

This sounds so unlike anything I would expect of Claren.

"Rumors—sketchy info blown up for huge access—can steal a good name and wreak havoc on a business."

"You keep repeating these are 'rumors.'"

"Never discount the importance of perception. Big business runs on it."

I don't tell Jade that Claren has fired us and that from this day forward her bill will be picked up solely by G&Z Investigation. I figure Gordy would agree this isn't the time to cut her off.

"At the moment, there's nothing concrete, nothing substantiated," Jade says. "No one's giving out names or any exact, supporting information. Two female employees of Claren Tech are making accusations of sexual harassment."

"Against Claren?"

"Started on Flitter. Then Friendline. Snapchat. Wheeler. Other social media channels. All the regular avenues of unreliable media, including the shock jocks, have hopped on. I'd characterize the charges, at this point, as 'innuendo.'"

She clicks a key on another keyboard. Distorted photos of Claren flash on the screen. He's holding a champagne glass and surrounded by women in low-cut evening gowns hanging on his words.

"That could be anywhere—the ballet, the opera, some fundraiser for something…"

Jade clicks onto another photo taken at a Boston University symposium—Claren is surrounded by female students. A willowy co-ed has pressed tightly against his side to assure her place in the camera's frame. Another picture of Claren in Las Vegas, presenting the winners' trophies at a Women Runners for Science Marathon. The winner, sweaty in skimpy t-shirt and shorts, is planting a pucker as close as she can get to Claren's lips. Next is an old photo of Claren in New Orleans, walking on Bourbon Street, with a headline "Over a dozen strip clubs within walking distance."

Jade snorts, "Anyone spending time in New Orleans ends up on Bourbon Street. Jazz clubs and restaurants are also on that street…"

Another photo pops up. Claren is getting out of his car on a street in Boston. The headline reads, "Boston's Top Madam Who Charges 10K for the Night Lives in this North End Neighborhood."

"Is there evidence he's a client of this Madam's enterprise?"

"No."

"Should be called anti-social media."

"All depends on what headline is added. See this?" Jade points to the Boston University photo. "See how the blogger has circled Claren's left hand on the student's waist? It's a natural move when someone's up against you and you are posing for a picture. But the blogger suggests Claren's copping a feel."

"Can you find the original source of these stories?"

"Well hidden. Details are foggy and stink of organized character assassination. Gander this one—the photoshop is done badly…"

She clicks on a doctored photo of Claren on a yacht; his head is superimposed on a bare-chested playboy who is surrounded by large-breasted women in skimpy bikinis.

I'm flummoxed. "No one's proven any truth…"

"Social media is not built on truth. The goal is to get hundreds of thousands of hits and stay alive for a few hours. The story broke on Flitter and hits and retweets reached over 200,000 in six hours. Bloggers are already commenting, purporting to find facts where none exist."

The speed with which the technology can create havoc hits me. "Shit. What does that feel like—to have your life go public and implode in seconds—by insinuations."

Jade's fingers fly over keys and controls. "Proving our gullibility and tendency—even pleasure—to sit in judgment. Recovery, if possible at all, is very slow." She makes notes on a few links and webpages. "Numbers of internet stories are climbing."

"Is Claren denying?"

"Hasn't responded," Jade says. "Probably holed up with his lawyers. And hopefully, a reputation management consultant."

"Tell me there really isn't a job with that title."

"There are universities where you can make it a specialization—usually within a communications degree. How to help people restore credibility after a bad bout with media. Re-fashion, re-do, re-build, re-course damage."

"Well, that makes me think less of…humanity."

"Spin doctors. Been around forever. Nothing new."

"Who are these women who are accusing?"

"Names are being withheld."

"You can't accuse someone anonymously."

"No. But they don't have to make themselves known to the public."

Will Claren fight the rumors? I remember his words from our dinner. *"What's the endgame? Are advancements used for good or evil? To build or to destroy."*

Jade uses her remote to activate her television screens. The local Portland news stations have zeroed in on the story. "Portland Benefactor Accused" flashes across the WMFT screen. Christine Poole, Donato's ex-squeeze and the face of the show for the last five years, in her too-tight-and-bright red jersey dress and giant jewelry, sits at the anchor's desk.

"Daniel, two women have targeted Philip Claren with claims of sexual harassment. We don't have details, but in other cases like this, women have pointed to lack of promotions resulting from their withholding intimate favors to their bosses. Could this be at the heart of this?"

Co-anchor Daniel Zann wears a pink tie that hangs on a purple and white striped dress shirt; these fashion choices, along with his tanning-bed orange-y glow, make him look like a clown. "Christine, makes sense…"

"Does not," I grumble.

Zann continues, "Seems like a possibility. We'll certainly have to keep a close eye on this story."

I snort. "What story? There's no story—it's all chatter and garbage they're trying to push over as news."

On screen, Poole touches her ear, where the audio feed earpiece rests. "And now, there's something else…"

Jade turns up the volume as Christine Poole speaks directly to camera. "WMFT has learned that just yesterday, Philip Claren was called to testify in front of a committee at the Department of Defense. We'll also have to get to the bottom of that." She turns to her co-anchor. "Daniel, here's my question. Is Maine's golden boy heading for a downfall?"

Jade checks another computer screen. "Claren's being forced to take this seriously. And respond quickly. Shares in Claren Tech have fallen 12% already."

"Who speaking up on his side?"

"Claren Tech has been mute on this."

Poole's overly modulated voice catches our attention. "Daniel, in the last issue of *Social*—I love that magazine, don't you?"

Zann smiles wide, "All the news we love to know."

Poole takes over, "There was a photo of Lucy Claren with her new fiancé." The photo of Lucy and Peppard, standing in front of the Destiny Leader curtain, appears on the television screen. "It is a shame that the actions of a parent can lend a shadow on a happy engagement announcement. Daniel, what do you think Lucy Claren is wondering about her father at this moment?"

"Well, Christine, it can't be all warm and fuzzy."

"We now have live footage," Poole announces, "from our cameras positioned outside the Westin Hotel and I've just gotten word that Renae Claren, Philip Claren's ex-wife, is coming out…"

The photo of Lucy and Peppard is replaced by video of a small crowd of gathered lookee-loos. Renae Claren sweeps out of the hotel's sliding doors. A fresh-faced reporter closest to her, ventures a question. "Do these allegations of sexual misconduct against your ex-husband take you by surprise?"

Renae flashes her dental whites. "I'm not surprised at any news about my ex-husband." She flips her hair back off her shoulder. "He's brilliant, of course, but difficult. Work always comes before everything else." She has the temerity to tear up. "I tried to make our marriage work, because of our daughter. But he made it impossible."

I sputter to Jade. "That's a real toss under the bus."

Jade's surprised. "You sound protective…"

"Renae Claren nearly got me kicked out of the Westin. Not a nice person. Their marriage lasted for less than two years and her settlement's kept her in riches ever since."

"My research shows she goes through money very quickly. Last year she left a Monte Carlo hotel bill of over $30,000 unpaid for months—and some gambling debts at the casinos there. They kindly suggested she take care of her accounts and when she ignored them, they quietly insisted that they would sue. The bill was paid."

"By Claren?"

"Unclear at this point."

"Must be tough to keep up with the mega-rich."

"Oh, yes," Jade nods.

"And all that work to not wear your age. That's an expensive challenge."

Jade cocks her head, taking in Renae's performance. "She didn't have to leave her hotel room. She enjoys the attention."

There's a shoulder of a man, close to Renae. The camera moves back to include more of his navy-blue linen jacket, his starched shirt, and finally, his long, thin face and close-cropped silver hair.

"Damn." It's the man I saw waiting for Claren on the private plane. "I've seen him a few times in the last couple of days."

"Leon Wolff, head of Wolff Future Fund; he's German." Jade says. "For internet entrepreneurs—getting backing from Wolff is like winning the lottery. He'll finance start-ups, let them grow, and if they take off, find a way to gobble them up."

"Not one of those stellar tech minds himself?"

"His talent is predicting the next big thing and being attached for a huge payday."

Wolff's elegant physique is striking. The idea of him as a birdwatcher does not jibe. "What's with him and Renae Claren?" I ask.

Jade's fingers fly over the keyboard, she inputs the right words, and information pops up. "Been seen in certain social circles together. Wolff has a wife—but they've been estranged for years."

"So, technically unavailable but available." He's too slick, too smug for me. "I saw Wolff and Claren together. Flying to DC in Claren's private plane."

"Both headed to the Defense meeting?"

"Don't know."

"That's interesting," Jade says, typing. In a moment, highlighted information appears on the screen. She says, "Huh."

"What?"

She leans back. "Wolff is one of the initial investors in Claren Technology; has retained shares. But not enough for a controlling vote."

"Claren told me Bunny Luce recently was awarded patent profits on her twenty-second birthday. Any way to find out how many shares Bunny Luce owns?"

Jade makes a note. "Should be able to get that."

My eyes are locked on the television screen. Wolff and Renae have finished posing for pictures. A Lincoln Town Car pulls up. "Surprise, surprise," I say. Murphy Duncan, one of the duo chatting up Thomas Beene at Sparrows and Peppard's photo booth pal, is behind the wheel. "Something's niggling in my brain. Can you find out about Wolff's involvement in a company called Destiny Leader? It's represented by Yarborough Inx."

Jade makes a note to herself. "The company Lucy Claren's fiancé—Peppard—works at?"

"That's the one. The guy driving the car is connected with Destiny Leader. I checked. Along with Peppard."

"That's interesting," Jade notes.

Renae and Wolff get into the spacious town car's back seat and the vehicle moves off. Reporters and camera people pack up their gear and head back to their news vans.

A commercial for laundry detergent fills the television screen and Jade mutes the feed.

"The networks will repeat the same information for the next few hours," she says. "Social media and internet sites lead now—television news just tries to keep up."

My phone pings—it's a text from Gordy. Obviously, the news stations in Florida have picked up the story. His text reads: *What's this with Claren? What the hell is happening?*

I text back that I'm with Jade and she's into it. That he should calm down, because, at this point, the veracity of the news is unsubstantiated.

Can't calm down. Damn it. Getting permission from my doctor to get on a plane. Pick me up Sunday.

I text back that his health is the priority.

Stop treating me like an infant.

I text him that he should grab onto a security blanket and enjoy cartoons for an hour. That I'd be in touch.

"Before you go, Dee. Wonder if you'd seen this. On Flitter. And Friendline."

"What?"

She accesses two photos on her computer. One is of me, splayed on the front lawn of my apartment building. Streetlights, the moon, and the photo flash work together to illuminate the night scene—I'm flat on my back, having just slipped on the wet grass in front of Billy Payer. The caption reads as if a child wrote it: "Humpdee Dumpdee Rommel" The next photo is also of me, my butt is featured as I struggle into a pyramid shape, getting my good leg under me so that I can straighten and gain balance on the uneven, sloping terrain. The caption is more commentary: "Life ain't so perfect anymore."

"Where did you find these?"

"Billy Payer's shared them with all his followers."

Anger boils inside me. The shit.

I'm still steaming, a half hour later, as I near Portland. My go-to desire to gain justifiable revenge has ramped up even more, it's filling my mind, I'm imagining multiple scenarios of a verbal and physical thunderstorm blasting Billy Payer.

My phone pings, the caller ID comes up. "Hi, Winston," I say.

"Just got back to the island and saw the news on Philip Claren on television. About some scandal."

Why is he calling me? I never mentioned the Claren name to him, I've kept the G&Z case close to the vest.

"That daughter—Lucy Claren. She came to Chebeague and stayed at the inn for a night—about two weeks ago. She asked about booking a wedding, I told her we were about a year and a half out on our calendar. She said she couldn't wait that long. She didn't register under Lucy Claren, I would've recognized that name."

"Can you tell me the date she was there?"

Ten Days

"I'm over at Gram's—at the end of the island; it's her 98th birthday, you know she's got the TV on 24/7. I'll email you the information when I get back to the inn. Just that you called about wedding dates a few days ago—and thought maybe this was related."

"You're a prince, Winston."

Sounds of a group swinging into the *Happy Birthday* song come from Winston's phone. He speaks louder. "Gotta go. I'll email you later." He clicks off.

So, Lucy Claren is involved in the preparations, hasn't left everything to her cool, self-centered mother. Perhaps Lucy's on her way to Portland to take one of the suites Renae's booked at the Westin.

CHAPTER EIGHTEEN
Saturday

A surprising chill is in the air, temperatures have dropped. A wind has kicked in from the north and it smacks me in the face as I get out of my car in front of my apartment. Karla's father is there, next to his Jeep, looking out towards the bay, lost in troubled thoughts. I've met him only once before, at the opening of Karla's salon. He's smaller than I remember. As if this event has diminished him.

"Mr. Ackerman. I'm Dee, we met a few years ago."

"Yes." He's suffering. "Thank you. For. Finding my baby." His voice is flat, expressionless. Like he's done with feeling and done with seeing the ways that humans can hurt.

We occupy the time and space for a moment. I have no idea how to comfort him. "Do you want to come inside?"

"That detective is in there. I—couldn't…"

The back of the Jeep is filled, there's a box and a suitcase and hangers-full of clothes. "Is that Karla's stuff?"

"Doesn't wanna go back to her apartment. I went there, got a few things. She wants to go home with us."

I excuse myself and go inside.

Abshir leans against the wall; he catches my eye and I can tell it's been a tough day. Detective Stinner has placed a dining chair next to the couch where Karla's mother, round and small in an Indian print skirt and well-worn knit top, sits. She's wrapped herself around her daughter.

Detective Stinner is talking. "Karla, if you won't talk to me, it's gonna make it harder to find…whoever did this to you. Help us, for yourself—and so no one else gets hurt."

Karla's bruises are now starkly purple in her pale face. She's silent; her eyes show no life. Mrs. Ackerman whispers into her daughter's hair. "Can't you tell the detective anything, my sweetie?"

Karla doesn't respond.

Mrs. Ackerman makes the request to Detective Stinner. "Let me take her home. She needs time."

Stinner's annoyed but acquiesces. I walk outside with him and to his car. "Figured I'd try again—hope for different results," he says. "Big zero."

"She's scared. The world doesn't feel safe."

"Needs to help herself."

"Did you find anything in her car?"

"Listen." He stops, his tone is unpleasant. "Don't want you to be a problem."

"Me? What're you talking about?"

"You gotta stop spreading your opinions around. Billy Payer has an alibi."

"What? No way."

"Three guys swear Billy was with them at a bachelor party—at a cabin on Dyer Long Pond. Girls from Eden's Best were invited…"

"Eden's is a joint just outside Waldeboro. The invitations must've come with upfront payment."

"Not of concern right now. Three ladies and five guys were there. Lots of beer, whiskey, weed, and women ready to party. Lots of cell phone video and pictures of Billy. Geo-tagged with time stamps. He was there."

"There's something off. Billy did this."

Stinner gets into his vehicle. "A warning, Rommel. Don't shoot your mouth off making accusations—making trouble. Just because you want it to be Billy, doesn't mean it is. Don't make more shit for me to clean up."

"And that's it? You're moving on? What about the note that was left on my door? Someone wanted me to go there—he knew I was searching for Karla. Billy likes games."

He exudes a forced, unfriendly calm. "Rommel, get your emotions in check. My job is finding the 'right' bad guy. And Karla's not helping."

Stinner drives off. I hear Karla's mother behind me; she's calling to her husband who's across the street, sitting on one of the benches that overlooks the bay. He hurries over and they get Karla into the back seat of the Jeep. Her mother gives her a large pillow so she'll be able to rest her head against the window. Mrs. Ackerman, barely five feet tall, hugs me; there are tears in her eyes. "Karla had such belief in goodness and fun. Loved life, always bringing sun to rainy days. The sunlight's gone now."

The back door of the Jeep is open and I lean in. "Karla. Billy Payer has convinced the cops that he has an alibi, that he never took you to that motel and he was not involved in hurting you. Is that true?"

Karla's eyes dart to her mother. To her father. Then back at me.

"Did Billy threaten you?"

Karla gently pushes me away and closes her eyes. I duck out of the Jeep.

Soon the vehicle is disappearing around the bend of Eastern Promenade.

I block out the sky, the clean air, the sailboats gliding across the water, the sound of laughter from the beach. My mind is focused on finding a way to prove Billy Payer was at PemaPond Motel, violating a woman who had defended him, who believed there was some merit to him. Obviously, he did not value her best quality—instead he decided to destroy that spirit.

Abshir comes out, carrying his backpack. "Your friend, Winston, took the noon ferry back to Chebeague, had to go to a birthday party."

"I've talked to him."

"What can I do now?" he asks.

"Can you set up again at the Westin? Gordy wants results."

"I read the reports on the internet about Dr. Claren. Are they true?"

"Who knows. If his ex-wife comes back to the hotel, call me. Take note of who she's with. And if Bunny Luce shows up—or her fiancé. You have the photos?"

"*Haa.* Okay."

"Abshir. Are you on Flitter?"

"Not much."

"Billy Payer is. Can you keep track of what he's posting?"

"I will try do that. What will you be doing?" he asks.

I speak through gritted teeth. "I have a few things to check up on."

* * *

The Gull Roost, Billy's latest watering hole (according to Reader), is down an alley off Veranda Street, behind a Thai restaurant and an auto body shop. I'd been there when I was active on the force—more than a few times—to break up fights and haul off drunks. The place attracts loud rednecks and those who like to hunker down for the night and drink away their paychecks.

My hands clench the steering wheel and cause a crick in my neck. I drive slowly on the alley's narrow blacktop, my eyes checking out the bar's pitted parking lot. There, backed up into a space that poaches on the auto shop's property, is Billy's white Chevy pickup.

Ten Days

There's one parking option left, next to Gull Roost's overflowing dumpster. The stench is of discarded onions, rotting potato peelings, lemon rinds, grease, and beer. Matches my mood. I wind my thick hair into a knot and tuck it under my Sea Dogs cap. Slip into the bar.

It's three-deep at the bar. Sports TV blasts, along with nineties' grunge music. I squeeze in behind two young women dressed in short jean skirts and polyester tops, bought a size too small for comfort. Hoop earrings, a few chains, and platform sandals finish their ensembles. I hear the blonde talking about celebrating her twenty-first birthday and I long to ask how the hell Gull Roost became the choice for this big occasion. But they're too busy testing out their 'flirt.' They're laughing too loud and trying to catch the eye of a not-averse-to-a-hook-up male. Which pretty much includes every guy—from twenty to fifty—in the rat-trap.

I try to get the bartender's attention, but he's taking an order placed from across the room. "You got it, Billy!" he shouts out. He leans into the birthday girl and tells her the next beers are being paid for by the stud in the corner.

The flirters giggle and wave to the corner booth where Billy, his brother Marvin, and two range-y assholes sit at a table already laden with empty pitchers. A small tier of a wedding cake, with a bride and groom statuette on top of it, is half-eaten in front of them. Booty from a reception? Maybe this was the crew that was at the bachelor party. Billy's got on a white shirt and tie under his denim jacket, Marvin's got a tie and vest in place and the others have knotted their ties around their heads like warriors. I know the jerks by reputation; they were a couple of years ahead of me in high school. The one with the lazy eye goes by Flea, he's chunky and hairy, works at the U-Tow office behind the counter; the other's name is Tad Nicker, he's a dockworker with biceps the size of cannonballs. Both have spent time at Cumberland County Jail for drunk and disorderly.

Another guy, wearing a dirty yellow Techno Shack shirt with a loose red tie under the collar, carries a container of freshly-poured brew through the crowds to join them. It's Hector, the unfriendly guy who lives in the apartment below Karla's. He doesn't fit in with the rest of Billy's hard-body pals. He places the pitcher on the table and waits behind Billy's chair, smirking with happiness—like he's been anointed jester to the prince.

I notice Marvin's chair is positioned a foot away from the others; he's not participating in the conversation. In high school, Marvin was always unfavorably compared to Billy and made fun of for his pear-shaped torso and big ears. I used to feel a leniency towards him, but he never stopped standing up for Billy and it got old. Even family should have its limits.

I grab my beer and move to a dark end of the packed room. The young flirters straighten their shoulders and push their breasts forward. Beers in hand, they head to the corner to thank Billy.

Bartender yells over the music, "Billy! Let's pay up for these two ladies—I'm going off shift!"

Billy elbows Hector, signaling him to pay the bill. Hector, obedient, pushes his massive flesh through the crowd, hands a bill to the bartender. It gets slapped back: "Don't take hundreds, fatso. What do you think this is—a bank?"

Hector's flummoxed and peeps back at Billy, but Billy's chatting up the flirters. Hector leans over the bar, maybe saying he doesn't have anything smaller. The bartender points to the corner gang and says, "Go get it."

I decide not to make a dent in my beer, don't want even a light buzz mixing with my emotions and sleep-deprived state. I lean against the wall, try to take the weight off the LiteGood. I've missed my Physical Therapy session, haven't done my reps and stretches in days and the ache is accelerating. The outrage that's been fueling me persists, but my plan's fuzzy; am I going to walk up to Billy and get him to confess? Am I thinking I'll do this superhero style? Maybe with eyes flashing, melting him with a glance? I remind myself I have no authority; my uniform is packed deep in my closet. I'm striking out—on all fronts.

Time to go home.

A smelly dolt in a cut-off sweatshirt pushes against me and my beer sloshes upwards and splashes my neck and shirt. The drunk leers with false contriteness, "Can I help clean you up?"

I swallow the expletives dancing on my tongue and head to the Ladies Room. There, I make a point of not touching the walls, the counter, the handles on the sink, everything is sticky and beer sloshed. I grab a paper towel and soak up the wetness on my shirt. The flirters enter. They're excited because their prep work—the clothing, hair, and perfume—has paid off. "Can you believe it?" says the Blonde with the Baby Fat. "We've only had to buy the first beer and we've each had three so far and I'm already…happily buzzed."

The Brunette squeals, "Did you give that guy your real number?"

"I had to." Blonde Baby Fat repaints her lips in red. "He's so cute."

"I love his dimples."

Tossing the paper towel in the trash can, I ask, "You're not talking about the creep with dimples and a skull patch on his denim jacket?"

They sneer at me, resent my uninvited question.

"What do you mean, 'creep'?" asks the Brunette.

"His name is Billy Payer. Just got out of prison. He's got a habit of beating people up. Doesn't care if you're a man or a woman."

They frown, maybe I punctured their dreamy clouds of romance.

I want to tell them to stop being laughable, that feeling 'hot' for a night in a trashy bar won't bring them happiness. But all I say is: "Be careful."

They huff and leave the restroom. Through the swinging door, I see Billy waiting. The young women hurry past him and head out the front door. He calls after them, "Hey. Hey. Thought we were goin' for a drive. Where you going?" The Ladies Room door swings shut. Has Billy followed the birthday girl and her friend to dissuade them?

Just then a barmaid pushes in. The door opens wide. Billy's in my sights. If he looks towards the Ladies Room, I'll be visible. I step to the side just as his eyes glide by the closing door.

I don't think he saw me. There were plenty of people jostling and drinking between us. Besides, I had my cap pulled down on my forehead.

I wait another minute, then hurry out of the Ladies Room and move through the crowd. I'm almost at the door.

Billy steps in my path. "Rommel. Never sheen you shere before."

He's slurring; there's the smell of beer and sweat. Plus he's jittery, not the normal sluggish swagger of too much alcohol. Maybe he's added another component to his high.

"You've been out of town for a while, Billy. How could you keep up with my habits?"

"One of 'em has always been stickin' your nose in." He grabs my forearms, presses hard. "Better let me be, damn it."

"My knee's about to connect with your crotch, Billy. Step back or everyone here will know I've got a problem with you manhandling me. Wouldn't want to tarnish your stud reputation."

He opens his mouth and calls up a wet, stinky burp that dampens my face. Then retreats—all the way back to his gang of idiots.

Seething, I push through the door to the wind-filled night. No one is in the parking lot. The bar's neon sign reflects off Billy's white pickup truck. I flash on Karla, outside Sparrows, climbing into its cab, just four nights ago.

As a cop I'd listened to people's stories; they were furious, angry, and fueled with a desire for revenge—that's why they hurled rocks at windshields, keyed shiny finishes, and slashed the tires of a perceived enemy. Right now I relate; a large part of me wants to go bonkers on the Chevy.

I move to the truck, climb onto its side step and survey the cab, hope for something that will point to its being at PemaPond Motel and Karla as abductee. I grunt; what would that be exactly? A bloody handprint on the dashboard? Wadded-up duct tape waiting to be checked for traces of Karla's skin?

Nothing so overt. Just a few candy wrappers on the floor, a half-empty Slurpee in the cup-holder. I consider the truck's bed. There's a black plastic rain tarp stretched over it, held in place by bungee cords hooked under the truck. Karla's bruised shoulders, the purple marks on her cheeks and forehead, maybe they were caused by crashing around the back of a truck? Her wrists and ankles had shown marks of being tied. She wouldn't have been able to control her movement.

My blood boils. Now that Billy's alibi has checked out, no one will be looking his way. There's got to be something. I walk to the rear of the truck and unhook the rear bungee cords, flip back the edge of the tarp.

I climb onto the back bumper, swivel to sit on the edge of the truck, and gently lower myself to the bed, keeping my prosthesis in front of me. My butt settles, I roll over to my belly. There's a split second of clear thinking. What am I doing? I tell myself to rewind my movements, get out of there. What if someone comes out, what if Billy comes out? But the next moment, I'm telling myself that although desperation and exasperation are dangerous playmates, if there's even a chance to find something—anything—the risk is worth it.

I slither forward and move under the tarp. The air is closer and feels wet in here. Sweat forms on my forehead. The flashlight option on my cell phone gets activated and light illuminates the near empty space. There's a pile of movers' blankets in the corner. A duffel bag. An attached toolbox is at the front, near the cab.

The zipper on the duffel bag is broken. I use the phone to push its canvas fabric apart. The bag contains one thing: a gray, soiled towel. Streaked with what? Dirt? Oil? Sweat?

The toolbox has a combination lock on it. Manufacturers set locks at 0000 or 1234, something innocuous. Maybe Billy Payer didn't engage time or energy to re-program it. I spin the numbers to all zeroes. Pull on the lock. Doesn't release. Try 1234. It opens. I hold the cell light over the contents. Inside are objects typical of a Mainer's toolbox—fishing stuff, hiking stuff, a small axe for chopping kindling—its blade is sharp, its handle well-worn. There's a length of rope, an air pressure gauge. A few tools are in a pile: a hammer, screwdrivers, a set of various-sized Allen wrenches held together with a thick rubber band. There's a small spool of fourteen-gauge wire.

Ten Days

Nothing screams Karla's presence. Disappointed, I finally come to my senses. Billy's wrath would be spectacular if he found me. And me getting hauled in for trespassing will not help Karla.

Something on the bed's floor catches the cell phone's bright light. A thin piece of red plastic stuck under the edge of the toolbox. I lift the fish-cleaning knife out of the toolbox, use its thin blade to extricate the red plastic—it loosens. It's the size of a credit card and it skitters across the bed of the truck.

Then there's a low and nasal voice—sounds like an allergy sufferer. "Shit. Too cold and windy out here. Let's do this quick."

I turn the flashlight app off. Hold my breath.

Another male whines, "Need five sawbucks."

There's a sneeze. Then a question. "What's with the increase?"

"Supply and demand," is the answer. "With drum-roll on the demand."

Allergy Guy blows his nose. "How come you don't get your teeth fixed with you making so much money?"

"Not smart to wear wealth."

"Where you getting this good stuff?"

"Like I'm gonna tell you. Want your mind-fuck or not?"

"I go home without it, the wife's gonna be sore."

"Fifty big ones."

The exchange is made.

Allergy Guy is startled. "Hey. You want something?"

There's a muffled sound of another man, asking a question I can't make out.

"Around the corner, dumb piss," says Allergy Guy. "Front door's around the corner."

The men wait. Probably rolling their eyes as the lost soul finds his way to the entrance of Gull Roost.

"Know him?" asks Whiny.

"Naw."

They head towards the Gull Roost entrance, their footsteps crunch on the blacktop.

I dare to use my cell phone light for a short moment. Locate the red plastic and wriggle over to it. I pocket the card, close the toolbox, reset the lock to its previous random number. I press my hands against the metal bed—push and belly slide backwards. At the rear of the truck, I raise my head slowly to check if anyone's nearby. No one. I get myself to the ground, impatient that it takes too long. I reattach the bungee cords and a minute later, ease my Outback away from the dumpster and head back towards Veranda Street.

On the corner of Veranda and Washington, I catch a stop light. It's a bright corner, features a gas station and a mini-mall. I fish the plastic card out of my pocket.

The name on the credit card is *Thomas H. Beene*.

Holy shit.

The light turns green.

My breathing is shallow. I turn towards the highway.

Five minutes later I'm parked in the front of 109, the Police Headquarters on Middle Street.

CHAPTER NINETEEN
Saturday

Sergeant Tiffany Gregerson is on the desk. "Hi, Dee. Whazzup?"

"Hoping Robbie Donato's here."

"Saw him go up a while ago." Her voice is deep, as if it echoes in her chest. "He expecting you?"

"Can you tell him I'm here?"

She presses buttons to connect with Donato's extension. "Dee Rommel's here. Wants to speak to you," She presses disconnect with her stubby fingernail. "He's coming down." She logs in my visit. "Geez, it's almost eleven." She leans forward, puts her elbows on the high desk. I notice the dark, feathery hairs on her upper lip. "We're all wondering, I guess."

"Wondering what?" I ask.

"Are you coming back? Here. You decided?"

"Finding decisions elusive right now."

"I get it. Sometimes someone's gotta crack me on the head just to get me to decide what socks to put on in the morning." She grins as if to ensure me she doesn't mean to be pushy. "You wanna see pix of my kids?" She scrolls through the photos on her cell until she finds ones of her kids at Disneyworld. I notice the geo-tagged time stamp above the photo. "You were there in April?"

She nods. "Toughest month for me in Portland. Spring always takes too long to show up." She points to the larger of her kids. "That's Hunt, it was his sixth birthday. Thought he was going to tackle Mickey Mouse…"

I hear the elevator door open. Donato interrupts us. "Rommel. Come on up."

Tiffany puts her phone away. "For another time."

I join Donato, can't help but be snarky. "Thanks for returning my calls."

The doors close, the elevator ascends.

"Didn't have anything to tell you and I thought if I told you that—I'd have to talk you down."

"Could've told me Billy came up with an alibi."

"Stinner told me he let you know."

"Gotta be a sham. Have you seen the cell photos and videos from the bachelor party Billy says he was at?"

"No. But Stinner says they're legit. He doesn't have to share anything."

The elevator doors open on the fourth floor and we get out.

"Well, got some news. Billy showed up at my house last night—just after midnight."

Donato's body tightens. "And?"

"He pretended he'd just heard about Karla. He was pretty pleased to show his concern."

"He was taunting you?"

"I took it that way."

Donato sighs. "Prison knocks some sense into some. Others—take a turn for the worse."

"And our paths just crossed at Gull Roost. Billy warned me about keeping my distance."

"Which you should, dammit." He points to the room straight ahead. "Let's go to the break room. No one's there."

We enter the small room; it smells of adrenalin and burnt coffee. Posters illuminating the steps of CPR, union information, and flyers for OSHA and equal opportunity pay are tacked to the walls.

Donato motions to a well-used chair at one of the tables. "Can't you get Karla to talk?"

"Not yet." I sit, aware of how amazing it feels to give my legs a break. "What about DNA?"

"Not back yet." He rubs his shoulder, tired. "But no AFIS help at the motel site; there's Karla's fingerprints and that's it. Maybe gloves were worn. The motel owner's like a sphinx—claims he doesn't pay attention, just takes money. The room was rented for two nights. He took two one-hundred-dollar bills for a room that goes for thirty-six dollars a night."

"Hundred-dollar bill per night. Incentive to not pay attention."

"He's also a sitting duck at the motel. If he talks—someone knows where to find him."

"Right." I lift my hair from off my neck, feel a momentary cooling. "What's another plausible story? That some stranger or strangers grabbed Karla, drove her and her car to a decrepit motel, raped and beat her just 'cause she was—what?

Available? Is Stinner searching for a roving crazy-scary duo—or trio—a gang of predators who've descended on our fair town? Too random."

"Nothing's clear yet."

"If what Billy says is true, that he dropped Karla back at Sparrows Wednesday night to pick up her car—did she drive home to her apartment? It's on a busy street—not the best place to grab someone. She didn't show up at work Thursday morning, so it happened the night before. When I climbed up the tree in her backyard Thursday, I could tell her bed hadn't been slept in…"

"You climbed a tree?"

"…to look in her bedroom window."

"Rommel, you ever tell yourself 'no'?"

"Gretchen was worried so I went to check on Karla."

Donato sighs. "Let Stinner do it his way." His eyes narrow. "You look worn out." He reaches to the counter behind him, grabs a Holy Donuts bakery box; it's half full with Portland's famous donuts, the ones made with potato flour. "Hungry?"

I choose a lemon blueberry and take a big bite. "Got something to show you. But don't want you to get too mad."

He's wary. "Too mad? I'm already mad you got face-to-face with Billy at Gull Roost. What else?"

I carefully take the credit card out of my pocket, trying to hold onto its edges, and put it on the table between us. My prints will be on it, but maybe other prints can be found.

"What's this?"

My finger points to the name on the card.

He reads:

Thomas H. Beene.

Donato's eyes travel up to mine. What the hell? "Where'd you find this?"

Just then, Tiffany enters. "I'm on break. Any donuts left?"

Donato cups his hand over the credit card and slips it into his shirt pocket. He moves the donut box over to Tiffany. "Sergeant, lucky night. Your choice."

Tiffany chooses a red velvet. "This has its name on my hips." She plops the donut on a paper plate. "Mind if I join you?"

"Just talking about basketball. The secret sauce the Celtics need."

"Donato, you're Italian," she says. "How can you like the Celts?"

"Always been my team." He gets up. "Sorry, Rommel, gotta get back to paperwork."

Tiffany chews on her donut, not totally buying my stop-by is to discuss basketball. "Wow. Basketball nuts."

But I fall into Donato's game, "He still owes me, I won the fantasy league."

Donato nods to me. "Right, I'll bring the bucks by—you're staying up late?"

My tired brain almost misses his clear hint. "Yeah. Okay."

I leave the break room and Donato heads back to his cubicle. I press the button to call the elevator. Tiffany calls after me, "Dee. Don't let that decision get you down."

* * *

Ample clouds have moved in, making the night very dark. I park in front of my apartment building. My neighbors are in for the night; the jungle gym and swings in the park across the street are empty.

Just the thought of getting out of the car feels like a huge effort. The lack of sleep hurts.

There's a rap on my car window. I jolt upwards. Reader's nose is pressed against the glass.

"Hey," he says. "Didn't appear you were home. Guess you weren't."

I tell my heart to go back to its steady pace. It's unsettling to know he's been waiting for me. I get out of the car.

"Thought I'd swing by." Reader waves to his motorcycle, sleek and black.

"Don't have to check in on me." I hit the lock button on my fob; the sound of the car's locking mechanism is sharp. "Been a long day, have to get some sleep."

He moves closer. "Sure you're okay alone?"

My hackles rise; he's too chummy, too familiar. "I don't do midnight booty calls."

"Whoa!" He raises his hands in mock surrender. "Misunderstanding of intent. Just a guy on a late-night ride, checking in on a new friend."

"You checked in this morning too."

"And you shared your coffee while in your bathrobe."

"I was in my bathrobe because Gretchen told me your visit was urgent."

He takes a step back. "I'm putting my foot in it. Didn't mean to imply your bathrobe was an invitation."

My teeth are clenched. "It wasn't."

"Mention it only 'cause it seemed to be a sign you were comfortable with me. Friends."

I can't get a clear read on him. And I don't want to deal tonight.

Reader continues, "And we discussed concerns we have in common."

"Not up for a continuation of the conversation," I say. "My temper's short, lack of sleep can be my excuse."

"Cultivate a heart that doesn't harden, and a temper that doesn't tire and a touch that never hurts. Dickens again."

I finally laugh. "You're very weird."

"Come by Sparrows tomorrow? Lunch on me."

"On your family plan?"

"Why not share perks?" He winks. "And Pat—he likes you."

"In the middle of something, won't have time for lunch."

"Take a break once in a while." He swings a leg over the motorcycle. There's the clicking sound of his fob; the engine hums. He ventures one more incentive. "If you change your mind, promise not to chew with my mouth open." His boot presses downwards, he's got the cycle in gear and glides away.

* * *

My apartment feels empty. As much as I'm not used to hosting an overflow of people—like last night—its current quiet feels wrong. Bert's special bowl is in the corner of the kitchen—but no sound of his padded feet.

A text comes through on my phone. Abshir's asking if he should spend the night outside the Westin. Was it just hours ago that Renae Claren was enjoying the media's attention and showing no support for her husband? That she left the hotel with Leon Wolff? It disturbs me that Claren hasn't returned my calls. His latest jump in social media attention is puzzling. Likewise, the cat and mouse game that Bunny Luce is playing. The Clarens have introduced me to a tiresome guessing game, there are not sufficient clues to move forward in any direction. And Gordy's determination to find answers seems to be an ego trip.

Keeping eyes on the sliding doors at the Westin is not a good use of time or money. I give Abshir permission to go home and get some rest.

My cell phone dings. It's a text from Donato—he's arrived, he's walking up to my door.

I unlock the door and he's there. With his beagle.

The hound's soft brown eyes gape up at me, a gentle bark escapes from his throat as his nose twitches and he checks out the scents of my home.

"This is Thor?"

"The god disguised as a twenty-four pound, four-legged, spotted creature. My neighbor takes care of him while I work."

Thor settles back on his rear and holds a front paw up to me. "You've taught him to shake?"

"My neighbor's a dog trainer. Believes in politeness."

I shake Thor's paw. "Good to meet you, Thor."

"Noticed you have a fenced backyard," says Donato. "I can put Thor there."

"No need."

Donato and Thor move into the living room, I click the door's locks into place.

"I thought you had Gordy's dog." Donato scrutinizes the place. "Where is he?"

"Gretchen has him. Too late to pick him up."

"Too bad. Thor likes to make friends." Donato takes out his notebook as Thor sniffs the furniture. "Start at the beginning. Where'd you find the credit card?" Donato chooses the reading chair my dad had always favored. "I assume the find was not on the up-and-up."

"It was in the bed of Billy Payer's Chevy truck. Which was parked outside the Gull Roost."

Donato rubs his forehead like I've dug a sharp spike into his brain. "Why were you in the back of Payer's truck?"

I tell him about my misguided search; finding the credit card wedged under the toolbox.

He groans. "Where was Billy when this was happening?"

"I saw him at the far end of the bar. At Gull Roost."

"And you were there—why?"

"Sometimes I crave greasy onion rings."

Donato's not laughing. "You went looking for him."

"Happened to guess right. But the bar was super crowded and my plan of instigating some kind of confrontation began to stink of carelessness."

"Or stupidity."

"So, I left. And—well, his truck was—just there."

"You know I can't use this."

"I didn't plant the credit card."

"Not in your character. But whatever—it won't hold up."

"You have any other leads on Beene's murder?"

He plays the card I expect. "Need to know, Rommel."

"Always the stickler." Damn trustworthy. So damn predictable.

"Best for all concerned. Not that I don't trust you."

"But in the Friday meeting with the Chief and the Senior Lead Officers…"

He gives me a clue. "We didn't have a lot to report."

Thor makes his way to the kitchen. I follow and fill Bert's water bowl. Thor's pink tongue dips into the water, over and over. When he looks up, his lips are pulled back in a smile.

"Full disclosure. I also overheard a drug buy. Two guys in the Gull Roost parking lot."

"And?"

"Didn't recognize the voices, didn't see the faces."

"Location's not surprising."

"One of the guys mentioned that his wife was pushing for the buy, expecting it would prime them for taking off their clothes and having mind-blowing sex."

"What does that tell you?"

"Nothing. But something about how much his wife likes being naked when she's imbibing."

"Party drug? MDMA something, maybe," Donato says. "I'll pass it along, but there's not much there. How does it relate to Beene?"

"Right. Right."

Donato's in the doorway. "Let's go back to the credit card. Why would Billy Payer take out Beene?"

"You said there are reports that Beene visited other bars that night and he was flashing his wallet full of hundreds. Billy could have been in one of those bars and found temptation too tasty."

Donato nods. "Maybe."

"Last night at the Gull Roost, Hector Manfred…"

"Who's that?"

"Lives in the apartment below Karla near Deering Park. Now he's Billy's errand boy. He tried to pay for some beers at the Gull Roost with a hundred-dollar bill."

"No law against that."

I give him a moment. Let it sink in. "Room #5. At the PemaPond Motel. It was paid for with two hundred-dollar bills."

Donato's good at being the devil's advocate. "We don't have serial numbers of the bills in Beene's wallet. We can't match them up." He hands me his pen. "You got paper here?"

I fish a legal pad from a drawer.

"Make a list of what you saw in the truck—all the info I can't use to nail Billy's ass."

I sit at the kitchen table, make the list, include the food wrappers and the half-drunk Slurpee in the cab area. "Putting an asterisk next to the axe—just in case you missed it."

He waves his notebook at me. "Didn't miss it."

"Beene's head was split in two."

"Right. Don't need the asterisk."

"And he's got a broken taillight."

"Who does?"

"Billy."

"You break Billy's taillight?"

"No. It was broken. Just noticed it."

Thor lays on the kitchen floor and lets out a loud sigh. His eyes begin to close.

Donato sits in a dining chair next to me. "You're sure no one saw you in Payer's truck?"

"Pretty sure."

"Not one hundred percent positive?"

"Can that ever be?"

He takes a moment. "Rommel, this adventure. Not a good idea."

I lean back in the chair. "It was foolish."

"Do I also have to point out that this can't go beyond you and me?"

I'm too tired to argue.

"If you ever want to come back to the force, you can't engage in these kind of antics."

"Antics?"

"Antics."

"Message received," I say. "Okay. But it's done. And now you have this information. Look, Beene's body was dumped the night before Karla was abducted. Billy's truck had mud and sand all over it—hadn't been through a car wash or been sprayed off. Something important could be found."

Donato writes in his notebook. He's quickly making lists, detailing the information, marking items with an asterisk.

Thor's snoring nearby. I support my head with my hand, tell myself to fight off sleep's seduction. I'm sure I'm succeeding, that I'm totally present, ready to contribute. But then I startle myself when my hand slips and my head jerks, attempting to stay upright. I must have drifted off. I straighten. Stay alert, I tell myself. I'm succeeding at the waiting game; Donato is so concentrated on his lists. Not sure how much later, but I hear a soft mumble. Donato's repeating my name. "Rommel. Rommel? Hey."

His face is close, there's heat from his body. "How long's it been since you slept?"

I mumble, "Didn't want to last night, in case Karla needed something."

All I hear is the tenor of his voice—it's not a rumbling bass, it's somewhere in a well-modulated middle. Words become a jumble. My eyelids are so much more comfortable in the closed position. I wonder what happened in his relationship with picture-perfect news anchor Christine Poole?

The next thing I know, there's a warm breath on my neck. He's sliding his arms between the seat of the chair and my upper thighs. I pull away. "What are you doing?"

"Was about to carry you to your bed."

"You mean lift me up?"

"That's the idea."

My brain feels a bit thick. I muddle, "No. No. Not happening."

"Dee Rommel. You need to get some sleep."

"I can walk." I focus on pressing my hands into the table and coming to a standing position. My body feels like it's weighed down by a ton of bricks, but in my half-dream state, I'm valiant and entirely capable of proving my independence.

My legs are set onto my bed and someone puts a pillow under my head. There's a tenor-throated whisper in my ear. "You okay like this?"

"What?"

"Your leg? Is it okay?"

"Mmmm?" Sleep pulls me under and dreaming stops.

SIX DAYS

CHAPTER TWENTY
Sunday

It's morning; there's the sound of Sunday church bells. Thick gray light is visible outside the high windows of my bedroom. A June fog has rolled in. I'm still in my jeans and shirt, my LiteGood attached. I've slept, flat on my back, and my body feels stiff. Across the room, in the chair where my iWalk and crutches usually rest, is Donato. He's asleep, his head is cocked to one side, resting in his hand. His mouth's slightly open, his breathing deep and steady. He must've brought in a dining room chair—because there it is, supporting his long legs and feet. The soles of his dark socks are worn.

Thor, in slumberland, breathes deeply at Donato's feet.

I vaguely remember Donato putting me down on the bed.

My room, my private place. The iWalk. The wheelchair. My jeans and shirts, dropped into the corner three days ago, earmarked for Peter D's Wash and Fold on Congress—a block from Sparrows. My bureau and its mirror, the snapshots of my parents that I'd taken from old family albums—and stuck into the mirror's frame. A photo of Gordy and me, fishing, in his boat. And now Donato, in the middle of my space. His dark brown hair has passed its regular length. He usually keeps it short; maybe he's been too busy to get to the barber. I like the slight curl in it. Curl is not the right term. *Wave.* Nice to touch. It crosses my mind how nice it might be to have him stretched out beside me.

I need to get him out of here, take off the LiteGood. Feel a shower on my skin. Massage my half leg. Stretch. Don't want to show any weakness.

Thor raises his head, eyes closed. Sniffs. Then puts his head back down. Way too comfortable.

I don't even try to be quiet as I swing my legs to the floor and sit up.

"What time is it?" Donato yawns.

"Clock says nine-thirty."

"I could sleep more. We didn't hit the hay until three."

"You didn't hit the hay at all. You slept in a chair."

Thor raises his head again. This time he opens his mouth wide for a morning lip-stretch. He puts his paws on Donato's knees. Donato rubs Thor's tummy. "How you doin', boy?" He retrieves his boots. He's not uncomfortable, doesn't find it odd to be in my bedroom. With—everything—that is in my bedroom. "Well, I gotta go," he says. "Figure out how to make the most of what you did last night. I did tell you it was a really dumb thing to do."

"You told me."

He reaches his hand out to me.

"I'm good," I say.

"And I'm here. Go ahead, take my hand, make it just a bit easier. What's wrong with that?"

His hand is large. Cool.

I stifle a grimace of pain. The LiteGood's been on too long. "You probably need to take Thor out." I move out of the bedroom and he follows me. "The park across the street is full of dogs in the morning. Thor should run."

Donato follows me through the living room. I unlock the front door. Thor races out into the fog, speeds to a row of bushes and lifts his leg. Donato grabs his jacket from the back of a chair. "You're going to let me handle what comes next—about Beene's credit card. And the hundred-dollar bills. And your other ideas."

"Right."

"Rommel, need your word…"

We notice it at the same time. A piece of paper, folded into a tight square, stuck into the frame of the screen door. "What's that?" he asks.

"No idea."

Donato takes out his cell phone, snaps a picture of the wad of paper.

I pluck it from its place. The paper's thin, it's lined, it's been torn from a small, cheap notebook. There's one word, scratched in blue ink.

bitch

I show it to Donato.

bitch

A sickening tightness builds in my chest. I reach to a small catch-all table by the front door; it's where I drop my mail. The table has a small drawer where I keep envelopes. I grab an envelope, drop the note inside.

"This a normal thing?" Donato asks.

"Looks like the same handwriting as the note that was sent to me about Karla."

Donato takes a long gander at my neighborhood. A few cars move slowly through the thick grayness. The fog wraps around the pristine Victorians, the well-kept lawns, the trimmed trees. Joggers and dogwalkers wear reflective gear. The park across the street—the benches placed in an orderly fashion; each with a dedication plaque to a grandparent or wife or husband or friend. The world had always felt kind—and safe—here.

"Go beyond Billy. Anyone else think you're a 'bitch' for any other reason? No dating problems? Anything to do with one of Gordy's cases?"

I shut that down immediately. "We're trying to get someone to talk to her father. And she's doing such a good job of eluding me that I'm sure I'm no threat at all. Besides, I got fired."

He holds his hand for the envelope. "Maybe we can find something on it."

"You'll put it through the system?"

"Not too hopeful, but we should." He looks across to the park again—and the water beyond. "I used to keep a kayak at East End Beach. Early morning—soul-invigorating to be on the water. Sometimes, like today, a person would have to wait for the fog to lift—wouldn't want to be run over by a lobster boat or cruise ship."

"The big ones that won't stop."

"No concern for the little guy. So. Everyone's gotta be vigilant." Donato waits until I meet his eyes. "You gonna stay here—at your place—this morning?"

"Things to do at the office."

He weighs my answer. "The Somali guy—what's his name?"

"Abshir."

"He'll be there?"

"It's Sunday. But we've got work to do, he said he'd come in."

"Watch your back." He taps the pocket of his jacket, where the envelope now rests. "Someone's not happy with you." He whistles for Thor. "You hear me?"

"Heard you."

* * *

Ten Days

As soon as Donato leaves and I turn the locks into safety position, I take off the LiteGood and my liner. Rub a towel over the limb, massaging it to encourage blood flow. A quick shower, leaning against the tiles. The water pings against my skin.

'Bitch.' My imagination fills in images relating to last night's darkness. A person padding up to my door between midnight and dawn. Why not accuse me, face-to-face, of insult? Real or imagined. Why the silent jab? To remind me the unexpected can be disturbing? I turn the shower off. My crutches are within reach. Did the person delivering the message know that Donato was inside my apartment? Did Donato's presence keep the deliverer from breaking a window and crawling inside? Was it a tease or was it a mean prank? A petty power play? That'd be something Billy Payer would enjoy. Billy Payer likes power—at least what he surmises as domination. One of his methods is to get people to back down because of his unpredictability.

I roll my mat onto the dining table, scooch my backside onto it, and swing my lower body into place for stretches and core work and replay the New Year's Eve night—when Billy broke Pat's nose—the act that sent him to prison for four months. I'd spent the day in the rehab center. Gordy wanted to be together—family-esque, didn't want me thinking about the ex-boyfriend that had taken off. Gordy had cooked dinner for Gretchen and me at his place, Bert had licked up the last of the chicken gravy. Gordy's date for the Veterans' Dance had pulled up outside his house and he was off to party with people his own age. I asked Gretchen to drop me off at my place, but, by the time we'd reached Congress Street, I'd agreed to stop at Sparrows for the neighborhood gathering. Bennett and Terry who run the East End Beach Kayak Rental in the summer and Snow Removal Rental in the winter were showing off their brochures for their Bahamas break. The head cook was filling platters with chicken wings. Pat poured beers, made martinis, some people were in their ugly Christmas sweaters, determined to get one more wear out of them.

I ordered my Rittenhouse, found a place in the corner, pulled an extra chair over and put my leg up. Gretchen was singing karaoke with a neighborhood couple celebrating their fiftieth anniversary and Pat announced discount pours for his steady customers.

Billy had pushed in, Karla in tow; they'd already done the House of Music's Band Night. Karla rushed over to me and Gretchen and kissed our cheeks. "Wanted to wish you a Happy New Year. I insisted." Billy was lit, and alcohol made him belligerent and nasty. He avoided Gretchen and me—probably pissed that Karla wanted to make the stop. He grabbed one of the special pours and downed it, demanded a shot of whiskey. Then, he focused on Hilary, who had come directly from the hospital; she had a sweater pulled over her scrubs. Hilary was panic-stricken and Billy, sensing vulnerability, pounced. He pulled her into the small dance floor and Hilary, trying not to dampen the holiday spirits, kept her eyes on the floor while Billy did a bump and grind around her, hooting while the speakers blared Foreigner's "Hot Blooded." Then he grabbed her close because he was angry she wasn't looking at him. I told Karla she'd better reel Billy in—she saw him wrap his arm around Hilary's waist and made excuses. "He took a little something, don't know what it was, but it's just fun," she said. "And he's drunk. Gets a little too happy and full of himself." Not too sober herself, she yelled over to Billy to leave Hilary alone and he yelled back at her to shut up.

The crowd was beginning to notice. Billy, fueled by the attention, lifted Hilary so her crotch was in his face. He shook his head, motor-boating her pelvis and making lewd sounds. Hilary screamed for him to put her down.

It happened fast. Pat cut off the pounding music. A few guys from the bar got off their stools, headed towards Billy, but I got there first. I hadn't even realized I'd stood and grabbed the chair in front of me. But then I used it—swung it at Billy's legs—the chair clipped him behind the knees and he hollered in pain. He dropped Hilary and he cursed a blue streak and kept on, "Rommel, disappear already! You can't mess with me!" His hands went under the lip of a table and he toppled it towards me, called me all the insults men revert to when women stand up to them. I stumbled backwards and used the wall behind me for balance. The bigger guys gathered together as a force and stepped towards Billy; he picked up a chair and did high kicks as he swung it in a wide swath. No one dared get close. Gretchen was holding Karla back from launching herself at her out-of-control date. Billy yelled at Pat to provide a whiskey and free beer back because he was providing the entertainment, "Serve me up!" Pat was on the phone calling 911 for emergency help.

Billy beat his own chest. "Beer back! Beer back! Beer back! Now, you fuckin' ancient codger!"

Pat put a beer and whiskey on the bar to appease him. Billy backed up to the bar, chair in hand—dropped the shot glass into the beer and chugged it. Pat, striving to stay steady, told Billy he wanted him to leave. Billy roared with rage and tossed the chair over the bar, liquor bottles toppled and crashed. And then he grabbed Pat's head and slammed it, three times, into the bar. The crack of Pat's breaking nose echoed in the room. Pat's knees buckled and he fell to the floor behind the bar.

The guy-force tackled Billy. Hilary and I got to Pat, tried to stop the blood. Sirens blared as two patrol cars pulled up. Billy was handcuffed and wrestled into the squad car. The ambulance arrived. The neighborhood's New Year's celebration was over.

I had attended Billy Payer's sentencing hearing and wished the judge had been harsher—had taken Billy Payer from our midst for a much longer time.

Ten Days

* * *

My exercise regimen, ending with core strengthening, is completed. I fire up the computer. Maybe Jade's checked in. She's sent a short missive: that the news on Claren has stalled—reporters and bloggers keep repeating the same information. Nothing new. She added that the fickle attention of the public had moved on to news of an American movie star announcing her engagement to an Indian prince. She noted that she's busy on her research into Leon Wolff's stake in Claren Tech and the distribution of the company's voting shares. There's a postscript at the end of the report: See separate file for results on drug analysis.

I open the file and read the results from the chemist. The dominant ingredient in the aqua pill stamped with a pouty lip is the 'club drug' MDMA, the psycho-stimulant chemical with many street names including Ecstasy, Love Drug, E-tarts, Scooby Snacks. The chemist noted that this particular pill is triple-stacked in potency.

Danger signals go off in my head. So many first-time users don't get that one small pill that a two-hundred pound person might ingest for a party-high, does not affect a hundred-pound person the same way. Potency has to be checked; the balance of psycho and sensory stimulant ingredients with the various combinations of calcium, phosphates, sulfates, and even sugars in the tablet. A triple potency pill could knock tiny Bunny Luce off her feet, play with her brain in treacherous ways. The chemist listed other elements found in this particular aqua pill: cocaine and the synthetic hallucinogenic para-methoxyamphetamine. I was part of a few drug raids during my time on the force. MDMA drug users, depending on the strain, often reached a state of increased physical sensitivity and sexual arousal, increased heart rate, accelerated self-confidence—and sometimes hallucinations.

Why were the pills in a bag behind the Einstein poster? Was Lucy hiding them from Peppard? Why did Lucy want me to find them? Was Hogan involved with these drugs?

I re-read Jade's last comment: In the last twelve hours, she'd found no visible trail of Bunny Luce, Tyler Peppard—or Philip Claren.

I call the Westin and ask to be connected to Renae Claren's suite. I'm told she's checked out of the hotel. Shit. Renae had felt pinned down. Now, I've lost my line on all of them. The Clarens could be anywhere. "One more request," I get the clerk's attention before he hangs up. "Can you transfer me to Murphy Duncan's room?"

"Mr. Duncan has also checked out."

"Really. Okay. Thanks." I click off. I toss my notebook. I don't have answers to anything. I'm not happy. Gordy will not be happy.

CHAPTER TWENTY-ONE
Sunday

A pounding, tinny rendition of Foreigner's "Hot Blooded" blares from the street; my windows are rattling. I step outside, a black and white PPD cruiser arrives. Hilary's rusted Volvo is parked at the curb, on its roof is an oversized, vintage boom box, speakers on at full blast. A small gathering of parents and children have come up from the swings and jungle gyms nestled at the base of the hill and are on the sidewalk across the street; they're curious. I move down the sidewalk, look to Hilary's apartment. Is she in there, asleep after a long night in the ER?

The two cops are strangers to me; the rookie, Cassler, has a round face and pink cheeks and walks with a swagger. He takes cell phone shots of the car and the boom box. The seasoned cop, his name tag reads "Vickers," reaches up a gloved hand and presses the 'off' button. Rookie Cassler shrieks, "Holy shit."

I'm close enough to take a gander inside the car. Hilary's pristine interior is swarming with rats.

It's that moment that Hilary steps out of her apartment; she's got on sweats and Birkenstocks, looks like she just rolled out of bed. She hurries to her car. "What is it? Dee, what's going on?" She sees the squirming, squeaking furry bodies inside her car. She gasps, stumbles back; I catch her arm as she sways—she's half upright, half crouching.

Another black and white cruiser arrives. Two female cops get out and shepherd the rubberneckers back across the street. Vickers takes down Hilary's details and asks her about anyone who might want to make her life miserable. Hilary's eyes dart to mine; she doesn't want to voice our suspicions, she doesn't want to attract more shade, more unwanted attention.

"What's that?" The pink-faced rookie points at the back seat.

"Squirming rats, Officer Cassler," Vickers snorts.

"Under 'em."

Ten Days

I peer inside. There's something skeletal, the rats have gnawed meat off the bones. "Some small carcass—looks like a skinned rabbit," observes Vickers.

Cassler's wits take a hike; he opens the door to get a closer look.

"What the hell you doin'?" Vickers yells and reaches over to slam the door shut—but not before two long, fat rats slip out and tumble to the street. "Get those buggers!"

Cassler pounces but the rats are too fast, they scurry towards the weather drain, scurry quickly through the metal grid. Cassler's pink cheeks burn brightly; he's not going to hear the end of this.

"Now what?" Hilary asks Vickers.

"If you need a car, suggest you call a friend or a rental company," says Vickers. "We'll tow yours—see if we can find anything."

"Are you going to clean it?"

"Can't promise."

"Doesn't matter. Couldn't drive it again." Hilary sounds hollow. She heads to her apartment. I start after her—feel a hand on my arm.

"You're Dee Rommel, aren't you?" It's one of the female cops. "I'm Officer Vera Sandrich. You were two classes ahead of me at the Academy. You live around here?"

"Couple doors down."

"Any ideas about who could've done this?"

Stinner's advice to keep my suspicions to myself rings in my ears. I realize Sandrich's trying to get something unique for her addition to the report; she wants to look good to her superiors. Can't help her.

* * *

Hilary, now dressed for work, drinks coffee at my kitchen table. Her chin trembles, she's upset. "I don't want to regret testifying against Billy Payer. What he did to Pat—breaking his nose and scaring people half to death on New Year's Eve. W-want to do what's right. But I... I don't want to be afraid all the time. My sleep is crap. I'm nervous at work. It was Billy, wasn't it? Who put those rats in my car?"

"Gotta find some proof," I tell her.

"It's not a stupid prank by some kids. Who else but Billy? He doesn't let anything go, I should've known."

"He likes to scare people. Can't let him win."

Hilary's hand shakes. She puts down the coffee cup. "Where does someone get all those rats?"

"Traps, maybe."

"Karla had rat bites on her," Hilary says. "We cleaned them when she was in the ER."

"I know."

* * *

It's noon. Hilary's car is being towed. I head down the hill towards town. The fog has burned off, but not my dark temper. No cruise ships are in port today; the town belongs to the locals. I veer into Nivas to get a coffee and stop by Doggie DayCare. It's closed, but Gretchen had emailed me that she'd slept in the back room; she does this when she accepts a few four-legged weekend boarders. Bert rushes from the outdoor play yard to the front desk; yelping with joy. We're separated by the wooden gate, but he's licking my face like I'm a popsicle. "I didn't know he liked me," I tell Gretchen as I rub Bert's head. "Wanna come with me to the office today, big buddy? Snooze under my desk and help me write a report?"

"Leave Bert here," Gretchen says, pushing her hair back. She's finally stopped wearing the cap, her lavender hair is swept off her face. "He can run in back, enjoy the sun—and he's got a new friend—Ivy Blue."

"Bert's got a girlfriend?"

"They shared a nap bed yesterday. And again this morning."

"Fast mover. Where does Ivy Blue reside when she's not here?"

"With a guy named Kevin. New lawyer in town."

"Heterosexual?"

"All seems to point that way."

"Single?"

Gretchen allows a small gleeful nod. "He's making the move from New York City so he's commuting for the next few weeks to finish up a few things." She pats her lavender hair. "Said he liked my hair."

"Good taste."

"Don't think he's a bull-shitter. But too soon to tell."

"Well, Ivy and Bert are gonna have to separate. Gordy's coming home tonight. Bert'll be back with him."

Bert barks happily at the sound of Gordy's name. Did his eyes get brighter? Did I just feel a twinge of jealousy?

Bert canters off, presumably back to Ivy Blue, and Gretchen shares her tuna fish sandwich with me. She asks about Karla. I tell her things have not progressed much in the last twenty-four hours and tell her about Hilary's car. Gretchen puts her sandwich down, no longer interested in eating.

"Karla's too scared to talk and Hilary wants to point a finger, but can't," Gretchen says. "Everyone's too afraid of Billy."

"And scared of something happening to people they care about." Karla's frightened eyes when I pressed her about naming Billy as her attacker haunt me. I break more bad news to Gretchen—about the bachelor party alibi that has taken Billy Payer off Detective Stinner's suspect list.

Gretchen's angry. "Is he going to get away with all this?"

"It's not over, Gretch," I say.

"You, Hilary, Karla, and Pat did the knock down testimony that sent Billy to prison." Gretchen grabs my hand. "Pat's got that protective guy with the ponytail and leather jacket."

"Reader."

"Who do you and Hilary have?"

"Hilary's gonna stay with a friend for a few nights."

"What if he targets you next?"

I don't tell Gretchen about the *bitch* note in my door. I want to keep her calm. "It's three days since Karla was attacked. Something's going to break, Gretchen. Soon. It has to."

* * *

Malio waves. He's sitting on the bench in front of Starbucks and quickly digs into his ratty shoulder bag and pulls out the latest Press Herald he's been saving for me. "Where have you been? Did you know that the guy floating off W-Widgery W-Wharf is a murder?"

"Heard that, Malio."

His arms jerk skywards. "But t-then you don't show up at the office. M-Murder's happening right close to here, and you don't show up."

"Sorry you worried."

"Life's full of bad stuff right now. Geez." He twitches, his neck shuddering with every word.

"Something else, Malio? You unhappy?"

"It was my girlfriend's m-movie pick yesterday. We watched three Disney animated movies. They were all the same story and there were no surprises."

"Sorry about that, too."

His eyes fill with tears. "So damn predictable. Kids aren't d-dolts. I'm not a d-dolt. We deserve more."

"New day, Malio," I say. "What're you gonna watch this afternoon?"

His chin juts forward. "My pick. M-mob stuff. *Good Fellas*." He brightens, realizing the truth. "Somethin' to look forward to." He heads across the street towards the Lobster Shack; there's always a good chance his cook-buddy will ask him to sample the first batch-of-the-day fries, just to make sure the oil is up to the right temperature.

"Malio, wait up," I say. "Your girlfriend's a dancer, isn't she?"

"An exotic d-dancer," he says proudly.

"Where does she work?"

"Mostly at Rocket D-Doll, off Riverside."

"She know anyone who works at Eden's Best?"

"Outside Brunswick?"

"Just north."

Malio squishes his eyes shut, something he does when he's thinking. "V-Vicki worked there for a while. Didn't think the owners appreciated her talent. She was voted the b-best pole dancer in the state. Didn't get a raise at Eden's even after that."

"Will you ask her if she has time to talk? I'll buy her lunch or…"

"She wakes up at noon. Then we watch the m-movie. I'll ask her if she can fit you in before work."

I head towards the office building. "Thanks, Malio."

* * *

I activate the locks, settle behind my desk at G&Z Investigations, and call Karla's mother. She tells me Karla's not eating—just staring and sleeping. But today, Mrs. Ackerman is going to try to change that, she's made a pot of chicken soup. I try to focus on the Claren report—a listing of its twists and turns. Gordy will want it as soon as I see him. Bunny Luce Claren—whereabouts currently unknown. However, I do know she'd been staying at Hogan's farmhouse, piggybacking on his footprint to stay off the grid. I add details on Hogan, his background in the military, his injuries, his meticulously set-up home. And how he hustled me out of his house. How Bunny Luce had given me a clue—'Einstein'—and finding the pills behind the poster. *"Let us not forget that human knowledge and skills alone cannot lead humanity to a happy and dignified life."* I add that Jade had sent the pills on for chemical analysis, I detail the findings. I detail Brad Hogan's quick rise in status as a trusted co-worker, his name on the emergency call list at LC Labs. I add that, despite Hogan's denials, I suspect he has feelings for Bunny Luce. Question: Are they reciprocated? I download my cell phone photos of Hogan's farmhouse—Lucy's room, the strip of photo booth pictures from Peppard's room, the Einstein poster, the baggie of pills.

Ten Days

Questions: Why the wedding? What's to be gained? Why the break-in at LC Labs? Why the sudden social media attack on Claren? Who instigated it? Claren has yet to offer a response. I glance at the newspapers Malio saved for me and the headline questions the reports of Claren's fall from grace. The front-page article written by Selma Puls, is focused on the fact that none of the information was substantiated. Kudos to the writer, she's the lone journalist searching for veracity. Why did Claren come to Gordy for help? And then dismiss us so quickly?

A lot of questions. Not many answers. I make a list of what has been verified in some way: The wedding is being organized by Shannon Styles, and catered by Chef Sean Prinn's company. They will be using a floating kitchen—probably on a yacht parked at a dock on Chebeague. Houses have been rented for the occasion and there are plans for lights in a tent—so, one could deduce that the event might start, or continue, past sunset. There will be helicopter rides.

A light buzz sounds, it's announcing a visitor at the door of G&Z Investigations. My stomach tightens, half-expecting trouble. It's Sunday. Who knows I'm here?

I turn on the camera feed to check on the presence in the hallway.

An unexpected visitor has found his way into the building.

CHAPTER TWENTY-TWO
Sunday

I flash on a cheetah—one I saw in a nature documentary that relentlessly pursued its prey, racing at nearly 75 miles an hour. And then, once clamping onto its victim, it surveyed the world with cool, golden brown eyes that revealed no empathy, no feeling—just expected, familiar triumph. Leon Wolff, who's responsible for bringing that prince of the African grasslands to mind, is dressed in a goldish nylon jacket, the white shirt beneath the jacket looks crisp, his dark jeans are pressed, and his shoes are shined.

"This is G&Z Investigations, yes?" His tone is haughty, his German accent noticeable. "I hope you do not mind I have stopped by without an appointment. Is Mr. Greer—Gordon Greer, I believe is the name—available?"

"He's out of town." The adrenalin-buzz that comes with an unforeseen opportunity kicks in. "If you'll give me contact information, I'll make sure Gordy—Mr. Greer—gets back to you. I expect him to be back in Portland later today."

"You are an excellent employee. In the office. On a Sunday."

"Good time to do paperwork."

"And you are…?"

"Dee Rom…"

"Yes. Yes."

It's clear he knows my name, he's going through some pretense, testing me. We're at the beginning of a hunt—the stalking stage.

"I am Leon Wolff."

I keep my face expressionless. "Can I get a phone number, Mr. Wolff? Where Mr. Greer might reach you?"

Wolff takes a leather card case from the inside pocket of his jacket, puts a thick, embossed card on the desk. "This is the number of my assistant, yes? He will be able to connect Mr. Greer to me."

"Would it be easier if we had a direct contact?"

"I travel extensively. I find it more efficient to have a central person to filter, yes?"

"Anything I can tell Gordy? About what you might want to discuss?"

He tugs at the cuffs of his nylon jacket. "I am a friend of Renae Claren, Philip Claren's ex-wife. She is trying to reach her ex-husband and I told her I would help, in any way I can." He sits in the chair, claiming uninvited territory. "She tells me Gordon Greer and Philip have a friendship."

"Think they grew up in the same neighborhood in Portland."

Wolff raises his pointer finger and taps his temple, as if just realizing something. "Wait. Let me think here. As a matter of fact, it could be beneficial for us to talk. You might have some insight."

"Me?"

"If my memory serves, I saw you in Philip Claren's car when he arrived at the airfield last Thursday morning. Perhaps you will have information on how to contact him."

I put my pointer finger to my temple, as if I, too, have just remembered something. "If my memory serves, I saw you and Mrs. Claren on the television news yesterday."

"Yes. I offered to shepherd Renae away from the hungry media. The rumors of Philip's sexual harassment charges and questionable business practices are concerning to her."

"Is that what she wants to talk to her ex-husband about?"

"She has her daughter's interests at heart, yes? There is a wedding being planned. She wants to keep the day special for her daughter."

"Lucy. Lucy Claren."

He nods.

"Are you invited to the ceremony?"

"Renae considers me a family friend. I will be there, of course."

"You've met Lucy's fiancé?"

"As a matter of fact, young Mr. Peppard works for a company I have invested in. But I did not play matchmaker." He taps his temple again, shakes his head. "No time in my schedule to be involved with young people's romances."

"Mother and daughter must be having fun, planning the wedding."

He sidesteps. "Lucy takes after her father. She, too, has an excellent mind and is a leader in the areas of myoelectric—the electric properties of muscles—and its possible connection with artificial intelligence. Perhaps she is not the normal young woman who puts the details of planning a festive occasion, such as a wedding, at the top of her priority list. You understand."

"Tech is not my area of expertise."

"Perhaps that is a blind spot that needs to be sighted?"

"Hard to ignore. Face its pervasiveness every day."

"Ah, you deprecate, perhaps you side with that part of the population." There's pity in his inflection. "Perhaps wanting to turn back the clock to—what? Seventy or eighty years ago? But what would you give up? Your cell phone? Your computer? How difficult would it be to do your banking, your research, organize your calendar, keep your client information, check the news. Without technology, a person would be stranded. Out of touch." Wolff's manner is disconcerting; part arrogance and part seductive faux-friendliness. "Some resent social media, makes them feel too naked. And perhaps you don't need much verification of worth. You are strong."

The conversation is getting too personal. But Wolff doesn't notice my frown. "We must agree that social media has proven to be a boon for those desperate for contact and validation and Happy Birthday greetings. It's a service for the common people." A quick wink. "And of course, a gold mine for developers. The brilliance is clear—software and hardware designers convince consumers that they will gain pleasure in sharing their lives. And more brilliant: those customers do a giant share of the work. They create the content. They invite friends to share with them—who also upload data to share with their circle of contacts—all who have likes and dislikes, families and dogs and cats and shallow thoughts, anxieties, and hopes. Designers and marketers have convinced the populace that sharing data is what can enhance their lives and give them a voice. Perhaps make them feel noticed."

"You're telling me that social media companies are altruistic? There to make people feel good about themselves?"

He scratches his ear. "Of course not. It's all about data. Data allows the founders and site managers to put people in categories and appropriately target them for marketing and campaigns of any sort. It's all about data—and how fortuitous for the developers that the common Jack and Jill and Heinrich and Greta provide it for us for free."

"Us?"

He waves his hand, dismisses my attempt to steer his lecture. "It's not just Silicon Valley and New York anymore. Berlin is a center in Europe, of course. Our start-ups have become worth multiple billions. Munich and Hamburg follow Berlin. I've created a new company, Minds4u, it's the joining of the hottest think-tanks of Israel and Europe. Global data collection is important—worldwide. And it's at our fingertips. What do many of the poorest spend their money on? Cell phones. Providing the underprivileged with phones—as well as computers and iPads—is presented as benevolence. But, is it? No. It's collection of data. Data is power. Philip Claren—and I—understand that."

His aligning himself with Claren feels forced. Pushy.

"You are a businessman reliant on others to come up with new products and ideas?" I ask.

"I assist the process with financing."

"Very important."

"Indeed. Philip and I had been discussing a project where we hold mutual interests. We parted in Washington, without arranging our next meeting. He has been unreachable. I wonder if something has happened to him?"

"I have no information on Dr. Claren."

Someone is accessing the office's security pad; I click on the computer to activate the hallway camera. It's Abshir. He enters, ducking his head under the door frame. His backpack is slung over his shoulder and he carries a shopping bag; a warm, spicy lunch must rest inside the bag for the room is suddenly fragrant with the scent of cinnamon and cloves. He stops when he notices Wolff and glances at me. "Should I come back later?"

"No, please stay, Abshir," I say. "We have bookkeeping things to go over."

Abshir understands my coded response, straightens to his full height and waits directly behind the chair Wolff has taken.

I lean towards Wolff. "I'm sorry, G&Z Investigations is not able to help you at this time. I'm sure Gordy will be in touch."

"Please tell Philip—when you see him or speak to him—that he will benefit in a significant way—financially—in continuing our conversations."

Wolff rises to his feet, smooths the front of his jacket against his lean frame. "Good day." He moves to the door.

Abshir's aware of the brush of my finger across my eyebrow. He nods and follows Wolff into the hallway, calls after him in his melodious accent. "Good day to you, sir. Just press the elevator button. I will wait here, to make sure the machine will come."

The elevator's arrival is announced with a whine and a ding. A moment later, Abshir waves to me from the opened office door and moves to take the stairs to the first floor. I go to the window. Leon Wolff's leaving the building, getting into the Lincoln Town Car. It moves off down the street.

Abshir's out the front door. Malio and he exchange a high-five and Abshir fires up his van. If Abshir can follow Wolff and find out where he's staying, perhaps it will lead me to Renae Claren. Maybe Lucy Claren will be with her mother.

I call Gordy's cell and get his voicemail. Damn. I try his brother's house in Florida. Gordy's sister-in-law answers. "Hi, Dee," moans Janette. "Gordy's in the shower. That man needs to sit, my goodness. And my Stuart needs to rest. Florida is slower, Dee, and Gordy doesn't understand. It's why we have screened porches and put daybeds in them, to remind us to slow down, take naps. But Gordy's always searching the ponds for alligators—him and his binoculars. What's he gonna do if he spots an alligator? You can't arrest an alligator for doing what he's born to do…"

I interrupt. "Janette, can you ask Gordy to call me as soon as he can?"

"He's just spent an hour trying to find flights back to Portland. Think he got the last seat. He's already packed his bag. I don't think he should travel, Dee. Not that it won't be nice to have it quieter here. He's a very noisy man."

"You'll tell him to call me?"

"I'll tell him."

"Thanks, Janette."

My cell phone buzzes. It's Donato.

"Busy?" he asks.

"At the office. Catching up on paperwork." I wait for the reason for his call.

"Want to go to a Sea Dogs game this afternoon? First batter's up in about an hour."

"You're taking the day off?"

"Billy Payer's got season tickets on the third base line, right behind the visitors' dugout."

"How do you know he'll be there today?"

"He just announced it on Flitter."

CHAPTER TWENTY-THREE
Sunday

We move inside the entry of Hadlock Field. There's the sound of the national anthem, styled by Portland's star bugler. Late arrivals pour in and join the baseball fans lined up at the food stations to purchase regular stadium fare—popcorn, hot dogs, corn chips slathered with cheese sauce, pretzels, beer, and sodas. The line for crisp, freshly fried dough, sprinkled with powdered sugar, is especially long. A family—mom and dad and three freckled kids with grins on their faces—pass us; each carries a bowl of local soft-serve ice cream covered in sprinkles and chocolate sauce.

Donato leans in close to my ear so I can hear him over the bugler and the crowd. "Lobster roll?"

"Never say no."

He hands me my ticket and heads towards the third base concession area where Shipyard sells beer and lobster rolls. I go in the other direction, towards section 'L.' Our box seats are three rows up from the field, halfway between home plate and the first base coach. I find the assigned aisle and let my eyes head over to the visitor's dugout. Billy's moving into his seats, Hector following like a grateful puppy.

My cell phone pings. "Abshir?"

"Reporting."

"Were you able to follow Wolff?"

"Down to Ogunquit. There is a private beach road that leads to Mary Cove. Very fancy. There is a guard stopping anyone who doesn't have an acceptable reason to be there."

Ogunquit is less than an hour south of Portland. Picturesque, with white sand beaches. Homes in Mary Cove go for millions of dollars.

"What do you want me to do?" Abshir asks.

"Accomplished what we needed. Just come back. We have a location for Wolff. Gordy will have to make some decisions."

"*Haa*. Okay. Good-bye."

I click off just as Donato arrives with two lobster rolls; thick, sweet chunks of lobster meat barely tossed with mayonnaise and resting in a toasted, buttered bun. "You wanna take the aisle?" he asks. "In case you need more room for your leg?" He's casual. Doesn't make a big deal of it. He moves into the row, checks to see if Billy is in his expected place, observes, "Appears Payer doesn't have a care in the world."

A familiar voice rumbles from behind me. "Hey."

Reader's there, leaning against the railing. The teasing is gone. He glances down at Donato, then back at me. "Guess you didn't fancy lunch at Sparrows."

"Was working at the office." Why am I explaining myself to him?

"Well, so am I. Working." Reader looks towards the third baseline, to Billy buying a hot dog from a guy wearing a Weiner Box over his shoulders. "Good to know where he is." He looks towards Donato again. There's an oppressive pause, it's laden with the expectation of an introduction. I let it hang.

Donato, oblivious to the awkward undercurrent, reaches his hand up. "Robbie Donato." He goes back to his lobster roll.

Reader mumbles into my ear. "Didn't peg you as someone who goes for the safe choice."

This guy can really piss me off. "What're you talking about?"

Reader tugs at his hat. "Callin' it as I see it. Bye." His long strides create quick distance between us. What's his problem?

Donato turns to me as I sit down. "Friend?"

"Pat's nephew. Hangs at Sparrows, to make sure Billy stays clear. Met him just a few days ago."

"He's keeping Billy in sight too?"

"Thought he was staying close to Pat, at Sparrows." Donato's question sticks with me. Has Reader followed Billy at other times? If so, what might he know?

Reader takes a seat a few rows behind Billy, in the General Admission section. His hat is low, it hides his face. Billy's finished a beer and Hector is handing him another. The Sea Dog's best hitter is up at the plate. Billy leaps up and extends his arms. "Homer! Homer! Homer!" The batter swings at the first pitch and it sails over the right field fence. Billy whoops and hollers and chugs his beer.

Donato tells me about the timeline he's put together on Beene's whereabouts the night of his murder. "We've got his particulars for Tuesday. Beene got to town, noon-ish. Did the Fore Street route, up Exchange Street, West End places like Jewel Box and LFK, worked his way down Congress, stopped in at the bar at Katahdin, tried a few others. If he didn't have an appointment, sometimes he didn't get to give his pitch—some managers don't like reps just dropping in. Didn't get the impression Beene was that good at his job—but he enjoyed the perks of sharing the product. You talked to him at Sparrows at around ten…"

"Right."

"We think, after that, he headed to Commercial Street. The manager at Spotty's Wharfside told my team that Beene came in close to midnight. Higher than a kite."

"You mean, drunk on his ass?"

"Whiskey mixed with something that was making him sweat and grin and talk a blue streak. About thirty minutes in, Beene felt a hand on his pocket. He made a beeline for Billy. Bouncer told him to take it outside."

"You think Beene added drugs to his alcohol?"

"His choice, or someone helped him along. Autopsy came back—stomach mid-digestion of greasy fries and a burger—and evidence in the system of a new strain of a happy club drug. MDMA; laced with all sorts of crap. There's a lot of it around lately, especially around Cumberland County."

The same sort of pill I found behind the Einstein poster at Hogan's farmhouse? "Kind of an aqua color? Pouty lip stamp?"

"You familiar with it?"

"Not directly." I can't break the confidence on the Claren case, so I change the subject. "Find anything on the credit card I found in Billy's truck?"

The Sea Dogs' next hitter bunts and makes it to first base. "Sent it to AFIS to check on fingerprints," says Donato. "Can't ask Billy about it yet, he'd bring in his lawyer and the lawyer'd ask how we found it. And that's not good for us. Or for you. So, we're going to take a longer way around."

"What longer route?"

Donato takes a sip of his lemonade. "Wonder if you keep up at the shooting range."

"I've logged hours."

"Stay current. Good idea. For when it's time to come back on duty."

He assumes that's my plan. I keep waiting for the lightbulb in my brain to blink bright—show me the path I'll be walking. Don't know what the signposts will read—is going back on the PPD force what I want?

By the sixth inning, the Sea Dogs were ten runs ahead. The home team was hitting and the New Hampshire Fisher Cats went through four pitchers, each one starting with over-anxious bravado and after line drives and bunts and a home run or two, each crumbled, aware their chances of being called up to the majors were diminishing.

At the seventh inning stretch, Billy and Hector got up, gathered their jackets.

"They're leaving," I say.

Donato and I descend to the entrance level. Fans are stocking up on nachos and beer. We spot Billy and Hector heading to the exit. "No re-entry!" the security guard bellows at them. Billy waves off his concern as they hurry out. "Not coming back, old codger."

Donato takes out his cell phone, engages in a conversation I can't hear and then clicks off. "You want a hot salt pretzel drizzled with mustard?"

"No. Why are we letting Billy out of our sight?" This doesn't feel right. What's Donato's plan?

"Best to wait here, just a sec." Donato moves to the hot pretzel line.

Reader's coming down the stadium stairs, he stops at the t-shirt kiosk. I move to him. "Hey, got a question."

His gaze is cool. "Might be too busy to answer."

"Thought you were hanging at Sparrows, near Pat."

"Is that a question?"

"Were you at Sparrows—or marking Billy's movements on Friday night? He was out at Dyer Pond."

"Friday's chili night at Sparrows. Couldn't miss that," he says. "But I can tell you where I was last night. Gull Roost, where Billy was after his asshole friend's wedding. Weird things is, I saw someone in the parking lot, climbing into the back of Payer's truck. Didn't look like Billy." Reader's monotone delivery—it sounds as if nothing warrants an emotional response—is plain irritating. "It was dark—I was about 100 yards off so didn't get a super clear mark on the interloper." He gives me a long sideways glance.

Is he waiting for me to admit it was me?

"Rommel! We gotta go." Donato hurries to us, puts his hand on my elbow, ushers me to the exit. "Shit, this just got screwed up."

A moment later we're on street. "Shoulda been there," Donato says. "I had him stopped."

"Who?"

"Billy Payer. But it got messy."

"Stopped him for what?"

"Broken taillight. You called it. Traffic violation we could pull him over for—could give us an excuse to get a good scout on the pickup."

"Who stopped him?"

"Our cops. But he ran."

"Billy ran off?"

"Yep."

"We going after him?"

We climb into Donato's department-issue Taurus. "There's a whole crew already on the lookout, including a K-9 unit. Two guys have been sent to Billy Payer's mother's place, a search warrant is being processed in case we need it. My job's at 109, keeping all options in play."

"What happened?"

Frustrated, Donato bangs his hand on the steering wheel. "Cruisers were minding Billy's truck. They saw where he parked up the road from the baseball field, stuck close by—I called them when he was on the go. They followed for a block or two, made the stop for the broken taillight—went through the drill. One cop stayed in the vehicle calling it in, checking on the license—wanted to make it look like a regular bad-luck stop. Billy got belligerent and this rookie named Cassler smelled beer on Billy's breath and told him he was going to administer a breathalyzer. Billy slammed Cassler's head into the frame of the truck's back end and took off through Deering Park—now is god knows where. But we've got Hector. He peed his pants when he was read his rights. That guy's scared of something."

"How can you hold Hector?"

"Reckless endangerment. Since Hector has a driver's license, and since he should've noticed Billy was intoxicated, he's technically putting the public in danger by allowing Billy to drive."

"That doesn't usually hold up."

"Allows us to keep him for bit."

* * *

Assistant Police Chief Harper barrels down the hallway towards the interview room. He's short and squat and his nose looks like it was ironed into his face. "What the hell is going on, Donato? I got a wonked cop and ten others out searching for an absconder. How'd this get screwed up?"

"Sir, it was supposed to go smooth…"

"But it didn't." Harper notices me and wheezes, "What're you doing here?"

Donato speaks before I can. "Officer Rommel's been instrumental in pointing us towards specific suspects in the Widgery Wharf case."

Harper's eyes don't leave my face. "You're on medical leave."

"But she's got knowledge of key pieces," Donato says. "Would like some leeway on this…"

Harper cocks his head towards the interview room. "You like this guy in there for the liquor salesman murder?"

"Very possible he's involved or—he knows something."

"Payer's a possible?"

"We got some questions for him. Along with this guy, Hector Manfred."

Harper folds his lower lip over his top lip, his bulldog-visage now complete. "Keep the boundaries clean, Rommel. No actual participation."

"Absolutely not, sir," I say.

"Doc Fogel's not sure you're giving your all in therapy," Harper adds. "Maybe you've lost your calling."

Donato butts in. "Not the priesthood, Chief."

"Close to it," Harper says. "No one's doing police work to get rich."

"Correct, sir," Donato says, heading to the interview room. "We're ready to get started, if that's okay with you, sir."

"Report to me, Donato. How everything goes down—every step of it."

* * *

I move to the next hallway, head to the viewing room. I pass an open doorway; it's one of the small coffee break rooms. Inside is round-faced, pink-cheeked rookie, Officer Cassler—the one who opened Hilary's car door and let two rats scurry off. He's got a bandage on his forehead, dried blood on his nostrils. Vickers, his training officer, leans against the counter, pissed. Cassler defends himself, "Police are supposed to get respect, I'm in the uniform."

"What did I tell you we were stopping him for?"

"But a DUI is a hell of a lot more than a broken taillight."

"Cassler," Vickers snarls. "You're supposed to follow orders—not over-reach."

"Guy sees an opportunity and gets in trouble. What's the deal?" Cassler whines.

I give Cassler a year to find his way. He'll either quit, or morph into an angry cop who figures out a way to take the first punch. Or maybe he'll learn how to consider the bigger picture. Somehow, I think he's too much of a pissant for that—but why not hope?

CHAPTER TWENTY-FOUR
Sunday

Out of sight, behind the one-way mirror in the viewing room, I watch Donato take the solo chair across from Hector. Junior Detective Preston Banford sits in the corner, pen and notebook in hand. Banford's the son of a Portland cop who was killed in the line of duty ten years ago and he's just moved into the detective squad; we've never met, but the word around the station—when I was on active duty—was that he's smart and dedicated. There's a recording device in the interrogation room, but I'd do the same thing Banford's doing—jotting down answers and impressions of the suspect.

Karla's hefty neighbor is whining to Donato. "I don't know why Billy took off running. Not my fault."

"He's just out of prison. Driving Under the Influence would be a problem for him."

"Never heard about reckless danger whatever. Didn't think I should drive his truck—I mean, it's his truck. He seemed okay." Hector wipes the sweat off his upper lip. "But won't make that mistake again. Really sorry."

Donato nods. "We can't take this lightly, Hector."

"But no one was hurt—so that's good, right? Didn't even know that was a thing, like I said, so how can you pick me up for some crime I never heard about? I'll do roadside shit or just pay some fine. Tell me."

"You want us to call somebody?" Donato asks. "Lawyer? Family?"

"No. N-no, don't call my dad," Hector stutters. "Just tell me what I gotta do."

"You and Billy Payer are good friends?"

Hector swallows hard. "Met when I helped him set up his phone. Added some apps—got him on Flitter, Friendline, Instafame, and Mutter and you know…. I work at Techno Shark."

"When was that?"

"About a week and a half ago."

"So you two met right after he got out of prison."

"I guess." Hector puts his hands together and pleads. "Can't I just do community service and promise I won't make the mistake again?"

"I don't make those kind of decisions, Hector." Donato sounds friendly, like he wants the best for Hector. "Other people decide on sentencing. My job is to write up the charges… We have reckless endangerment here—could be a Class A or a Class C—depending. Right, Detective Banford?"

Banford nods. "Misdemeanor or felony. Right. Depending."

Hector straightens, now on alert. "Depending on what?"

"You know when you get brought in like this, you empty your pockets and give us your wallet—that kind of stuff."

"Yeah?"

"You carry hundred-dollar bills with you all time?"

"Huh?" Hector's tone shoots up an octave.

"You have seven one-hundred-dollar bills in your wallet."

Hector pulls his shirt away from his body. The pit stains are growing. "Uh, uh…cashed my paycheck."

"Hector. Are you sure they weren't bills you found in Thomas Beene's wallet?"

"Who?" he whispers. And blinks rapidly.

"The liquor salesman who was killed and dumped off Widgery Wharf."

"Don't know anything—anyone…" The beads of sweat on Hector's forehead are the size of buckshot; they bead and slip down his cheeks.

"You were drinking at Spotty's Wharfside on Commercial Street on Wednesday night, right?"

"Can't remember."

"You have to pee a lot, Hector?"

"Huh?"

"Take a whiz."

"Why?"

"A lot of hallways—in bars—leading to bathrooms have security cameras."

Hector doesn't pick up on the fact that Donato is not specifying that Spotty's Wharfside has a camera near its men's room. His shoulders slump. "Okay, guess I was there."

Donato continues, "So was a guy named Thomas Beene. We have witnesses who saw Beene flash his wallet there on that night—which happens to be the night he was killed. It was full of Ben Franklins."

"Huh?"

"Hundred-dollar bills."

Hector's plump cheeks jiggle as he tries to hold back tears.

"Who were you with at Spotty's, Hector?"

"Just there."

"Were you with your new friend that you met at Techno Shark? Billy Payer?"

"Just…there." Hector's dodging, trying to find a self-protection mode.

"And a few nights later you were with Billy Payer, trying to pay for beers at the Gull Roost with a hundred-dollar bill. Fingerprints are pretty good evidence, Hector."

Donato leaves out the part that fingerprint evidence has not been retrieved from any of the bills. Hector has no idea that these things take time to process and analyze.

Hector's tears merge with the beads of sweat on his reddened face, he looks like he's been unhappily bobbing for apples. "Give me my community service. My dad doesn't need to know about this."

"What do you think your dad will say, Hector?"

Hector lets out a howl. "He'll say 'I told you that you were a fuck-up.'"

Donato lets Hector wallow in his misery. Then suggests, "You could show your dad you're not a total fuck-up."

"Huh?"

"Beene was a big, tall guy. You're not tall, and giving you a quick appraisal, I'd bet you're not spending a lot of time at the gym. What do you think, Detective Banford?"

Banford gives Hector a slow look-over. "No indication of lean muscle mass. Agree."

Donato's focus is on Hector. "Beene yelled at the manager that someone lifted his wallet."

"Not me."

"Taking Beene on yourself—grabbing his wallet all by yourself—might not have been a smart thing. And you're smart. You work at Techno Shark, so you must be smart."

Hector presses his lips together so hard there's a pale bloodless rim around the edges of his mouth.

"But maybe someone convinces you to help lift a wallet from a drunk guy. And you're drunk and feeling invincible."

"No."

"Someone says, Hector, you can be my friend and join me in a joy ride with some sweet hundred-dollar bills. Someone convince you of that?" Donato presses. "You want your dad to think you're smart. That you figured out how to shave a little off your prison time here."

Hector's panic escalates. "Prison?"

"Sorry to tell you but this has gone beyond doing simple community service."

"The wallet was just there. On the street." Hector's latched onto a story, gains a little strength. "Someone pointed it out to me that it was on the ground just off the sidewalk and that guy was acting like a Mr. Big Shot in Spotty's. Called me fat and he was fat too, so why was he picking on me? So when I picked it up, I took out the money. Cause he was an asshole."

"You didn't happen to accidentally take a credit card too?"

"Naw, just cash."

"Beene's credit card was last used at a Cumberland Farms for a couple of sandwiches and six Milky Way bars. Given that we know Beene's time of death—we can be sure he was not the guy feeding his face."

Hector looks trapped.

"You like Milky Way candy bars, Hector?"

"Yeah." Hector's the kid in school who just hopes the teacher accepts his answer. But then worries he's got it wrong. "But…"

"Let's go back to you and the wallet. Who pointed it out to you?"

"Someone driving by." Hector's blinking double-time. "I left Spotty's and was going to my car to go home and that was it."

"You were out drinking—by yourself?"

"That's why you go to bars. So you're not alone."

"So you're lonely and you really need strangers around you to pretend you have friends?"

Hector's cheeks redden; he's defensive. "I was at the bar with people."

"Who? Give me their names."

"Ahmmmm…"

"Need a timeline on when this wallet was found. Did your friends leave before you?"

"Yeah." Hector's happy to have found a safe answer. "Yeah."

"Then you left Spotty's and you were walking to your car and the same friends that you were with at the bar drove by in a car—no wait, you said pickup…"

"Huh?"

"Pickup or car?"

"Pickup."

Nicely done, Donato. One step closer.

Donato keeps on Hector, "And yelled that there was a wallet on the ground."

Hector fidgets, now not so sure he's in a safe zone. "I didn't say exactly that."

"What'd you do with the wallet?"

"Huh?"

"You said you took the money out of the wallet. Hector said that, didn't he, Banford?"

Banford flips back a page of his notebook. "Yep."

Donato leans in. "What'd you do with the wallet?"

"Tossed it into the bay," Hector answers.

Donato grimaces. "Not very eco-friendly, Hector."

"Huh?"

"Polluting."

"You can't arrest me for tossing a wallet into the bay—right?"

Donato leans back. "Did you take the credit cards out too?"

Hector closes his eyes. "Said I didn't."

"A lot of people would, Hector. It's a smart, short-term thing. Use the cards before the person realizes they're missing. Smart creeps will do that and you like Milky Way bars."

Hector's jaw clenches. "Don't have to make fun of me…"

"You don't like it when people make fun of you?" Donato feigns apology. "Sorry. Let's get back to that night. So, someone in the truck—white truck, right?"

"I said it was a pickup truck. Did I say…"

"Driving by, pointed out a wallet on the ground. Where were you?"

"Um. Um. On Commercial Street." Hector swallows hard, blows out air. "That's where."

"Near the wharfs."

"Across from the bakery with that weird name."

"Bam Bam Bakery?"

"Yeah, they don't use regular flour for the health nut people…"

"That bakery's kind of close to Widgery Wharf. Did you kill Thomas Beene, Hector?"

Drool drips off the corners of Hector's mouth. He's too panicked to wipe it away. "No. No. No. Didn't know anyone was killed 'til I heard about it on the news the next day."

"Not sure this is falling into place for me, Hector," Donato acts confused. "Who was driving the truck—white truck, right?"

"White. Not a lot of lights around, that's why white is good at night…"

"I agree. Easier to see a white truck."

Another tick for Donato.

"And who pointed out the wallet? Why were you asked to pick it up? Who thought it'd be a good idea for you to hold onto the hundred-dollar bills that were in the wallet? Was it someone who wanted to set you up to take the blame—for murder—if anyone noticed the flashing of big bills and connected them to Beene?"

"Huh?" Hector's beginning to register that he's got himself in a hole. That maybe he'd been used.

"You were the one noticed at Gull Roost with a hundred-dollar bill. Heard you were acting like Billy Payer's errand boy. And you're the one holding onto the evidence today. Be smart, Hector. Don't make this 'fuck-up' even more fucked up."

Hector puts his head on the table and pounds his plump hands into the back of his neck. "Stupid. Stupid."

Donato looks across the room to Banford. "Billy Payer has a white pickup truck, doesn't he?"

"Yeah. And we got it in our basement. Looking close at it."

"What are we going to find in that truck, Hector? In the cab. In the truck bed. Candy bar wrappers?"

Hector does not raise his head.

Donato stands. "Let me do this, Hector. I'm asking Detective Banford to get you the rough perimeters on sentencing for reckless endangerment and what kind of time you might get for accessory to robbery. And then we'll tell you how the charges are amped up if we add murder to that list."

Hector squeaks, "Didn't murder!"

"Accessory to murder?"

"Huh?" Hector's tears are flowing again. "Come on. Can't tell you anything."

"Because you don't know anything or because you're scared?"

Hector nearly gags; it's because his emotions are blocking the path to a deep breath.

"We do have to inform you," Donato continues, "there's this crime called 'withholding information.' You can't keep a knowledge of a wrong-doing to yourself without being punished by our judicial system. We wouldn't want that to be a surprise to you—once you get to court."

Hector wails, "Don't want to go to court. My dad'll..."

"If you help us find Billy Payer—that'd make you smart. Your dad would recognize that."

"Billy said he was my friend." Hector exclaims. "And then he just ran off."

"Not what a friend does, huh?"

Hector whines, "Don't know where he is."

Donato moves to the door and exits. Hector looks at Banford, hoping for something—understanding? Sympathy? But Banford closes his notebook and when a uniformed cop enters, slips out of the room. The uniform leans against the wall, keeps cold and steady eyes on a very nervous Hector.

I step out of the viewing room, hoping to meet up with Donato. Marvin, carrying his motorcycle helmet, is walking down the hall. He sees me, heads the other direction. But Donato's rounding the corner and Marvin's now between us. He stuffs his large hands into the pockets of jacket.

"Hey, Marv," Donato says.

Marvin, defenses up, anticipates the question. "Don't know where Billy is. My mom doesn't know where either. You can keep sending guys to ask her, but she's a few sheets gone already. Alcohol's her hobby and she starts at dawn." When we were partners, Marvin was mum about his family, like if he didn't talk about them, they couldn't reflect on him. I knew Billy was an all-out bully, got an idea his mom was too—and that Marvin absorbed most of the blows.

"Tough situation," notes Donato.

"Billy's always been a crappy situation."

"Why do you think that is?"

Marvin's confused by the question. "What?"

"You're here," Donato says. "Trying to do good—keep crime at bay. Billy's the opposite, wouldn't you say?"

I stay casual. "Do you know of friends he's contacted since he's been out of prison? Who might let him hang at their place or…"

Marvin doesn't look my way, just sends a verbal jab, "She shouldn't even be here."

Donato pushes in another direction. "How well you know Hector Manfred?"

"Don't. Met him once at Gull Roost. Little prick thinks Billy walks on water. Billy collects guys like that." Marvin pulls his shoulders back. "I'm taking time off, using the time I saved up 'til this is settled. Don't need everyone talking behind my back."

"No one's blaming you."

"I see it on everyone's face."

"But if you hear from Billy, you'll check in?"

"My paycheck comes from this place, it's been made clear to me." Marvin, continuing to ignore me, strides past Donato.

When Marvin's turned the corner, Donato turns to me. "Feel any sympathy?"

"Want to," I say. "But he doesn't make it easy."

* * *

Ten Days

I'm back at the viewing glass. Donato and Banford enter the interview room, take their places. Donato presses the record button. Hector wipes the sweat and tears from his cheeks. "I didn't kill anyone on Widgery Wharf. And I don't know where Billy is."

"Just need it to make sense to me, Hector," Donato says. "Who was it that told you to pick up the wallet?"

"I left Spotty's and I was gonna walk home 'cause I couldn't remember where I parked my car." Hector stopped. "Billy threw the wallet out the window at me."

Banford immediately starts writing. Donato feigns informality but wants verification. "Billy was driving the white pickup truck."

"He had that big fat guy in the back of the truck and the fat guy was cursing and kicking and Billy stopped and threw me the wallet. Then he hopped out of the cab and into the back of the truck and opened his toolbox."

"What did Billy take out of the toolbox?"

"Don't know. I ran. Just took the wallet and ran."

Hector shuts his eyes. Like he's trying to block us out. But his lips move. "I just ran."

The door behind me opens. Stinner enters the viewing room. "How's it going?"

"He gave up Billy. On Thomas Beene."

Stinner raises his eyebrows. "Excellent. What else?"

"That's where Donato's been working. On Beene."

Stinner nods. He leaves the room and a moment later, Donato responds to a knock on the interview door. He sees Stinner and slips out.

Banford keeps his eyes on the hunched Hector. "Want something to drink?"

Hector keeps his eyes downcast. "No."

"How 'bout a sandwich?"

Before Hector can answer, Donato comes back into the interview room. "Few other questions, Hector. One is about the bachelor's party at Dyer Long Pond on Friday night. Were you there?"

Hector is startled. His eyes go wide.

"Did you drive yourself to Dyer Long Pond on Friday night? In your own car?"

Hector shakes his head. "No. My car's a piece of shit."

"How'd you get there?"

Hector looks down at the table, a deep purple redness collects in his neck. He wiggles in the chair. Maybe he's going to pee himself again.

Donato leans in. "Hector, you know Karla Ackerman?"

"Huh?"

Banford's surprised by the shift in questioning. He flips a new page in his notebook; his pen moves quickly.

"Karla Ackerman," Donato says. "She lives in the same apartment house as you."

Hector blinks hard. "Ahhh. Oh. There's a Karla who lives upstairs from me. Is that her last name?"

"When was the last time you saw her?"

Hector stumbles over his words. "Can't—can't remember. She shoved diet crap at me. Didn't ask for 'em."

Donato makes a show of studying his small notebook. "Billy Payer and Karla were an item, before he went to prison. Did you know that Karla Ackerman was raped and beat up pretty bad—and found on Friday night at PemaPond Motel?"

Hector puts his head onto the table and folds him arms over the back of his head.

Donato keeps going, "Not too far from Dyer Long Pond. Crappy motel that rents by the hour. We've got a forensic team going over the motel room now. That room was paid for with two hundred-dollar bills. And we're thinking Karla Ackerman didn't drive herself to the rat-infested PemaPond motel, so we're also going over her car for fingerprints and since we've gotten yours tonight—you sure you don't want to tell us something?"

A wounded animal sound ekes out from Hector's throat.

Donato gets up. "You ever had the privilege to spend time in our fine jail, Hector? Let's get you processed and settled in there. You'll be able to think about how smart you want to be. The arraignment will be first thing in the morning."

Hector mumbles into the tabletop. "Can someone call my dad?"

CHAPTER TWENTY-FIVE
Sunday

My phone pings just as Donato concludes his time with Hector. It's Abshir, telling me that Malio is in the G&Z office saying his girlfriend has to be at work in two hours. It's nearly five. Maybe girlfriend Vicki's shift at the club starts at seven. I tell Abshir to tell Malio I'll be at their place in fifteen minutes, and to please wait.

In the hallway, Donato's huddled with Banford, going through his notebook. Envy creeps in for a moment; working as a detective had been part of my long-term plan. Banford's only a few years ahead of me; he'd obviously set his goal and already reached it. Banford moves off and Donato joins me. I tell him about Vicki, and her experience working in some of Portland's best exotic dancing clubs. "I'm going with you," he says.

* * *

We park in front of a down-at-the-heels clapboard apartment house off Oak Street. Malio and Vicki sit on the front stoop. Her bleached blonde hair is piled on top of her head, her dancer's body evident in a tight shirt with a Betty Boop cartoon on it and spangly aqua dance pants. She wears three-inch wedges with pink ties around the ankles. She motions for us to follow her. "I'll have the burger at Oona's Natural. Made of farm raised beef, cows grazing all natural—in pastures. No additives. Served on gluten free buns. It's around the corner and I only have forty-five minutes."

Minutes later, Malio and Vicki dig into their burgers. Vicki gets right to it. "I left Eden's Best because of its slave wages—the bosses there expected us to live mostly off tips. And it was not clean." She takes out a small packet of baby wipes and cleanses her fingers and the edges of her mouth. "In my business, cleanliness is very important."

Malio swallows the last of his burger and adds, "She's why my clothes smell good."

"Is it usual for the dancers to book bachelor parties?"

"Eden makes it known they'll arrange for girls to show up wherever."

"For extra cash?" I ask.

"Why else? Of course, the cheapskates at Eden's take a cut of the fee. But the girls opt in or out. My girlfriend, Lyla, she sticks with Eden because she lives in a trailer not far from there and she doesn't want to travel too far for work. She put in a real patio and nice steps leading up to her trailer with the extra cash from private parties. It's not illegal."

"We don't want to make trouble for anyone," Donato says. "Appreciate you answering a few questions."

Vicki's inspecting me. "You ever consider blue eyeshadow? Your eyes would really pop if you added a little shadow."

"Thanks for the tip," I smile. I don't add that I wouldn't be caught dead wearing blue eyeshadow.

"Malio says you're a good person," Vicki says. "If it was a private party, Lyla is usually asked first. She's does a special grab thing with her butt cheeks. You want me to ask Lyla to talk to you?" Vicki gets her car keys from her bag. "She might need an incentive. Lyla's hankering for a L.L. Bean outdoor grill. A gift card for Bean products could encourage her to talk to you."

* * *

Stinner meets us at an Irish pub situated a block from Eden's Best. A shiny award plaque is on the passenger seat of his car. "Looks like you got your award," I say.

"Talking to Eden's Roost girls is on my list, Donato. Why're you jumpin' in?"

"Rommel had a contact," Donato explains. "Thought it might be good to use it—sooner rather than later."

"Sorry shaking the Governor's hand slowed you down," I mutter as I walk towards the pub.

"What did you say?" Stinner calls after me.

The bar is dark, neon beer signs provide the only light. Lyla waits at a table in one of the darkest corners, a club soda in front of her. She's a cat person, wears a baggy sweatshirt with two Siamese cats embroidered on it, drop earrings featuring enamel cats' heads and L.L. Bean Wicked Good Moccasins with mini-stuffed animals—cats—safety-pinned to them. Her bag is enormous; there are stilettos, sparkling bras, and feather hairpieces sticking out of it. I put the L.L. Bean Gift Card on the table. "Thanks for meeting with us, Lyla. My name is Dee, and these two men are policemen—detectives."

Stinner takes over. "Want to ask if you attended a bachelor party a few days ago—on Dyer's Long Pond."

Lyla picks up the gift card, purses her lips, wondering how much this plastic represents. I explain, "Vicki mentioned you needed to pay off your outdoor grill."

Lyla winks at me. A heavily mascara-ed lash nearly sticks to her cheek. She puts the card into her pocket and turns to Stinner. "I accepted an invitation to a party in that location."

Stinner presses for the specific. "Party for a guy getting married, guy named Fred Nicker?"

"We called the groom 'Loser' all night. For fun. Didn't get names."

"What time did this party start?" I ask.

Stinner's eyes shoots me a warning—he would prefer I not open my mouth. "'Bout ten o'clock," Lyla says. "I punched out of Eden's at 9:30 or so. Three of us went over to the party."

"How many party guys there?" asks Stinner.

"Six or seven. The groom-guy had a few cousins…"

"This one of the guys?" Stinner shows her pictures of Billy. "He showed us his cell phones pictures of the night, said he was there. You talk to him?"

"Yep. The hot one. He was with the fat one who didn't know where to put his greasy hands. He ended up using them to eat Doritos all night. The hot one was full of himself, he had someone stashed in a back bedroom behind the kitchen. Bragged it was a bachelor party present for everyone, that she was willing and able."

Alarms go off in my head. I didn't want to consider that Karla was this 'someone.'

Stinner presses, "Tell us more about this…present."

"They made it a game," Lyla says. "If a guy drew the short straw, he got to chug a beer and have fifteen minutes in the back bedroom. The hot one called her 'his blindfolded pet.'" She points to Billy's picture again. "That's the hot one. The other guys took turns having a 'banging' good time. I assumed. I was never in the back. Never good to get curious at these things. Just do what you're paid for." She tapped her long nail on Billy's picture, "…but he shelled out ten bucks once in a while so he could gawk."

Stinner asks, "You're sure the person in the back room wasn't a dancer from Eden's Best."

"We're booked for stripping and lap dances. Pratt makes sure we aren't giving away anything else."

"Who's Pratt?" Stinner asks.

She points to a corner in the pub. Pratt is built like a sumo-wrestler; he's stuffed into a Patriots jersey, puffy down vest, and lime-green sweatpants.

Ten Days

Lyla continues, "Pratt drives us in the Eden's van. We go with him; we return with him. He finds a corner, goes into a Kung Fu, eagle-eye zone till it's time to call it a night. That right, Pratt?"

He gives her a thumbs-up.

Lyla gets up. "If you talk to any of them guys, tell 'em to give my feather boa back. Need it for my show—my extra-long boa."

* * *

Lyla's left us to start her shift at Eden's Best. We head to the parking lot and I start the conversation, "So Billy's alibi now sucks."

"We don't know that the person in the back room was Karla," says Stinner.

"Come on," I argue.

Stinner moves to his car. "I should have the forensics report on the motel room soon." He gets into his car, smooths his hand over his award, and drives off.

Donato and I head out of Brunswick; the early summer sun is dipping over the horizon. It's getting close to the longest day of the year.

"That party cabin's a short drive from PemaPond Motel. Makes me sick to think about it," I say. "Has to be Karla."

"Feelings don't make cases," Donato counsels. "Stinner's building this one."

"And we don't know where Billy is."

"It's only been three days since you found Karla in the motel, Rommel."

"Feels longer," I sigh. "Anything from Karla's car yet?"

"Stinner expects a report in the morning. He's getting results first."

"He'll share?"

"Think so." Donato shakes his head ruefully. "The more frustrated you get, the more you dig in. That's good. But don't get stuck—all possibilities have to be taken into consideration."

We pass the exits to Freeport and the L.L. Bean store. I check my watch. "Damn. It's going to be tight. I have to get my car so I can pick up Gordy at the airport. Can you drop me off at my place?"

"How 'bout we pick him up together? We can keep talking this out."

"I have to pick up Bert first."

"Then let's go get the dog."

* * *

A woman in a burka, one of the airport's customer service employees, pushes a wheelchair. Sitting in it is a scowling, gray-haired man wearing an old fishing hat. A light jacket hangs on his frame and he's wearing Croc sandals with pineapples on them.

It takes me a moment. "Gordy?"

He's lost weight, his face is thinner, his neck not as thick as it was when he went to Florida a month ago. I always thought he was a giant of a man when I was younger, and even when I reached his height, he outweighed me by a hundred pounds. Not so giant-ish today. His scowl gets deeper. "Get me to the Hill, I wanna get some cold salt air in my lungs."

The customer service attendee won't let me push the chair. She explains that her job doesn't end until Baggage Claim is reached. The three of us head there.

"Damnit, medicals in Florida think everyone's a sissy." Gordy grouses. "My doc there wouldn't let me fly without a note—and the wheelchair chaperone was part of the deal. I told him he must be pretty crappy if I'm an invalid a week after routine surgery."

"It's not routine."

"Nearly twenty thousand kidney transplants this year—that takes into account only America."

"You feel any different?"

"I still can't abide my sister-in-law so I guess there's no significant change." He glances over at me. "Are you limping?"

"No."

"You're favoring your left side."

"I have an appointment at P&O tomorrow—it's no problem."

We reach Baggage Claim and I collect Gordy's rolling duffel. The customer service rep helps Gordy out of the chair. He barks at her. "Am I supposed to tip you?"

"It is not necessary, sir."

Gordy gives her his card, there is a twenty-dollar bill wrapped around it. "Gordy Greer, private investigator. Call me if you need me."

We walk through the sliding doors to the curb. Donato's next to his car; Bert on a leash beside him. Instant recognition. Bert jumps high into the air, his happiness impossible to contain. Gordy rubs Bert's ears, puts his face in place for happy licks. "Yes, yes. Big licker." Gordy looks up at Donato. "What're you doing here?"

"Wanted to tell you the Sea Dogs won today," Donato grins. "Record now 30-19, not bad for late June. Fisher Cats folded, but we had the best pitcher."

"Too early in the season to get excited," Gordy snaps back. "What're you doing going to a baseball game?"

"Doin' a vigil on Billy Payer," says Donato. "Thought we had him on a traffic violation but he assaulted the arresting officer and took off. Now he's 'at large.'"

"That's a screw-up," says Gordy.

"Tell me about it." Donato opens the back door. Gordy settles into the seat and Bert sits next to him like a super proud dog. I get into the front next to Donato. He pulls away from the curb and we head towards Munjoy Hill. Gordy leans forward, taps my shoulder. "What do you have for me?"

I hand him the report on Claren. He leans back and opens the folder. I thought he'd have some choice words of frustration, but he's silent. Unusual for Gordy. I've printed copies of photos—the flashdrive, the Einstein poster (front and back), newspaper photos of Renae Claren and Wolff talking to the press outside of the Westin Hotel, and the photo strip from Peppard's room at Hogan's farmhouse. Finally, he rumbles, "This marriage ceremony is totally bogus?"

"Doesn't fit into a happily-ever-after story."

"What would you know about those kinds of stories?" Gordy asks.

Donato chortles. "Can't imagine you reading fairy tales."

I explain, "I'm saying, the wedding is happening for another reason. Don't know what it is, but Bunny Luce is counting on her dad."

"For what?"

"Unclear. What does 'tell him I have "it"' mean? They tell us they want us at the dance but won't let us hear the music. They parse out info, but nothing connects. You got us into this, Gordy—it's irritating."

Gordy sighs. "Let's stop at Figgy's. Fried chicken."

We take the Congress Street exit and wind our way to a West End side street and arrive at the take-out shack. The fragrance of chicken frying in cast iron skillets reaches us as we pull into a parking space across the street. The outdoor picnic tables are full, customers are glad to be eating. Gordy tells me to hurry, he's hungry for 'real food.' I ask if this is on the diet his doctor gave him; he tells me to mind my own business.

Ten minutes later we're driving to Munjoy Hill and its clear views of Casco Bay. Gordy's munching on a buttermilk-coated chicken leg and muttering happily with each chew. Finally, he brushes the crumbs from his chin and powers his window down, breathes in the cool breeze. I follow his lead, admire a ferryboat heading towards Peaks Island, moving across the water, its night lights soft in the windless night.

Donato pulls up to Gordy's narrow clapboard house, it's across the street from Sparrows. Gordy grew up in this house, his dad was a dockworker and his mom taught first-graders. When he was a kid, the neighborhood was considered rough blue-collar, a place immigrants settled. With each influx of another nationality, there came territorial chips on shoulders and kids had to be tough. Gordy was no exception. In the last decade, the homes on either side of him have been bought and renovated by young architects, and lawyers and doctors decided to raise their families on the Hill. Gordy calls it goddamn gentrification. Developers have offered Gordy more than twenty times his parents' initial investment. But he's not moving.

"Sparrows is packed," Gordy says. "Must be a Red Sox game on."

"Yankees and Sox tonight," Donato tells him.

"Sox'll take it…"

"I don't know, Gordy…"

"Think positive, Robbie."

Someone sits in the shadows of Gordy's porch. "Who's that?" I ask.

Gordy powers down the back window. "Hello, beautiful lady."

Marie Bianchi, fifty-ish and svelte, waves and bounces down the steps. She owns a neighborhood art gallery. She leans in Gordy's open window. "I missed you, sweet man."

Bert leans over Gordy to lick Marie's hand. I give up on jealousy, Bert appreciates nearly everyone.

Marie busses Gordy's cheek. "Pat sent over some of Sparrow's baby-back ribs for you." She waves at me. "Hi, Dee. Don't worry, I'll be gentle. No sex for a month after the operation."

I close my eyes. "Too much information, Marie."

She pats the top of the car. "Let's get your bag inside—my *dolce uomo*. My sweet man."

"Dee's staying here too," Gordy says.

"She is?" Marie frowns prettily.

"I am?" I ask.

Gordy growls back at me. "You're staying here 'til Billy Payer's off the street."

"I like that idea," Donato adds.

"Maybe I don't," I retort.

"Better than me moving into your basement place," says Gordy.

Marie weighs in. "Dee, Gordy has to sleep in his own bed. If he wants you close, you'll have to stay here."

Donato gets out of the car and grabs Gordy's duffel. He walks with Marie and Bert towards Gordy's house. I grouch to Gordy, "Don't need to stay here."

"Won't be able to sleep if I'm worried and my doc told me to get good sleep." He calls to Donato. "Robbie—can you go with Dee to her place to get her toothbrush and whatever else?"

Ten Days

Donato, going in the front door, calls back to us. "No problem. Give me a sec."

I'm steaming, don't like decisions made for me. But Gordy ignores my silent heat and he gets out of the car. "Don't forget. You and I have to be at the taxi wharf at eight in the morning."

"What? Why?"

"We have an appointment with our client. Claren's ready to talk to us."

CHAPTER TWENTY-SIX
Sunday

Donato waits as I quickly re-pack the bag I'd taken for the overnight with my mother. I throw in another pair of jeans, underwear, and a t-shirt. I pick up the collapsible forearm crutches. Donato moves to take them. "Got 'em."

"I can carry them."

"So can I." He takes the crutches, slings the strap of my bag onto his shoulder. "Got your toothbrush?"

"I do."

We're close, he's half blocking the bedroom doorway. "We can go," I say.

He steps to the side. "Since we're technically not working together, and since I'm not your training officer anymore and—and since both of us aren't tangled in other relationships…" He waits.

I haven't moved. There's only a foot or so between us.

He's serious. "And since cops now give talks at schools telling kids they have to ask permission to move into someone else's personal space…"

"I gave that talk a few times. Suggesting they use their words before a booty grab and lip lock." I'm trying for lightness but know if we are inches closer, I'll feel his body heat.

"Right. So here goes. I've wanted to kiss you for a long time."

"Out of curiosity?"

"Curiosity?" He's surprised, thinks about it. "Ahm. Maybe we could call it that. You curious?"

There's a fuzzy energy of anticipation.

"Yeah."

Donato takes a step to close the space, leans in. His breath touches me first. Then a brush of a day's growth of beard. He grazes my cheek, slides his mouth towards my ear; he's exploring my form, the shape of my face, using his lips to move my long hair back and expose skin. Soft exhalation and inhalation as his mouth travels to my temple and forehead. I lift my chin. "Okay. Permission." I want his lips on mine.

The kiss goes on for a very long time. We lean into each other, balancing as one. Desires I'd pushed aside for the last year rise and pulse and my arms tighten around him.

And then his phone pings. We ignore it. The pings persist. Donato's voice comes from deep in his chest, "I better get that." He moves away from me.

Donato clicks on, listens and answers: "Okay. Got it. Be there in five." He punches a finger to his cell phone to end the call; he explains, "That was Chief Harper. Wants me at 109 for a sit down."

I take a step back. "He doesn't like to be kept waiting."

"He's got the Evidence Report on Billy's pickup."

* * *

We switch gears quickly, head to Donato's Taurus. Within minutes we're back at Gordy's, my bag is deposited in the front hallway. Marie leans over the railing. "Dee. Gord's exhausted. I'll be next to him, if he wakes up and needs anything, so don't worry. I made up the guest room down there for you. *Buonanotte*, sweetie." She waves her manicured fingers at Donato. "Good night, Detective."

Donato and I stand in the entryway. "We okay?" He puts his hand on my arm, but I inch away. He's confused. "Wanna weigh in?"

"That—what happened—out of curiosity—back at my place…"

"The kiss." He makes it sound like a momentous moment in a major motion picture.

"Shouldn't be a big deal."

"Maybe we don't talk about this now," he says.

"You called it curiosity. That's exactly what it was…"

"Not exactly."

"I think so."

"That's how you want to leave it? Curiosity?"

"Best thing to do. Leave it."

His eyes narrow for a split second. "If that's what you want. Okay." The door swings shut behind him. He hurries to his car; I hear a final call out to me. "Make sure you lock the door."

* * *

Jule Selbo

An hour later, I try to keep my mind off Donato and our kiss; it's been over a year since I was close to someone like that. Donato, as far as I know, has always kept his personal life uncomplicated and eschewed departmental relationships. He had visited me in the hospital after my injury, gently digging for more details of the event that might be stored somewhere in my memory. He and Gordy set up a plastic Christmas mini-tree in the corner of my room and decorated it with candy canes. They played corny holiday music and then there was a call from Christine Poole; she was done at the television studio and she was ready for him to drive them to her family's home in Kennebunk. I distinctly remember my disappointment as he walked out of my festive hospital room. I'd pushed that feeling aside and told myself that he had stopped in only because he was investigating the case and the event happened on his watch. I push my feelings aside again.

What was found in Billy's pickup? I hate being on the outside, can imagine Chief Harper making it clear to Donato that all information was to be kept in-house.

Another list. This one turns out to be a timeline. Wednesday night, Billy picked Karla up at Sparrows. Twelve hours later, Thursday morning, Gretchen told me she'd heard from Karla's salon that Karla hadn't shown to open up. Less than an hour later, I was in a tree, looking into Karla's bedroom window and seeing she hadn't slept in her bed. I arrived at the Payer residence before nine in the morning and Billy, in his tight t-shirt and fake concern, denied knowledge of Karla's whereabouts. A few hours later, I stopped at Karla's salon and L-vis lied about Karla calling, told me she was at her parents' home in Augusta. Why did he lie? I refuse to think it was a knee-jerk reaction to my not wanting a manicure. The next day, Friday afternoon, after returning from Boston, I found a note tucked into my door frame. It was a few hours later that Abshir and I saw Karla's Camry in front of Room #5 at the PemaPond Motel and I found empty-eyed Karla, bruised, frightened, and forever changed, inside the motel room.

Lyla, of Eden's Roost, told us about the woman in the back room at the camp at Dyer Long Pond. My gut tells me it was Karla—but I don't have proof. I open the pictures app on my phone and view the images I took at the PemaPond Motel Room.

One of the photos catches my attention. I zoom in on an area of worn carpet near the bed. Is that what I think it is?

I ignore the late hour. Stinner answers my call on the third ring.

"What do you want, Rommel?"

"Something that Lyla said to us at the Old Pub. About things missing from her bag."

"What about it?"

"I noticed—when we were at the Irish pub—that she likes feathers. Feathers are all over her costume, on her bras, her shoes, lots of feathers on her scarves."

"Isn't her routine called Feathers and Fluff?"

"Exactly. She said her extra-long boa was missing from her bag. The cell phone pictures I sent you—the ones I took of the motel room. Check the one with the bed in the corner, the overturned lamp on the floor. If you zoom in—notice that white fluff on the carpet? Could be a feather?" I expect a reaction but Stinner's mum. "And if that is one of Lyla's feathers, that might put Karla at Dyer Long Pond."

He takes a long moment.

"You there?" I ask.

"Heard from Donato."

"You did?"

"Found traces of blood in Payer's truck."

Eagerness and trepidation kick into higher gear. "And?"

"Being sent to the lab. See if there's a match."

"To Karla."

"And Thomas Beene, liquor salesman."

What will that matter if Payer can't be found?

Stinner takes another moment—then makes a decision. "I convinced the judge that the bachelor party cabin might have something to do with what happened at the PemaPond Motel. Had to work for it—but got a warrant. My team got back from the cabin and the motel room. They've documented everything and brought items back to the station. Maybe you want to go through them."

He's opening a window and I jump through it. "I'll come to Brunswick now."

"How about first thing in the morning?"

I have to meet Gordy and Claren early. "Now is better for me."

Stinner sighs. "Why not? My wife and kids are not waiting up for me. And I've got paperwork to finish."

"I can be in there in twenty."

"Don't speed."

"Okay, maybe twenty-five."

CHAPTER TWENTY-SEVEN
Sunday

Gordy's house is a hundred years old. The floorboards creak under my weight as I head to the front door. But no one stirs, not even Bert. I step out into the cool night. Sparrows is busy, strains of Joan Jett's "I Love Rock 'n' Roll" fill the bar as baseball fans linger after the televised game. I swing the mag-light I took from Gordy's hall closet. There's a dog walker rounding the corner of the first block. Portland's a friendly town, but not a talkative one. We leave each other to personal thoughts and space.

My car's parked near my apartment, six blocks away. The night air is cool, the sound of my footsteps echoes in the empty street. Two cars are jammed into the spaces on either side of my Outback. In front of me is a Prius, not the first choice of most Mainers, they think they're not hefty enough for our icy winter and they ride too low to maneuver over deeply rutted country roads. It probably belongs to a new transplant or to a visitor. Its back fender touches my front bumper. The SUV behind my Outback is an inch from my bumper and there's no need for that—there's at least four feet behind it before a driveway starts.

I'm trying to figure out how to maneuver the Outback out of the space when the SUV's darkened passenger-side window powers down. A shadowed face leans out of the car. "Thinking of going somewhere?"

Now I wish I'd woken Bert and insisted on his company. He's only a labradoodle but he would have been some sort of ally.

I swing my mag light upwards so it blasts in his face.

"Shit," he complains, putting his hands up to protect his eyes. "Fuck." It's Flea, the guy who works at U-Tow, one of Billy's pals.

The passenger door opens. Thick shit-kicking hiking boots hit the ground, the kind that ward off snakes, ticks, and rabid animals in the backwoods. A whiff of late-night snack wafts from the SUV, it's like a brewery and a taco truck have married in the interior. I press on my Outback's horn with my left hand and the fingers of my right hand try to punch 911 on my cell but it slips out of my hand—damn it—hits the pavement and bounces under my car.

Flea's thick-bodied, over-pumped body is coming close. I lean on the horn again, short bursts of the strident, annoying sound fills the neighborhood.

"You're no cat, no five lives." He sounds like a moron.

"That's *nine* lives, Flea."

"You don't have that either." He sounds even more moronic.

"I'm not a cat." I try to get a closer look at the driver, but he's just a shape.

"A cat falls off the top of a building and doesn't go splat."

He's making no sense. But he's got a four-foot pipe in his hand and I'm not going to diss him. I slam on the Outback's horn, loud, insistent honks screech through the air.

A window opens. "Hello? What's going on? Is my car in the wrong place? That's my Prius. Sorry."

I yell, "Call the cops, please."

"About my Prius? I can move it."

The window is on the second floor of the condo building; the Prius owner doesn't have a good view of me. I'm basically a voice coming from the darkness, a person hoping for trust and help.

"Tell them some guy, goes by 'Flea,' works at U-Tow and is a friend of Billy Payer, is threatening to beat me with a pipe."

Flea's forehead creases into dark ridges and he spits out, "Fuck you."

The person in the condo freaks. "Beat you up?" He calls to someone in the room. "Honey, call 911, get the cops here now." He yells into the night, "Hey—we called the cops!" He's back to me. "I'll be right down. Do you want me to come down?" He definitely doesn't sound like he wants to get into the fray, but he's left the window.

Flea and his shit-kicking boots retreat to the vehicle. He slips inside and the driver reverses the vehicle, changes gears, and squeals out into the street. The SUV speeds to the corner and heads west towards the highway.

The door of the condo opens and a skinny guy in his sixties, dressed in plaid pajamas, sticks his head out. "They gone?"

"Took off."

He blows out a grateful puff of breath. "Okay. Okay. Good." He holds up an umbrella. "Brought this. Didn't want to bring a knife—figured that could be asking for it, probably end up having it shoved into my own ribs."

"Thanks for opening your window." I balance myself on the car door and shoot my good leg out to bend down to retrieve my phone.

My pajama-clad reluctant hero shuffles towards me in his furry slippers. "Cops should be coming. We're new to Portland—but cops in Portland do come when you call them, don't they?"

* * *

The man in the pajamas had introduced himself: Forrest Rankin. We'd waited for the squad car to arrive. Turned out to be Officer Vera Sandrich, the one who wanted my opinion on the rats in Hilary's car. She took my statement. "You didn't get a license number?"

"Plate was in the shadows," I said.

"And you don't know where this Flea lives. Or his real name." She'd been disappointed. "Not living up to your reputation."

"What?"

"That you were crackerjack when you were on the force."

I hoped she'd heard the sarcasm in my comeback. "Sorry I can't make you shine tonight."

"You didn't get a look at the driver of this SUV?" She said it like the situation might have been a figment of my imagination.

It pissed me off and I snapped, "No."

Sandrich had taken down Rankin's contact information. He was anxious to get back inside, slip into a warm bed, and forget about me. I'd gotten into my car and headed north on I-295 towards Brunswick. I kept looking in my rearview mirror, half-expecting to see the SUV following me. But no sign of it.

The Brunswick Police Department, Stinner's domain, is off Highway One, close to the Androscoggin River that starts somewhere in New Hampshire and drops about eight feet per mile heading south. The river provided waterpower to paper mills and textile mills for centuries. The environmental clean-up is on-going. The small town is full of Bowdoin College professors and administrators, students, small business owners, former mill workers, gas and oil companies, and BPD cops who fill the roster of the best police department softball team in the state.

I park on Pleasant Street and wait a moment. But there's no traffic. No one walking the streets. Finally, I head towards the long, two-story brick building. Stinner meets me in the lobby and leads me to a workroom. "We got a call from the neighbor next to Smith's Fishing Camp Rental—the place used for the bachelor party. They were pissed that their garbage bins were overflowing with chicken buckets and trash—raccoons and other critters got into the crap and messed up their property. Neighbors told me that Smith, the owner of the fishing camp, lets the place out by the night and it's an ongoing fight with the other homeowners around there. We've got the non-food garbage laid out in the evidence room along with what was left in the cabin."

"What was in the back room where the 'pet' was stationed?"

"Empty except for a narrow iron bed frame; no mattress on it. We found the mattress floating in the low end of the pond, half submerged in the mud. Don't know if we'll be able to get anything off it."

Stinner nods to one end of the table. "You can start there—what we found in the neighbor's garbage can. See if anything shouts out."

Beer cans. Liquor bottles. Empty fried chicken buckets. Pretzel bags. Oreo cookie bag. A sweaty t-shirt. A hoodie. A broken fishing pole. Plastic bat and cracked whiffle ball. Pair of old water shoes. A poster of a Playboy pinup, dart holes evident on it; five frayed darts rest next to the poster.

One item catches my eye. A mud-spattered piece of material. I lean in to study its shape. It's a felt flower, with torn threads hanging off its base. My heart quickens, I call to Stinner. "This is from Karla's sweater. She was wearing a sweater that had a flower like that on it when she went off with Billy. Last Wednesday night." There's something metallic—it's the clasp of the brass cupid pin. The angel is half-gone, but a wing and the fastener remains.

Stinner bends, gets low for better scrutiny.

I open my cell phone and show Stinner the picture Karla took of us with my phone. Sparrows in the background, she's pointing to the felt flower where she'd attached her pin, I'm holding up the strap of my purse, Gretchen's proudly thrusting out her chest and looking down at her pin. We're all at the tail end of saying 'love ya, Karla' and grinning for the camera.

Stinner motions to one of his officers. "This is Dee Rommel. She's sending us a cell phone photo now. Get it blown up. ASAP."

"Got it, detective."

I forward the photo to the department's computer.

Stinner leans against the table. "Guess this is tough for you."

"Finding out it was Karla at Dyer's Pond? Yeah. Knowing she was used, beat up, knowing she was terrified. Yeah. Tough."

"It's gonna be made right."

"Never can be made right," my words catch in my throat. "Damage is permanent."

"Understand."

"We gotta find Payer. He can't get away with this."

"The note left in your door—about PemaPond Motel," Stinner continues. "Donato got results—couldn't get any significant prints off it. And the paper's torn from a cheap spiral notebook—kind you can get from Staples or Walmart or grocery stores."

"He tell you about the opinion piece stuck in my door last night?"

"'*Bitch*.'"

"Right. Same kind of paper." That threat was not direct, not like the one tonight. A guy swinging a pipe at me in the dark, making it clear I was in line to be another victim.

* * *

It's almost midnight. There's a parking spot a few doors down from Gordy's. The lights in Sparrows are flashing, signaling closing time and neighborhood regulars have left their barstools and are moving out into the street. Pat walks out, Reader lagging behind to lock the doors. Pat peers across the darkness, sees me locking my car door. "That you, Dee?"

"Hi, Pat."

"Need to eat? Can grab you a container of soup."

"No, I'm good. Staying at Gordy's—so…" I point to Gordy's house, right across the street.

"Gonna take care of him?"

"Marie's here too."

"Word at Sparrows is Billy Payer ran away from the cops. No one knows where he is?"

"Not that I've heard."

"So, stay at Gordy's. Not that Gordy could beat off the creep—but I'd lay bets Marie could." Pat laughs, but it's not a joyful sound. He takes the stairs. "I gotta hit the hay. Too old for this."

"Uncle. Flip the lights on and off when you get in…"

"Worried I'll get hacked to death?"

"Do me the favor, Grumps."

Pat grunts and keeps climbing.

Reader and I are in the middle of the street. A Portland Police vehicle passes by on Congress, a half-block away. The light in Pat's apartment flicks on and off.

"Sit on Gordy's porch?" Reader takes a flask out of his pocket. "Rittenhouse—your favorite, right? I'll share with you."

Ten Days

It's my chance to ask him about where he might have followed Billy, where he's been when not at Sparrows. "Can't sleep anyway."

We settle into the two rockers, put our feet up on the railing. The whiskey scorches down my throat, makes my chest feel hot. Reader takes a sip. "You find something in Payer's truck that night that the cops could use?"

"What if I say I haven't been at the Gull Roost for months?"

"Doesn't mean I'll believe it."

There's no way I can admit to finding Thomas Beene's credit card.

He hands me the flask again. "Guess we'll leave it at that."

I float my question. "Any other times you were checking out Billy's whereabouts in the last week?"

"No. You mentioned Dyer Pond? Where is it?"

"Close to where Karla was found."

He holds out his hand for the flask. "How's your friend?"

"She'll be better when justice is served. I hope."

"That's what gets you going? Justice?"

"Important to me. Bad guys shouldn't be free to terrorize people."

"And you want to be part of making sure the rotten eggs are put away. Written all over you."

I'm rankled. "You're really judgmental, you know."

"Not really. I'm about getting to the bottom of a person."

I swallow my irritation. "Tell me your story."

"Took a left here, a right there, flipped a coin at roundabouts, followed the weather, and avoided anything that felt like a noose."

"So, constantly on the move—with no ties. Sounds 'free.'"

"Pros and cons." He breathes in. "But…nice little city you got here."

"Could never leave it."

"Because of Gordy?"

"'Cause it's my home."

Reader's rocker moves back and forth. "What makes this place feel so good? The people or the familiar streets and bars and…"

"Both. Like tonight—there's a half moon, enough light to give a glow to the crooked, lumpy brick sidewalks. To make the waters in the bay shine. Enough wind to fill a sail. I like knowing tomorrow I can walk to the pier and pick up fresh lobster and oysters, wave to people who knew my dad. So it's a blend of both—people and place."

"Didn't figure you for the warm, fuzzy, sentimental type. You hide it pretty well."

I take another sip of whiskey.

"What're you doin' out this late? By yourself."

"Was up in Brunswick. Evidence piling up, case closing in on Billy."

"Good."

"Can't be soon enough."

"How come Billy Payer hates you so much?"

"Maybe 'cause I'm not good at keeping it a secret that I don't think much of him. Sets him off."

"Billy ever ask you out?"

"His style is late night hook-ups. Whoever looks most willing."

"That isn't you?"

"Sex is kind of wrapped up in respect for me."

He grins. Hands me the flask again. "So if I told you I respect you?"

My scornful sigh is ornery.

"Sorry," he laughs.

We sit, silent for a moment. Reader's many facets play through my brain: smart-ass, kind, aggressive, bossy, cold—and now this—companionable.

"What's with Charles Dickens?" I ask.

"Like his writing. He gets to the raw of people—all the warts. Some of the characters are heroic—but flawed nevertheless—majorly flawed."

"Wow. Look at you," I tease. "Some deep thinking."

"Nothing a high schooler isn't taught. Just rings truer to me every time I re-read the books." He finishes the whiskey. "You and that cop. Donato. You two got something going?"

I hesitate. Then I shake my head. "Being solo is better for me right now."

"That's a waste."

"Excuse me?"

"I said, that's a waste."

"What's a waste?"

"You being solo."

"Don't need your opinion." I get up. "Gordy and I have an early meeting. Night."

"Night." He doesn't move.

I unlock the door to Gordy's house, step inside, and flip the latches after the door's closed. Reader and his opinions have raised my hackles again. I can hear his rocker rocking; hate that he can get under my skin.

FIVE DAYS

CHAPTER TWENTY-EIGHT
Monday

The smell of a mouthwatering breakfast wakes me before my alarm sounds. Pancakes, coffee, bacon. I get ready as quickly as I can and head down the stairs. Reader is at the stove, Gordy, Marie, and Pat sit at the small round table near the kitchen window, Bert is happily situated at Gordy's feet.

"This is cozy," I say.

Marie purrs. "Nothing wrong with cozy, sweetie."

Gordy glares at me. "Pat said you were out late. Alone."

"Too late," Pat opines.

"Went up to Brunswick PD," I explain. "I was with cops."

"Not when you were driving. Your mother'd kick my ass if she…"

"No need to fill her in."

Gordy glares. "They get Billy yet?"

"Sick shit," says Pat.

I hold up my phone. "Received the most recent text from Donato. He's out there—no one knows where."

Gordy nods towards Reader. "This the guy you were talking about, Dee?"

"Pat's nephew, yeah."

Reader winks at me. "Glad to hear you were talking about me."

"He slept on my porch," Gordy says.

Reader jokes, "You thinkin' of charging rent?"

"Better to expect the worst from Billy Payer, someone's gotta be alert," Pat observes, chewing on a soft pancake.

Reader forks a hefty-size pancake onto a plate and hands it to me. "Syrup's on the table."

Gordy finally stops glaring at me and chats up Reader. "You're Pat's sister Debbie's kid?"

"I am," says Reader, flipping another pancake.

"To Debbie," Gordy raises his orange juice glass. "Homecoming queen two years after Pat and me graduated. Never could convince her to go out with me."

Marie laughs. "Her loss."

Pat disagrees, "She had taste, Gordy."

"Where's cute and *bellissima* Debbie now?" Marie wants to know.

"Cancer got her," Pat says. "Five years ago—isn't that about it?"

Reader serves pancake-laden plates. "Yep."

"My nephew's a nowhere guy. That's what the family calls him. Mr. Nowhere."

Gordy speaks with his mouth full. "Gotta be somewhere in all that nowhere."

Pat nods. "Montana. Utah. British Columbia. Up to the Yukon, too."

Gordy shoots a question towards Reader. "Not a 'roots' kind of guy?"

Reader pours pancake batter into the skillet. "Never had a reason to stay in one place."

Pat slices a banana on top of his pancakes. Smothers the mound with syrup. "Got through Harvard."

I sip my coffee, take in this unexpected information. "Stayed in one place long enough to do that?"

"Figured out the minimum on-campus days I needed to get a degree. My mom said it'd make her happy," says Reader.

"What'd you major in?" I ask.

"English Language and Literature," Reader says.

"Books," grunts Pat.

I press. "You remember the night we met?"

Reader grins. "Sure do. Is this going to get romantic?"

Gordy's now interested. "What? Something I should know?"

I focus on Reader. "I have a question about your powers of observation."

"Try me."

"Couple sitting in the corner by the fireplace?"

"All New York cool? Saw the guy using the facilities a few too many times, thought he was young to have prostate problems…"

Pat interjects, "Not like me."

"So, I checked out the Gents' Room next time the guy made a move. Didn't see the exchange, but some money was being pressed into New York cool guy's pocket and a pretty guilty young guy hurried out as I came in."

Pat's face hardens. "Drugs? In my place?"

"I got rid of him, Uncle."

"That New York guy's name is Duncan," I say. "Did you see what he was selling?"

"I hung at the door and stared at him while he made a big deal of washing his hands. Gave it a full ten seconds. He knew I was onto him. Especially when I followed him back to his whiny friend. They left. Better than making a scene with the cops. Let everyone else keep on with a nice neighborly time."

"My nephew." Pat's proud. "Always thinkin' of me."

Gordy asks if I'm ready. I down the last bite of my pancake and nod.

Marie grabs the car keys and heads out the door. "Bert'll spend time with me at the gallery today. No worries."

"You don't have to drive us," says Gordy.

"Yes, I do," Marie tells him. "Doctor's orders—you're not allowed to drive for three weeks."

Gordy grouses and follows Marie. Reader flips a pancake onto a paper plate and holds it out to me. "Take this. As a reminder, I hate wasting anything."

This guy never lets up.

"Stop at Sparrows later, Dee," says Pat, focused on folding a pancake around a slice of bacon. "We have a brisket special tonight."

* * *

Marie drops us off a few minutes before eight. There's not a breath of wind; the water in the bay is absolutely flat. We're at the water taxi dock and can see workers load the groceries from Whole Foods and supplies from Home Depot and other venues onto the ferries—the products will arrive at the various islands and be picked up by locals who rarely leave their more isolated environs.

Malio spots Gordy and races across the street. "My m-man is back." He shakes Gordy's hand. "I've been k-keeping eyes wide. There was a m-murder on Widgery Wharf."

"Heard about it."

"Violence all around, man."

The water taxi, painted a bright, deep yellow, pulls up to the dock. Gordy waves to Antonio DeMiguel, the driver. Antonio's got the biggest boat in the taxi fleet, it's got a wide berth and a heated cabin. "Morning, Gordy. Morning, Dee." Antonio holds out his large, rough hand; I step onto the boat. "Help yourself to cuppa joe."

"I will."

Antonio gives his hand to Gordy. "How's your brother doing in Florida?"

"Gonna be fine. And I'm dandy, if you're wondering."

"You're too cantankerous to let anything slow you down." Antonio takes his seat behind the wheel.

Gordy sits next to him in the elevated passenger seat. I pour coffee from Antonio's super-sized thermos and hand Gordy a cup before I move to the outside deck. "Too nice to sit inside."

"Suit yourself."

I head for the stern, sit on a cushioned bench. I can hear Gordy asks Antonio about his family.

"Son's finally got his lobster license," says Antonio. "Ten years it took him. All that waiting, but I guess patience pays off. Ah-yup. It does."

"Ah-yup. Patience pays off," Gordy repeats.

Antonio backs the boat out of its space. "'Cept now the big lobster pods are moving north. Water's getting too warm here. Never thought Casco Bay'd come to this. My son's thinking of moving up near Mount Desert next year to be near the larger population."

"Pretty up there," says Gordy.

"Ah-yup. Pretty up there," Antonio agrees. He concentrates on getting us out of the harbor and headed into the waterway between Peaks Island and Little Diamond.

Gordy comes out on the deck, sits next to me. Seagulls glide by on the slight breeze. "You're being hard on yourself."

"Payer's out there. I don't know what he's planning…"

"You're thinking he's targeting those that testified against him."

"Karla. And Hilary with the rats; she's terrified. Pat's nervous, but how long can he keep his nephew around?"

"And you."

"Do I wonder what he's got planned for me?" I don't share last night's interaction with Flea and the shadowed man in the darkened SUV. Not in the mood for a lecture right now.

"Put it aside for the morning. Trust Donato and the PPD. Focus on Claren now."

"That's another failure added to my list. Claren hired us to get him and his daughter in the same room. Haven't been successful at that either."

"Yet. We have a few days before the wedding."

We pass the daily mailboat on its regular route. I envy its task, looks so ordered and simple.

"What is it between you and Claren?" I ask.

Gordy grunts. "Lived a block from each other. Phil was always getting picked on, bullies followed him home to shove him, kick him—didn't like he was so smart, that teachers were impressed with him and all. I was bigger than those bullies and had a boxing title attached to my name and didn't like that he was being punished for just being who he was."

"You became Claren's bodyguard?"

"After he had both legs broken and had to have his jaw re-wired."

"Serious?"

"Munjoy Hill was a tough place back then. Made it clear if anyone messed with him—they messed with me."

"So he owed you—but why do you owe him?"

Gordy closes his eyes, appreciates the salt air on his skin. "It was after he got married and then split with Renae. He'd bring Bunny over to my house when they visited Portland. She never sat still. Once, when she was a month or so out of diapers—she took apart my turntable. Never did get it back in working order. Pretty soon after that, she emptied a box of cereal on my living room carpet and counted each Cheerio. Finally, when she was about four, Phil bought her the entire Nintendo collection—he'd travel with a whole set up. Pretty clear she was taking after him. When she was six, she took the casing apart, tried to rebuild it using my pitiful toolbox. I was finding parts under the couch and chairs for a year."

"You're not answering my question."

"Bunny was cute."

"Gordy, why do you owe Claren?"

"When I stepped away from boxing—I got into betting. New England bouts, but sometimes Vegas—the big fights. Wasn't good at it. A particularly bad bet became a disaster. Coulda lost the house my parents built. My business that I'd started. Claren Tech was doing well. Phil let me buy in at a good time."

"You own shares in Claren Tech?"

"Not anymore. Sold 'em, made a good profit; paid off my debts. Got tough on myself. Quit gambling. Phil keeps telling me it was small potatoes—but it saved my ass and everything my family put their sweat into—couldn't've lived with myself if I'd lost the house my dad built."

"You sure Claren's giving us the truth?"

"As much as we need to know."

Antonio maneuvers through the waters, steering clear of the buoys that mark the location of the lobster pots on the route into Hussey Sound. He calls back to us. "Starboard! Seals—off starboard."

Sleek, silvery-black seals glide near the surface—their flat noses and whiskers visible above the surface of the water.

"You make your decision yet?" Gordy asks.

"What decision?"

"If you're going to go back on the force. Doesn't Chief Harper want a decision by the end of the month?"

"Something like that."

"There's another option. Join G&Z full-time. Get your PI license. I'm thinking of slowing down." He takes my hand; his has become thin, the skin dryer. "The plan could be for you do most of the work and let me sit back and consult."

"You'll get back to your old self," I tell him, not wanting to think of Gordy underestimating his stamina.

The water taxi heads past the shores of Long Island and twenty minutes later we're passing Chebeague Island's Chandler's Cove. The wide lawn in front of the island's stately, yellow-sided inn comes into view. We continue east to the deep waters of Broad Sound. Antonio pulls up to a multi-million-dollar Sunseeker yacht; it's a hundred feet long, super-sleek and pristine. A crewmember, in a navy polo shirt and khakis, drops a gangway to connect it to the taxi. Gordy holds onto its rails and shuffles on board.

CHAPTER TWENTY-NINE
Monday

Claren, in a gray striped shirt and gray Dockers, takes in Gordy's pallor. "Too pasty and too skinny."

"You look worse." Gordy's got a point; there are dark-as-mud circles under Claren's eyes. His freckles are prominent on his pale face, his ginger hair unruly.

"Left you messages, Dr. Claren," I say.

Claren leads us into the yacht's sleek salon. White leather couches form a u-shape sitting area; teak cabinets and side tables gleam.

"Have a seat, Gordy, don't want you falling over."

Gordy sinks into one of the couches.

"Wanted to tell you I saw Bunny Luce." I want Claren's attention. "At Bradley Hogan's home."

"That was after I terminated your services."

Gordy's gruff. "Phil, one minute you're adamant to know where Lucy is and now you don't care anymore?"

"I care, Gordy." He signals the crewmember. "Coffee and tea ready?"

A cart, with hot and cold beverages, is wheeled into the salon. I wait for the crewmember to move off and continue. "Lucy had been staying there. And Peppard. She asked me to give you a message."

Claren goes to the cart, pours coffee for himself. "What's the message?"

"That she wants you to show up on June 22."

"So that hasn't changed," he says.

"And that she has 'it,'" I add.

Claren slowly turns. "She said that?"

"Phil, what's 'it'?" Gordy asks.

Claren keeps looking at me. "What else did she say?"

"Peppard came in before she could give details. And they took off."

"You scared her off." Hogan's wheeling into the salon.

My jaw practically hits my chest. "What're you doing here?"

"He invited himself," Claren says.

Hogan's light flannel shirt is crisp and ironed. His jeans are folded under his knees, his fingernails buffed and light on the controls of his machine.

Claren's voice is cool. "He filled me in on your visit."

"Did he tell you about the pills behind a poster in the upstairs hallway?" I snap.

Claren nods. "He told me of the discovery."

Gordy takes charge. "Time to get everything on the table. No one's holding back anymore. It's four days before the wedding and time is of the essence. Phil? Is everything fair game here?" Gordy nods towards Hogan.

"We can speak freely," Claren says.

Hogan's powerchair slides into an open space at the end of one of the couches, we all take seats. Claren nods towards him and Hogan takes a deep breath. "A month ago, Lucy and I were in the LC Lab. One of the office staff brought in a letter—wasn't stamped. Must have been brought by messenger."

"Did you ask her about it?" I ask.

He takes a moment. "We were in the middle of recording findings…" He looks to Claren, seems to take care to remain vague. "On some working theories…the letter seemed…personal. Maybe from Peppard. Didn't think it was my business."

I'd seen the photo of Hogan and Lucy, looking happy, drinking martinis on the Miami beach. Lucy choosing an intimate relationship with Peppard might have thrown him.

"She said she had to get something from her office," Hogan continues. "That was the last time I saw her—until she called and asked if she could stay at my house."

"At your home—near Lincoln," I say, "Lucy and Peppard were using separate bedrooms. A few items made me think Peppard had other romantic interests."

Hogan's eyes darken. "I flat-out asked him. Told him Lucy deserved someone great and I wasn't thinking he was enough for her. He didn't care for my opinion—just yelled up to Lucy that she should make it clear—to me—who she was going to marry."

"And she did?"

"Lucy asked me not to get involved, not to make a scene."

"How'd she come to stay with you?" Gordy asks, wanting the connection between Hogan and Lucy to be clearer.

"She called, said she needed a place to think, get away." Hogan glances at Claren again. "Thought she meant away from…"

"Peppard. That maybe she was going to call off the wedding?" I say. "Is that what you thought?"

"I wanted to do what she needed. Lucy came alone. He showed up an hour later. She was weirded out that he tracked her. I told her I'd call the police—but she didn't want that."

"Why'd you let him stay?" I ask. "It's your house."

"Like I said. Lucy asked me not to kick him out. Not to make a scene."

Gordy vents at Claren. "Damn it, Phil. We're dancing around the reasons for everything. Come on."

I nod. "We know Peppard works for the Destiny Leader account, a company owned by Leon Wolff. Wolff was on your plane to Washington. Yesterday, he came to our office and asked for our help in getting in touch with you. Said you've been avoiding him since Washington. The puzzle pieces need to start clicking together. What are we missing?"

Claren pushes his glasses higher on his nose. "Wolff's pressuring me to license one of our new projects to the Pentagon. We're not interested."

"Why does he think he can put pressure on you?" Gordy asks.

"He's an early investor in Claren Tech—he's got interest in some of the intellectual property that feeds into our new project. Could be a significant payday. Plus he likes to hob-nob with big government. But he doesn't have controlling interest in Claren Tech, he has no say in company decisions. Bunny and I do." Claren leans back on the couch. "You've heard of Radio Frequency Identification—RFID."

"Not familiar," I say.

"You will realize you are. Implanted microchips used as tracers to track animals—birds, seals, ducks, elephants, the list goes on. Lets them be studied in their natural habitats. Ostensibly to aid in their well-being."

"Okay, heard of that," I admit.

"There are ultra-microchips in our many phones that can tag us. Some can determine our locations within centimeters, to the very row we might be sitting in at a concert. Our phones can connect to wi-fi hotspots, count our steps, take our pulse, and more."

"But if we don't carry or activate our phones…"

"We mitigate the tracking possibilities," Claren says. "There are instances of non-medical microchip implantations in humans as well."

Hogan takes up the explanation, "Several companies in the USA, and others around the world, have given their employees the choice of having a chip implanted under their skin…" He turns his hand over, shows us the thick, flat area below his thumb. "Usually here. When the area is scanned, the chip is activated and works as a signal; it can be used instead of a key or password or fob to get into a secure building, into a company's computer system, to pay for meals in the company cafeteria—that sort of thing."

"Why would people volunteer for that?" I'm an immediate non-fan.

"Convenience," Hogan says. "To please their bosses. To be on the cutting edge."

"No way." I know I sound stubborn.

"Low-powered, signal-processing chips are being perfected for those with serious hearing problems," Hogan continues. "They can be implanted and externally charged—taking the place of the comparatively bulky cochlear transmitters. Some pacemakers gather data from heart-embedded chips through radio frequency, similar to the RFID tagging." Hogan's eyes meet mine. "Deep Brain Stimulators are electrodes implanted in the brain that can help the physically impaired. Help a patient with advanced Parkinson's control their involuntary tremors. There is work using DBS chips to help amputees control advanced prosthetics. This is the work I've focused my energies on. When Lucy and Dr. Claren shared the work they'd already taken to an advanced level, it was clear there could be overlap."

Claren continues, "Lucy and I started work on a project four years ago…"

This goes against what he's told me before. "Dr. Claren, you told me Lucy did not partner with you on projects."

"There is a long-term project, started when she was at MIT…"

I press, "Did you hire G&Z to force a meeting with your daughter for business purposes?"

Claren looks at Gordy. Gordy holds his gaze, he wants the answer to this question.

"It's part of it. I was worried," Claren admits. "The last message I'd gotten from her is that she—and Hogan—had fashioned a new code, moved us through our last obstacle."

"This code. Is that what she's referring to as 'it'?" I ask.

"More than a code—well…" Claren shrugs. "You can think if it that way. We've done extensive work beyond the mere microchip technology that can implanted under the skin," Claren explains. "Understanding the dangers and benefits of human-centric AI is necessary for certain applications. Knowing that, we believe that policy mechanisms must be put in place. You've heard of the Future of Us letter?"

"No," says Gordy. "Educate us."

"Written around 2015, it's signed by the best minds in technology and science. It asks for a study of the societal fallout of AI. It stated that innovators must not create something that cannot be controlled. Knowledge of the endgame must be understood."

Gordy holds up his hands. "Without going into more detail, what's this code or 'it' or formula or secret sauce worth?"

Claren provides. "The semi-conductor memory chip industry, last year, took in over 130 billion dollars."

"Damn." Gordy is as grumpy as an old dog. "Wolff wants his payday."

"There are possible benefits that we—along with other companies—have been working on. For example, individual medical information could be entered into the chip. A person is in an accident, needs immediate attention but a hospital hesitates because they need pertinent information such as blood type, allergies, medical history. Insurance. Let's say someone with a chip ID collapses in the street. Strangers call 911. Medics arrive, quickly scan the chip, find out if the person is insulin dependent or has Tourette, or is anemic, or has an allergy to penicillin, or has a do-not-resuscitate order in place. The ambulance personnel can call ahead to the hospital, where all the arrangements for this particular person can be arranged and when they arrive, medical help is already set in motion. Could save a life."

"But who really controls the information stored in the chip and who—really—no matter what privacy crap is advertised—controls access?" I ask.

"In other words, what's at stake?" Gordy asks. "Besides money."

"That's the ethical question. Washington has already considered using a similar chip, not as sophisticated, to mark groups of people—like migrant workers at the border before they enter the United States. There's talk of chipping anyone who joins the military, using the excuse that once Uncle Sam has been accepted as boss, Uncle Sam owns every movement. Talk of using it as a way to keep records of voters. Of requiring chipping of anyone found guilty of a crime."

"Anyone who gets a DUI or a traffic ticket gets forcibly chipped?" My heart rate is going up.

"The government's already shown their hand," Claren says. "It's an ongoing ethical discussion—debatable *ad infinitum*. Should chipping be added to the American fingerprint database of over 50 million? The larger proportion of that number are ordinary citizens. There are already iris scans on file, facial recognition data. Long-term information storing on CCTV recording devices is gaining traction. Chip ID can be seen as a logical next step."

"And your work takes it to another level."

"Potentially," says Claren.

"Lucy and I alluded to it when we received the Near Future Award," Hogan says. "It got attention."

Ten Days

Claren nods. "The research attracted government attention. They are interested in an experimental level; we are not inclined to fulfill their interest. Wolff wants Claren Tech to make a deal with the government—use their money to speed the process. However, that would give them priority status in use. We think that's a slippery slope."

Gordy slaps his hands together, wants to focus. "And this discussion of bio-memory chip, RF whatever, tracking technology whatever, has to do with Bunny Luce wanting you, Phil, to show up on Chebeague—for a wedding—four days from now?"

Claren looks to Gordy. "We have to find her."

I look to Gordy. Then back at Claren. "Is G&Z back on the payroll?"

"Yes."

"You have the harder-to-trace burner phone I gave you when we met a week ago?" I ask.

"Thought it was wiser to destroy it."

"Anticipated that." I hand Claren another burner phone and we activate the connection to the red phone that I still carry.

* * *

Standing on the back deck of the Sunseeker, I gaze out at the sublimely cozy island of Chebeague, green with summer leaves and dewy grasses. I half-envy its residents, content with being more connected to the land and sea—and to each other—than to Portland's pace and problems. Hogan moves in next to me. We're silent for a moment. Finally, he sighs, as if he knows my thoughts. "How easy would it be to stop trying to change the world?"

"Yeah." I think of my friend Winston Barry and his decision to dedicate his time and passion to Chebeague and its inn, to the ghosts he believes are there. Let the rest of the world be.

"Why'd you choose LC Labs?" I ask Hogan.

"Lucy."

"Simple answer."

"She's extraordinary."

"That picture of you two. I keep thinking about it. You looked happy."

"She's not afraid to put effort—money—time into the next newest." He nods towards his lower body. "Total twenty-eight surgeries, not the typical candidate for prostheses. There are others in my situation and we can do better. Lucy offered me my own lab, the ability to focus on that goal."

"Mind me asking? Where were you?"

"Afghanistan. Hindu Kush, south of Kabul. Intelligence unit out on a run; four Humvees. One minute we're cool, the next, rocket-propelled grenades were pounding and my vehicle ran over an explosive. C4—stuffed with crap—literally. Taliban add feces and blood to the explosives—so if you did make it through—you got a better chance of infection—which gives you a better chance for amputation. I'm the only one in my truck who made it. My sergeant got me away from it all, got me airlifted out."

What can I say? I sound lame. "Sorry."

"Thousands like me have been dealt a bad hand but that's how it is. I want to turn 'the bad hand' around."

"Build the million-dollar body."

"Won't cost a million. Not if it's done right."

"How does this myoelectric thing—this memory bio-microchip fit?"

"As you know…" He glances at me. "Prosthetics get better and better. This could take it another step. Bionic limbs can help people achieve full range of motion—and a sensitivity."

"Sensitivity?" I'm skeptical. "Come on…"

"We're not close yet—but it is the goal."

"You think that can be done?"

"Once you aren't 'the norm' anymore, big chunks are spent thinking about how streets, sidewalks, offices, homes, clothing, tools, getting on a bus—lots of things—are obstacles that take time, energy—sometimes in a humiliating way. With work on hydraulics, nanotechnology, biotech, myoelectric, computation… Best possible scenario? Those with adaptive needs, people who've lost the ability to do the things that used to feel 'normal,' could feel more connected. Reach closer to 'the norm.'"

Antonio's water taxi is motoring towards us.

"If you took the government money…"

"Controlling the use of this kind of property is important. To Claren Tech." His statement is delivered in a tone that shuts down further questions.

"Dr. Hogan," I say. "Do you have any idea why Lucy is playing this game?"

"I wouldn't call it a game."

CHAPTER THIRTY
Monday

Winston, in khakis and white cotton shirt, waves to us from Great Chebeague's landing dock. The island was once considered a suburb of the mainland town of Cumberland, in 2007 it seceded and became an independent township. It's got a school, a library, a pastor, a grocery store, and intense community spirit. No one is left to deal with any problem that a neighbor could help fix. In the winter, when snow, storms, and winds keep everyone inside, there's a weekly resident check-in—a sort of health and well-being review. Winston's been the point person for the last five years and the position suits his personality. I used to kid him that he was born with a priest's soul—that he was too intent on making others feel good about themselves. He'd tease me, call me judgmental, and tell me that I was also driven—that my desire for justice was as all-consuming as his was for trying to provide peace and tranquility.

Antonio maneuvers the water taxi to the dock. I toss a line to Winston; he makes a loose wrap on the cleat.

"You guys staying for lunch?" Winston asks.

Antonio's lined face brightens. He glances at Gordy, "We got time?"

"Not today," Gordy says. He remains seated on the back bench of the taxi, expending little energy. "Thanks for the offer, but we're in the middle of stuff. Dee said you called with some news about the June 22 wedding we're interested in."

Winston pushes back the brim of his straw hat. "Word on the island is the Robinson enclave had tent poles and canvas pieces delivered from the mainland yesterday. The Robinsons don't show up until July 4th every year—then they spend the rest of the summer. I called them in Baltimore to make sure they knew what was going on. Eric Robinson—the owner—said a company called Shannon Styles rented their place for an event and he couldn't say 'no;' said the rental was more than enough to pay for the new roof and a few other things the house needs."

Ten Days

I turn to Gordy. "Shannon Styles is the event planner out of Boston I told you about. Renae hired them for the party, the event, the food…"

"Has a couple of rental cottages across the street from it," Winston adds. "Anyway, I told Eric I'd make sure all was copacetic, so I took one of our golf carts to check things out. Didn't notice any activity—but saw the tent pieces in a pile on the front lawn. High winds expected tomorrow and the next day—probably waiting to get the tents up. Dee, didn't you tell me they were using a floating kitchen?"

I nod.

"A yacht with a good set-up could anchor nearby, use a smaller boat to transfer food and whatever to the private dock. You can view it from the water." Winston turns to Antonio. "It's round Ricker Head."

Antonio knows the island. "Sure, we can scoot by there."

"Let's do that." Gordy goes back to Winston. "No one's checked into the hotel in the last few days?"

"Like I told Dee before, summer season. We've been booked up for a year—birthdays, wedding parties, and a couple anniversaries. No room for anyone who wants a late reservation."

"Speaking of that," Antonio says, "I'm dropping off the bridesmaids for that Chen/Kennedy affair later this afternoon. Chef harvest any of the island strawberries from his garden yet?"

"Ah yup," says Winston. "Small and sweet. And he's made short biscuits this morning."

"Maybe I'll pop in for a lobster roll and strawberry cakes with cream after we get their luggage off the taxi?"

"Sure, Antonio," Winston gives a thumbs up. "I'll tell the kitchen."

I yell my thanks to Winston as Antonio maneuvers the taxi away from the dock and we head west. A few minutes later, we're contemplating the Robinson place; it's a two-story white Federal style home; it sports a wide and flat side lawn. A steep staircase leads down to its low dock and a thin, sandy beach, large enough for a clambake. I figure any bride would find this as a picturesque place for a fairytale wedding—but I don't get a good feel about it.

* * *

Antonio lets Gordy and I off at the water taxi landing. We head to J's Oyster, hoping to grab a haddock sandwich. We hit it when the 'open' sign is set into the window. Crowds haven't gathered, so we get a table at the window where we can eye the high-end powerboats that line Custom House Wharf. Gordy orders a dozen local oysters, dabs vinegar and horseradish on them, then lets them slide down his gullet.

"Five days 'til the wedding," I say. "We've got a few little pieces in place in the big puzzle, but not enough to get a sense of the entire picture."

"Which is getting Claren and Lucy in the same room so they can talk."

"And understand why she's run off with a dipwad…"

"Our job is getting Phil Claren and Lucy in the same room so they can talk," he repeats. "That's Claren's ask. All the other pieces are not our worry."

"What about the 'it'?" I ask. "The 'it' that Lucy's protecting."

"Maybe part of this AI project?" Gordy replies. "Claren gets buttoned up."

"I thought he trusted you."

"He knows I understand how to use my phone and my laptop, that I don't comprehend what's general knowledge in this tech stuff or what's important to keep quiet about. Therefore, he wisely chooses not to confuse me."

Bessie, the wiry, pony-tailed waitress who has been at J's Oyster since I was a kid, brings us our iced teas and oysters. "Hi Dee. Good to see you back in town, Gordy."

"Same," Gordy beams.

Bessie squeezes his shoulder, rushes off to greet new customers.

"Got your notes with you?" Gordy leans towards me. "Let's go through them—maybe there're connections I might have missed."

I take out my notebook. Gordy reaches across the table and extracts the folded copy of the photo of Lucy Claren and Peppard at the charity event in New York City. He studies the photocopy. "Peppard. Don't like the look of him."

"You're negative on any guy who wears pointy shoes."

"Pointy shoes with those metal tips—they're a statement; they say 'don't think, just cause I'm a skinny wimp, I can't kick your ass.'" He adds sugar to his iced tea. "The steel toes are weapons. Seen 'em kick into a person's chest, puncture skin, give one last swift kick and rip into a lung."

"Where'd you see that?"

"Back in the 70s. Outdoor rock concert. Some guy with a really bad temper. Took out a scrawny guy who ogled too long at his gyrating naked girlfriend."

"You went to rock concerts."

"With your dad. We tackled the shithead, held 'im till the cops could take him away. Your dad wasn't always the history buff and laid-back nice guy he morphed into. He could be a tough guy, with moves."

Gordy's recollections about my dad were usually good excuses to sit back, relax, and enjoy stories. But we both knew the clock was ticking. "I thought you'd pick on Peppard's haircut."

Ten Days

"Don't like that either—may as well be one of those topiary things. Hate bushes and trees that have been trimmed and cut to mimic squirrels or donkeys or whatever." Gordy licks the briny taste of the oysters off his lips, sops off the remaining with a napkin. "That haircut looks like too much time in front of a mirror. Too much primping, a waste of time."

"Hard to think of Peppard as a dad. In high school he and his girlfriend got pregnant."

"You follow up on that?"

"That wife moved on, has two more kids with a guy who sells cars in hometown Omaha. Hasn't talk to Tyler for five years, but he sends his child support."

He taps at the photocopy image of Lucy. "Describe Bunny Luce to me again—when you saw her at Hogan's house."

I think back—two days ago. Lucy's emaciated body, her sunken cheeks, the hot flush on her cheeks and in her eyes. "She was exhausted, unhappy, twitchy—and weak. I told you about Jade's chemist—and the analysis of the pills. Cousins to the classic MDMA…"

"That's a feel-good pill, right? So why is she looking so bad?"

"We took drug classes at the Academy, but it was never my area of expertise. Here's surface knowledge: Ecstasy usually gives the user a sense of euphoria. Things feel brighter, nicer—you feel better about yourself. More confident. More open to intimacy."

"I repeat, she looks awful."

"Her pills were laced with Special K…

"The roofie. I've read the stories."

"It's slipped into a cocktail, the imbiber can get hazy, pliable—even pass out. There are instances of memory suppression too. Jade's chemist also found cocaine in the pill. The three elements together? Get someone high—and low—and anxious, paranoid, horny, and maybe cause hallucinations. Basically, send someone all over the place."

"Geez. Beer was always a good enough for me."

"Claren thinks Lucy walks on water and wouldn't waste time with anything that could cloud her fine mind. You agree?"

"Last time I saw Lucy was when LC Labs opened. Two and a half years ago. She was the focus of the celebration, so I didn't get a chance to have any private talk with her. But she looked happy."

"A year later," I remind him, "She took time off from the LC lab and was on her own, in New York City, teaching at Columbia. Getting in touch with being a 20-something with other 20-somethings."

Bessie brings our sandwiches to the table. The lightly battered and quickly deep-fried haddock is on a grilled bun slathered with tartar sauce and fresh-made coleslaw. The first bite sends my taste buds to food-euphoria; the salty-sweet bread, the creamy slaw, the crunch of the fried batter and flaky, steaming, thick hardiness of the haddock. How many of these sandwiches have Gordy and I ordered and enjoyed, sitting across from each other with the summer sun warming the windows? Or during the wet, cold winter? Or the golden autumn season or during spring rains? This is 'family dining' to me. I tell Gordy I want him to eat, to fatten up, to get a healthy glow back into his tired eyes.

"Sure. I'm eating, okay? I'm eating." He chews. And talks with his mouth full. "Time for 'maybes.' Can you write them down and chew at the same time?"

"Do you doubt my dexterity?" I wave my pen in the air, flip to a new page in my notebook. I start, "Maybe Lucy, when she moved to New York, wanted to explore the scene—check out clubs…"

"Doesn't seem like a thing for Lucy…"

"Maybe she wanted to kick up her heels, try something new. Maybe she was nervous, maybe she wanted to smooth some edges. Decides to experiment. Maybe she ended up in a drug crowd."

"Or maybe someone spiked her drink," Gordy suggests.

"You're like Claren," I chastise him. "You want Lucy to be the victim, keep her on a pedestal."

"Maybe Peppard met her." Gordy says. "And maybe he realized who she was. Pursued her. One night, spiked her drink, compromised her."

"Why? What would the Peppard plan be?"

"Maybe to marry an heiress," Gordy suggests. "Gain access to a fortune."

"Maybe it is just about money. Separate from the 'it.'"

"Maybe," Gordy say.

"Too convenient to be separate, Gordy. Two problematical entities working parallel to each other?"

"Maybe."

"Maybe Peppard makes a point of meeting her. Maybe it wasn't random and 'it' has everything to do with it. Which could make sense because Peppard, in some probability, is in an affair with Murphy Duncan, the guy who's driving Leon Wolff and Renae Claren around. Duncan is connected to Peppard. He's connected to Wolff. And if Reader is correct, Duncan was selling drugs out of Sparrow's men's room…"

"Reader? The guy making pancakes..."

"That's his name?"

"That's who he is."

Gordy grunts. "Back to Lucy. So, is this Peppard a bisexual guy?"

"Don't know anything about his and Lucy's sex life. But he looked romantic with this guy—his name is Duncan—in the pictures I saw in Hogan's house."

"Didn't you tell me Peppard's last boss was the Golden Boy of Destiny Leader? Then he took a wrong turn, was asked to leave the company, and is now spending time in drug rehab? And Peppard moved up a notch because of this guy's demise?"

"From assistant to junior executive. Only took him a year." I get where he's going. "You're saying maybe Peppard finds a way to introduce people to drugs. And then takes advantage."

"Not the first time an underling is called on—or gets the idea to impress by the ability to provide contraband."

I sit back. "You really don't like his pointy shoes."

Gordy stabs at his pickle. "Don't tell me you think Peppard is a good guy?"

"No. Too many connections. Are Peppard's actions and interest in Lucy is directly linked to Leon Wolff and Wolff's interest in Claren's AI project?"

We sit for a moment.

Gordy puts down his sandwich; it's as if simple eating tires him. "Not our job to get to the bottom of drugs or business dealings. We were hired to accomplish a simple goal. Get Bunny Luce and Phil Claren in the same room. Father and daughter. Let them talk it out. We're not here to control an outcome."

"You mean we can't arrest any assholes."

Gordy smirks, but his eyes are serious. "That's a different job. You want to be the one who handcuffs the bad guys and puts them behind bars, you might want to sign that reinstatement request waiting for you at 109."

I don't want to open the gates to this discussion. "Let's focus on getting Lucy and Claren together."

Gordy takes a slow sip of iced tea. Nods. "Figure I should talk to this Leon Wolff."

"Abshir followed him to Mary Cove. That's a private development in Ogunquit. Wolff told me he planned to be at the ceremony so assume he stuck around. Renae Claren could be with him."

Gordy's eyes narrow. "Think Renae knows where Lucy is?"

"She's chummy with Wolff and I'd take bets Wolff knows a lot about a lot. We need to find out if Lucy's playing her dad and working on Wolff's team."

"Don't want to consider the possibility."

"Maybe we should. And not keep Lucy on that pedestal." I finish my fries. Gordy's lunch remains half-eaten. "You're not a member of the clean plate club today."

Gordy's mind is somewhere else. "What about Hogan?"

"What about him?" I ask.

"Friend? Co-worker? Any connection to Wolff? Something we might not have considered?"

"Hogan worked closely with Lucy, they traveled to conferences and won awards together."

Gordy shakes his head. "And he didn't notice she lost weight and looks like hell?"

"I asked him. Hogan said she doesn't confide in him. He allowed Peppard to move in because Lucy asked him to. Maybe only because his paycheck comes from LC Labs and she's kind of his boss."

"You think he's hiding something?"

"His feelings for Lucy. I'd bet the next haddock sandwich that he's in love with her."

Gordy takes a moment. "Sentiment returned?"

"Unclear."

"Maybe he's angry if they're not."

I scrunch my napkin and toss it, frustrated, on the top of my empty plate. "Maybe he's a Soviet spy or an AI bot or an alien or a guy with no legs who wonders if someone will ever love him."

Gordy eyes bore into mine, looking for signs that my anger might come from similar experience. A self-esteem check-in. I push through, "What do we do next?"

"Can you set up a time to meet with Leon Wolff?"

I take out my cell phone. "He gave me the number of his service. The drill is to leave a message, it's relayed to him and he calls back whenever. Likes control."

"Sure. We all do." Gordy reaches for his wallet in his back pocket and heads to the cash register. "Set it up for today, if you can. After your appointment with Ebenberg about your leg."

"I can postpone…"

"No, you can't."

I grab my jacket from the hook by J's Oyster's front door. Gordy's handing Bessie his credit card and she's telling him about her daughter's violin recital.

"How was lunch?"

I turn towards the voice; Dr. Fogel sits at the counter, a bowl of clam chowder in front of him. I don't think I've ever seen him outside the Police Department; his wrinkled, brown tweed jacket and unkempt, tight-curl gray hair seem to fit in here at J's, which also has a down-at-its heels charm.

"Had the haddock sandwich," I say. "Always good."

"Heard you're helping Robbie Donato."

"A little. Billy Payer's making trouble for people I know."

"It's personal for you?"

I think of rats in Hilary's car. And of Karla that night at Sparrows, thinking she was going to get an apology and spend quality time with a repentant Billy. "He beat up my friend and used her as a sex toy. Also uses rats for scare tactics."

Fogel sighs. "Heard some of the details. Your ex-partner's brother, right?"

I nod. "Stories are legendary. If you cross him—or maybe if he just feels like it—he leaves misery in his wake. Isn't that called being a sociopath?"

"Capable of superficial charm, no regard for the feelings of others, everything is about them and their power. Don't feel remorse. Often narcissists. That's the textbook answer. Does he fit that?"

"I'd say so. When Marvin and I started our first days on the job—we were on traffic duty. Billy harassed us on and off for hours, turning in front of our vehicle, yelling at Marvin through his window—cheers and raspberries when we stopped someone for gliding through a stop sign, getting into the road ahead of us, speeding up and slowing down…"

"What did Marvin do?"

"Asked me to ignore it. Billy was clearly the big brother bully that Marvin didn't confront."

"Did you ignore him?"

"At first. Marvin was a mess. I thought he'd explode. Then, after the fourth or fifth hassle, Billy passed us in a thirty-mile zone—he was going sixty and barely missed clipping a station wagon with five kids and a mom in it. I was driving at the time, got the siren on, called for back-up, and we ended up trapping Billy in a dead-end street. Ended up having his license suspended for a few months. Any interaction Billy and I had after that escalated our dislike. Can't imagine what living in the same house with him did for Marvin."

Bessie's voice carries over to us. "More iced tea, Ken?"

"Sure, Bessie. Bring it on."

Gordy comes to my side. "Good chowder, huh?"

"Not too creamy," says Fogel. "More clams than potatoes, the way I like it."

"Doc Fogel, this is my boss, Gordon Greer."

"We met a few years ago, at some event," Gordy says.

Fogel frowns, trying to place when their paths crossed. "Details escaping me."

"Hope Dee isn't as stubborn with you as she is with me," Gordy jokes. "Tough to know what's in her head sometimes."

"Are you blatantly baiting me for privileged client/doctor information about your office manager?"

Gordy snorts. "You think she's doin' okay?"

"Officer Rommel's always interesting."

I jump in. "Gordy and I need to get to the office."

Fogel dips his spoon into the rich clam broth. "Wednesday, Officer Rommel."

"That's not our regular day."

"We're doing Wednesday this week, remember? Don't be late. I'm sailing to Camden right after for the Penobscot Schooner Race."

"Okay. Sounds like we talked about this."

"Should be on your calendar. If it's not, I wonder how important you think our time working together is."

Gordy grunts. "She gets that it's important. Don't let her fool you. Enjoy your lunch, Doc."

CHAPTER THIRTY-ONE
Monday

Abshir's waiting for us at the office. His eyes light up when he sees Gordy. "Boss, it is good you are able to walk and look grouchy and normal with just one kidney in your body."

Gordy goes into his office and sinks into the couch. He heaves a large sigh. "Heard you been doing a good job."

Abshir shoots me a grateful nod. "I try to fulfill what is asked."

"Keep it up." Gordy lifts his feet up to perch on the arm rest; he's too long to fit on the couch.

"I do want to inform you," Abshir says apologetically, "That I have my final exam today at one o'clock in 'History of America's Racial Politics.'"

"Not an uplifting topic," Gordy grouses.

"My exam will be over at four o'clock," Abshir says. "I am happy to be where you need me the moment after."

"Dee has a prosthetics appointment."

I check the reminder on my phone. "Same time as your exam, Abshir."

Gordy closes his eyes. "Both of you get out of here and let me take a nap."

The office phone rings. I answer it.

"Miss Rommel. It is Leon Wolff."

Sooner than expected. "Your call center is very efficient, Mr. Wolff."

Gordy waves at me to put the call on speaker.

Wolff's voice comes across as light, friendly. "It will be excellent to meet Gordon Greer. Has he been in contact with Dr. Claren?"

"Gordy wants to fill you in on particulars in person. We could come to you later this afternoon."

"That will be fine. You know where I am."

Gordy raises an eyebrow. Abshir hangs his head. But I realize I'm not surprised Wolff was aware Abshir had tailed him to the Mary Cove enclave.

Ten Days

Wolff continues, "I will alert the guard at the entrance to the development to expect you. Shall we say early dinner? I will have steaks grilled for us."

Gordy holds up six fingers.

"We'll be there at six o'clock, Mr. Wolff."

I click off. Gordy motions to Abshir. "Get out the good car."

"Gordy," I remind him, "You can't drive."

In 2000, a client was short of cash and offered to sign over a custom model 1997 Grand Marquis to Gordy for payment. Maroon, with a shiny grill and white leather interior. He gleefully agreed. Turned out it was the last year the second generation of the car was manufactured, and Gordy appreciated that the large sedan was built in nearby Canada and shared a chassis with the Lincoln Town Car, and put its ugly cousin—the classic cop Crown Vic—to shame. Around the city, Gordy uses his decade-old Subaru for errands and bad weather drives; he parks that vehicle outside his house spring, summer, fall, and winter. But when he wants to impress, he drives the Grand Marquis out of the covered parking garage across the street from G&Z Investigations.

"You think Leon Wolff's going to get how special this car is?" I tease him.

"Men notice that other men have certain tastes."

Abshir gets the car keys from the reception desk's drawer. "I drive that good car very well. I will be happy to do that."

Gordy closes his eyes. "That solves the driving issue. Now, everyone, go do what you gotta do."

I close Gordy's office door. There's a frown on Abshir's face. "I know," I say.

"His skin is gray. I will ask my mother to make his favorite sambuusas and cambuulo."

"He'll appreciate that."

"Maybe he is too tired to go and meet with this Wolff."

"He'll push himself. We gotta keep an eye on him."

***

"Dee Rommel?"

I get up, give the assistant a wave. "That's me."

"Mr. Ebenberg's ready. The blue room."

She walks ahead of me, I read the clinic's logo on the back of her shirt: *Portland's Prosthetics and Orthotics*. "Gonna be a hot one today," she says.

"And rain tonight," I reply, so she doesn't think I'm anti-social.

The clinic walls are white, the linoleum floor gray, the doors to exam rooms are painted bright colors—green, purple, red, yellow, pink… We reach the blue room and the assistant smiles and leaves me. Through the open door, I see my prosthetist, Randall Ebenberg, sitting on a stool next to the exam table, reading my file. He's the lead of P&O; forty-five, married, moved away from Philadelphia and his job heading up Prosthetics at its Children's Hospital ten years ago to get away from crowds, pricey private schools for his kids, and traffic. He's no nonsense, which suits me.

"I'm listing a bit to the left," I say before he can ask. "Hope we could adjust something."

"Okay. Walk straight away from me. Across the room so I can take a look at the sagittal gait. You tell me your sensations, where it feels off."

I do as he requests. "My hips. Seem out of balance—like I wanna straighten up but can't manage to get there."

"Your body and mind are going to take a couple years to get used to the new you, we talked about that. It's been a little over a year with this device, that's all. Your muscles and tissue need this adjustment period."

"Want to get used to it quicker."

"Okay. Now walk straight towards me."

I do. He's studying my shoulders, my torso, hips. He focuses on my knee flexion. "You been doing anything out of the ordinary lately?"

I leave out the names, details, and the reasons, but tell him about climbing the tree outside Karla's apartment. Skidding on the wet, slick grass in front of my place when Billy Payer showed; the twisting to get up while he took cell phone photos of me. The cramp in my hamstring. About crawling on my belly like a reptile in the back of a pickup truck. Slipping on the ice cream that had been dropped on the slick concrete floor of the Sea Dog stadium and how that aggravated the hamstring strain even more.

Ebenberg considers me, then observes, "When I advised you to stay active, I figured you'd weigh the difficulties of certain situations."

"Sorry. Things happened."

He goes back to my file, adds a few more notes. "Still planning on running those 10Ks again?"

"Soon as you tell me I can be fitted for a running blade and I save up a big chunk of money to buy one."

"Mmhm. Let's adjust things. Can you take off your device?"

I doff my prosthesis, the two socks, and the liner. He checks the residual limb for any sign of bruising then uses his wrench to adjust the screws that connect my 'unfoot' to the 'unleg.' He adds a thin adhesive cushion to the right side of the device, where it rests against my stump. "This should help." He concentrates for another moment, takes photos of his work with the camera hooked up to his computer. "We have the monthly meetings here. It's a good group, they share experiences. You haven't taken advantage of them."

"Been busy."

He goes back to adjusting the prosthesis. "What about the Friendline group? Check into it online?"

"Have an aversion to social media."

"Use it as a source, a good place to pick up tips. Could be beneficial."

"I'll try check it out."

"The Ryryx help with the phantom pains?" He checks my file. "You were feeling a ghosting—an intense squeezing and pressure in the foot and calf."

"You mean the foot and calf that are no longer there."

"Phantom limb. Yes. Abated?"

"Calmed down—sleeping better. Would like to stop taking the medication."

"I'll put in a call to your surgeon and we'll talk." He makes another note. "You're impatient, but it takes time. Your body, your memory bank, your nervous system—all need to acclimate. Takes time." Ebenberg hands me back my prosthesis and I don it. "See how that feels."

I walk the room again. "Might be better."

He opens a drawer and takes out the latest medical rep's sample; it's a three-socks-to-a-bag item. "New sock on the market. Has good wicking fabric. Designed to keep the sweat factor down. Now it's summer and humidity's going up, you can experiment with them. They're one-ply so you can fool around with thickness; might work for you."

"Okay."

He makes a note in my file. "Call me in three days. Let me know if the adjustment helps."

"Okay."

"Try to cut back on climbing trees."

"Okay."

"I'm here, Dee. Don't ever hesitate."

"Thanks." I walk out, appreciative—because he's no nonsense and doesn't pry into the personal.

Standing in the hot sun outside the clinic, I check my phone again.

No message from Donato. I push down my irritation. I want to hear any news about the search for Billy. I also know that, technically, I'm not owed an update.

My phone pings—a text is coming through. It's from Jade. *Urgent. You and Gordy should come to me.*

* * *

Abshir waits beside Gordy's shimmering Grand Marquis. "Put it through the car wash," he says. "We are ready to go."

I slip into the back of the Marquis and remember my first ride in the car. I was nine years old. My dad was in the passenger seat, Gordy was driving and the wide, leather backseat was all mine. It felt as big as an entire house and I stretched out and took a nap.

Now I appreciate its size all over again, because I can settle near one door and sit nearly sideways and prop up my leg.

Gordy is already in shotgun position. Abshir's behind the wheel; the Grand Marquis moves out of the shadows of the parking garage.

CHAPTER THIRTY-TWO
Monday

Jade leads us down the stairs off her kitchen to the work sanctum. "The contents of the flash drive were hyper-protected. Initially when I got it into my USB port on computer 4, it brought on a malfunction alert, but I connected with the Device Manager to delete obstacles and scramble passwords…"

Gordy pushes her to get to the specifics. "Jade, can we get to the 'urgent'?"

Jade activates the center computer screen. "These photos might open a window of understanding as to why Lucy Claren is evading her father."

"What photos?" Gordy queries.

"They're disturbing. Not 'PG' or even 'R.'"

A prickle of alarm moves up my spine.

"Go ahead," Gordy says.

Jade opens the file and clicks on the first photo. A naked Lucy Claren is pictured. Her eyes are rolled back, mouth open, back arched, her hands clutch at her breasts.

I nearly choke on my words, "What's this?"

Jade moves to the next photo. Lucy is on her hands and knees; a naked male body positioned at her rear. The man's face is out of frame. Lucy's got a dog's collar around her neck and a male hand holds the leash so that her head is pulled back. Another photo: naked Lucy is spread eagled, a laptop computer between her legs. Another photo: Lucy holds a dildo in one hand, the laptop computer in the other. Another: Lucy's nude backside is thrust towards the camera, her head lolled to the side; she gives a sloe-eyed gaze at the camera. Jade observes, "If you can disassociate from the images, and compare them with internet porn sites, the photos are pretty cliché."

"Not disassociating here," mutters Gordy.

"The props are typical adult-erotica shop items," Jade says. "The suggestive images using the computer—I suppose are commentary on Lucy's rarefied place in the tech field." She goes to the next photo. "Here's a shot of Lucy on her knees, mouth positioned at the naked man's crotch."

"Don't need the descriptions, Jade," Gordy says through gritted teeth. "Can see what I'm seeing."

Jade becomes aware of Gordy's growing agitation. She hesitates. "Shall I show you the next photo?"

"How many?" I ask.

"26 photos."

Gordy sits, leans his head in his hands.

"Can you summarize?" I ask.

Jade nods. "Some show explicit penetration, some have Lucy glassy-eyed, putting aqua pills on her tongue, and in some, she even grins—a crazy sort of grin—at the camera. There are five that show her naked, tangled with two men—whose faces are unclear—on the hotel bed."

Gordy catches the detail, doesn't raise his head. "Hotel?"

Jade goes through photos quickly for me, points to various clues. "Notice the requisite clock on the bedside table, identical lamps with electrical outlets at their base. High-end but no personality. In this photo: a corner of a breakfast placard that can be hung on the doorknob." She moves to the next photo. "And here—on the headboard. You can hardly make out the monogram, the thread is the same color as the fabric."

Jade zooms in and I can read it. "M.O.H."

"Marvin Onley Hotel," Jade says. "Fancy boutique hotel in the village in New York. On Barrow Street. Thousand dollars a night."

Gordy blows out a deep breath. "We have a time frame?"

"We got lucky," Jade says. "See here? A few of the photos are date and time stamped."

"There is one identifier you haven't mentioned," I say.

A frown appears on Jade's forehead. "What?"

"Can you magnify the hip on the skinnier guy?"

Jade zooms into the photo. She reads. "May 1. May."

"Peppard's got a daughter," I say. "Named May. That's her birthday, May 1st."

Jade magnifies the photo even more. "That's right. Good catch, Dee."

A pall slips over the room. The evidence brings no sense of celebration in finding a possible insight into Lucy's recent behavior. "Here's another 'maybe,' Gordy," I say. "Maybe the acceptance of the marriage proposal came right after showing Bunny Luce these photos."

"You're assuming Lucy was coerced. That these were taken without express permission," Jade says.

She's right, I think sourly. I'm like Gordy and Claren, I do lean towards seeing Lucy on a pedestal, a victim. Assumptions cannot be made.

Gordy nods. "Jade, print copies of the photos. Want to take them with us."

Jade sends the command to her photo-printer. "And I have one more thing."

"It gets worse?" I ask.

Jade hands me a sheet of paper. "There's recent activity on Bunny Luce's credit card; one hour ago. Two plane tickets to Rio de Janeiro for Sunday, June 23. Isn't that the day after the wedding?"

* * *

We're silent on the drive to Mary Cove. Was Lucy the shy, socially inept wallflower Claren believed in? Or is it possible she's a willing participant—that the invitation, the troubling disappearance, and the pleas to show up at Chebeague are a ruse to take advantage of her father?

I ask Gordy, "Rio de Janiero? You think it's a real honeymoon destination?"

"We have to find out."

"Disturbing information. The photos. But—it's the teaser we needed."

"What are you talking about?

"To getting to the bottom of the whys and wheres and hows. Like some crossword puzzle. There's always one word—it's usually the longest one that's elusive. You can't get to the bottom of the clue, you can't figure out the letters, none of the across and down lines jibe. You get down on yourself, figure you're incapable of solving the puzzle…"

"Why are you talking about crossword puzzles?" Gordy asks.

"Then some letter falls into place and the answer feels within grasping distance—you can feel it come together, fall into place. Maybe it just needed time for the brainstorm to brew…"

"Never get too excited about hope. Things don't always come together."

"No guarantee of a happy ending," I agree. "But the tease is there."

* * *

The cantankerous guard at Mary Cove's welcome station checks to see if our names are on a list of expected visitors. He tells us to look towards the camera mounted above the window of the kiosk. A click of the photo being taken. He hands us a map of the development and circles the house where Wolff is residing.

We drive half a mile through lowlands before we come upon the first of five mini-mansions gracing wide lawns. Each is bedecked with grayed cedar shingles; all sport white shutters and blue tin roofs. We pull into the circular driveway of the third house and Abshir parks near a stone fountain featuring a mermaid with flowing hair. Gordy holds his hand up; he wants to clarify our goal before exiting the car. "Reminder: we're here to locate Lucy. Drugs, photos, assumptions about who did what to who, ethics of sharing intellectual property—everything else is secondary. Dee, are we on the same page?"

"Got it, Gordy."

"I'll take the lead." Gordy turns to Abshir. "Stick with the car, will you? Text Dee immediately if anyone goes in or comes out."

"*Dabcan*, Gordy. Yes. The rain will come soon."

The oversized front door is opened by Leon Wolff. He's in pleated linen pants and a crisp, striped, cotton shirt. High-end Sperry boat shoes are on his feet, the ones that are suede and hand-stitched—really not the kind of shoe anyone would choose to wear on a wet boat. "Mr. Greer and Miss Rommel. I expected you earlier."

Gordy grunts. "Had to make a stop on the way."

Wolff spends a moment admiring the Grand Marquis. "Vintage car. A tribute to a different generation of design."

"Yep."

"Mint condition," Wolff says.

"Almost."

"German cars are superior, of course. But America was once the king of style." Wolff waves us into the house. "I'm half through my first cocktail, you must catch up to me."

"Fancy place," notes Gordy as we enter the massive living room with floor to ceiling windows providing stunning views. The building breeze causes a rippling effect on the silver-gray waters.

"It belongs to a CEO of a company I invest in. I am fortunate he was not using it at this time and decided to do me a favor."

"Quid pro quo, I'm sure," Gordy smiles, as if they are men who perceive how the world really works.

"Always give and take," Wolff agrees. "My chef is there—that's him on the deck at the grill. He is seasoning grass-fed steaks and preparing us something very special. The clouds portend rain, but not until the steaks are cooked perfectly."

Gordy questions, "You've made a deal with the weather?"

"I like deals. Especially ones that benefit all concerned. May I offer you beer? Wine? I'm partial to whiskey sours in the summer." He picks up his glass.

"Got some water?" Gordy says.

The rasp in Gordy's throat makes me glance more closely at him; his lips look dry, his skin shines with a thin layer of sweat.

"Sparkling? Flavored?" Wolff's being the gracious host. "We also have those vitamin waters—with a slight cranberry flavor."

"Maine tap is good for me," Gordy says.

Wolff turns to me. "Miss Rommel?"

"What Gordy's having. Thanks."

At that moment, Duncan, in a pink cotton polo shirt, enters from the kitchen through double swinging doors. He carries a large wooden board; it's excessive with cheeses, nuts, olives, and crackers. He puts it on the buffet next to the dining table set for four. Wolff relays our drink preferences. Duncan nods and goes back into the kitchen.

Wolff explains, "Behold an ambitious young man. Actually, he is top salesperson in a company I invest in and this honor earned him the privilege to shadow me for an entire month. It's known throughout all my companies, that I am in constant work mode and it is good for a young man of ambition to be aware of how that plays out on a daily basis." Wolff chuckles. "Admirable, don't you think?"

"It's you." Her voice cuts through the forced pleasantries. Renae Claren has entered and is pointing at me. "She's the one who pretended she wanted Lucy to speak at her university. She came up to my table at the Westin Hotel. During my breakfast."

"Oh dear. How inconvenient." Wolff's tone is overly solicitous.

"Rude." Renae's flowing white maxi-dress is nearly see-through; there's a turquoise body stocking under it. She moves to sit next to Wolff. Her gait seems unsteady; maybe her cocktail hour started early as well.

"I agree, Renae," Gordy says. "Breakfast should be sacrosanct."

"Gordy's sarcasm," Renae snipes.

"I've always been straight with you, Renae," Gordy replies. "Haven't seen you for a while. You haven't changed."

"That's because science and beauty experts are finally making anti-aging a focus. Thank you for noticing." Renae's smile is nearly imperceptible, the muscles of her face are reluctant to move. She looks to Wolff. "Time for prosecco?"

"Duncan is bringing in libation." Wolff motions to the two chairs arranged to take in a view of the water. "Please, let's relax."

Gordy settles into a chair. I stay standing next to him.

Renae's eyes dart back to me. "Are you here to try to take advantage of Lucy again?"

Duncan enters with another tray. This one holds a stemmed glass brimming with bubbling prosecco and two crystal goblets filled with Maine tap water. He delivers the drinks and moves to the buffet table to slowly fork bites of cheese, almonds, salami, and olives onto individual plates; doing his shadow best to linger unobtrusively.

Wolff gets to the point. "Miss Rommel—I believe you inferred that Mr. Greer and his friend, Dr. Claren, had time to talk?"

"I don't think I inferred that," I say.

Gordy clears his throat. "But, as a matter fact, it's true. Phil and I did have a chance to chat. About his daughter."

"Our daughter," Renae slurs, sips her prosecco.

Gordy continues, "Phil's hoping to spend time with Lucy, before the wedding. It's reasonable. A father's last chance to be with 'his girl.'"

Renae rolls her eyes, causing her thick false eyelashes to flutter. "He wants to guilt her. He wants her back at Claren Lab."

"He might want to ask why she's marrying so quickly, without a pre-nuptial contract in place."

"There's an agreement," Renae says. "Leon helped with it."

"As a friend of Renae's, I was happy to help protect Lucy's financial status," says Wolff. "If the marriage doesn't work, there can be an official divorce and it is understood that no profits on new work completed after that, are to be shared. It's a common agreement. I told Renae that."

"I'm sure Phil would've liked to help work out the details," Gordy says.

Renae swings one thin leg over the other. "Phil wants to take hold of Lucy's energy. Forever."

Gordy's hand trembles as he reaches for a napkin to wipe his damp forehead. "I was under the impression Lucy concentrates on LC Labs and there, she has autonomy. Her own space, her own staff, her own projects."

Renae scoffs, "Phil and Lucy have been thick about the project they're doing together—ever since she was at MIT. Three years and some. I told her to cut herself loose. She told me they were done. Not to worry." Renae swings her head, her hair rearranges on her shoulder. "Doesn't matter now. She's getting married," Renae sniffs. "Her fiancé lives in New York City. She'll have her labs there. Leon has arranged it."

Gordy cocks his head towards Wolff. "You arrange a lot of things."

"It happens I own an interest in a facility there," Wolff says. "Lucy will be able to move into a very well-equipped space right away."

"Leon is generous." Renae puts her hand on Wolff's arm.

A distant sound of thunder rumbles. Wolff looks out the wall of windows. "Nature gives us warning."

"Renae, where is Lucy now?" asks Gordy. His voice is harder now, impatience evident.

"Getting ready for her big day," Renae responds smoothly.

Wolff leans in, presses Gordy. "Did you tell Dr. Claren that it's important that we talk?"

"He did wonder if you, Mr. Wolff, had any part in keeping Lucy from contacting him."

"Lucy is her own person," interjects Renae. "A mother recognizes that, Gordy. Why would Leon have anything to do with Lucy not talking to Phil? And why is this your business?"

Gordy wipes his forehead again, takes a moment to retain his calm.

Duncan delivers two small plates to the side table near Gordy's chair. I reach for an almond, pop it into my mouth, and change the subject. "Are you a birdwatcher, Mr. Wolff?"

Wolff sees me eyeing the binoculars on the window and the high-powered telescope next to them.

"New hobby," Wolff says. "Maine is quite the state for birds. And the telescope—that came with the house. I find I also enjoy taking stock of the tankers, sailboats, lobster boats, and…"

"Yachts? The yachts that go by?" I finish his sentence.

"Large and small boats," Wolff nods. "The waters are filled with all sorts of them. One can often read their registration numbers and names, and I task Duncan with the challenge to gather up the provenances. There is also an app on Duncan's phone. Yesterday a rather large vessel powered by, it's owned by someone involved in controlling capacity of one of the NFL teams in America. What team was that, Renae?"

She ignores the question, doesn't care.

"It was Atlanta something," Wolff ventures.

I press, "Is there a particular large boat—or small—that piques your interest, Mr. Wolff?"

"It's more important that we talk about arranging a meeting for Dr. Claren and myself."

Gordy leans back. "Claren is interested in a personal meet-up with Lucy. That's paramount."

"I do need to talk to him about our project."

"He didn't mention he had a project with you."

"I'm an investor in Claren Tech. We have been discussing a groundbreaking project. There is a time clock ticking on bringing it to intrigued parties. Interest can wane quickly, and one never wants to give competitors an edge."

"Some sort of AI thing?" Gordy says.

Wolff pounces, "So he did talk about it."

"Only that it's some intellectual property of Claren Tech that he felt was not quite ready for the marketplace."

"What other impression did you get?"

"As I said, we talked about his desire to see Lucy."

Wolff gets up to make himself another drink. "An idea can't be owned. It cannot be 'intellectual property.' The idea has to have taken form, the creation has to be worked out to a certain degree—has to be able to be patented or trademarked. Really, it's like any piece of property that can be bought and sold. Part of a person's portfolio. It is my belief that property should be monetized and implemented when it is of use. Getting products into the working world only serves to push the universe forward."

Renae, in her attempt to savor the last drop of her prosecco, leans her head back so it touches the back of her chair. She's disappointed, her glass is empty. She frowns. "Philip can be so precious about his work."

Wolff stays on track. "It's simply a question of who should get access, for the greater good."

"Shared for greater good or shared for a price?"

"No one should have a problem with people being rewarded for the power of their intellect. The work it takes to harness the intangibles. Hours of gathering data, cogitation, designs, experimental phases. It's all worth something."

"How do you perceive your participation in Dr. Claren's work, Mr. Wolff?" Gordy asks.

"My talent, if I may be bold to suggest, is to recognize potential. Provide resources for potential to flourish. My largesse in supporting others, who, without my financing, may never have brilliant work recognized, is, of course, worthy of reward. I take risks, therefore I should reap."

"Of course you should, Leon," says Renae.

Wolff raises his glass to Gordy. "And so should you, Mr. Greer. I am always willing to reward those who are conduits."

Gordy ignores Wolff's inference and concentrates on Renae. "Your shares of Claren Tech have made you a rich woman."

"It takes more to be rich these days," she sniffs. She holds her empty glass up. Duncan hurries over to fill it with prosecco.

Gordy doesn't take his eyes off her. "Do you know when Lucy got into drugs?"

Renae shakes off the question. "Lucy is brilliant."

"That's why it must be concerning for you."

"Lucy does not have a drug problem."

"But she *is* in the middle of a problem. Wouldn't you agree, Renae?" Gordy's voice is soft.

"You're taking liberties, Gordy. Lucy is my daughter. You sound like you have some special permission to claim a space in her life."

"I care about her," Gordy says. "That's my investment. I don't turn my back on anyone I care about."

Renae's petulant. "You never liked me."

Gordy keeps his voice low, non-confrontational. "Unfortunately, Renae, we never got to know each other well. But I know you love your daughter. So that gives you points in my book."

"You take Philip's side in everything. I told you, he only thinks of himself."

"You love Lucy," Gordy says. "You do, don't you, Renae?"

"Of course I do."

Wolff puts his glass down. "Renae's feelings for her daughter are not at issue here."

"I think they are," Gordy challenges.

Wolff stands. "This no longer feels like a social call."

"This was never a social call, Mr. Wolff," Gordy replies.

"I thought you had influence with Dr. Claren."

"Not in any way that could benefit you, Mr. Wolff," Gordy says.

"Perhaps, then, we should forego the steaks and call this meeting short."

"Don't give a shit about eating steaks with you. I want to make sure I discern Renae's feelings—about Lucy, her only daughter—before I show her some photos."

"What photos?" Wolff takes a step towards Gordy. I move to ensure there is a physical barrier between the men. Wolff hesitates; but he's not a man who fights his own physical battles.

Duncan, the silent specter at the buffet table, slips through the swinging door to the kitchen. I glance at Gordy. He shakes his head; his sign that I should hold my ground.

Ten Days

Gordy takes photos from the inside pocket of his jacket. He holds one out. It's the photo of five-year-old Lucy Claren, red hair wild in the wind, sitting on the shoulders of her father at the Grand Opening of Claren Tech. Lucy's waving, grinning, watching balloons float into the sky. "And you must have seen this young girl that day, Mr. Wolff. Since you were an early investor. Did you see this young girl, proud of her father, excited about life and envisioning the future of a technology he was promising…"

"I was there," says Wolff.

Gordy looks to Renae. "That was a good day, wasn't it, Renae?"

Renae stares at the photo. Flicks of jealousy register on her face. She'd divorced Claren by then. Her participation in the celebration would have been marginalized.

Gordy persists, "I was glad to be included—to witness his hope in endless possibilities." He passes the next photo to Renae. Peripherally, I see the one he's chosen: Lucy Claren, only weeks ago. She's naked, her eyes rolled back, her lips open, her hands groping her breasts. Large tears visible on her cheeks.

"Oh my God," Renae's face pales under her perfectly applied make-up. "Where—what is this?"

Wolff goes to Renae's side. "That's not Lucy."

"It is Lucy." She turns to Wolff. "Who took these?"

Gordy leans forward. "Why are you looking at Mr. Wolff as if he has the answer?"

Wolff's nose rises in the air. "Renae's looking at me out of friendship." Wolff puts a hand on Renae's shoulder. "The photo must be a joke. Young people play games like this. It's all pretend."

Gordy hands Renae three more photos. "These are not pretend, Renae. Note your daughter's glazed, half-closed eyes. Her mouth is slack. Her body is slumped. See how lax her muscles are? Lucy is drugged. She's clueless. She is either under the influence by choice, or she was a victim of others' bad intents."

Renae's whine is thin, angry. "I don't want to envision my daughter like this."

"You can perceive the danger inherent in these photos—if they get into the wrong hands," Gordy warns. "If any sort of media finds them—her work at LC Labs could be compromised. Claren Tech has already had a setback with questionable attacks on Phil's character. Stock prices don't like scandal."

"Those allegations had no traction," Wolff says.

"Do you know how they started, Mr. Wolff? Or how the traction was lost?" Gordy turns to Renae. "Think about your daughter's life, how it could be affected, in a very harmful way, throughout the years ahead of her."

Wolff waves this off. "Mr. Greer, you are not in the high-tech game. There could be short-term consequences if a scandal hits the media. A Board might have to make decisions to save face. However, when things settle down, the needed, desired, appreciated person—whoever that might be—can be strategically reinstated. It's done all the time."

"Renae," Gordy says. "Where's Lucy?"

It's as if Renae's false lashes have become too burdensome to lift off her eyes. Her lipstick-ed mouth is downturned—clear defiance of her latest Botox treatment.

Gordy offers another group of photos. Renae shakes herself, as if she does not want to escape this moment. She accepts them gingerly, with the tips of her manicured nails.

"But what about Lucy?" I ask. "If she's been taken advantage of, can she ever resurrect faith in humankind, in herself? In her mother?"

Wolff turns on me, eyes afire. "Don't be maudlin. Americans can be so maudlin."

Renae's up, her arm sweeps across her, the photos frisbee through the air and land on the polished floors.

Wolff cajoles, "Renae, whatever this is—it can be fixed."

She half-runs out of the room, unsteady in her high heels.

Wolff's voice is steely. "What do you think you've accomplished here, Mr. Greer?"

Gordy moans as he stands. "I saw what I needed. The truth of what Renae knows."

"What other 'truth'—that you can prove?"

Gordy's voice is soft, but has an edge. "Do you know Lucy's location, Mr. Wolff?"

"No."

Gordy presses. "Because you refuse to know 'specifics'? Makes it easier for you to distance yourself?"

"Please, show yourself out. I should go to Mrs. Claren."

CHAPTER THIRTY-THREE
Monday

The hefty doors of the Grand Marquis close; it's as if we're being sealed into an airless tomb. "Gordy, I must tell you something that I did without your permission," says Abshir.

"What?" asks Gordy.

"A blond man with a beard, perhaps 30 and some years old, he wears a pink shirt, hurried out the back door and jogged quite fast to a white Honda car parked over there." Abshir points to a parking area on the side of the house. "Here is the license plate of the car." He hands Gordy a piece of paper torn from one of his college notebooks. "But it looked, to me, as if the car were a rental, so that, perhaps, would be difficult to trace to the driver quickly…" Abshir puts the massive car into gear and we turn from Wolff's driveway onto the road.

"We know who the driver in the pink shirt is," I say, wanting Abshir to get to the core of his story.

"I hurried over, and as he was putting a bag in the trunk, I asked if he knew the closest place for me to get gas. I was lying, I did fill up the Marquis' tank at the car wash, but it was the first thing I could think of. He told me to fuck off and get my black ass out of his face. As the pink-shirted man got into the driver's seat and as the trunk was in automatic close mode, I dropped my G&Z business cell phone inside the trunk compartment."

Gordy gives a grunt of appreciation.

"If it is necessary to find out where the person in the pink shirt is going," Abshir continues, "the GPS on that phone is activated and I can track it with my personal phone." He's already got the system activated. He hands me the phone; the marker is moving on the screen's map. "At this point, the white Honda is passing the guard house…"

"Keep following him and don't be shy on the gas," says Gordy.

"He's got to be going to Peppard," I suggest. "And Peppard's keeping a close hold on Lucy."

"Abshir," Gordy says. "I like the way you think ahead."

"It is always necessary, my family taught me that when I was very young." Abshir accelerates on the road.

Gordy shoots back at me, "See if Jade can get on it, too."

I call Jade, give her the details. She tells me how to share our screens, so she can connect to the phone. The tracking shows Duncan's car getting off at Exit 7. This leads of Highway I-95 to Route 1 and that leads into the small village of York, the second oldest town in Maine. He's at least ten miles ahead of us.

The sky has darkened and large droplets of rain splat onto the Grand Marquis' windshield. Gordy turns to face me, reaches his hand out. "Give me another one of those water bottles. Can't seem to get enough water." I give him the bottle; he chugs half of it.

Ten minutes later, the clouds have opened and we're in a downpour, surrounded by tourist traffic on the main street in York. The wind has kicked up, gusts of wet drench the pedestrians crossing streets, running into restaurants and stores for cover, creating more havoc.

The GPS shows the Honda somewhere nearby—but it's impossible to pinpoint the exact location.

"We followed Duncan to York, we're in the village area," I tell Jade, who has stayed connected to us on speaker. "There's a pile-up at a stoplight that's gone out. The traffic cop's slow and indecisive."

Abshir, frustrated, taps his finger on the steering wheel. The heavy windshield wipers produce a swish and click on every sweep.

Gordy finishes the water in the bottle. "If he's meeting this Peppard, where would they be holed up?"

Jade must have a view of the village up on one of her computers. "There're a couple dozen hotels and motels in the main area. Wait. This is something. 'M.O.H.'"

"What? That's the hotel in New York City, we're in York, Maine."

"M.O.H., York," Jade responds. "Opened a month ago, part of the boutique line."

Gordy nods at me. It's worth a try. "Got an address?"

I search for it on my phone. "Found. We're a block from it." Traffic's not moving. I hop out of the car and am immediately drenched as I stride down the street, not bothering to skirt the quickly forming puddles. My thick hair hangs heavy, its saturated wetness drips and soaks my shirt. I get to the corner of the block; there's the canvas awning: M.O.H. York Boutique Hotel. The white Honda's in the alleyway, to the side of the hotel. I approach and concentrate on a tall twenty-something valet in a white shirt, checked blue and lavender bow-tie and black khaki shorts. He's got on a thin rain jacket that fits tightly over buffed pecs and abs. He holds the alley-side door open for a patron and then races to the man's blue Mercedes and gets the car door, allowing the guest to quickly get inside and ward off a long connection with the rain. He accepts his tip and folds the bill into his already-large stash as he walks towards the awning and me. My cover story is lame, but I aim for sincere. "That's Murphy Duncan's car, right?" I pant. "Supposed to meet him here, I'm a little late, we're going to this thing together…"

The valet smiles; his teeth are startling white. "No worries, didn't leave without you. Said he'd be five minutes, might be coming down the alley exit, to be closer to his car."

"That's a relief. Did he seem hassled? Maybe I should go up and help him with the…presents we're bringing to the party. Big boxes." I'm scrambling, trying to sound plausible. "I forget his room number…"

"Like to help, ahm…" The valet takes his time, finishes folding his tip into his wad of money. I get the hint and offer him a ten-dollar bill. He immediately recalls my request. "Oh, right, that room number."

The sliding door at the top of the three broad steps that grace the front of the hotel, is now opening.

"No need for it now," says the valet. "There he is. Guess he decided to take the front door…"

Duncan's at the top of the steps. Tyler Peppard, in black t-shirt, jeans, and metal-toed boots is beside him. They both carry large duffel bags. The valet is way too helpful. "Mr. Duncan, your friend is here."

I'm in their eyesight, and they are not pleased to see me. Duncan holds out a twenty-dollar bill and his room keycard. "We're out of here. Need my car, under the awning, so we don't get wet."

The hunky valet takes the money and keycard and hurries to the locked cabinet, punches in the code. "Right away."

I stay at the bottom of the steps, feel the rivulets of water drip from my hair and down my back. "Where's Lucy?"

Peppard smirks, "She's not feeling like having fun tonight."

"Where is she?"

"Lucy's kind-of famous and has the habit of not making a big deal or announcement of her comings and goings, because there's always someone around to take an unflattering picture, isn't there?"

Ten Days

"Where is she?"

"Wouldn't want to tell you anything without her permission. Kind-of famous people get their noses out of joint about things like that."

"Hey, you," Duncan grumbles at the valet. "Need my car."

"Got it! Found the key. One second…"

Duncan moves back to the hotel's sliding door. "Left my glasses at the concierge's counter." He slaps Peppard's shoulder. "Ignore her. Nothing's going to happen." The door slides shut behind him.

I take a leap because I'm pissed and feel I'm running out of time. "Little careless about what you left behind at Brad Hogan's house, Tyler. I have a few pictures of you in not very flattering positions."

"Bullshit."

There's a crack of thunder. A gust of wind lifts the awning, it nearly breaks off from its supports. I wave a copy of one of the printed photos in the air. "If you study it closely, that tattoo on your butt cheek is clear. Isn't your daughter's name 'May'?"

He snarls. "Fuck off…"

"Cute name for a little girl born on the first of May. You must have cared about her at some point. You think little May would be proud of what her daddy's up to?"

He's two steps above me and he kicks forward; the sharp metal toe of his boot connects with my wrist. I can feel the skin tear, the bone bruise. "Yeow, shit!" I yelp.

The photo falls to the ground, lands in a puddle.

"You won't use that." Peppard's face is contorted in anger; his dark handsome look is gone. "It'd ruin Lucy Claren."

"Lucy can decide what she wants to use when she presses charges."

"She won't."

"I had a chance to share some of the photos with Lucy's mother, who is staying with Mr. Wolff. She wasn't pleased. As a matter of fact, Wolff was also interested in the photos of one of his company's employees…"

There's a twitch of nerves. "Wolff won't do anything…"

"Are you saying that because Wolff knew what you were doing? Drugging Lucy and posing her?"

Peppard picks up his duffel. The valet's backing the Honda out of the alley and maneuvering it into place under the awning.

I don't have much more time. "You and Duncan have a little side business in the Destiny Leader offices."

Peppard wrenches his head around to look back into the hotel, hoping Duncan's found his glasses and is on his way out.

"Providing drugs to fellow employees and taking photos documenting out-of-character, lewd, and questionable behavior must be lucrative," I observe. "If anyone looked closely, they could see you were always in the right place for bonuses and promotions."

"You're pitiful," he spits, dismissive. "No idea what you're on about."

"I'm pitiful?"

He sneers at my dripping hair, my soaked shirt and jeans. "Look at your reflection in the glass. See what you look like."

I'm not ready, I know that truth a moment too late. He kicks again and the steel toe gets me under my chin. My head snaps back and my blood spatters into the air; there's an immediate metallic taste of adrenalin in my mouth.

I stumble back and slam into the valet, who is getting out of the Honda, and surprised to have a body falling into him. "Geez, what happened?" he shouts. "You're bleeding…"

Duncan's hurrying out of the sliding doors; he pushes Peppard forward. "Tyler—what the hell? Get in the car." Peppard's light on his feet, quickly gets into the passenger seat. Duncan shoves the valet, who is holding onto me. "Get outta the way, asshole, out of the way." Duncan slides into the car, puts the car into gear and the Honda speeds off.

The valet's slow on processing. "What's going on? What happened?" He leans me against the cabinet that holds the keys and grabs a small towel. He forms it against my chin, the white towel turns crimson in moments. "What do you want me to do? This wasn't my fault, was it? Am I gonna get blamed for something? What should I do?"

"Give me that key card." I wipe the blood that drips from my mouth. "And the room number."

CHAPTER THIRTY-FOUR
Monday

The suite's on the fifth floor, at the end of the hallway. I hold the towel to my chin, ignore the bloodstains on my shirt. My wet jeans feel heavier with each step. Peppard and Duncan have given up their oversight role so easily. Will Lucy be in the room?

The keycard unlocks the door. I enter, the lights are off. The furniture in the living room resembles overstuffed shadows. The rain pounds against the windows.

"Lucy?" I call out. No response.

I turn on a table lamp. I'm dripping on the thick, beige carpet. "Lucy?" I enter the bedroom through the open doorway. The bed is tossed, sheets crumpled on the floor. I turn on another light, it bounces off the dark gray walls.

I push the bathroom door open. The faucets, set on the thick marble vanity, gleam. I find the light switch on the wall. And see her. Lucy, small and immobile, is in the bathtub. The water laps at her lips. Her eyes are closed. "Lucy. Lucy!" Her naked skin is pasty white, her head is slumped forward, her chin nearly on her chest. I can't help but think how easily she could've slipped down an inch below the water. And drowned. No one would have found her until the maid arrived in the morning. I bend over, grab her under her arms, pull her towards me. "Lucy. Can you hear me?" Her head slumps against my shoulder and her eyes flutter open for a moment.

I lift her, hope her ninety pounds won't tip me over. I step back and her legs trail over the lip of the porcelain tub. I have to lean against the wall to make sure my balance doesn't desert me. I'm finally able to lay her out on the bathmat.

Lucy makes a sound like a stunned, wounded creature, plaintive and mournful.

I call Gordy; my voice sounds breathless. "I have Lucy. Peppard and Duncan are gone. Where are you?"

"Outside the hotel…"

"She's passed out, don't know what's in her system. Doctor needs to look at her."

"Don't want to call any attention here. Is there a back way out?"

"Stairway is across the hall from the room. I'm on the fifth floor…"

"There's got to be a rear entrance…"

"In the alley. Saw it."

"We'll get the car there. Can you get her downstairs?"

"I can get her dressed. But don't trust that I can get her down five flights of stairs."

"Abshir can come up."

"He'd need a keycard to come up the elevator. The valet's in front, the Baywatch lifeguard type—lots of abs under his rain jacket. He might have a bit of my blood on him…"

"What?"

"If he's there, give him fifty bucks to get Abshir in the alley door. He responds to tips."

"Be ready in five," Gordy says.

I click off, grab the dress that's been tossed into a heap at the base of the tub. Lucy moans, as if her brain cells are crawling back towards consciousness. I sit on the edge of the tub. "Lucy, my name is Dee Rommel. I'm Gordy Greer's friend—he's a friend of your father's…"

"Gordy…"

"He's downstairs, in a car. To take you someplace safe."

"Don't want Gordy to see me."

"He cares about you. Your dad cares about you. I'm going to get you into this dress, and we're leaving the hotel. Can you sit up a little?"

"Tell my dad…. Chebeague. That I tried…"

I get Lucy's dress over her head, it covers her thin body. I help her to her feet. My jaw and wrist are now throbbing, but adrenalin keeps me focused. We move out of the room just as the stairway door opens. Abshir's there. "We can put her between us," I say.

Abshir quickly calculates Lucy's size and weight and announces it'll be easier if he, alone, carries her down the four flights of stairs. "It will be safer, you do not look so good."

I agree.

* * *

It's past midnight; the downpour's become a drizzle. The city's in a post-storm pause. Gordy and I wait for Hilary at the water taxi dock; she's getting out of an Uber, wearing a hooded raincoat tossed over her hospital workpants and a light sweater. A rainproof carry-all is over her shoulder.

"Thanks for coming, Hilary," I say.

"What happened to you?" Her eyes are on my chin.

"Someone didn't like me asking questions." I was lucky I'd fished an old rain poncho out of the Grand Marquis' trunk and she couldn't get a load of the bloodstains on my shirt. "You can look at it on the boat. We're in a hurry."

I've shared some information, but Hilary's face registers the thousand questions. "Just to let you know," she says, "I've worked with Dr. Julian Gil at the hospital a few times. Highest caliber."

"Expect no less from Claren."

"Claren? As in…"

"His daughter needs medical attention. Dr. Gil—and two security guards—are already in the taxi. He asked if she'd thrown up. I told him 'no.' He took her temperature, muttered something…"

"I'll get the information from Dr. Gil." Hilary heads down the dock to the boat.

I linger with Gordy one more moment. He's not happy that Claren had informed Dr. Gil about Gordy's recent surgery and that Gil had made a medical decision: Gordy was not to be allowed on the water taxi. Gordy had sputtered, insisted that he accompany Lucy. Gil made it clear that, as the doctor, he needed to focus on Lucy—and the chance that Gordy could make that problematical was not attractive to him. Gordy had barked a question: did he look that bad? I told him that yes, he looked worse than roadkill, like a critter that'd been flattened, pissed on, and kicked into a ditch. He'd sputtered again that he was the one who called in the favor, got Antonio out of bed, and arranged the taxi transport out to Claren's yacht. "And that's your last job for the night," I told him. Finally, he went to sit inside the Grand Marquis.

Now I turn to Abshir, "Make sure Gordy gets home—that Marie's there to get him to bed."

"Got it. *Haa.*"

"I'll call you with updates." I hurry to Antonio's water taxi.

* * *

By two o'clock in the morning, Lucy has been settled into one of the Sunseeker's state rooms, with Dr. Gil administering care. Hilary is with them; Gil wants her taking notes and recording instructions. The short, beefy bodyguards are in the bow, sipping hot coffees.

Claren, a clean-shaven Hogan, and I are in the yacht's salon. My chin has been bandaged and a painkiller administered. Antonio's headed back to Portland because Claren insisted I spend the night on the yacht. I'm wrapped in a blanket because my clothes are damp, a nearby heat lamp has already nearly dried my hair and I have a hot toddy in hand. Claren sits next to me. "Since Dr. Gil—Julian—has given Lucy a mild sedative, we'll leave off getting any answers tonight."

"Makes sense."

"Julian doesn't want to push anything." Claren's frazzled. Relief, worry, guilt—all are etched on his face. He swallows a large drag of whiskey. "I don't want to think of what could have happened—if you hadn't found her."

"She's here now. With you."

"Yeah." He empties his glass. Millions of questions must be swimming in his brain, but it's as if he doesn't know where to start. "She looks so frail. Fragile."

I broach the delicate subject. "There are circumstances—details—that Lucy may have trouble sharing with you. We're not sure how things went down, how things played out. What was done to her, or what she was involved in."

Claren runs his freckled hand through his untamed hair. "I should've protected her."

"She did mention Chebeague to me. That 'she tried.'"

"Tried what?"

"I don't know."

Claren looks to Hogan. "Do you?"

Hogan's face is a pained mask; his scar seems more prominent. He smooths his dark hair back off his face. "No. I'll clear my stuff out of the lab as soon as we get back, Dr. Claren. You'll have my resignation."

"I can't accept it. You work at LC Labs, with Lucy," Claren says. "You'll have to wait until Lucy's able to discuss things."

It's an hour before dawn when I enter my state room. Two rubber-tipped walking sticks lean against the full-size bed. The private bathroom in the cabin is as large as the one in my apartment. The drawers have safety clip locks, I release them and find a packaged toothbrush, toothpaste, sunscreen, facial wipes, hairbrush, a manicure set, and an array of other offerings for the unprepared guest. I doff my LiteGood, grab the walking sticks, and take advantage of the shower. Minutes later, I ease back onto the freshly ironed pillowcase and pull cool sheets over my body.

Sleep comes quickly.

FOUR DAYS

CHAPTER THIRTY-FIVE
Tuesday

The sound of lapping water soothes me as I rise from sleep to groggy wakefulness. Soft footfalls move by in the passageway. Muted conversations. I grab the walking sticks, half-hop to the curtains on the bull's eye windows, and pull them back. The sun is high. Amazed, I check the time on my cell, it's mid-day. I grab my clothes, they're dry, but feel stiff. My wrist and chin ache, but I'm ready to join the world in record time.

Claren and Hogan sit in the salon, their heads close together, deep in conversation. When they hear my approach, Hogan looks perturbed, wheels himself portside. The dark circles are deeper under Claren's eyes.

"Coastline has changed. Where are we?" I ask.

"Moved northeast. I didn't want to stay in one place."

"You think someone's looking for you?"

"Privacy is a wonderful thing. I never take it for granted." He hands me a cup of coffee.

"Have you been able to talk to Lucy?"

"Just to make sure she knows she's with me. Doc Gil thinks she'll sleep off the sedative in an hour or so."

My phone pings. It's a text from Jade, asking me to call. I excuse myself and head to the starboard passageway and punch in her number. "It's Dee. We're on Claren's yacht. We found Lucy last night, in bad shape, but she's here now. With her father."

"What story does she tell?" Jade asks.

"Hasn't talked to any of us yet."

Jade continues, "Sorry this is late news, my system must have stalled during the storm last night. The tickets to Rio de Janeiro for the flight on Sunday I told you about?"

"Bought on Lucy's credit card."

"Right. The tickets, issued to Peppard, were exchanged for a flight that took off last night from Boston Logan. Duncan's registered on the second ticket. It's already made its connection in Houston. Should land in Sao Paulo Guarulhos International in about four hours. Are there any arrangements that should be made with authorities there?"

"Hold on."

I share the information with Claren. He takes a moment and then shakes his head. "I don't want to take a chance on alerting any media. There'll be time, later, to take care of them."

For the first time, I hear a determined coldness in his voice. I have no doubt that, when the time is right, money and connections will be used to make sure Peppard and Duncan face consequences.

I relay Claren's wishes, tell Jade that no action will be taken at this time, but to keep me informed about the flight. Claren may be able to shake off a penchant for immediate revenge, but I want to be in the loop. And Gordy will want the information. I connect with him on his cell. "Afternoon, boss."

"How come you're not answering your phone?"

"It was a big day yesterday and sleep won out."

He grunts.

"How are you feeling?"

"Marie's got me sitting on the porch, a blanket over my lap." Gordy doesn't want to chitchat. "What's Claren doing?"

"The doc gave Lucy a sleep-enhancer. She's still in dreamland. Claren's waiting to talk to her. Doesn't look like he slept at all. Hogan's as creased and buttoned-up as usual, but he looks haunted. He talking about resigning from LC Labs, but Claren told him he can't accept that decision, the LC Labs is Lucy's domain."

"What else?"

I tell him about Jade's latest message and Claren's decision not to try waylaying Peppard and Duncan at the airport in Brazil. "The shits will probably be eating barbecue and chimichurri in a few hours."

Dr. Gil's coming out of Lucy's state room, I tell Gordy I'll call him back if there's anything he needs to know.

Claren meets Gil in the passageway to ask questions; he nods a few times, then shakes Gil's hand. They join us. An attending crewmember hands Gil a plate, it's got a chicken sandwich on it. Gil thanks the crewmember and turns to Claren. "Hilary has agreed to stay on. She's an excellent nurse and has managed to clear her schedule. I'll stay in touch with her, on the hour, until she feels Lucy is properly stabilized."

"Thanks, Julian."

"I'll have to get back to Portland."

"Of course," Claren says. "The first mate will get the tender ready."

"Whatever you need, Phil. Whenever. I'll collect my bag." Gil, finishing his sandwich, moves off.

The Sunseeker's support boat is a 37-foot Axopar, a boat designed in Finland that can move smoothly through choppy waters at over 40 miles an hour. Dr. Gil joins two crewmembers and the tender quickly motors off just as Hilary steps down the passageway and advises us that Lucy wants to talk to her father. Claren straightens, hurries towards the stateroom. Hilary touches my arm. "She'd like you to join him, Dee."

The uninvited Hogan is at the portside railing. His shoulders are stiff, he's concentrating his gaze on the water.

* * *

The state room is twice the size of mine. It's actually a suite, in addition to the bedroom, there's a sitting area, with a desk and computer set up, and large windows that provide an ocean view. Lucy's in the bed, she looks miniscule; it's not only her thin body, but her entire demeanor.

"Bunny." Claren sits, gently, on the bed.

"They won't ruin everything, Daddy." She takes his hand. "I'm sorry I was imbecilic. Ludicrous."

He's gentle. "Trust is tricky, Bunny. Naturally, we want to believe the best of people. Mistakes can be made—understandable mistakes."

"Daddy. I was idiotic. A sucker."

He interrupts, soothes her. "I understand how it happens—from experience."

I wonder how many times he'd trusted that someone was interested in him—and not his money or his connections.

Claren leans in so she can connect with his eyes. "What we rely on is each other. Trust that."

Lucy blows out a deep breath of air, as if she wants to expel her gullibility and recent past. She looks to me in the corner of the room. "What did you tell him?"

"Your father knows I found a flash drive, taped to the back of a drawer in the room Peppard was using at Hogan's house. That we had someone access the files on the drive and found photos."

"I haven't seen them, Bunny," Claren tells her. "I don't want to see them."

Lucy's jaw tightens. "They're smutty. I'm high, I'm drugged. I was scared…"

"You can't blame yourself…"

"Yes, I can. And I do. I shouldn't have been drawn in. When they showed the photos to me, I puked. Nauseating images. Claren Tech—the work could lose respect. End up disregarded."

"Lucy," I ask. "Were you being blackmailed?"

Tears brim in her eyes and drop down onto her cheeks. "It happened because of my own neediness."

There's a knock on the door. "Dr. Claren, it's the Captain. Sorry to interrupt, you have a call from Washington."

Claren hesitates.

"Go ahead, Daddy."

Claren gets up. "I'll be back in a few minutes."

She grabs his hand. "I have 'it.'"

Claren kisses Lucy's forehead and hurries out.

He leaves the state room. Lucy wipes the tears from her cheeks. "You saved my life."

"Don't be so sure you were going to give up."

"I did have a thought—that self-immolation—slipping under the water in the tub—would solve a lot of things."

"No. Would not have been true."

"I thought anything would be better than seeing the disappointment on my father's face."

"Dads can be special. They see deep—beyond the mistakes."

Lucy squeezes her eyes shut. Blows out another gulp of air.

I move to a chair near the bed. "Your dad told Gordy and I a bit about this pressure he's been getting to share—or sell—the work you collaborated on with him."

"And Hogan."

"Hogan's part of the project?"

"Working together was productive. Synergistic." She stops. "And then it wasn't."

"You trust him?"

She looks at me, her eyes huge. "Hogan? Shouldn't I?" She clenches her hands tighter.

"How did you meet Peppard?" I ask.

"Hogan introduced us."

"What?" Is Hogan, with his military background, aligned with Wolff—and thus with Peppard and Duncan?

"Tell me about Hogan."

"When I got to NYC and worked at Columbia," Lucy's face brightened, then clouded. "I was still the oddity. Didn't matter that I was twenty-one, same age or younger than most of them—that I'd prepped by watching popular shows—*Bachelorette, Survivor, Mr. Pickles, Robot Chicken*, so I could have conversations outside of the lab." Her laugh holds no joy. "Didn't work out so great. But Brad—everyone calls him Hogan—he'd just finished his doctorate and asked to assist in my lab because I was working on bio-memory and myoelectrics. We were interested in similar mechanics and joined forces on a project."

"The one you presented in Miami?"

"At the Festival of Ideas. We were awarded a prize, it was validation of the work. I invited him to pursue his interests at LC Labs. He was willing to relocate, make the commitment." Insecurity creeps into her voice. "We were asked to present our paper at this big conference in Philadelphia. After the final conference meeting, Hogan asked if I wanted to go out to this club near the hotel. To celebrate. I even got dressed up. We were sitting at a table, watching people dance. The staff was setting up karaoke. We joked about how most scientists suck at karaoke. I said I'd never tried it but I was probably terrible. Hogan went to get us another drink and when he came back, he said that someone at the bar had noticed me, thought I was pretty. I figured he was kidding."

"This person was Peppard?"

"Hogan joked that he told the guy to buzz off. But it turned out Tyler had followed him back to the table. He sat down with us, introduced himself. Tyler was funny, said he liked the sweater I was wearing, made me laugh…"

"Peppard horned in on your date?"

"It wasn't really a date, it was casual…"

"What did Hogan do?"

"We both let Tyler go on talking. About music, about art, about living in New York. He said he was in town on work too, talked about working on the Destiny Leader account, his responsibilities. He was really charming. Then Tyler asked me to dance. I said 'no' but Hogan said go ahead—that he had to use the bathroom and he went off. Tyler pulled me up onto the floor and we danced…"

"Until Hogan came back?"

"Hogan never came back to the table. He'd left." Lucy ducks her head. Had she felt abandoned? "I mean, of course, Hogan could split; like I said, it wasn't like we were on a date."

"You kept dancing…"

Ten Days

"And drinking. I was embarrassed and angry—that Hogan didn't even tell me he was leaving. But Tyler was attentive—and he had these pills. He was handing them out to everyone. People were happy, having a good time. Finally, I took one too. The next morning, I woke up in his hotel room. I didn't remember getting there, what happened the rest of the night. Tyler was making coffee—told me we kissed and messed around but since I was drunk—and high—he didn't want to take advantage even though I begged him to have sex with me."

"Do you recall that?"

She shakes her head. "No. I just wanted—needed—to get back to New York, I was giving a lecture that night. He said he was heading to the city too; we went to the station together."

"Where was Hogan?"

Lucy frowns. "We'd planned on taking an earlier train together, but I'd slept through it. So Tyler got me a ticket on the train he was taking. And when I got back to Columbia, Hogan didn't show up for my lecture. I was so mad—but I had no right to feel that way. It was his choice. It wasn't an official date."

"Maybe Hogan thought it was."

She looks surprised. "He could've said so."

"Then what happened?"

Lucy puts her head into her hands as if realizing her insecurities and desire had put her in this position. "After the lecture, I went to my university office and Tyler was waiting for me. Invited me out for a glass of wine." She sighs. "Very attentive. Hadn't heard anything about my work and I thought, 'good.' A person who doesn't know what my father does…"

There's a tap on the door. "It's Hilary."

I look to Lucy, she nods. "Come in," I say.

Hilary enters, comes to the side of the bed. She quickly moves the wand thermometer across Lucy's forehead. Feels her pulse. "Do you feel hungry, Lucy? The chef's preparing broth and toast."

"I don't want to eat…"

"Dr. Gil recommends it. So, we should try."

I tease, "Is that the royal 'we'?"

Hilary raises an eyebrow. "I know I'll feel better if Lucy eats."

Lucy emits a light laugh. "How long have you two known each other?"

"We've been neighbors for—two and a half years? Is that right, Hilary?"

Hilary's busy recording Lucy's vitals. "Almost three. Dee, you'd just gotten out of the Police Academy and I was halfway through nursing school."

I nod. "We lucked into the smallest apartments on Eastern Promenade."

"Munjoy Hill, where my Dad grew up." Lucy's voice gets softer. "Near Gordy. I like it there…"

Hilary takes in Lucy's slumping shoulders, her fading words. "Would you like to take a rest?"

"No… No."

"I'll get the broth." Hilary leaves us.

We sit quietly. Finally, Lucy mumbles, "You're older than me."

"Couple years, yeah."

She grimaces, looks up at the ceiling. "When do you get to feel—an ease—a contentment about yourself? I keep waiting for that."

It's a question that's familiar to me, but I don't think I ever actually put it into words. "Maybe that feeling's meant to ebb and flow? Somedays it looks more accessible than others?"

"That's not fair."

I chuckle. "No."

"When I'm engrossed in a project, I can experience an equanimity that sticks…" She exhales another large gulp of air. "When Hogan and I landed on the new code that accelerated our blueprint on the Near Future presentation, that was an exceptional day. Lasted a week. Almost a month. Doing something together—that felt extra special. And then we weren't talking, and things didn't feel as satisfying." She sighs, goes from heart to head and adds sarcasm. "So, looking at it as if it were a formula: work alone is not as gratifying as work shared."

"Okay. If those are your findings. You're the genius."

She remains in self-deprecation. "Could've learned that on Dr. Phil or the New England Patriots' handbook."

"Life as a team sport."

"Exactly."

I let the moment hang. Then, "Lucy, when did you meet Murphy Duncan?"

Lucy frowns. "Guess it was when Tyler and I had our first official date—he asked me to the ballet and a nice dinner. Duncan drove the car, joked that he was our chauffeur."

"When were the photos taken?"

"A few weeks after that, Tyler invited me to his place. He told me he lived in a hotel suite in the village because he liked maid service and his company paid for it. Seemed proud to show it off. Gullible me. I was flattered. Not happy, but I didn't focus on that. Flattered. Stupid. That first night, when I'd taken one of the pills that Tyler was handing out—I felt this crazy wild abandon. And this confidence that I was desirable. At his hotel suite, he offered me another, turned on the music, we danced and—the rest of the night I can't recall." Tears fill her eyes. "They showed me the photos they took of me about a week later. Said they'd be on media sites if I didn't agree to an engagement. Said if we were married, Tyler wouldn't want them to come out because he wouldn't want to take down the latest work of LC Labs and Claren Tech. His profit-sharing would be at stake."

"You told him what you and your dad were working on?"

"No, don't think so. He knew. Somehow." Her hands scrunch into fists. "Everything my dad had worked for. But I wasn't going to let them ruin everything."

"Your mother—Renae. She saw the photos."

Hurt is mapped on Lucy's face. "My mother knew?"

"When we showed them to her—she was pretty incensed. Pretty sure she didn't know about them."

"She knew Tyler wanted to be engaged. Called me the next day; Mr. Wolff had told her. She was all about wedding plans. There must have been cash involved."

"Why do you say that?"

"My mother never has enough money." She sighs. "She doesn't really have anything else—and she needs money for her distractions." I realize Lucy feels sorry for Renae. "I wasn't the daughter she wanted. Dad and I—we had more in common."

"Leon Wolff got involved, in some marriage contract?"

"My mom insisted on the contract, said I could trust Mr. Wolff. He's been around Claren Tech since the beginning. I didn't know him, but I'd seen him. I just wanted to get it over with."

"Why didn't you call your father?"

"I wanted to make my stupidity disappear."

"But you sent him the note. 'Chebeague.' Your cryptogram."

"Just in case."

"In case of what?" I ask.

She doesn't give me an answer. I can hear Gordy's edict, that the whys and wherefores are not part of our job, but my curiosity wants to be satiated. I want Peppard and Duncan to pay for abusing Lucy. I want Renae to question herself when she looks in the mirror. I want to know if Wolff hatched the plan to compromise Lucy or if greedy Peppard and Duncan were the instigators. "In case of what, Lucy?"

"I wanted to take care of it myself. I'd ask for pills and then hide them—and act sleepy so—at Hogan's—Tyler'd leave me alone. I offered him money for the photos, but the wedding was all he talked about."

Claren could be back at any moment, he could shut down the discussion. "What about the break-in, at LC Labs," I ask. "Who broke in?"

She furrows her brow. "I heard about the break-in from Hogan. When I went to stay with him. That someone used my fob to get in."

"Where did you keep it?"

"Inside a compartment in my work bag. It's not labeled. Someone would have to know what it was for."

"Peppard? Duncan? Plenty of opportunity to rifle through your work bag when you were out of it."

"They didn't find what they were looking for."

"Which is?" I ask.

"It's safe." She closes her eyes, her mouth tightens.

"What's safe? What's 'it'?"

"My father understands."

"And Hogan? He's on deck, not sure if he should be here or not."

Her voice becomes even smaller, breathless. "Hogan is here?"

There's a soft rap on the door and Claren slips in; he carries a small dinner tray. "I told Hilary I'd deliver this."

"Daddy. Hogan's on the boat?"

Claren puts the tray down on the table. "He is. Wonders if you want him to resign."

"Does he want to resign?"

"You'll have to ask him." Claren turns to me. "Miss Rommel, your dinner is on the deck. And could you, please, ask Hogan to join Lucy and me?"

* * *

Hours later, the waters are absolutely calm. In the far distance, a super freighter, its night lights the size of pinpricks, glides by, heading south. Goods from Canada? Timber, maybe? Claren's yacht is positioned off Boothbay Harbor; it feels far from Portland, especially because the clouds cover the moon, and the darkness is thick. Claren, Lucy, and Hogan have been sequestered together since dinner and I have the second-tier deck of the boat to myself. My conversation with Lucy plays in my head. I wonder if ease—or contentment—is reachable.

Has it ever been within my grasp?

Not when I watched my parents grow apart. Not when I decided on the Academy, full of a desire to balance the scales of justice. Huh. I'm ducking behind lofty ideals, giving myself more credit than I deserve.

My unease is really more personal. And I'm a coward to hide behind idealism, thinking my only goal is to help promote a fair and just world.

Ten Days

Take a closer look, Dee, I tell myself. Stop screwing around. Be honest.

My discontent. It's directly due to my thwarted hopes and visions for myself and how, after one night on top of a building where I thought I'd secure a very large feather in my cap and move up the ladder in my superiors' estimation by bringing in men who robbed an old man and murdered a young boy? The night I looked straight into failure. And permanent injury. And a loss of confidence in my own body and its capabilities. And lost a solid sense of where I could fit into those prior ambitions.

Accomplishing Claren's ask—getting him together with Lucy—is one thing. Being kept out of the bigger picture—the larger problem—smacks me back and I feel like a kid whose hand is deemed too big to fit into the candy jar. Something very important is out of reach, I'm not allowed involvement in it—and my desire to feel vindication, for a correction of wrongs—creates a very strong itch. I can't reach it.

What have I been able to do for Karla? Billy Payer's out there, ready to create more chaos.

What would my father tell me? "Dee, everything in life is a challenge. Get your nose in there. Don't back down."

Hilary's coming up the ladder-stairs behind me. "Can I join you?"

"Sure."

With characteristic quiet gentleness, she takes the lounge chair next to me. We watch the clouds as the wind picks up. They're moving fast.

"They're still talking down there?" I ask.

"Door's shut. Big doings, I guess." She leans back. "Nice to be where it's beautiful. Isn't it?"

I can't allow myself to relish the beauty. My brain won't rest. But I won't ruin Hilary's ability to take this opportunity for appreciation.

"Yeah. Beautiful," I say.

THREE DAYS

CHAPTER THIRTY-SIX
Wednesday

It's morning. I sit in the protected cabin of the Axopar. The winds are blowing, the water's choppy and the salt spray hits the windows. There's a blanket next to me on the seat and I pull it across my shoulders.

Claren had walked me to the tender, told the first mate to take me back to Portland. He thanked me again. "For getting Lucy back to me. You did what I asked."

The echo of Gordy's words reminds me our job is complete, once father and daughter are within talking distance, in one room, we've earned our fee. The goal is accomplished.

"Are you going back to Boston, to Claren Tech?" I had asked.

He's non-committal. "I'll see how Lucy's doing."

I'd gotten on the boat. The yacht quickly became a spec on the horizon.

* * *

My cell phone pings. It's Donato. "Where are you?" he asks.

"On a boat, coming back to Portland. Finished stuff for Gordy."

He hesitates. "Sorry, but I called with bad news."

The unsettled feelings that stirred in me last night ratchet up another notch. "You gonna tell me Billy hasn't shown his face yet."

"That's true. It's been nearly 48 hours. Canadian borders have been alerted; I don't think he could've gotten across. But he might be halfway across the states. We have someone minding the Payer house but so far, just Marvin and his mom. She walks outside every hour, flips us off. Don't think Chief Harper's gonna keep a car there much longer."

"But that's not the bad news you called about."

"Right. Ready?"

"Why not?"

"Hector Manfred was found dead in his cell this morning."

"What happened?"

"Got the report in front of me. He ripped up a bedsheet, stuffed pieces up his nose, down his throat and wrapped a wide strip around his neck. Then tied that to the vertical heat pipe in the corner of his cell—about six feet up, around a joint. Probably tipped forward and hung there 'til he had no more air."

"Did that all by himself?"

"There'll be an investigation."

"Someone motivated to take it seriously?"

"When did you get so cynical?"

"Did he have visitors?"

"Public defender connected with him yesterday. That's it."

The image of chunky Hector, eyes bugging out, his face blue from lack of oxygen and salt tears caked on his chubby cheeks, flashes in my mind's eye. "Hector's father—who suggested he was a fuck-up—he never showed?"

"No."

"That sucks."

I'm traveling at nearly fifty miles-per-hour. I almost miss the seals that pop their heads up out of the water, their whiskers and noses twitching in the breeze. They ride the waves for a moment, then slip back under the water and disappear. I wonder if they know that sharks have made their way up to Maine in the last years? That as the waters warm, they've gained new predators.

"Got time for a quick dinner later?" Donato asks. "Can fill you in more. But sorry, gotta go now." Donato clicks off.

* * *

The tender drops me at the dock at Fore Points Marina at noon. It's only a fifteen-minute walk to my place, but it's uphill. Maybe working up a sweat will make me feel better. I cross the footpath. Reader is in the nearby parking lot, sitting on his motorcycle.

"Pat made a chicken soup. Gordy and Marie sat down to bowls of it at Sparrows when Gordy got your text—that you were on your way. I told him to keep eating his soup, I'd pick you up."

"On your motorcycle." The thick, polished, two-wheeled steel frame with glaring chrome details.

"He probably thought I was taking Pat's car. But Pat couldn't find the keys and I didn't want you to be waiting." He dips his head to see my eyes. "You're glum."

"Not seeing a lot of positives right now."

"Buddha teaches we have to free ourselves, accept that things take their own course."

"Too impatient for that mantra."

"Why so pissy?"

"Hector Manfred's dead. They found him this morning, with a sheet wrapped around his neck, hanging forward from a pipe. What would Buddha say to that?"

"He'd ponder on how screwed up life can get. But maybe he'd add, 'when one door closes, another opens.'"

"For who? Not Hector."

"Who knows where he is now."

"You're way more evolved in your thinking than I am. Life is life and death is death."

"Let's talk about it sometime."

"Buddha say that too?"

"Buddha's about doing."

I look at the burly motorcycle; I don't want to envision getting on it, trusting a foothold for my unfoot, feeling balanced.

"I'll drive slow," Reader assures me. "You'll be fine. The old fart wants to see you."

"Old fart?"

"Gordy. He's your old fart, Pat's mine."

Reader takes a helmet out of a sidesaddle compartment, hands it to me. "Put your left hand on my shoulder for balance. Keep close to the bike and swing your right leg over. It's not rocket science."

"How did you know I'm miserable at rocket science?"

I follow directions. Reader continues, "Put your arms around my waist. Or chest. Or anywhere in-between."

We turn onto Fore Street and motor up the hill, where the breezes get stronger. The sailboats come into view on Eastern Promenade; the ferry's heading from Portland to Great Diamond Island, its pace steady. And so is Reader's, he's keeping his word.

We take a left on Atlantic Avenue and can hear sirens blaring. The firetruck is parked four blocks ahead of us on Congress Street, right next to Sparrows. Reader picks up speed and we're there. He kickstands the cycle and jumps off, grabs me around the waist, plants me squarely on the ground. "Go, go," I say. He sprints to Sparrows; I'm moving right behind him.

Gordy yells. "Dee! It's okay. It's okay. Dee! Over here!"

My heart slows to a mere frantic beat. I veer from joining the group of firemen gathered at the back door of Sparrow's and reach Marie and Gordy. Marie's face is flushed, she grabs my shoulders. "*Terrifacto*, Dee. But no one's hurt." She turns to Gordy. "*Che cosa*, what do you call what it was, Gordy?"

"Arson."

"Details?" I ask.

"Someone poured a can of gasoline at the back kitchen door—by the garbage bins."

"You were inside when the fire started?"

"Story is, one of the busboys went out the back door to catch a smoke, smelled the gas. A car drove by, driver tossed lit cherry bombs and sparklers. Busboy screamed like a stuck pig and raced back inside yelling 'Fire!' Everyone got out fast. Pat had the firemen here in minutes."

Marie puts her head on my shoulder. "Gordy couldn't finish his chicken soup."

I pat her back. Amazing what remains uppermost in people's minds when they're rattled.

* * *

An hour later we're sitting in the living room at Gordy's. Marie's gone upstairs to take a nap, Reader's made coffee, Gordy and Pat sit on opposite sides of the long, well-worn couch. Gordy's frown forces his jowls below his jawline; he wants Donato to find Billy Payer. "It's been two days since he ran off."

"Billy's getting what he wants," I say. "Riling people up, making people nervous 'cause they're worried he'll strike any time he feels like it and wreak havoc."

"Sick shit," Pat complains bitterly.

Gordy eyes me, his voice harsh. "Dee. What haven't you told me?"

"Told you everything." I'm defensive. "All about Karla…and the rats in Hilary's car."

"Things happening to other people. If Billy's targeting Karla, Hilary, and Pat—you're on his list too. You testified along with them."

"He knows hurting people I care about will get to me. I'll get drawn into his game."

Pat, getting irascible, repeats, "Sick shit."

I remind Gordy of the note left in my door, the one that led Abshir and me to finding Karla at PemaPond motel. "And another note was left in my door—just said 'bitch.'"

Reader throws a look at me. "When was that?"

"Night before the Sea Dogs baseball game—when I saw you at the stadium."

"I came to check in on you that night," Reader remembers. "Basically, you told me to get lost because you needed shut-eye."

I don't tell him, that for a split second when he was curt and judgmental the next day at the baseball game and resented Donato's presence, I had wondered if he'd left the note. "It was left hours later," I say. "Long after midnight."

I fill Gordy in on Hector Manfred's death in jail. "Hector was scared. Scared of what his dad would think, but—more scared of Billy."

Pat bellows, "Sick shit's gotta go down."

My cell phone pings. I answer. "Yeah?"

"It's Tiffany, at 109. Dr. Fogel says to tell you you're late and asks what time you'll get here?"

"Damn," I eject. "Forgot. Shit. Can you tell him there was a fire at Sparrows and Gordy, my boss, was there and I'm with him now… I can't get over there."

Tiffany takes a long moment. "You're canceling?"

"I'll be in next week. Can you tell Fogel that?"

"You're sure?" Her tone reminds me that these sessions are required, that missing an appointment does not go over well with Fogel—or Chief Harper. "Your boss is okay?"

"That's the good news. But, I can't break away. You'll give Fogel the message?"

"Okay. But he's not going to like it. Take care." Tiffany hangs up.

Gordy's pursing his lips and studying me. "You coulda gone."

"Now's not the time to be talking about my feelings for an hour. There are other things to do."

* * *

Tipo's is a small corner restaurant on Ocean and Walton, it's been converted from a small house into an eatery. I join Donato at an outside table. It's early for the dinner crowd, so we're the only two on the patio. He's already ordered meatballs to share, and they arrive as I sit down. "Figured you like 'em," he says. He's got his corduroy jacket on over a navy t-shirt. Looks comfortable.

"Yeah. Fan of the meatballs here."

"Drink?"

"Club soda and lime."

"Pizza will be quickest," he says. "Pepperoni or veggie?"

"Like the veggie, but either way."

"Veggie's got these charred peppers on it."

"Like those too."

He gives the order and I take a lengthy draught from the water glass already in place on the table. The waiter moves off.

"What happened to your chin?"

"Little altercation on the job Gordy and I were doing. A doctor checked it; don't need stitches."

His gray eyes study the wound. "Might leave a mark."

"I'll heal."

"Okay." He lets it go. "About this quick meal; sorry, gotta get back in an hour."

"Appreciate you filling me in."

"The guards at the jail are sticking to the same story. Walk-throughs at three and four am, all copacetic. Walk-through at five, Hector's dead."

"You talk to Hector's dad?"

Donato cuts one of the large meatballs into quarters. We each fork one of the chunks, dip them into the rich marinara sauce and chow down. "Not part of the job."

"Who's job I wonder? Isn't he a line cook at Denny's? Is the dishwasher gonna listen to his regrets?"

"If he has any?"

"Yeah. If he does."

"You gotta cut that thinking off."

"And Beene's family. Who do they talk to, to figure out the senselessness? And Karla. How does she move on from Billy's attack?"

"Not that we don't care. But that's someone else's expertise."

"Gordy puts up those fences too. Perimeters. The narrow job description."

"Can't make everything surrounding everything right. Gotta focus."

"You and Gordy should write a book."

Donato's not cold. Just reasonable. "We identify the bad ones and get them off the street. Hector's dad's not a suspect in a crime. His feelings are his own."

"Any of the guards connected to Billy Payer?"

He cuts the last large meatball into quarters and we share it. I like this method; it's efficient. "This group happens to be on the older side. Going into their fifties. All have good records. No reason to think they even knew Billy. But we'll find out."

"How is this going to affect the Beene case? If Billy's ever apprehended..."

"*When* he is. We've got the DNA. The manager at Spotty's saw Beene go apeshit when he realized his wallet was gone, saw him lumbering after Billy. Got the couple in the parking lot who saw them tussling..."

The pizza arrives. Zucchini, pesto, charred peppers, and mozzarella. The smell of garlic oil makes me salivate. We each grab a slice. Donato tells me he thinks the fire at Sparrows makes it clear Billy hasn't left the area.

"Agree. Totally a Billy Payer move."

"We gotta hope he'll keep doing stupid stuff." He leans back. "Think Marvin knows anything?"

"You were there at the station when he said he didn't."

Donato doesn't let it go. "He's been holed up in his garage apartment. Hasn't even gone across the driveway to talk to his mom."

"Don't blame him."

"Got a case of Jack Daniels delivered yesterday. That's it."

"Billy's always been screwing up Marvin's life."

"Maybe he wants it to be over," Donato says. "Feel like calling him?"

"Who?"

"Marvin. Doing the old 'partner' thing?"

"He doesn't consider me a friend."

"Went in the ambulance with you after the roof. When you were pushed off."

"Visited me once. Two days after. Don't think he's said more than ten words at a time to me since."

"But the partner code. Solid. More important than friends. How many times did you have his back at a domestic dispute or a bar fight or a road rage?"

"Went both ways."

"There was that thing, Labor Day. Your first year. Some ass wouldn't get off the tourist Bay Cruiser at the end of the night—what was the deal?"

"Marvin went over the side. Water was 50 degrees. We got him back on board..."

"You got him back on board. I saw the report."

I flash on when Marvin and I were rookies. Our first run-in; we cornered a guy from Brewster who'd come into Ben's Clam Shack with a knife, determined to slash the jerk who stole his truck. I lost a tooth, Marvin broke a finger. But we bagged the arrest. There was the Chinese restaurant in the Deering area. Husband and wife—owners and cooks—ready to toss hot oil on each other. Marvin slipped on the floor, I pulled him away from the fryer, and he grabbed the woman before things got really nasty. And that tourist Bay Cruiser incident, some blockhead had stormed the helm and wanted to take the boat over to the islands so he could howl at the moon. He was behind bars that night.

"You don't have to be friends to be solid partners," Donato says. He's already given the waiter his credit card; he signs for the check and we head to our cars. I press the button on my remote, hear the creaky Outback's lock release.

"Can I bring up one more thing?" Donato asks.

"What?"

"Nothing about Beene or Karla or Billy."

"What?"

"I remain curious."

It's a recall to my sluffing off any importance of the kiss we shared in my apartment. My face feels hot. He waits.

"You have work to get back to," I remind him.

He opens my car door, stays close while I slide in and bring my left leg into position. "Thor says 'hi.'"

"You gave him an impossible name to live up to."

"He does a fine job."

"He is a beagle."

"You're sticking at Gordy's." He's checking up on the fact.

"I'd rather be at my own place."

He leans in, we're nose to nose. "Give it a little more time. Let me know if you talk to Marvin."

* * *

I pass the surveillance vehicle at the end of the block. The cop on duty is eating potato chips from a super-size bag. I pull up to the Payer house. The curtains in the main house are closed. Marvin's old Jeep is in the driveway. I take the side stairs up to the garage apartment, hear ESPN blasting. "Marvin? It's Rommel. Can I talk to you?"

I get a shout back. "No."

"One quick word?" I ask.

"No."

"Favor to your old partner?"

"Screw you. Go away."

CHAPTER THIRTY-SEVEN
Wednesday

As soon as I enter Gordy's house, I sense something's wrong. Marie's not bustling in the kitchen, Bert's not bounding to the front door to demand a scratch and an 'atta boy.'

"Marie? Gordy?" I climb the narrow stairs to the second floor.

Marie juts out the open door of Gordy's bedroom, her fingers to her lips. "Gordy almost fainted when he was walking up the stairs. Doing way too much." She looks like she's blaming me. "He's gotta rest, Dee."

I peer inside the room. Bert's moving slowly off Gordy's bed, he ambles over to me, gives a soft yip. I rub his head. "You guarding him too, Bert?"

Gordy flags a weak wave from the bed. "Don't listen to Marie, she's getting bossy."

Marie's hands are on her hips. "If you don't listen to me, I'll hire the biggest, hairiest nurse I can find to make your life miserable."

"She sounds serious, Gordy. And I agree with her. Stay in bed and rest."

"Stop ganging up on me," he snarls. "Claren left a message. Lucy's up and walking around."

"Good. Anything about Wolff and the project?"

"Doesn't owe us news on that."

"Didn't mention anything?"

"No." Gordy wipes a wad of tissue over his sweaty forehead, shuts down that line of inquiry. Again.

Marie grabs my hand. "Tell the police to find that Billy Payer. How can anyone think of anything else?"

"I'll pass your message along, Marie."

"I've been reading to Gordy."

"To put me to sleep," Gordy rolls his eyes. "It's poetry."

Marie defends herself. "Lovely thoughts for lovely dreams."

"You two go back to that." I head downstairs.

"Come on, Bert." I hear Gordy sigh and Bert jumping onto the bed. "Good boy."

The kitchen refrigerator contains Gordy's favorite beers. I grab one and let my frustration fester. The waiting game is not for me. I call Karla's mother's house in Augusta. Mrs. Ackerman picks up, tells me Karla's not talking much, but she's eating oatmeal this morning and Mrs. Ackerman holds onto that as a positive sign. A text comes through from Gretchen; she's heard about the fire at Sparrows. I text her back that no one was hurt. Maybe her lavender hair is faring well with that new lawyer that's moved to town. Would be nice to hear something positive. But I don't call her. Don't want to rehash anything right now. I text that I'll check in with her tomorrow.

The desire to be active pulls at me. I phone the Gull's Roost, ask if Billy Payer is there. "Guy's banned," is the reply, followed by a quick hang-up. Next is PemaPond Motel; the phone keeps ringing. The hunched, ugly man who paid no attention to Karla's rape and terrorization in Room 5 has probably decided to lock his doors in case Billy Payer shows up to make sure he keeps mum. Maybe he's sitting in the motel office right now, fingering his Penthouse magazine, scared, ignoring the phone.

My cell buzzes; don't recognize the number. "Yeah? Who're you trying to reach?"

"Rommel. It's Marvin. Maybe I do have something for you."

I straighten. "What?"

"Flea just called. Asked me to put stuff together for Billy."

"What kind of stuff?"

"Clothes. Toothbrush kind of shit." Marvin sounds drunk. "The fuck wants mouthwash. Asked me to drop them off at the U-Tow place."

"So Flea knows where Billy is?"

"Maybe. Don't care. He didn't tell me, if that's what you're suggesting."

"Wasn't suggesting anything. Glad you called."

"Wouldn't be so glad if you knew everything."

"What do you mean 'everything'?"

He's silent.

"Marvin?"

"You know, Rommel, I coulda—I wanted to be—a good cop."

"You're still a…"

"Billy's really tanked me now."

"No one's gonna blame you."

"Don't make me laugh. Done tryin'."

I need to get him back on track. "What else did Flea say?"

"I told him to fuck off. Wasn't gonna lift a finger. Told him to fuck off."

Marvin hangs up.

Donato's phone goes to voicemail. I leave a message, telling him Marvin called, that I'm going to check out U-Tow. I click off. Maybe I can reach him at 109. Tiffany answers, tells me Donato's not at the station; she'll track him down. I ask her to find Stinner too, share the information.

I figure I'll drive by U-Tow, see if Flea shows his hand. Maybe follow him when he leaves work, hope he'll lead to Billy. I can keep Donato updated if anything seems promising.

* * *

It's five minutes later, the sun's descending in the western sky. I sit in my car, a dirt field away from the office building of U-Tow, binoculars held up to my eyes. Flea's visible through the plate glass window of customer reception; he's behind the counter. There's a dozen tired trucks and trailers in the black-top lot behind the office building. The rest of the fleet dot the adjoining field next to me. It's noisy here; sounds of traffic on the nearby highway, crows and seagulls fighting over rows of trashcans filled with take-out food from the neighboring Chipotle and Subway restaurants. I wait. A hundred yards down the street, I notice a new brewery is about to open. The sign, not yet affixed to the building, leans against the brick facade. *Owl's Brew; Established Yesterday for All Your Tomorrows.*

Marvin's rusty-red Jeep pulls into the U-Tow lot. I slide as far down in my seat as I can. Marvin gets out of the Jeep, pops the hatch, lifts out a cardboard box, and hurries into the reception area. So he's acquiesced to Flea's request. Brotherly duty has trumped sound judgment and he's now officially aiding and abetting a criminal. Billy's hold on Marvin is too strong. I feel for my ex-partner, but he's clearly made his choice.

Flea takes the box. Marvin storms out the door, gets into his Jeep, and drives off.

U-Tow's neon sign, on the top of the office building, clicks off. A moment later, the lights in the office extinguish. End of the business day. And there's a cloud cover tonight. Everything feels dark.

The office door opens and Flea steps out; he's carrying the box. He locks up and heads to the parking lot. I expect he's going to put the box into his own car—give me the chance to follow him. But Flea crosses the narrow street and enters the field—heading straight towards me. I start my Outback, not ready to confront him by myself. I curse under my breath. How did he know I was here?

Before I can move my car from the curb, Flea veers off and heads to a row of the larger U-Tow trucks; they're parked against a chicken wire fence at the far edge of the field. I lose sight of him in the shadows and darkness for a long moment, and then he slips by a safety light. Stops at the rear cargo door of one of the 15-foot trucks. Raps his fist against it. A moment later, one side of the back doors open. Flea shoves the box inside, and then jumps in, using his beefed-up arms to heave himself up and over the high back end.

Shit. Has Billy Payer spent the last two days holed up in the back of this moving truck?

I punch in Donato's cell phone number. Again, it's voicemail. I tell him where I am, that I don't have eyes on Billy yet but I feel the possibility. I click off and my fingers move to auto-punch 109…

Just then the passenger window of my Outback shatters. Small rounds of safety glass storm at me, I cover my face with my arm. Then a long iron crossbar rams through my window, shoots past my eyes. It's quickly retracted and shoved forward again, this time it connects with my temple. My blood spurts onto the steering wheel and my vision instantly blurs. Can't see. My phone topples from my hand, it thuds onto the floor mat. The driver's side door opens. Blindly, I grab for the handle, try to keep the door shut but my fingers are slippery with blood. Someone grabs my hair, yanks me so I'm half-hanging outside the car. A black garbage bag is thrown over my face. I punch into the air, try to tear at the bag over my head, but strong arms drag me out, slam me against the car, and a knee pounds into the soft spot under my ribs, my organs register the assault. I double over and hear the crack on my skull, it echoes relentlessly in my ears. A searing jolt of pain shoots through my brain…

* * *

There's a sound. I tell myself to open my eyes, but another part of me wants to stay in this mournful nothingness. An overwhelming sadness permeates me; does my life add up to this? Fading out alone. Never letting anyone get close, too determined to be stronger than I am, never letting on about my fear that my limitations now define me and will forever keep me separate.

Another part of my brain rears up, commands me to find my spine. Fight.

But my head is pounding, the pain excruciating. No energy to resist.

Stop focusing on that, don't give up.

The sadness is seductive. It's over, it says. Let it go. It's all right.

No. The bossy inner voice muscles back into my mind. Battle.

Why? The bleakness feels easier. Sink into your disappointment. It'll be over soon.

My survival side won't release. I manage to open my eyes enough for a narrow slit of vision; there's only blackness. Where am I? I take a breath, succeed only in drawing dirty, slimy plastic into my nose and mouth. The garbage bag. I try to lift my head. Sharp agony in my neck. I'm thirsty.

Taking stock: I'm propped up onto my right side on a cold metal floor, something solid and hulking is rammed up close to my back, keeping me in place. My prosthesis is angling oddly from my knee, but I can't reach it to determine if it's in one piece because my right hand is tied to my belt, the other attached to the object at my back. I pull, wriggle my arms as much as I can. The rough, spiny hemp cuts into my skin; I'm going nowhere.

A sound. Like the release of a spring-dagger knife. My heart accelerates its pace, pounding so loud it blocks out the hissing slice through the plastic, so close to my ear.

The bag is pulled off.

I'm in the cargo area of a 15-foot U-Tow truck. Small pools of light, from battery-operated lanterns, illuminate the metal corners. There's a camp cot against a wall, a twelve-pack of water bottles, empty cans of beer. Billy's pacing. "Not quite sure of yourself now, are you Dee Rommel. Gotcha."

"Billy," I mutter.

"Couldn't leave my city—my guys, shmy mom, shmy bro-brother, my waterholes—until you and I got to spend more time together." He comes into a vague focus. Wild eyes, a jerky motion in his shoulder. His words are slurring. Is he high? He opens a McDonald's take-out carton, pinches off a piece of burger, drops it on the ground near his feet. A fat, brownish-gray rat, two feet long from nose to end of its bald tail, ambles out from behind a long, low plastic container. Sniffs at the thin, over-cooked meat. The rodent's red eyes glance at me. No fear. Grabs the food and glides back into the shadow.

Billy uses his foot to move the crate closer to me. He pulls on a pair of leather gloves; he's talking fast, as if now that he's got company, he can reconnect with his old self, be the center of attention. "Lots of field rats out here. People toss their garbage, and birds and rats and critters take advantage. I got traps like thish one all over the field." He rolls his neck, breathes in through his nose, sniffing up draining mucus. "Met a guy up at MCC, that shit hole prison you helped put me in—he loved rats. He'd get guys to steal bacon and peanut butter from the chow hall, then he'd make sticky globs of the stuff—about the size of a fucking golf ball." Billy prowls the perimeters of the inside of the truck, like an animal in a cage. His words trip over each other. "Once the snow, the shnow, melted and outdoor sports time started, always saw him sitting out in the field, by the fence. I was playing

Ten Days

basketball, still good after high school. Never lose my touch. Asked the rat-wacko what he was doing. Told me he was communing with the stronger species. The rats would smell the food—come up and take nibbles—one or two of the biggest would keep the smaller ones away. All this guy wanted to do was catch one, make it his friend. One day he snuck out an empty tomato sauce can—hid it down his pants somehow. When one of the rats was busy licking and nibbling on the bacon-peanut-ball, this rat-guy slammed the can on top of the critter. Guards saw the slam, made him let the ugly rodent go. They checked him after that—kept confiscating his rat treats, which made him mad." He stops, picks up the McDonald's carton again. "Peanut butter and bacon work better, but this gets their attention too."

The truck smells. Body odor, beer, over-salted meat product from McDonalds, sweaty t-shirts, rat shit.

Billy bends his knees and scrunches down close to me. His breath stinks. He strokes my hair. "Like your hair. And like that you're tall. You used to be someone I'd want to see fucked."

"Never woulda happened," I croak.

"Only a matter of time." He takes a cell phone from his shirt pocket, clicks on the photo app, a small flash bursts in my face.

"You liked watching Karla get fucked?" I'm trapped in whisper mode, can't get enough breath to get louder.

"And squirm. She'sh not gonna tell anybody anything this time. She sent me letters like 'so sorry, so sorry' she said those things about me in court. Well, they sure came out of her mouth easy enough. She won't do that again."

"Where's Flea?"

"Don't need him for what'sh gonna happen."

"What's going to happen?"

"You'll ask for m-mercy."

"Did Karla?"

"I have pictures on my phone."

"You shit."

"Me? We were having fun that New Year'sh Eve. Tease was all over me. We'd just screwed in the truck, she was all lovey, we're out having a good time, then what? She doesn't stand by her man. Not acceptable."

"You terrorized Pat's place, broke his nose, you wanted Karla—and Hilary and me—to lie?"

"To just shut up."

"And Pat?"

"It was New Year's Eve. Give a guy who'sh out having a good time a break."

"So everyone else is wrong," I mutter, wishing my head would stop pounding.

"What? What'd you say?" His shoulder twitches, he shakes his head as if trying to dislodge a fog.

I don't answer.

"Bitch."

My eyes sweep as far as they can through the truck. The rear doors are closed, the squared-off metal crossbar in place. Bare walls. The roof, nine feet off the floor of the truck, is solid. I twist my wrists, the packing twine is scratchy, strong, but not thick. Would take a sharp object to cut through it. Billy had used a knife to cut into the bag over my head. Where is it? I move my neck, try to get another vantage point, but the pain is excruciating.

Billy opens the cardboard box that I'd seen Flea deliver to the truck. He takes out an extra-large plastic bottle of Listerine, a box of Cliff energy bars, and a couple rolls of toilet paper and puts them on the floor. He leans into the box to check out the rest of the contents. He lifts out a towel, a plastic bag full of socks, another one of underwear, two large bottles of Jack Daniels. "Marvin told me you wouldn't let go. You shoulda. Told you at Gull Roost. You shoulda."

"You hurt my friend…"

"Dee Rommel thinking she knows best. Wrong this time."

I imagine Donato—anyone—getting my messages and driving by U-Tow. Flea had left the building, turned off the lights. Even if someone finds my car, with its window smashed, my cell phone on the floormat—nothing would lead them to the field of trucks. To this truck.

Billy grabs my nearest hand, it's attached to my belt. He yanks me upwards at the waist, shivers of torment race through my ribs and back, I can't swallow the shallow scream. "Shut up," he snaps. He uses the heel of his boot to position the plastic container in front of me, there's a small sliding door built into its side. He opens it to reveal a thin, metal crosshatch barrier keeping a half dozen curious rats from spilling out onto the floor of the truck. Billy presses a button on top of the container and the crosshatch barricade begins to slide up—he releases the button and it clinks back into place. The rats' noses are pressed against the screen, they're unhappy not to be set free.

Billy twists the top off one of the bottles of Jack Daniels and swigs the alcohol.

"Flea'sh gonna give up his dead-end job, we're getting' outta here."

"Flea's going with you?"

"We'll have fun, I tell him."

"What's he doing now?"

"Getting his monster truck ready. Told him to give me an hour."

I want to keep him talking. "Better get out of town," I rasp. "There's DNA from your truck and a few witnesses. You with Thomas Beene."

He hunches down again. Strokes the rat cage. "Who's that?"

"Liquor salesman. In Portland for a night or two. Wallet full of hundreds…"

"That smelly guy was sharing his whiskey with the bartender at Spotty's—and half the people at the bar. I was ready for a taste and he walks—walksh—right by me."

"You killed him 'cause he didn't notice you?"

"I noticed his money." He touches my cheek. "The critters like this sh-soft part."

"Rats carry a lot of disease…" Can't help that my mind goes there.

"It's not their fault. It'sh the crap we leave around for them to eat."

"Weird, Billy. You feel more for the rats than…"

"Shut up. They like toes, but since you only have five of 'em now…your cheeks and fingers can be their first meal."

The pulse in my throat quickens. It's hard to swallow.

"Want to show you something first." He takes his cell from his pocket. "You're my home screen, bitch. Got excellent shots of you not being all you can be…" He chuckles, holds the phone in front of my face. "Put it on Friendline too. Got a lot of 'likes.'" He presses a dirty finger onto his camera app. "Probably need the flash for this one." A quick burst of light hits my face. "Now I got a pix of this."

"You're a shit," I hiss.

"Yeah. People don't mess with me."

"What other pictures you have on that phone?"

"They're mine. Shut up." He takes his time, positioning my hand at the rat screen again.

"Why'd you have to kill Thomas Beene? Why not just take his money?"

"Started hollerin' when he figured I'd lifted his fat wallet from his fat pocket. Had to kick the snark out of his face and roll him into the back of my pickup—loudmouth slob. Fuckin' hurt my back. Wouldn't shut up."

"You used that axe in the back of your pickup to split his skull?"

He twitches. "How'd you know I had an axe?"

I leave out my first glimpse of the weapon—when I was crawling in the back of his pickup at Gull Roost. "It was in the truck when the cops stopped you for a broken taillight."

"And shit, want my truck back—that'sh my truck! Want it back!" He attempts to shake off the loss, but his agitation grows. "That'sh my truck!"

"Beene's blood was found in the bed of your truck."

"Hector was supposed to clean it up."

"Hector Manfred told the cops you bragged about swinging the axe at Beene. You hear that Hector was found hanging? In the jail."

Billy grabs the knife off the cot. "Yeah. Yeah."

"You have anything to do with that?"

"He couldn't make the grade."

I'm running out of gas. Can't see a way out of this.

He uses the sharp knife to cut my hand loose from my belt. "Probably sorry you didn't croak falling off that building. Slippery as hell, huh, from the sleet, huh? Fuckin' cold, huh? Fancy condo building now; too many rich people moving to Portland." He positions the rat crate in front of me, crouches close.

What's he going to do with my hand?

"Marvin was freaked. Shakes like a squiggle head when he gets freaked. Told him he shouldn't've fished you out of the dumpster. Little brother, the cop. Squiggle shake little shit." He strokes my fingertips. "First they'll lick you, then use their sharp teeth."

I groan.

"Couple guys in MCC didn't have an arm. Or leg. Or fingers. I kept in shape. You don't know what it'sh like being cooped up, you bitch."

"Like now?" I try for a deeper breath; fear makes it difficult. Keep him talking, I tell myself.

"What?"

"Like now. We're both cooped up."

"This is your prison. Gotcha." Billy shoves my hand against the small sliding door of the rat crate. I writhe, want to shift my body, but can't. My left hand's still attached to that bulky, cold object in my back. He places his finger on the release button, prepares to open the barricade.

Suddenly, the 15-foot truck jerks roughly, quakes. Something's slammed into it. Billy loses his grip on my wrist, falls on his butt. "What the hell?"

The heaviness at my back skids a foot across the floor, drags me with it. I collapse onto my back. I reach, with my free arm, to my LiteGood. It's in place, but has the fabrication been compromised? If I get the chance, will I be able to get up?

Billy's up, grabs for the knife. "Who's here?" He kicks me, his boot sharp and hard on my shoulder. "Who knows you're here?" He moves to the back of the truck.

That long, cold object is beside me. It's a 75-quart, thick, molded plastic ice chest—probably weighed down with ice and beer. It's two feet high, five feet long. The twine attaching my hand to it is sloppily tied around the handle, the knot's come loose. My shoulder aches as I swing my free hand over my body, my fingers fumble with the knot, every movement sends slivers of pain through my neck and torso, but I keep at it. One thread of the twine disengages from the ice chest's handle.

Outside the truck, a strained engine revs, there's a screech of gears and the U-Tow is rammed again, there's high speed behind the strike and the incredible force rocks the truck.

"Shit!" yells Billy as he slips and hits his head against the truck's metal wall.

Wanting to use every moment of the distraction, I tug, pull, and pitch forward so I can move closer to the ice chest, lessen the tension of the twine holding me to it. I maneuver myself into position and manage to get two fingers inside the careless knot to separate it even more.

The vehicle slamming into the U-Tow backs up, moves forward, backs up, moves forward again and again—the metal against metal punching and knocking escalates Billy's anger. He storms towards me. "Who the fuck is…"

I imagine the attacking vehicle's front end smashed, its engine blown apart. Apparently not, there's sound of it withdrawing, the driver's blowing on the horn, gears are grinding and—another hit. The U-Tow pitches. The heavy ice chest slides on the floor. I'm still attached. Billy's heels flail into the rat trap; it tips it over and the rats topple out; they're loose. Two large gray rats, tails long, skitter over my chest.

Outside the sound of the charging attack machine whines, the U-Tow lurches as the vehicle attempts to back up, but it can't disengage from the U-Tow frame. We jounce and sway; we're stuck together.

"Billy! Billy!" Someone's calling from outside.

"Shit. Marvin." Billy races to the back, grabs the iron crossbar and pulls it out of its lock-pocket. He pushes one of the double doors open. More than a dozen rats, screeching, their claws scraping on the metal floor, clamber towards open air. They tumble out, disappear over the cargo truck's high edge.

I give another massive jerk on the twine, another wrench and this time my skin rips open, but the coil connecting to the ice chest disengages from the handle— I'm panting, watching it fall freely to the floor. I can use both arms now, I grab onto the ice chest, use it to help haul myself up.

Over my shoulder, I see Marvin, on the roof of his half-crushed Jeep, weaving drunkenly. He's got a gun pointed at Billy.

Billy bangs his fist on the inside wall of the truck, his anger high. "What the hell you doin'?"

"Saw you—you got Rommel—she's in there."

"So what? You hate her guts."

"Marvin," I shout. "He's got a knife!"

"She's my partner!"

"She thinks you're worthless. Like you are! Sorry—ashamed to sh-ay that, brother—"

"I'm ashamed. You fucked up bad this time, Billy!"

"Get lost," Billy says. "Flea's gonna be here—you stay—we'll cut your ass."

"Tell her about the roof, Billy."

"Shut up!" Billy bangs his fist against the side of the truck.

"If you don't, I will."

Marvin gives a deep guttural yell, "Rommel! Ask him…"

Billy screams, "Marvin, don't go against me…"

"Throwing the beam off the roof, Billy. Tell her about it."

"You're dead!"

Billy leaps off the back of the truck—Marvin takes aim and shoots. At the last moment, he moves his arm and the bullet flies into the night, into the field. Can anyone hear it? Is the noise of traffic too loud? If someone heard the gunshot, would they report it?

Billy's feet hit the ground. He's fast and the driver's side door of Marvin's Jeep is open, so he can step up into it and grab Marvin's legs. He yanks and Marvin's upended, topples to the ground on the other side of the Jeep. "Don't get up, asshole," Billy's scream is raspy; his throat dry. "You're getting the shit kicked out of you…" Marvin's shouting back. Is he scrambling to his feet? I hear Billy's racing footfalls as he runs around the Jeep, pounding on its sides to increase intimidation as he makes his way to Marvin.

I'm using the ice chest as leverage, pressing my hands into its top, getting my right leg in position and dragging the left so the unfoot can find steadiness. Something feels off, but I can put pressure on the unfoot and that's what I need. I hobble to the rear of the truck, realize the vehicle is now on an angle; I use the side for support. "Marvin, heads up on a knife!" I call out.

Another gunshot, and a loud bellow of pain from Billy. "You fuck—ahhhh. Damn damn damn…"

It's silent.

Standing near the open rear door, I wait. The dark night feels eerie. Traffic on the highway speeds by. Far off there's light from the streetlamps, but here, right here—the field is pitchy, dank and hushed.

"Marvin?"

I lower myself to my butt, sit on the lip of the truck. The iron crossbar used to break my car's window is tilted against the inside wall of the truck. It's five feet long, has square edges and is substantial. I flip over to my stomach and use my arms to lower my body to the ground.

"Help me." It's Billy.

I don't want to walk into a trap. "Marvin? Talk to me, Marvin."

No response.

I reach into the U-Tow and grab the crossbar. Marvin has fallen off his Jeep and landed on the side of the field that's not in my sight.

My hands tighten around the crossbar. I shuffle forward carefully, steady balance is not my friend right now. Hear no movement, no voices. I round the Jeep. Billy is on his back, splayed; his dirty, scuffed hunting boots look stiff at the end of his legs.

Another two tottering steps to gain a full view. A wide, red splotch stains the fabric of Billy's upper chest and shoulder. His chest is moving, up and down. Up and down.

Next to him is Marvin. The spring-dagger knife is jammed into the base of his throat. Blood oozes from the corner of his mouth and out his nose. His eyes are open. I use the crossbar as a steadying stick, lean down to feel a pulse in Marvin's carotid artery. There is none.

"Help me," says Billy.

"Your brother's dead," I tell him.

"Help me," Billy repeats.

His phone is in his shirt pocket. I use it to make the calls.

* * *

The ambulance and patrol cars notice me under the safety light in the dirt field. I hold up my arm to caution them to stop a good distance from the truck and Marvin's Jeep. I've wrapped my jacket tight over Billy's wound, he's unconscious but alive. I said a prayer for Marvin, but I couldn't touch him or move him. The scene had to remain unmolested—so it would be clear how Billy Payer murdered his brother.

Officer Sandrich is the first out of her vehicle, she jogs to me, insists I look grubby, lousy, and wobbly. She helps me to the back of her squad car. I hand her Billy's cell phone and tell her, "He likes to take pictures when he's terrorizing people. Make sure people see this."

Sandrich grabs an evidence bag from the back seat's pouch, drops the phone in. She flips open her notebook. "Let me get your statement…"

She's excited, she knows this will make her stand out. Earn a few kudos. I'm too spent to launch into a monologue.

"You ask the questions," I say. "I'll answer."

TWO DAYS

CHAPTER THIRTY-EIGHT
Thursday

The hospital room is small. Gordy's on one side of the bed, my mother's on the other. She looks worried—but perfectly groomed in her blue silk blouse and pleated slacks.

"Look at your hands, all cut up," she says.

"And your face. That cut on your chin opened up again." Gordy adds.

"Opened again? You didn't get that cut last night? When did you get that cut?"

"It's okay, Mom. My chin just connected with someone's boot."

"Steel-toed," Gordy adds.

"What?" My mother glares at Gordy.

"I'm fine, Mom."

She sits next to me. "We'll get you a good facial surgeon, honey. Don't worry."

Gordy had called my mother without asking me. He didn't want the grief she'd give him if she found out in another fashion. She and Chester had gotten into the car right away, arrived at the hospital at dawn. It's now mid-afternoon, the doctor has taped my shoulder and told me not to lift anything and signed my discharge papers. I'm dressed in clothes Gordy gathered for me from my apartment—sweatpants and sweatshirt.

"You'll come back to Boston," she says. "You can recuperate with Chester and me."

"You're supposed to be going to Japan, Mom."

"I'm changing my plans."

"Don't. The doctor told me I can go to my own home. Nothing's broken, I've got bruises but I'll heal. All I'm gonna do is sit around, watch classic basketball games on television. Don't need someone to babysit while I zone out…"

"Are you sure your prosthetist…"

"Ebenberg," I fill in his name for her.

"Says your LiteGood is adjusted properly?"

"It's adequate for now," I say. "We'll check on the finer points later in the week. Got it covered."

"Dee's always got a room at my place," says Gordy. "Marie and I can give her whatever she needs."

My mother pats his arm. "Thank you, but Chester's waiting in the lobby." She turns to me. "Chester says to tell you he needs someone in the house who can beat him at backgammon."

I try for a deep breath, but my ribs are not happy. "Mom, you need to learn to play backgammon."

"I'd rather read a book, honey. So, there's a very good reason for you to stay with us."

"If she wants to be at her own apartment, it's only a few blocks from me," Gordy say. "Marie'll want to bring over lasagna—she's making it now. And cannoli."

A voice from the doorway. "That sounds good."

My mother turns to see who's interrupting us. She cocks her head to one side, trying to place him. "I've met you."

"Robbie Donato. We met at your daughter's graduation from the Academy."

"That's right. I'm Gayle." My mother offers her hand. "You're the one who brought Dee to the hospital last night."

"Got there after the big moments. Didn't like that."

"I called you," I defend myself.

"And I wish I'd gotten there sooner." Donato turns to my mom. "Rommel wouldn't leave the scene until Billy Payer was officially under arrest and Marvin was…"

"Taken to the morgue," Gordy finishes the sentence.

My mom places her hand on my shoulder. "He used to be your partner, is that right, Dee?"

"He stepped up last night," Donato says softly.

The image of Marvin on top of his rusted Jeep, telling Billy to release me is clear in my head. His cry for self-respect. Donato and I share a look. Out of the corner of my eye, I notice my mother studying us.

Donato fills me in, "Flea's at 109—the station—the cousins of the groom who were at Dyer Long Pond that night are with the Brunswick PD. Photos on Billy's cell phone—everything's there. Karla, Beene, you in the U-Tow truck—and lots of rats."

My mother's eyes go wide. "What? Rats?"

Gordy gives a pointed look to Donato. "Billy's going away for a long time. No more details needed at this time."

Donato realizes the subject needs to be changed. "And, I'm happy to eat lasagna tonight at Rommel's place."

Gordy grunts, "Marie didn't say she'd cook for you."

"She'll be fine with it. Plus, I have a few days off. Rommel likes my dog. Thor and I can be helpful."

"You like his dog?" My mother pounces.

I don't help her. "Thor's an okay dog."

"An animal of the highest caliber." Donato winks.

My mother's very curious. "All right. Chester and I will stay at the hotel for a few days. We'll be over for lasagna tonight. Gordy, I hope Marie's making a big pan of it."

"She always does," assures Gordy.

Donato takes charge. "I've got my car in the parking lot. I'll bring it around, give Rommel a stylish ride." He moves out of the room, heads down the hallway.

"He's a good watch guy, Gayle," Gordy says. "Solid."

My mother sits next to me. "Honey, why does he call you 'Rommel'?"

"Habit. From Academy days."

"Remind him you have a first name."

"Mom…"

She reaches for her purse. "Chester and I will check into the Harbor House Hotel. We'll be over for dinner, I want to make sure you eat well."

* * *

My spot is on the living room couch, and everyone insists I don't move. The conversation from the long table in the kitchen is lively; my mother, Chester, Pat, and Marie grill Donato about the crime numbers in Portland. Gordy sits with me, his plate of half-eaten lasagna is on the coffee table. He looks up to see if Marie has eyes on him. Satisfied he's in the clear, he pours himself a glass of Chianti. "Better you stick with water, Dee. Not the best with lasagna—but better until you heal."

There's a knock on the front door, Gordy answers it. "Hey, come on in."

Reader, carrying his helmet, wearing his jacket and chaps, ducks his head under the door frame and enters. "Wanted to make sure Dee's alive and kicking."

"She is. Sit down. I'll get you some lasagna." Gordy heads to the kitchen. "Marie, we need another plate…"

"You have enough leather on?" I ask.

Reader keeps his monotone delivery. "Top quality. Like having butter against your skin." He sits in a chair next to the couch. "So—Billy's off the streets. And you took the brunt of it."

"And you wanted to beat his ass…"

"You bet I did. And looks like you didn't." His eyes travel from my eyes, past my taped shoulder, torso, and legs. "But you're in one piece."

"That's what the doctor says."

"Came by the hospital, but you had a crowd in that room. Didn't know you were so popular."

"I'm not."

"Wouldn't be so sure. *Family's not only those who we share blood with, but those we'd give blood for.*'"

"Is that more Dickens?" I moan.

"He was prolific, and I like to paraphrase." He looks to the kitchen. "Who's here?"

"Gretchen's in the backyard with two dogs—Bert and Thor—she's tossing some gummy tennis ball to them. My mom and her husband are at the kitchen table—with Marie and Donato."

"The cop."

"Detective." I try to straighten up, but the pain makes me decide not to. "So, Pat can sleep better now."

"And he'll be glad to have me off his couch."

"You're leaving?"

"Got a few things out West to take care of."

"Harvard grad spreading the word of Charles Dickens to those who only read Cliff notes in high school?"

"Usually save that sharing for special people."

There it is—his ability to keep me off-center. "Is that flattery?"

He adjusts the straps on his helmet. I realize he's got the whole outfit on—not only the jacket and chaps, but a balaclava scrunched down on his neck, ready to be pulled up and over his nose and mouth if bugs—or cold—become a problem. Heavy boots. Gloves sticking out of his jacket's pocket. "You're leaving tonight?"

"Like the space of the night highway. Already said goodbye to my old fart." A lopsided smirk creases his face. He sits on the edge of the couch. Close to me. "You wanna take a break any time, you could fly out West, I'd pick you up, show you some excellent vistas. Always good to get a fresh perspective."

"On what?"

"That gaping empty feeling you're gonna get when you walk into Sparrows and I'm not there."

"You're full of yourself."

"Keep this in mind—I'll be here for Uncle Pat's Thanksgiving feast."

"Thanks for the heads up."

"So, I'll be back."

I laugh. "Isn't that what the Terminator promised?"

"He's a charming fellow," Reader says. "But I'm more charming."

He gets up; I'm aware again of how his presence fills a room.

"You won't forget me."

He's out the door just as Gordy comes back with a plate heavy with garlic bread, lasagna, and green beans. "Where is he?" he asks.

"Wanted to get on the road," I tell him.

ONE DAY

CHAPTER THIRTY-NINE
Friday

Thor and Bert sleep on the rug. My mother and Chester are in the backyard, appreciating Maine's night sky. Donato, Gretchen, Abshir, and Marie are doing the dishes in the kitchen. Gordy and I sit in my living room, his eyes are closed, I expect the snoring to begin at any moment. Donato, a glass of Chianti in his hand, joins us, complaining. "They don't like the way I dry dishes."

Gordy keeps his eyes closed. "Marie's very particular."

"Thought you were asleep," I say to Gordy.

"Waiting for you to tell me what's running through that brain of yours."

Donato sits in a chair. "What isn't she talking about?"

Gordy opens one eye. "Dee, can't get into deep slumber here. Feel you cogitating."

Donato takes in a healthy hit of wine. "Worried about Fogel? He's gonna have a field day unpacking your U-Tow experience."

"He's not happy I missed our appointment."

"Yep. That'll be in his report," agrees Donato. "But Harper's gonna give you some credit for the Billy bust-up. That'll help when you sign back up."

Gordy clears his throat. "Is that what you're thinking about? What comes next?"

"Got something else."

They wait.

"Something Marvin said," I tell them. "Right before he took on Billy. About Billy being on the roof—part of the robbery—the guys we chased up to the roof—you know, November before last."

Donato and Gordy, as if they're connected, lean forward.

"Last night, Marvin—he was drunk—he told Billy to tell me about the beam thrown off—the one that came after me."

Ten Days

"Why's he asking Billy that?" Donato says. He's been working on this cold case for over a year. "Payer's whereabouts were checked. He was in Florida for two months. Working on some boat, hunting big tuna. Wasn't in the state of Maine that night."

"When Marvin called about Flea wanting the box of supplies for Billy, he said something about wanting to be a good cop—that he lived with one big mistake that made it clear to him he was never going anywhere in PPD. Ashamed of the kind of partner he was. Something to do with that night, the roof. And then in the U-Tow field, Marvin kept repeating it…"

"We've got Billy," Donato says. "Soon as the doctor gives us the go ahead—we'll work it."

"I thought Billy and all his shit was over," I say.

* * *

The gathering powered on, no one wanted to leave. I was fine with that, didn't want to sleep, to chance that images of Billy or Marvin or rats would slip into my dreams. Donato found a classic on the sports channel. The Lakers vs Toronto, Kobe Bryant's 81-point game in 2006. It was amazing to watch it again, to appreciate that the Lakers were down 14 points at half-time when Kobe, on a mission, accepted the challenge and didn't stop until he found success. The final basket of the 122-104 point game had us all cheering. Even my mother, who insisted on making popcorn and Chester, who actually took off his shoes and hooted and hollered with Gordy and Donato, enjoyed it. Everyone stayed for the entire replay.

Now it's dawn, Abshir has left to plan his book-buying for next semester; he wants to get the best price and today other students will be selling their used copies at the university bookstore. Gretchen's stretching, tells me she plans to go straight to Doggie DayCare, catch some shut-eye there before she opens for the day. She's out the door with a wave. Chester's put on his shoes and my mother's kissing my cheek; tells me they'll check in later, she'll bring over lobster rolls from Luke's Lobster for dinner. Chester helps her on with her light coat and takes her hand as they leave. Bert and Thor raise sleepy heads, open their hairy jaws to yawn, probably imagining doggie treats.

I swing my legs off the couch and head to the kitchen.

"Where are you going? Get back on that couch," asks Gordy. "Let people wait on you."

"Can't just sit around. And there's still food here, for Bert. You can take it home. It's taking up space in my refrigerator."

"You've got a lot of space in that thing. When are you gonna learn to cook?"

"When the Celtics win the NBA championship."

"I won't hold out hope. For that—or for whatever it is you might decide to burn in that oven."

I come out of the kitchen with the plastic tray of pre-measured, all-organic dog food, each stamped with a date on the plastic baggie. "You were supposed to be away in Florida this whole week."

Marie has her sweater on, waits at the door for Gordy.

"Come on, Bert." Gordy takes the tray from me. "Marie wants some shut-eye."

"And you need sleep too, *mio caro*," she reminds Gordy.

Donato heads into the backyard with Thor, commenting that it looks like the weekend will be warm and sunny, an excellent time to be on the Eastern Promenade.

"I'm not coming into the office today, Gordy," I joke.

"Place is closed 'til Monday. For all of us," he says.

Gordy's cell pings. "Who the hell's calling so late? No wait, it's not late. It's early." He checks the caller ID, then quickly answers. "Yeah? … Really?" He listens. "Sure. See you then."

"You are not going anywhere, you're going to bed," Marie bosses.

Gordy looks at me. "Claren's going to be on Chebeague tomorrow."

"Why?"

"Didn't say."

"There's no wedding happening."

"Wants G&Z's presence. I'll take Abshir with me."

"I'm going."

"No, you're not," he insists.

"I'm going."

SATURDAY

CHAPTER FORTY
Saturday

June 22, the day that was printed on plain paper sent in a simple envelope, ten days ago. Lucy Claren's request for her father to attend her wedding. Thor's at my bathroom door when I open it after finishing my morning shower. He's sitting on his haunches and I swear he's giving me a smile. It takes me longer than normal to get ready, every movement hurts. But Thor's patient, he spends his time sniffing the corners of my room as I disengage my iWalk, towel off, and don my sock, liner, and prosthesis. We move to the living room; Donato's on the couch, in a t-shirt—his jeans are in a pile next to the furniture. He's just waking.

"Pretty uncomfortable couch?" I ask.

"Not complaining."

He'd insisted on staying the night. I didn't fight it; I liked the idea. Sharing the bed did not come up in the discussion. I'd closed the bedroom door, pushing the possibility from my mind. Not very successfully.

Donato sits up. Pulls me towards him. "Where are you taking my dog?"

"Quick walk in the park? Okay?"

"I'll come with."

"Thor and I will be fine."

"Ferry or water taxi to Chebeague?"

"Gordy hired Antonio for the day, to give us flexibility. On Claren's dime."

"What time are we due?"

"We?"

"Don't want your mom to think I'm not reliable. I'll hang in the background. Or even on the inn's porch, sipping beer, if I am absolutely not needed and in the way. For some reason, I don't want you out of my sight."

I pull back, his words make me anxious. And at the same time, I like hearing them.

Ten Days

***

The water taxi passes the Sunseeker yacht, it's moored a few hundred yards off Chebeague. Antonio drops Gordy, Abshir, Donato, and I off at the pier near the inn. The yacht's tender is already secured at the dock.

I've brought a walking stick today, knowing my LiteGood's in need of adjustment and not sure what uneven surfaces I might encounter. Winston meets us in an eight-seater golf cart. "The island's limo," he smiles. We pile in and he tells us the Clarens are waiting for us on Bunny's Point. "Didn't know Philip Claren even owned property out here," Winston tells us as he guides the electric cart around a few potholes. "Thought Bunny's Point was part of the nature preserve." He laughs, "Piece of land full of rabbits or something. Turns out, the point borders on the preserve—which Claren donated to the island twenty years ago under the name Bunny Luce. Who knew it was him? He held onto a couple acres, kept it natural, never really built on it."

We're heading to the more southern part of the island, towards Sunset Landing. Winston hands Gordy a *Washington Post* newspaper, the business section. "Philip Claren thought you might like to see this."

Gordy looks at the above-the-fold-story; I read it over his shoulder. Wolff is being interviewed, he's standing in Rio de Janeiro, in front of the Copacabana Palace Hotel. Apparently, the night before, he had announced at the Next Best Thing Conference, that his company, Minds4U, had invested in five Artificial Intelligence start-ups in the vibrant Brazilian market. "The atmosphere here," Wolff is quoted, "Reminds me of the early excitement at MIT and Cal Tech and Silicon Valley. I have recently made a deal with eSousaVenture and am ready to use my deep resources and contacts to ensure its success." The journalist asked about the Pentagon contract that Wolff had boasted of a month previously. Wolff assures him that all projects are ongoing, that having many fingers in the 'Future Pie' allows him to be part of shaping the world."

Gordy mutters, "Doesn't take him long to wheedle into new possibilities."

"Do you think Claren shut the door on him? With a huge thud?" I ask.

"Doesn't seem like they're of the same mind about things. But…"

"Right. Not part of our job to ask."

Abshir is enjoying the summer warmth. "It is my first time on this place," he tells Donato. "It is bucolic. Everything is peaceful, my mother would like it. There are many vegetable gardens…"

Winston veers onto a packed dirt, single-lane road; we're heading towards the water.

The trees surround—and camouflage—a grassy expanse. There's a gazebo, surrounded by Maine's early summer flowers—daffodils, clove currant, and lupine.

Hogan and Hilary sit in the gazebo. Hilary waves as we pull to a stop; she hurries down the gazebo's steps to join us.

"Lucy's getting stronger," says Hilary. She and her father are down near the beach." She points to a rugged pathway.

"Wait here," Gordy tells Abshir and Donato. He offers me his arm, I move my cane into position, and we follow the downhill trail.

Five minutes later, we're on a flat promontory. Tall trees edge this space too. Claren and Lucy stand on a solid porch that flanks a small, granite rock cabin. Gordy and I join them.

"Lucy," Gordy says. "How do you feel?"

"Better," she smiles. "Thank you for not giving up on me, Gordy. I will never forget it."

"You can thank Dee, also," Gordy says.

"I have." Lucy grabs my hand, squeezes it. "You're so strong, and… I hope we can be friends."

"Sure," I respond. "Who doesn't need a genius friend?"

Claren takes a thick envelope from the inside pocket of his jacket. "Tell me if this covers it."

Gordy opens the manila envelope, eyes the contents. "Very generous."

I can see banded hundred-dollar bills inside. Do quick math in my head. Forty percent of that was going to be more than enough to finance that Subaru I have my eye on at Portland's Best Used Vehicles.

"You can't see this place from the water," I observe. "Or probably from the air either." I put my hand on the rock walls of the compact edifice. There are two thick windows on the front, on either side of a heavy door.

"Lucy told me she wanted to build here. She's actually done it. And done it well." Claren puts his arm around Lucy's shoulder.

There's a momentary gleam of pleasure in her eyes.

"One more favor to ask," says Claren.

Lucy doesn't waste time. "Let me show you."

We go inside the rock cabin. It's one room; the plaster walls are covered with found arrowheads and softly rubbed, blue, green, and white sea glass gathered on the beach.

Lucy takes a key ring from her pocket. She folds back a loose arrowhead to reveal a small lock cylinder embedded in a flat stone—it's about the size of a basketball. She inserts the key and turns it. She presses the other key on the ring against a sea-green piece of glass to the side of the stone. There's a click. Claren takes a small remote from his pocket, presses its lone button. The stone juts forward. Claren reaches out, dislodges it, and reveals a deep, narrow, steel-walled storage area. Inside are stacks of small cases, each no bigger than a housing for a flash drive.

"Pretty cool," says Gordy.

Is this a simple sharing of a clever hiding place? Why are they showing it to us?

"Lucy inherited my interest in locking systems." His voice is so serious that I swallow a sassy retort, a comment on the multi-tiered security system he put in place for Gordy at G&Z Investigations.

"It takes three components to open this." Lucy hands Gordy a copy of the first key. She hands me a copy of the one to be pressed against the sea glass.

"You want us to keep copies of these keys?" Gordy asks.

"As a favor," Claren says. "Lucy and I will have access to the remote, its signal can be activated from a great distance."

Gordy is unsure. "Why us?"

Claren dips his head to the side. "Gordy, I've always trusted you. You're not leaving Portland, too attached to it. You'll always be close to Chebeague, to Bunny's Point. I'll know where to find you—and these keys, if it's needed."

"Why would it be needed?"

"Just overly cautious. As always," Claren says.

I turn to Lucy. "When you came out to Chebeague, two weeks ago, did you add anything to this space? Something that the people breaking into Claren Tech couldn't find?"

Claren answers for her. "Something that we, at Claren Tech, need to keep to ourselves. Until we are assured it will only be used in the best possible ways."

"That's why I needed my dad to come to Chebeague," Lucy admits. "To see this space—that it was ready to be used. If we required it."

"And we do," Claren adds. "Will you keep the keys?"

"I thought we were even," Gordy says. "This is another favor."

"I'll be happy to repay it, when needed."

Gordy looks at me. I nod. He gives Claren our answer.

***

Lucy and Hogan are ready to move onto the docked Axopar, her hand is on his broad shoulder. He leans over to it—his lips brush her skin. They look comfortable, at ease. Hogan backs up the powerchair, enjoying being the perfect gentleman, and lets Lucy traverse the metal gangplank ahead of him.

I join Hilary, Donato, and Abshir on the long porch of the Chebeague Inn. They're sipping lemonade and eating cookies. "Chocolate chip," says Abshir, chewing the cookie. "One of America's great foods."

Gordy and Claren are on the dock, shaking hands. Claren moves onto the boat. The plank is lifted and stored back on the tender, and the vessel glides silently off. Moments later, the Axopar saddles next to the yacht and the trio get on board and disappear into the salon.

Gordy makes his way up the hill to join us on the porch, arrives just as Winston comes out of the adjoining dining room. He announces that Antonio has already had two helpings of strawberry shortcake, and that it's time for us to come in for lunch.

* * *

Portland's sunset was golden, with pink striations rising just on the horizon. Lobster rolls have been eaten, my mother has agreed not to change her plans, she'll take the plane to Japan at the end of the week. Chester announces that he's decided to accompany her. My mother's made a point of using my first name, over and over: "Dee, would you like another club soda?" "Dee, do you like mayonnaise on your lobster roll, or are you a fan of just melted butter?" "Dee, does that Billy Payer remain in the hospital? When will he be transferred to jail?" Donato did not get the hint, he's fine with calling me 'Rommel.' We discussed the topics of lobster and incarceration, and finally, they got into their Mercedes, we waved, and they headed towards the highway.

Donato and I walked to Sparrows. We're sitting on the newly opened patio space; a sure sign it's time to take Maine's summer season seriously. We're enjoying our Allagash North Stars, a deep dark Belgian brew. There's a water bowl on the sidewalk at our feet, and Thor rests beside it. Moments after the sun goes down, Gordy and Bert approach. Thor yips, and moves aside for Bert to lap up the water. Seems like they're best friends. Gordy waves at Pat, who is behind the bar, and a beer arrives ten seconds later.

The six o'clock news is on the television above the bar; I can hear Christine Poole, she's sharing the daily stories, making a joke that she'd better make it fast before all channels are changed to tonight's Red Sox game. She reads from the off-screen monitor: "In a surprising turn of events, Claren Tech, the company founded by Portland's own Philip Claren, responsible for innovative work in semi-conductor memories and circuitry—and LC Labs, run by his daughter Lucy Claren, whose advances in bio-engineering have gained recent attention, have shut their doors."

I nearly choke on my Allagash. "What did she say?"

Ten Days

Gordy and I move inside to the bar. Flawlessly coiffed and crammed into a tight green dress, Poole reports, "Philip Claren, who gave no warning for this closure, has provided no statement and has not been located. We have received no responses to our queries to multiple officers and board members on the Claren Tech roster. 'Mum' seems to be the word. Daniel—what's your take on this?"

Daniel Zann, wearing his signature pink tie, this time with an orange-striped shirt, adds his vapid opinion. "Christine. Sure seems odd. Take a look at these videos of the Claren Tech campus." We watch the screen; WMFT news vans move through the abandoned space. There are no cars in the parking lots. No ultra-modern Electro Buddy carts whiz by on the paths from building to building. No security guards are in the kiosks. No lights on in any of the buildings. The entry doors of many of the buildings are open, as if security is no longer necessary. Poole continues, "Daniel, our reporter, Susie Bing, was able to speak to the one remaining official on the Claren Tech campus."

"That's right, Christine," Daniel fills in. "We're getting to that point on the video. Here it is." On screen, Susie Bing leaps out of a news van as an Electro Buddy approaches. Prudence Lopez brings the vehicle to a stop; her severe countenance is very much in place. Susie Bing, breathlessly, asks what Lopez can tell the public about the Claren Tech shut down? Bing thrusts the microphone towards Lopez's face.

"No comment." Lopez presses the pedal down on the Electro Buddy and speeds off.

I look to Gordy. "What do you think?"

Gordy purses his lips. "That this is the reason Lucy and Phil gave us those keys."

"What do you mean?"

"Maybe the intellectual property of Claren Tech and LC Labs is being stored on Chebeague? While the future of their work can be considered."

My head spins. Could we really have that responsibility?

"What's going on?" Donato's joined us. His intelligent eyes connect with mine. "It's just me and the dogs out there and I'm wondering if I'm missing something important."

"Something G&Z Investigations was interested in," Gordy sounds casual.

"But that case is over," I say, aware my statement could be totally wrong.

Gordy pats me on the back. We move back to the patio. Pat yells over to us, "Apple pie? Served hot, with ice cream."

We all give him the thumbs up.

* * *

The moon is high in the sky as Gordy and Bert pad up the porch steps of the house Gordy's parents built. Gordy unlocks the door and they move inside.

We wait. I hear Marie telling Gordy to come up to bed.

Donato's voice is gentle. "Don't you have a deadline at the Department? At 109?"

"Re-up papers. If I want to apply for reinstatement, the application is due tomorrow."

"*If* you want to…?"

I watch as Gordy's upstairs hallway light goes on.

"Rommel."

"Yeah?"

He puts his hand on my arm. "You've made your decision, haven't you."

In my mind's eye, I'm at that crossroad. The two signs still point in different directions. But one pathway seems illuminated now. The clear choice.

I nod. "Yeah."

The End

Acknowledgments

I feel it's taken me a long time to reach this life-long goal—to write the debut novel in a crime/mystery series. Lots of other writing has led up to this. So, sincerely: Thanks to every writer whose books I've read and been inspired by—you've kept my butt in the writing chair. Especially my peers in my writing groups (East Coast Pine Nuts and West Coast Big Boys, as well as Sisters in Crime), and the amazing scribes in Maine's literary community who share their work, worry and expertise so willingly. Thanks to every friend, film executive, producer, film and theater director, actor, critic, literary editor, publisher, teacher, and fellow writer who gave me sage critiques and support over my years of writing in different modes and genres. Their insights may have been focused on the story-of-the-moment, but their wise words absolutely affected this one too.

Special thanks to those who've been there with me on this particular endeavor: Sally Reinman, who always wants to know more about Dee Rommel, to Mark Winkworth for making the cocktails, to Kathy Aspden for her supportive, good ol' gol'dang honesty, Elgon Williams for answering every question. Thanks to Zara Kramer and Allan Kramer and Pandamoon Publishing and its amazing support teams—and to the New England's Crime Writers Community for pointing me towards incredible experts and research. Extra shout out to John LeMieux for sharing his own experiences with amputation. Of course, there's Becky's Coffee Shop, Navis Coffee Shop, Coffee by Design Coffee Shop, Porthole Coffee Shop, Woodlands after Pickle, and the one and only Armory Bar: each a writer's dream place to noodle a story.

When you're too tired to write—read good books. Energy will magically return.

About the Author

Jule Selbo is a novelist, playwright, and screenwriter whose original work explores an individual's need for justice and a sense of belonging. She grew up in Fargo, North Dakota, got her BFA at Southern Methodist University in Dallas, Texas, her MFA at UNC, Chapel Hill and moved to New York City where her plays were performed off-off Broadway, in regional theaters and in Los Angeles; these earned her gigs writing for network television and major film studios in Hollywood, both in live action and animation. While still writing for Hollywood, in the early 2000s, she became involved in academia, earned her PhD at University of Exeter and took on a professorship at California State University, Fullerton. She's contributed articles to many film journals and her books, *Story Structure: Building Story Through Character, Film Genre for the Screenwriter,* and *Women Screenwriters, an International Guide,* are used in universities across the globe.

Jule moved to Portland, Maine in 2019, to focus on writing novels—and especially her lifelong goal of writing in the crime/mystery genre. She didn't realize the state is home to some of the country's most accomplished and exciting (and welcoming) writers. She's glad to be part of the literary community in Maine, contributing to the vibrant theatre work in Portland, writing scripts for national drama and comedy podcasts, sailing with her husband, and playing pickleball.

Other books include award-winning historical fiction: *Dreams of Discovery, Based on the Life of Explorer John Cabot* (2018) and *Breaking Barriers, The Life of Laura Bassi* (2020, Finalist for the Goethe Award) as well as *Find Me in Florence* (2019, Chatelaine First Place Award in Women's Fiction/Romance).

https://www.juleselbo.com

Thank you for purchasing this copy of *10 DAYS*, Book 1 in the Dee Rommel Mystery Series. If you enjoyed this book, please let the author know by posting a review.

Growing good ideas into great reads…one book at a time.

Visit http://www.pandamoonpublishing.com to learn about other works by our talented authors.

Mystery/Thriller/Suspense
- *A Flash of Red* by Sarah K. Stephens
- *A Dee Rommel Mystery Book 1: 10 DAYS* by Jule Selbo
- *A Rocky Series of Mysteries Book 1: A Rocky Divorce* by Matt Coleman
- *Ballpark Mysteries Book 1: Murder at First Pitch* by Nicole Asselin
- *Code Gray* by Benny Sims
- *Crescent City Series Book 1: Crescent City Moon* by Nola Nash
- *Crescent City Series Book 2: Crescent City Sin* by Nola Nash
- *Evening in the Yellow Wood* by Laura Kemp
- *Snow in Summer* by Laura Kemp
- *Fate's Past* by Jason Huebinger
- *Graffiti Creek* by Matt Coleman
- *Juggling Kittens* by Matt Coleman
- *Killer Secrets* by Sherrie Orvik
- *Knights of the Shield* by Jeff Messick
- *Kricket* by Penni Jones
- *Looking into the Sun* by Todd Tavolazzi
- *On the Bricks Series Book 1: On the Bricks* by Penni Jones
- *Project 137* by Seth Augenstein
- *Rogue Alliance* by Michelle Bellon
- *Southbound* by Jason Beem
- *The Amsterdam Deception* by Tony Ollivier
- *The Juliet* by Laura Ellen Scott
- *The Last Detective* by Brian Cohn
- *The Moses Winter Mysteries Book 1: Made Safe* by Francis Sparks
- *The New Royal Mysteries Book 1: The Mean Bone in Her Body* by Laura Ellen Scott
- *The New Royal Mysteries Book 2: Crybaby Lane* by Laura Ellen Scott
- *The Ramadan Drummer* by Randolph Splitter
- *The Teratologist Series Book 1: The Teratologist* by Ward Parker

- *The Unraveling of Brendan Meeks* by Brian Cohn
- *The Zeke Adams Series Book 1: Pariah* by Ward Parker
- *The Zeke Adams Series Book 2: FUR* by Ward Parker
- *This Darkness Got to Give* by Dave Housley

Science Fiction/Fantasy
- *Children of Colonodona Book 1: The Wizard's Apprentice* by Alisse Lee Goldenberg
- *Children of Colonodona Book 2: The Island of Mystics* by Alisse Lee Goldenberg
- *Dybbuk Scrolls Trilogy Book 1: The Song of Hadariah* by Alisse Lee Goldenberg
- *Dybbuk Scrolls Trilogy Book 2: The Song of Vengeance* by Alisse Lee Goldenberg
- *Dybbuk Scrolls Trilogy Book 3: The Song of War* by Alisse Lee Goldenberg
- *Everly Series Book 1: Everly* by Meg Bonney
- *Finder Series Book 1: Chimera Catalyst* by Susan Kuchinskas
- *Finder Series Book 2:*
- *Fried Windows (In a Light White Sauce)* by Elgon Williams
- *Magehunter Saga Book 1: Magehunter* by Jeff Messick
- *The Bath Salts Journals: Volume One* by Alisse Lee Goldenberg and An Tran
- *The Crimson Chronicles Book 1: Crimson Forest* by Christine Gabriel
- *The Crimson Chronicles Book 2: Crimson Moon* by Christine Gabriel
- *The Phaethon Series Book 1: Phaethon* by Rachel Sharp
- *The Phaethon Series Book 2: Pharos* by Rachel Sharp
- *The Sitnalta Series Book 1: Sitnalta* by Alisse Lee Goldenberg
- *The Sitnalta Series Book 2: The Kingdom Thief* by Alisse Lee Goldenberg
- *The Sitnalta Series Book 3: The City of Arches* by Alisse Lee Goldenberg
- *The Sitnalta Series Book 4: The Hedgewitch's Charm* by Alisse Lee Goldenberg
- *The Sitnalta Series Book 5: The False Princess* by Alisse Lee Goldenberg
- *The Thuperman Trilogy Book 1: Becoming Thuperman* by Elgon Williams
- *The Thuperman Trilogy Book 2: Homer Underby* by Elgon Williams
- *The Wolfcat Chronicles Book 1: Dammerwald* by Elgon Williams

Women's Fiction
- *Beautiful Secret* by Dana Faletti
- *Find Me in Florence* by Jule Selbo
- *The Long Way Home* by Regina West
- *The Mason Siblings Series Book 1: Love's Misadventure* by Cheri Champagne
- *The Mason Siblings Series Book 2: The Trouble with Love* by Cheri Champagne
- *The Mason Siblings Series Book 3: Love and Deceit* by Cheri Champagne
- *The Mason Siblings Series Book 4: Final Battle for Love* by Cheri Champagne
- *The Shape of the Atmosphere* by Jessica Dainty
- *The To-Hell-And-Back Club Book 1: The To-Hell-And-Back Club* by Jill Hannah Anderson
- *The To-Hell-And-Back Club Book 2: Crazy Little Town Called Love* by Jill Hannah Anderson

Non-Fiction
- *The Writer's Zen* by Jessica Reino

mystery
SELBO
2021

1700783

Made in United States
North Haven, CT
19 October 2021